The Refracted

Michelle Medhat

MINDBLOWING
BOOKS LTD

THANK YOU FROM MICHELLE MEDHAT

I would like to thank you for reading this book.

If you've picked this up, and you haven't read the earlier books, please check out The Trusted (book one), The Dominant (book two) and The Resonance (book three). Direct links to these books can be found at the end of this book.

Also, at the end of this book you can find details on how to get the free eBook **Operation Snowdrop**. This book is only through sign up to my newsletter *'Fearless Spies, Amazing Realms and Ice-Cold Villains'*. It's not available anywhere else. Operation Snowdrop is the mission that is cited throughout *The Trusted Thriller Series*. Together with this free eBook you'll get early bird discounts, the latest news on this series and access to incredible free thrillers bundles to keep you entertained.

But for now....

Dive in, hold on tight and enjoy!

From the dark…

Two days have passed since the world had almost fallen to Al Nadir. Of course, the world didn't know that they had almost been crushed under the weight of Lord Aswa-da's mighty hand. But what they didn't know couldn't hurt them.

Ignorance had a kind of bliss attached. A rosy, warm feeling when you know, deep down, everything will be alright.

Oh, how wrong the world was…

Preface

The boy dove further, his body minuscule against the massiveness around him. A glorious turquoise sea, rippling with light, enveloped his thin frame. Shoals of iridescent fishes flashed past him. He gazed in wonderment at the world within a world so rarely seen. Everything was glistening, reflecting the brilliant sunlight above the waves. He sensed everything around him. The great light that saturated. The soft movements in the sand. The little undulations made by things unseen. All had a harmony. A living connection.

The boy stared at the seabed. It sparkled as if diamonds had been laid instead of sand. Shifting amongst the jewels, a starfish emerged and crawled across the bed. The boy was mesmerized. His eyes followed the starfish's trail. Another movement suddenly attracted him. Maybe it was a crab or even a stingray. Hoping for a stingray, the boy watched...

A tip poked through the sand. Grains tumbled down as the object started to reveal itself. Curious of the unfolding, glittering peak, the boy moved forward. Thinking it must be buried treasure and valuable, the boy reached out to snatch it.

His hands touched its smooth sides. The boy felt heat for an instant. Then he felt as though a double-decker bus had smashed into him.

The force sent the boy hurtling backward and the coral behind broke his fall. On impact, his mouthpiece dislodged, and oxygen rushed out. The boy saw the bubbles streaming but did not move. The mouthpiece floated in front of him. It was now an unnecessary accessory. Smiling, he breathed again as if the sea had always been his natural habitat.

The peak rose to its full height. The boy nodded, acknowledging its arrival. Uncovered, the object was a seven-sided crystal standing no more than two feet high. Inside, a burning white light pulsed rhythmically.

Intrigued and unafraid, the boy advanced again. This time, his hands were outstretched, as if welcoming an old friend. Wrapping his arms around the crystal, like a son's embrace of his father, the crystal was soon hidden by the boy's body.

The warmth was comforting and reassuring. Like a parent's love, it was bold, undemanding and always there, a love of such strength that had borne life. It filled him with hope. Tighter, he enfolded his arms. He never wanted to let go of that feeling. Inside, and all around him, was complete goodness. Nothing could harm him. Nothing could touch him. He was as old as time. But out of time. He was everywhere. And he was nowhere.

His hands glowed. He smiled. The light was coming. Expecting the surge, he gripped tighter still. White, shining light poured into him. He smiled and smiled and smiled. Water molecules moved away from him. His skin was dry as if he was standing on land. The light infused with purity. Unencumbered goodness raced through his shining body. Totally submerged in light, the boy stood like a gleaming torch on the seabed.

Slowly, the light in the crystal pulsed and the boy's torch-like appearance faded.

Releasing the crystal from his hold, he moved away. The crystal blinked and its light dimmed. Watching as the crystal lost its luminescent light, the boy felt pain. Tears streamed. The last vestige of light blinked and the crystal shuddered. Its clarity clouded. Turning an angry grey like the sky before the rain, the crystal burnt out.

The boy cried with a sorrow he could not comprehend. All he knew was that his heart hurt. He could feel it ripping apart inside him, flooding blood through his body until he drowned in those ruby rapids.

Sinking to his knees, he felt transparent. Barely there. Barely existing. In response, the crystal descended into the sand. Second by second, the grains swallowed up the small opaque tower. Scrambling desperately through the sand, the boy searched for the crystal, but it had vanished.

Resting back on his heels, he stared at the point where the crystal had been. He knew it wouldn't return.

He stood up. It was over. Now, the beginning. *The new chance.*

And he would not fail them...

Chapter 1

Earth Date – 28 March 2017

Crystal encases me. Day and night. If day and night existed. But here in Kudamun, we have no natural dawn or dusk. It's important to understand the difference between 'in' Kudamun and 'on'. For Kudamun is not a planet. It is a complete inner dimension that is everywhere and nowhere, and crystal defines this world. From the opulent rooms upon rooms to the staircases and towers, all is created from crystal. But this crystal lives. It is sentient and offers nourishment to us, enabling continuation without the need for food. I still haven't found out how this happens. It just does.

Kudamun is separated from the known Universe by the Reality Gap. Walking through the corridors, sitting in my quarters, wherever I am in Kudamun, the Reality Gap floats high above, removing the need for a ceiling. I stare up at it and imagine it's a sky. Deep blues, bursts of vibrant orange, and silver streaks left by the quantum particles in constant fluctuation. Lines crisscross, shine, and explode then coalesce and vanish. As I understand it, the degree of tilt of these shooting quantum particles keeps Kudamun from being seen by anyone in the physical world, which, I guess, is a good thing. It stops us from breaking through at inopportune times, such as, well, those times you need to be alone, or alone-ish....I'm sure I don't need to spell those moments out for you!

Sorry, I didn't introduce myself. I'm Ellie Noor, a Kudamaz-human hybrid attuned to the resonance pattern of everything on Earth. Yes, it is quite a mouthful.

I could, of course, say, "Hi, I'm the Protector of Earth." It's a little shorter, but it also sounds like I've just stepped out of a Marvel movie.

But you know what? I think I'll just stick with, "Hi, I'm Ellie Noor, and I'm a bit different."

It has been a very strange journey, and one, I can honestly say, I'd never want to repeat.

I've been here just over two Earth days. Strictly speaking, I haven't been here a second, as there is no time in Kudamun. Our lives here and any time passing is defined by the planets with which we are connected. Through symbiotic interactions with the planets in our care, we age. But it's not how humans age. In truth, the Kudamaz are almost ageless. A young Kudamaz may have an Earth age of millions of years.

It is a difficult concept to explain, let alone fully comprehend.

I mean, I am one of them. But even I have some difficulty in realizing that both Sam and I will live forever. Or until the time when we surrender our life forces to the Library of Ummia.

I look at Sam and I see it in his eyes. Although he would never admit it, Sam still holds himself responsible for what happened. Despite the fact that Aswa-da was the orchestrator, he feels answerable for the hell I went through.

Those last five days of my human life, I still remember with vivid clarity. Although my strength overpowers the memories during consciousness, they burrow up like maggots in my unconscious mind, rising from a dark place. When I sleep, the nightmares come.

That reality of knowing with absolute certainty your final breath will soon be drawn in the sadistic hands of Al Nadir, I came to know it. I whispered my peace. I shall never forget the vision. It captured and tore apart my soul. Sam, bound and broken in a chair, his size made even larger by the massive screen before me. Defiance radiated throughout his body, but his eyes were sullen, opaque orbs. Those beautiful, laughing eyes I remembered had lost their light. He had no fear. Just sorrow. Deep, trembling sorrow for a life followed that would lead to another's death.

The death of the woman he loved.

At that moment, I tried to give him strength. Through those satellite waves, I attempted to restore his faith. He was already adrift, but I had to try.

I couldn't break. He had to see the force of my resolve. Despite my then human frailty, the Kudamaz code in my DNA had started to break through, increasing my resilience to Al Nadir's barbaric interrogations.

Awash with selflessness, I accepted my fate. Beyond husband and wife, our lives were joined in the common goal to save thousands of lives.

As it was, those lives were a statistic, a flashing headline of breaking news to horrify and plague those governments who had allowed infiltration into their ranks. It was a time of turning. The reassertion of a battle for dominance at an eventually universal level.

And a struggle that would change me forever.

We all search for a purpose in life. Including me. How strange that my purpose in life was death. Okay, I'm alive now. But Ellie, old Ellie, Mark I Ellie, has gone. Well, more accurately, her corporeal body has gone. Ellie is still alive in me. I'm the Protector. Although, as I say, I still can't bring myself to be called that. It sounds too weird, too out-there.

Does that sound wrong? I am the Protector of Earth. I have been imbued with unbelievable, mind-blowing powers. I did save Kudamun, Earth, the Universe and, most of all, Sam. But, inside, where no one can see, I'm still that frightened woman who saw her husband with a gun and whose world shattered from that moment.

I was never the same after Aby-od's call. The scream, the confusion, the sheer terror of seeing a glimpse of a power no human should ever see, of experiencing the point of death before it happened. I felt emotions with no rational explanation. Even when I replay the memory, the pain is still too much. I can't control it. The memory delivers an agony greater than all of the torture Ellie suffered.

Without that moment, nothing else would have happened. The Protector would not be here. Ellie would still be alive, in her human form, and still blind to the truth by Sam's lies.

Aby-od often asks me if all is well, as if he knows. He is such a sage. A man of wisdom. And a man much maligned by Aswa-da's actions.

Sam hated him at first. But he's come around since his reconstitution.

Of course, destiny is written. Even mine. Or perhaps especially mine. A destiny of seven thousand years in the making.

Sam loves being Kudamaz. He always was a leader, always had super intelligence, and as I found out recently, was also a rather badass kind of guy. The transformation for him, I can see, has been a good thing.

I'm not so sure about me.

Everything happened so fast. I had no choice. It all ran away from me and out of my control. I gave my human life so that others would not die. I should be proud. So why do I feel a little cheated?

Why do I feel that I was betrayed by my own destiny?

I guess no one really asked me what I wanted. I was forced to accept such a dramatic change. There was no alternative. I had to evolve. As Darwin says, "to change is to survive."

After his reconstitution, Sam became obsessed with returning to Earth. A thirst for retribution carried him forward. He had a desire to annihilate all of Al Nadir so that they never had the chance to regroup again or do to another innocent what they did to me. That was the reason I supported Sam and entered into a whirlwind execution of evil.

No one in Kudamun can give an explanation as to why Sam wasn't overwritten by Dumuzi's life force. But I know, however, that the truth is very simple. It's very, very clear.

Sam was saved by love.

Chapter 2

Two Earth Days Earlier

Ashton sat at his desk, staring in silence at a point in the past. He'd dimmed the lights to just a flicker and shut down his laptop. He should've been hearing nothing, but Godley's scream played at full volume in his mind. Ashton closed his eyes. He'd seen Godley fall to his sudden death on those shiny, marble steps in Whitehall, and his scream still reverberated with ceaseless persistence. When he'd seen the contents of that foolscap file on Maide, he'd wanted closure on the whole Sam and Ellie thing. But he never expected the actions that Godley had taken.

Abduction, torture, death. He could never countenance what Godley had done.

The level of deceit.

How could he, the prime minister of the UK, not have known that members of his own Cabinet were Al Nadir? With all his past training. His private intelligence networks. Why couldn't something have been seen? How could he have been such a fool? How many secrets had ended up in Al Douri's hands?

Ashton chided himself for being so blind to what was really happening in his House. With the exception of Jensen Stalbridge, his confidante, Godley had been his closest ally. He was always Mr. Fix-It when Ashton needed a job solved, and not just in politics. It was true that Godley had enough skeletons to topple the entire government and decimate him completely. It was perhaps a blessing he'd died so quickly.

Of course, if he hadn't died and Sam had still identified him as the turncoat in his Cabinet, Ashton would have enjoyed creating the conditions to see true pain in his eyes. Never one for being squeamish, he would have pulled the trigger when the time eventually came.

In many ways, Godley had gotten off lightly.

Ashton wondered why Godley had become a spy. What drove a man like Godley, who seemed so principled, to embrace the dark side? Money, power, influence? Or was it just that he couldn't stop himself? An inherent, festering streak of evil that manifested and metastasized throughout his body?

In his life, Ashton had seen a lot of what mankind could do and he realized that 'kind' had no place in 'man'. He'd often gone to the very edge of the abyss. In killing for his country, he'd never questioned the reasons why. Like Sam Noor, he always believed it had been for the greater good.

Accept that and you could literally do anything to anyone.

Unexpectedly, the beautiful, naughty face of his lover Judy Katzenberger, or as he called her, Katzy, drifted into Ashton's mind, but then the vision was superseded with the horrific present delivered by Al Nadir's resident sadist, Sabena Sanantoni. The present was Katzy's heart and her eyes had been embedded into the fleshy muscle of literary love. The recall shook Ashton, forcing bile up inside him, and he shuddered so violently he had to wrap his fingers around the edge of the desk to steady himself.

Yes, man (and woman) are capable of doing anything to anyone.

Ashton breathed in. He had to calm his nerves. Despite his compartmentalization training, sometimes alcohol was the only thing that enabled that siloing of emotions. He dipped his head down toward the drawer at the side of his desk and pulled out the Talisker. He tipped the aged malt into a glass. As he lifted it to his lips, he noticed a stream of red light glint through the glass and reflect across his desk. At the very same second, screams and yells pelted from outside. He leaped to the window. All of Downing Street was daubed in a strange, eerie, red light. People had massed below, despite it being the most private and guarded street in England. Number 10 staff, police, and other officials had poured outside to stare at the strange phenomenon in the sky. Ashton followed suit and looked upwards.

The night sky, no longer black, twinkled and rippled with hues of crimson. Ashton watched the people below. They were terrified. He wondered why he wasn't.

Maybe what he'd seen already fortified his resolve.

Ellie turning up announcing she was a Kudamaz alien and doing that weird vanishing act. And now this strange aura. The two occurrences were too unbelievable not to be connected. Of this, Ashton was positive.

What had Ellie said about some high council wanting to obliterate Earth? Could this be a precursor to total destruction?

Ashton didn't have time to consider it further. His door flung open and security personnel stormed inside.

"Prime Minister, sir, we have to take you to the secure location. Your family is already heading there."

Ashton didn't respond. He looked down at the people milling below him. Their screams and shouts still resounded. He looked at his security team. Their eyes were frightened despite their rock-hard demeanors and years of training. He had to ask himself again: if this truly was Armageddon, why wasn't he frightened?

Something inside made him feel calm. He remembered the incredible force that was Ellie Noor. Whatever was happening, she was at the heart of it. And she would win.

"Of course," said Ashton, grabbing his briefcase and jacket.

Security personnel took up their positions in a diamond formation around the PM and ran down the back staircase to the waiting car at the back entrance.

The secure bunkers that his predecessors would have used in such an emergency were no longer viable. They'd been destroyed by Al Nadir after they'd infiltrated into Special Branch, London's elite police force. Al Nadir spies had used their embedded positions to deploy nano-bombs, and now the bunkers underneath Whitehall, Horse Guards Parade, and Pall Mall were mere rubble and dust.

Now Ashton's route to safety was via a secure armed escort with an armor-plated, bulletproof Range Rover.

"Does anyone know what's happening?" asked Ashton, once safely inside the car.

His chief security advisor shook his head and shrugged. "No, sir. All we know is this red sky is everywhere across the world. Intelligence sources say it's originated from Iraq. It has to be Al Nadir, sir. Some gas or airborne biological weapon."

Ashton nodded, but inside he knew it wasn't anything to do with those lunatics.

"Anyone died?"

"No, Prime Minister, but we're not waiting to find out."

Ashton looked out from the darkened windows and shuddered. He definitely didn't want to hang around to discover what came next.

Chapter 3

The car headed for a secure location several miles outside of London. It was one of only two locations that had never been compromised by Al Nadir. Its failure to be on Al Nadir's radar resided in its cover: a typical English pub.

Underneath the saloon bar, whilst pints were being pulled above, a bunker forty meters deep, encased in lead and reinforced with nanocoated smart materials, was the last place of retreat for the UK's political leaders. Built to stand any nuclear, biological, and chemical attack, it was deemed to be the safest hole in England.

Ashton had quickly been escorted through the secret entrance behind the pub's outbuildings. By the time his security detail arrived, it was way past eleven o'clock, and all the drinkers had departed. Even if it had been earlier, the structured positioning of the outbuildings enabled a car to enter without being seen. This wasn't just a convenience of the architecture; the building had been designed specifically so no line of sight could be made by anyone outside.

Once inside, the PM was maneuvered into the elevator by his head of security. The door slammed shut, sending a ringing in the PM's head. Ashton sat down on the small curved seat with his chief security advisor and pulled the straps across his chest. He snapped the connection together and the elevator auto responded, plummeting the PM and his chief security advisor to the bottom of the shaft at a vertical speed close to G-3. Wind rushed through Ashton's paper-thin body. Or at least that's what it felt like to him. His cheeks rippled back, exposing the side of his mouth. The speed wasn't just a novelty reminiscent of old spy films, but an absolute necessity. The designers had to ensure that the PM got to the safety of the bunker quickly. Speed was very much the design ethos, and a G-3 force was acceptable if it meant the UK's leader would be secure and out of harm's way.

Ashton barely had time to get himself acquainted with his surroundings when his head of security received the all clear. As mysteriously as it had formed, the red, sparkling aura had vanished.

It was probably just as well; his wife Natasha, who arrived a little earlier, had barely made eye contact with him during the time they'd been in the subterranean bunker. She pretended to fuss over their youngest, Mariella. But Ashton knew she hated being in close confines with him. His older daughter, Abigail, sat in a huddle in the corner, having hassled security for a securely encrypted Wi-Fi code, and now her fingers didn't lift from the screen.

Ashton ignored Abigail and gave Natasha and Mariella a wide berth. He wanted to leave. Natasha, when she slyly glanced in his direction, had radiated pure hatred for him. In many ways, he wished he could've chanced his luck outside. Far better than the killing stares he was getting down there.

Ashton thought for a moment about Ellie. What a wife she must be for Sam with her luscious figure and incredible intelligence. What a man could do with that in his hands. Okay, she was an alien, but if inter-species mating was called for, he'd be the first in line for experimentation. A slow grin slipped across his face as he imagined getting real with that proposition.

Chapter 4

The sparkling ceiling that was the Reality Gap pulsed with orange bursts and silver lights shooting across the navy-blue fabric of the quantum energy field.

Temenos glanced up for a moment, his mind tripping off somewhere else. He had much to think about after taking the mantle of the Head of the House of Etima, a position left vacant after Aswa-da's dive into utter insanity.

The House of Etima had, in the past, been in awe of Lord Aswa-da and his maneuvers to consistently undermine the House of Giznu. His latest endeavors, however, had brought shame and disrepute on the House of Etima. It was an embarrassment made even more acute by Etima elders having to work in collaboration with Giznu elders to search and develop tactics for the capture of Aswa-da, should he venture on any planet in the known Universe.

Temenos waved his hand across the dark crystal walls of the Hall of Etima-Si-Sig, the Hall of Dark Silence. The atoms parted to reveal an inner compartment. Temenos reached inside and withdrew a small item no bigger in diameter than twenty centimeters, the size of a sandwich plate. It featured a solid, crystal, opaque dome that sat on a base of about five inches in depth. The new Leader of the House of Etima touched the base and the crystal mound disintegrated, unveiling four ruby-red, elongated crystals standing upright in each corner. He pressed small gems around the base of the structure in a particular but erratic sequence. The four crystals lowered until they were horizontal with their four tips touching, resembling a beautiful snowflake. The crystals had an inner depth. Temenos watched the lights like sudden starburst shatter through the solid red color. The crystals were in connecting mode. They were attempting to find the target Temenos had just programmed them to find.

The starbursts flowed clockwise like a wave through the four crystals, each one experiencing intense explosions. The movement began slowly, methodical at first. But on the third revolution, the pace was upped until all that could be seen were pulsing flashes of bright light tinged with a hint of crimson.

The flashes ceased to be independent, appearing to Temenos as a stunning halo of spinning light. Inside the halo, some light particles appeared to detach and started to coalesce with each other. The action was similar to a Protector's reconstitution, when particles of light follow a life force framework to reconstitute a Kudamaz-hybrid being.

Rapidly, a structure of light particles started to form in the center of the halo. It was a strange-looking crystal with unbalanced configuration and geometries. As a result, the structure was angry and frustrated. The light that formed the uneven crystal darkened as weirder geometries took over, making the dark crystal not just angry but livid and insane as it recognized the fractured and unbalanced formation that it had become.

Temenos watched the structure solidify. From a matrix of particles, it took a solid form, if one could call it such. It had an abomination of geometric angles and a depth of darkness that caused even Temenos to momentarily shiver.

The crystal *thing* suspended a few inches above the spinning halo and levitated upwards. It then began to rotate as if caught in the spinning halo's own orbit. But, in parallel, it turned itself around and around in a spiral movement. Temenos patiently took in its weird but deeply organic movement.

He knew it wouldn't be long now.

The hideous crystal structure that had been created was a physical manifestation of a life force resonance of a very, very important Kudamaz.

It now revolved at a swifter rate, like it was caught in a spectral spin cycle. Faster and faster, until the darkness at the center of the crystal started to develop its own vortex, a small wormhole that pulled into itself bits of its own crystal particles. Temenos was amazed. He'd followed instructions, but he never believed it would work.

He'd heard of the process. Resonance implosion. But he'd only heard, never witnessed. And even then, what he'd heard had been whispers, hurried suggestions, nothing articulated.

Many Kudamaz believed that only the Ancient Ones had the power to activate resonance implosion. The Kudamaz did not have the knowledge. That was what his peers had heard, even Aby-od.

But here he was, in the Hall of Etima Si-Sig, undertaking the action that had been confined to legend.

Whatever they said about the House of Etima's former Leader, Temenos still venerated him. He was in true awe of Lord Aswa-da.

Chapter 5

It drifted back into Sam's mind. That memory would never go away, and now his databanks were forcing him to relive it all over again. Sam rested his head on the satin pillow, eyes closed, and remembered…

"Think the tip-off from your black market asset is legit?"

Sam listened to his MI6 colleague, Jerry, and doubt slipped into his mind.

"He's brought me the goods before. Why let me down now?" Sam glanced at Jerry, who sat across the street in a blue van, watching. He could see Jerry peering up the road.

"Not here, is he?"

There you go, genius, thought Sam. Tell me the obvious.

"I know that." Sam scanned the café tables, and then he clocked an Al Nadir top lieutenant, Palmero. "Jerry, he's here."

"Sanders, that novel energy weapons guy, is approaching on the left."

"Looks like all systems go," Sam said, moving into the café.

"You keep in the van and intercept Sanders. I'll get Palmero."

"Copy that." Sam sat down at a table and waited.

"What's happening?"

Sam grimaced. *Any louder and they'll hear, idiot.*

"Nothing. Palmero hasn't engaged and Sanders is looking away."

"Are they talking?"

"No. There's fuck all happening!"

In front of Sam, Sanders leapt up and ran out the café. At the same moment, Palmero maneuvered quickly outside in the opposite direction.

"They've been spooked. Must have made us. You take Sanders. I'll get Palmero."

Sam shot off after Palmero down Via Nicola Salvi. In his peripheral vision,

Sam saw Jerry jump out of the van and head toward Sanders.

Sam could feel Rome's mid-afternoon sun beat down on his neck. Even in January, it was close and claustrophobic.

Palmero headed into a side street. Sam followed on his tail.

In his ear, Sam heard Jerry. "The fucker's gone. Must've had a car waiting. I'm coming to you."

Sam heard a vehicle behind him. He looked over his shoulder as the blue van pelted down the side street and into a car park.

"Any exits?"

"No, Sam. Entrance and exit the same."

"Block it," Sam told Jerry. Then he stormed after Palmero, drawing his Sig. "Stop, Palmero. You fucker. You've got nowhere to run!"

Sam expected Palmero to turn around firing, but he stopped and revolved to face Sam, his hands raised high.

Sam grabbed hold of Palmero, pulled his arms back, and ring tied his wrists, just as Jerry arrived. Together, they dragged Palmero to the van. Sam could see that Jerry took pleasure in hauling Palmero inside.

Sam stared at Palmero, who didn't make any attempt to escape. He heard the dull thuds, followed by the sound of bones breaking as Jerry kicked and punched Palmero. When Palmero cried out, Sam turned around to see Jerry ram his boot hard into Palmero's ribs.

"That's enough," called out Sam. "Plenty of time to talk to him later. Let's get the fuck out of here." Sam jumped down from the back of the van.

"Shit! I think he's ill."

The moment Sam heard Jerry's words, he knew. Everything about the capture was wrong. No Al Nadir lieutenant allows himself to be taken.

Sam turned back. Palmero's skin was purple, his eyes bulbous and bloodshot.

"Jerry, get the hell away from him," Sam screamed, running away from the van.

He glanced back and saw that his colleague couldn't get away. Palmero had snatched Jerry's leather jacket and pulled him back inside the van. Sam noticed Palmero's face had taken on a maniacal smile.

He yelled, "Fuck you," and exploded.

On the pillow, eyes closed, Sam jerked fitfully, recalling the next events.

Sam had huddled down as the explosive fireball sent bits of the van flying in all directions. Hiding behind a parked Peugeot Estate, he could smell burning flesh in the air. Sam watched Jerry's body parts scatter across the small car park at the side of the Coliseum. He'd been ripped to pieces. Sam heard a hefty thud as Jerry's torso landed next to him. Metal shards stuck through the body like a grotesque human pin cushion. Another thump on the sandy ground by his feet forced Sam to look down, and he stared straight into his dead colleague's horror-struck eyes.

Sam moved back and forth in bed, feeling the emotions of that moment flood him.

He felt a hand upon him, and a soft voice followed. Sam opened his eyes.

"Baby, are you okay?" Ellie leaned on her elbow and touched Sam's face.

Sam pushed himself up, bent his head down, and kissed Ellie. As she reached up to him, Sam backed away and slid off the satin sheets.

"Come back," whispered Ellie, patting the bed.

"There's something I've got to do first."

Sam slipped into a heavy, white robe, covering his sculptured, naked body. He didn't react to Ellie's cries of despondency but headed toward the Knowledge Suite. It was the place in their quarters that would enable him to connect his inherent databanks directly to the Universe's knowledge field.

As Sam entered the room, the sentient crystals that made up the suite perked up and flashed through the walls, signifying their activated status. Sam searched his databanks to focus on the problem in question: reversing or obliterating the nano-bomb. Although it was a surprisingly recent addition to Al Nadir's potpourri of terrorist activities, Sam knew that the nano-bomb had been the biggest scourge on the world's intelligence agencies.

In his mind, Sam connected with the sentient crystals.

"What do you need from us?" the crystals asked.

"An integrated solution that will reverse all versions and upgrades of Al Nadir's nano-bomb technology."

In front of Sam, holographic molecular configurations of all types of nano-bomb appeared. Sam recognized the version that killed Jerry and the insidious upgrade that took the life of his best friend and colleague, Matthew Kinley, and his beautiful wife and young daughter.

Sam gritted his teeth, recalling the devastating explosion that had taken the lives of the Kinleys. The moment he came back as Kudamaz, his first thought was to solve the nano-bomb problem. Unfortunately for Sam, Ellie had other ideas, involving the most demanding bedroom gymnastics. After indulging in considerable pleasures for two days, Sam couldn't hold off any more. He had to find a way to finally negate the power of the nano-bomb forever.

Sam stared at the holograms.

He could almost make out the process, but seeing was better than assuming.

"Run mutation sequence," requested Sam to the sentient crystals.

In front of Sam, the single nanobot embedded at the quantum level started to replicate a copy of itself from its own parts, and then another from those parts, and so on. Sam stood transfixed, taking in the speed of the nanobots' replication inside the human bloodstream. Many hundreds were created in minutes. Sam could see how the nanobots changed the iron-sulphur structure, making the helpful enzymes harmful within a human's DNA. Sam watched as the structural change increased the acidic concentration, reversing the electrical charge.

Sam detected the completion signal that the principal nanobot sent out to an Al Nadir base station. This was the signal that had been detected by GCHQ, which had triggered him to track down the nano-bomb in Dubai.

Him and his CIA co-op Ricky on that mission flashed into his mind. Sam would never forget the look of sudden pain as the bullets from the M240 machine guns tore into Ricky, chewing up his body in a fountain of blood and gore.

"Some cakewalk," muttered Sam, recalling Ricky's fatal words about the mission.

"This solution is for you, Ricky. Rest in peace, mate," said Sam, feeling his throat catch with emotion.

Sam moved some of the images around as they floated in the center of the Knowledge Suite. He could see the massive catalysis that took place as a result of the enzyme suffering the polarization. Before his eyes, a huge, lethal, electrical current was generated. Almost in parallel, the Al Nadir base station sent back a detonation signal. It was a signal, Sam knew, that turned anyone with the nanobots inside them into a walking bomb.

Sam pushed aside the images and focused on the completion signal first. The Universe's knowledge field connection was working; knowledge about how to overcome the nano-bomb flowed into him.

First, Sam ran a few harmonic frequency tests and modelled the responses. The sentient knowledge crystals advised him on the best frequency resonance to use. The frequency resonance would block the completion signal from being sent and therefore would stop the detonation signal.

Sam shook his head. No. No, this wasn't good enough. The nanobot would still be in the target, harming their DNA structures.

"Show me an analysis on the nanobots' structural frequency resonance," requested Sam.

Sam received the complex frequencies making up the nanobots' vibrational energy pattern from the sentient crystals. Immediately, he knew this was the heart of the nano-bomb's existence on the universal plane.

"Program and run the frequencies for the vibrational energy pattern of a version one nanobot and target on a nanobot."

Sam watched the simulation run. As the frequencies reached the nanobot structures, their atomic configurations vibrated wildly and then exploded.

"Confirm status of nano-bomb under test conditions," said Sam.

He listened as the sentient crystals responded, "All nano-bomb functionality disabled and disintegration of nano-bomb structure imminent."

As he listened, the exploded nanobots' structures disintegrated and vanished.

"Please confirm whether the life of the host will be maintained during disabling and disintegration of the nano-bomb structure."

"Affirmative. The life of the host will be maintained. Nano-bomb structure will no longer be harmful to human host or to outside humans."

"Produce prototype for field test," said Sam.

Then he looked over at the Manufacture Pod in the corner of the Knowledge Suite. It was a large cube of crystal about two meters high. The crystal had sentient properties, just like the knowledge crystals around Sam. It acknowledged the sentient crystal interface and read the data stream. Lights inside the crystal flashed a continuous purple, and Sam heard "Ready" in his mind.

Sam knew that the Pod system integrated with the MD Modeler when designs were undertaken on Earth, or elsewhere in the Universe, but he'd interfaced directly with sentient crystals, and thus manufacture through the Pod was immediate.

Sam heard a loud, harmonic sound and the Pod flashed with purple light, and then from the front of the Pod, an elongated cone extended outward. From the cone, crystals flew out and arranged themselves into a device to broadcast the disabling and disintegrating vibrational energy frequency. Sam was intrigued with the crystals coming out of the cone. Although he understood their function as self-replicating, sentient nanocrystals that initiate and self-organize, he was awestruck at how quickly the broadcast device was built.

After a few Earth minutes, Sam had in his hand a small, rounded device with a red button in the center. Sam recalled the Martian weapons in the old 1960s B-movies and realized the device had similarities. He wondered whether he'd be able to convince others in British Intelligence and the CIA to use it, and not laugh it out of the water.

He shimmered to the Observation Room. The sentient crystals sprung to attention.

"Locate Nathan Cartwright, head of MI6, Dudley Gibbs, head of MI5, and Morgan Greene, divisional director, CTD, CIA, of this Earth moment."

Across the room, Sam watched lights flash up in different places across the globe. Cartwright and Greene were in the same place in Bursa, West Turkey. A black site. It was not so strange that they were together. But Gibbs, thought Sam, don't you ever leave your desk? Stuck in Thames House. Again.

Sam smirked and made to shimmer.

"Where are you going?"

Oh dear. Sam had left Ellie in slumber and hadn't told her anything about his plan.

Ellie's eyes glared at him.

"I said, where are you going?"

"I've got some things to put right."

"This is the bloody nano-bomb thing, isn't it? I said I'd help you, but no, you just want to do things all yourself. Typical bloody Sam Noor. Despite *what* you are, you'll never change *who* you are!"

"Ellie, that's not true. But this is something I needed to do myself. It's in honor of my fallen brothers. We lost so many to that fucking nano-bomb, I just want justice for them. I don't expect you to understand."

Sam looked down, holding the device in his hands. Ellie walked toward him and took it.

"It's a vibrational energy pattern set to a frequency that should disable and disintegrate the nano-bomb if it's inside the human body," said Ellie.

"How the hell? Ellie, did you watch me?"

"Nope. I just asked the device what it does, and it told me."

"Devices talk to you? Not just the crystals?"

"Yeah, of course. I can speak, or rather not speak, to anything. It's more like the way we mind-talk. But the language is in a different resonance. I thought you knew this?"

Sam felt his face flush with embarrassment. "No, I didn't. If you'll excuse me, I've got some deliveries to make."

"You're taking the blocker to your intel chums."

For fuck's sake, thought Sam. Can't I do anything on my own?

"Yes, I am. Problem?"

Ellie shook her head. "No,"

"Want to come with me?"

"No. I can see it's a boy thing. You go and play with your device. I'll wait for you back here."

Ellie faded as Sam shimmered away. She watched him, grinning, and gave a little wave.

Sam scanned the area in a degree out of reality before he locked his soul force with his quantum self and materialized against the side of a white building.

He turned the corner and ran straight into armed US soldiers.

"Who the hell are you?"

Sam flashed his MI6 badge, and the soldier snatched it for closer inspection.

"Are you expected?"

"Always." Sam grinned. "Tell Nathan Cartwright and Morgan Greene that I have a present for them."

The US soldier tapped at his intercom.

"Sir, I have a man here who says he's Dr. Sam Noor from MI6 in London. He has a present for Mr. C and Mr. G."

Sam stood in front of the soldier and waited.

"Right. Okay. I'll tell him."

The soldier beckoned, and Sam moved forward, his hands by his side. Total non-aggression. Not confrontational. Very neutral.

"Go through the entrance. Someone will meet you in the lobby."

Sam followed the soldier's pointed arm and headed in that direction.

He stepped into the sparse, rather dingy lobby.

"Sam Noor, I can't believe it. What happened to you?"

Morgan Greene, divisional director of the CIA and often the bane of Sam's life, walked over and wrapped him in a bear hug.

Behind Greene, Sam noticed Nathan Cartwright, head of MI6. Nathan stuck his hand out to Sam, who shook it.

"Good to see you, Sam. There was talk you'd been killed."

Nice to see you too, thought Sam, and nice to see I'm valued so much, you cold-hearted, uptight prick!

"Long story," Sam replied. "One to tell over a whisky or two. I can't stay long but I have got the solution to the nano-bomb. Here it is. Just press this button and the nano-bomb will disable and disintegrate inside the host."

Cartwright and Greene stared at Sam. Greene, in a daze, took the device from Sam.

You're welcome, guys. Brownie points all round, I think.

Chapter 6

Aby-od considered that maybe Sam wanted to vent a steam of vengeance. For after just an equivalent of two Earth days following his reconstitution, Sam, visibly restless to return, announced his intention. He understood what his new-found knowledge could do for the war on Al Nadir. He wanted to solve the nano-bomb problem first. That would give the edge that the security agencies needed to close the net on operatives and interrogate them without fear of detonation.

Aby-od was amazed at how quickly Sam had reverted back to his old role and attitude. Ellie had been very different. Aby-od knew her behavioral cellular memory had gone. Her form was human but that's where the similarities to Sam stopped. She was like Aby-od, totally Kudamaz.

After Sam's reconstitution, Aby-od had taken Sam and Ellie to their new Kudamaz home: stunning, crystal quarters that seemed to consist solely of a super king-sized bed with the most luxurious ice-blue silk and satin covers. Actually, it consisted of much more. But over those two days, that item of furniture was the only one that had any meaning for both of them.

Emerging from their quarters two Earth days later, Aby-od observed for signs of exhaustion. If Sam had been human, he would not have been able to stand, much less announce his readiness to take down Al Nadir. But Sam wasn't human, and neither was Ellie. However, his supercharged wife wasn't interested in returning to Earth, and she was annoyed by his insistence to do so. Aby-od recalled the clash of the Titan lovers.

"Why the hell do you want to go back to Earth now? I thought you'd have got it all out of your system after solving the nano-bomb thing. Can't you just wait a bit? We're having a beautiful time. We need to relax after all we've been through. We need to love each other more, not fight."

Ellie's furious voice bellowed through their crystal quarters, and at that point, Aby-od entered the chamber. He looked at Ellie, those unnatural, blue eyes shining iridescent and her arms waving wildly in synch with every word uttered.

"I have to go back. I'm needed there," shouted Sam with equal power.

"Oh, so I'm not? I save the Universe's ass. I save Kudamun's ass. I even save your sorry one. Then that's it? Goodbye. Time for big bad Sam to take over from wifey. Business as fucking usual!"

"Ellie, darling, that's not true. I need you. I want you with me. Don't you want to take Al Nadir down? I thought you'd be the first to pursue them after what they did to you."

Aby-od watched Ellie's reaction. She was caught in a moment of deep introspection. Aby-od couldn't read her mind, but he knew, having looked back at the observation data streams, what that moment was. Her face, so full and healthy, shining with light and love, drained completely. Her skin turned grey. Her eyes misted over and Aby-od believed she would cry.

Aby-od couldn't comprehend Sam's crassness. He shook his head sadly at him. Didn't he understand what he'd said? Couldn't he see how hurtful the impact of his words had been? Ellie looked crushed. Aby-od watched her, and as he thought about her being broken, Ellie visibly straightened. She regained her towering strength and undoubtable presence.

"You're right, Sam," she screamed, more banshee than woman. "I'm gonna teach those motherfuckers a lesson they'll never forget."

Aby-od smiled. What was he thinking? Ellie was solid, unable to crumble. A few inappropriate words delivered by her husband wouldn't break her. Nothing could do that. Even when she was human, she couldn't break. But now she was stronger than stone. Listening to her and that wonderfully colorful turn of phrase, Aby-od beamed with joy.

"We make beautiful music together." Sam slipped his arm around Ellie's trim waist, dropped it down and cupped her peachy backside, squeezing hard. Ellie breathed in. Aby-od could see that she was contemplating the return to their quarters, and that the gorgeous bed was a better idea than going one-on-one with Al Nadir.

"Let's see if we can't make some beautiful mayhem together for Al Nadir as well," suggested Sam.

Ellie nodded and Aby-od could see a chilling coldness in her smile. He knew she planned to give her tormentors hell.

He noticed the air slip and slide, and Sam and Ellie shimmered in unison out of Kudamun to Earth.

"Good luck", whispered Aby-od, as their soul forces were sucked into the quantum domain, through the Reality Gap and down to Earth. Luck, however, was one thing the Universe's power couple had in abundance.

Chapter 7

As we shimmer away from Aby-od, the terrible memories triggered by Sam's words still hang in my mind.

I remember the room. The stark coldness of the stainless steel trolley. Knowing I was naked underneath the medical gown they had wrapped me in. The vulnerability of it all. The way Sabena thought of me as her toy to use, abuse, and then rip apart.

And, of course, the pain. Not just my injuries caused by Sabena's unspeakable torture, but the pain of knowing that death for Sam and I was close, and to realize all those little things my passing would leave unfinished. The painting of a greenfinch. The herb garden in Winchester. Mastering bread baking, a skill that Sam had promised to teach me. Little things, but those that signify life.

I recall my attempt to escape, firstly by trying to slip out of the handcuffs and secondly by ploying to get Sabena to believe I'd flipped. Gone insane. Tripped over to the dark side and would happily be her lover. If she'd release me.

Both times my stupid body had given me up, and my attempts had ended in disaster.

The second attempt almost worked. It left Sabena seething. As my punishment, Sabena luxuriated in describing every hideous act that would befall upon my fragile, human body.

Sabena enjoyed this transfer of knowledge. She gave a detailed description of what I would be subjected to during her *floorshow*. That word, I still cannot hold in my mind without shivering inwardly.

I try to push out of my data banks those last few moments before Aby-od saved me. But those moments still return. Lying there in that sterile, ice-cold room, I'd cried myself out. I remember that empty feeling like I didn't really exist. I was a mere husk, a vessel awaiting savage violation and mutilation under Sabena's instruction.

But my soul had already departed. They could do anything to my body, but my soul, they could not touch. I'd already died in my heart.

As well as sadness, Sam's words had triggered a fierce will for action.

I could see the same ferocious feeling inside of him, and his drive to destroy Al Nadir for what they did to me, and what they'd been planning to do. I had felt the surging force run through me. I recalled Sabena and when I'd taunted her before obliterating her to smithereens, and the torture I'd inflicted on Salim, how I'd made him suffer to get to the truth.

More of those evil generals of that sadistic terrorist collective were still out there across the globe. I have to rid Earth of them completely.

'Darling, to our flat first,' I hear Sam say in my mind.

I target my quantum self and my soul force connects and streams me into the familiar surroundings of our London waterside apartment.

Out of shimmer, I look at Sam.

"Why here?" I ask

He grins like he's holding another secret from me, which is, of course, impossible.

"Some things I need," says Sam, scooting into his study.

"You mean the locations of Al Nadir bases?" I say, getting his urgency.

"Yes," replies Sam, preoccupied on his computer.

"Sam, you're Kudamaz. You don't need to go back to your old ways. Focus on their dark energies. You'll track them down in seconds."

I didn't realize it, but what I was saying wasn't completely true. Yes, Sam was Kudamaz, with incredible mental abilities, super strength, and the ability to shimmer across the Universe and into Kudamun. But he wasn't the Protector. He didn't have all the powers I did.

I suddenly understood the initial fear in Aby-od after I was reconstituted as the Protector two days before. Being the Protector was about responsibility and using my powers responsibly for good.

I watch Sam shake his head.

"Can't do that, sweetness."

"I know. Sorry. Don't worry. I've got all their locations. I can see their darkness in my mind. It's like a homing beacon for me. Link to my shimmer and I'll take you."

I go to shimmer and Sam pulls me back.

"We'd better clear this with Ashton and Hutchinson."

"Clear it? Sam, you're not working for MI6 anymore."

I stare at my husband, deeply annoyed by his insistence to maintain his Six persona. Although his reconstitution happened two days before, like mine, Sam still has issues with accepting his new form. Now he's using his past life as a safety net. It's something that he knows and can believe in.

"Oh, you know what I mean," he continues. "Check they have clean-up troops in the area to take the survivors and bodies. We have to align our activity with who is on the ground, Special Forces, marines, whoever. We need to abide by rules of engagement."

"Bullshit, Sam. We abide by nothing! We're Kudamaz. I'm the Protector. What did Aby-od say? 'I'm more powerful than any ground force on Earth'. And there won't be any bodies to clear up. I'll obliterate all with my rainbow light. Much cleaner that way."

"Okay, that's your choice. But we still have to tell the PM and the president. Just as a courtesy, so they know Al Nadir's days are completely numbered."

I agree that the two world leaders have to know what our intentions are, but I really hate the way Sam defers so much to Ashton. That level of subservience grates on me. I have to believe it's due to Sam's training and conditioning. His cellular memory patterns, although held in a Kudamaz energy, still have whispers of his former life ingrained with them.

I also feel that Sam enjoys the power play with the PM and US president, and knowing he has all the moves instead of them.

"We'll see Ashton first, okay?" suggests Sam, gauging whether I'm going to flare up and counter his decision.

"Absolutely," I say.

I focus on Ashton's 10 Downing Street dwelling. Sam links into my shimmer and then pushes forward ahead of me. That bloody alpha-shimmer, he has to do it. I feel my lips crack into a smile as I dematerialize into a rainbow sparkle.

Chapter 8

Ashton realized something was happening, but his senses didn't instantly confirm what it could be. The sensation was familiar. He'd seen it two days before when Ellie Noor, the wife of Dr. Sam Noor, an MI6 operative, did that weird vanishing act. He'd not yet completely reconciled what he'd seen to his physical understanding of the natural world. Ellie was alien, of that he was certain, but there was something more to her. He wanted to find out. He wanted to get right under her skin and find out what made her tick.

Leaning nonchalantly against the desk, his arms crossed, he watched the air in his private office oscillate and then grow thicker like a twinkling fog was appearing from nowhere. He raised an eyebrow. That gorgeous woman was returning.

He licked his bottom lip, remembering Ellie's edible figure, and he did his best to concentrate on her arrival. He smirked. The smirk turned into a grin, and then he noticed that the figure materializing was two people, and quickly the grin lapsed into a scowl.

Who the hell was she with? Surely not Sam.

"Hello, sir," said Sam, coming out of the shimmer. "Good to see you again."

The air twinkled and solidified next to Sam, and Ashton's eyes fell upon the goddess that was Ellie Noor. The bodycon clothes clung to her figure, and she dripped with pure seductive allure. Ashton had to stabilize himself and force down his growing arousal.

"Hi, Ashton. I told you I'd be back." Ellie smiled, her mischievous eyes twinkling.

"Actually, you didn't. Your exact words were, 'If we don't succeed, I'll tell you all in the afterlife. If we do succeed, then you don't really need to know.'"

Ellie laughed. "Great recall. Yes, I did. Oh well. We made it, as you can see."

Ashton stared at Sam, taking in his body from top to toe. His well-defined muscular form was so much more than what it was just a couple of days ago. Even his facial contours were sharper, and his dark eyes shone brighter like an energy burned within them.

"Obviously not without some changes occurring."

Ellie stopped laughing and fixed Ashton with a penetrating stare.

"Very perceptive of you. Yes, some changes. I had to bring Sam back from death. He got shot, you see, and now he's a Kudamaz-human hybrid like me. Aren't you, darling?"

Ellie grabbed Sam around the waist and pulled him tightly to her. Ashton's customary smirk hardened on his face at this show of blatant emotion.

Sam nodded and turned toward the sofa to sit down. Ashton beckoned for Ellie to sit down too.

"So why are you here?" asked Ashton, finally getting to the chase. It wasn't every day he was visited by a superhuman couple.

"I've solved the nano-bomb issue. Nano-bomb blockers have been issued to all operatives on dark sites. Gibbs and Cartwright in Five and Six and Greene in the CIA have all been briefed on its operation."

Sam produced the nano-bomb blocker from his pocket. "Here is your one."

Stupefied, Ashton took the blocker from Sam.

"Ellie and I are taking out Al Nadir base by base across the world. We just need troops on the ground to mop up after us and take away any survivors. Can you handle this?"

Ashton listened, still holding the blocker device, and prickled at Sam's inference that he was incapable of just arranging on the ground forces.

"Of course I can. I'll liaise with the US president to ensure a coordinated response."

"Good. Well, we better be off," Ellie said.

But Ashton stuck up a hand. "Wait a minute. You've just arrived. You've dropped a series of bombshells and you're just going to leave? I need a better explanation than that."

Ashton noticed Ellie flick a look at Sam and her eyes fixed tight.

"What do you want to know?" Sam said, staring at Ashton.

The PM held Sam's stare and didn't falter as he answered. "How about everything? Where do you come from? That red sky stuff? What's all that been about?"

"We're Kudamaz-human hybrids from Kudamun, an inner dimensional world. That red sky stuff isn't your concern."

Ashton stiffened with annoyance and glared at the Kudamaz couple.

"Everything is *my* concern. I'm the prime minister of the United Kingdom."

"Sorry, that's *all* we can say," said Sam firmly.

"It's not enough," argued Ashton, looking between the couple for answers.

"That's all you're going to get. You're human and not ready to hear the answers," Ellie snapped.

"Okay, if that's what you feel, I won't tell you my grand plan to unite the world under one purpose."

Ashton sat back. A smug smirk rippled across his lips. Ellie creased her forehead, narrowed her brow, and flicked a look back at Sam who sat motionlessly.

"Grand plan?" she asked finally.

"Yes, my grand plan."

"What is it?" said Sam.

"Oh, can't you just read my mind?"

Ashton watched Ellie glower with irritation.

That's obviously not something in your skill set then, he thought to himself.

Ellie sat back on the sofa and regarded Ashton.

"What is it you want, Ashton? We've got work to do cleaning up Al Nadir. We can't hang around playing your party games."

Ashton's lip pouted downward like a little boy who was told he couldn't go to a party.

"Right, well, if you think global harmony and everlasting peace is a party game, I may as well leave the room."

Ashton crossed his legs, languished on the sofa, and stared in the opposite direction. His body language was clear; he couldn't be bothered to talk anymore.

Ellie was instantly riled by Ashton's posture and inferred insolence.

"Global harmony and everlasting peace? How do you propose to do that?" asked Sam, astounded by the prime minister's incredulous proposition.

Ashton turned back, sat straight, and uncrossed his legs. He placed his hands palms-down on his knees and moved toward Sam and Ellie. He rubbed his hands on his trousers to signify that this information was exciting.

"It's something I've been working on for a while, an idea that came to me some months back. But it has built in intensity after all that happened two days ago with the momentum of events. How you, Ellie, gave freedom back to Earth on that day of the red sky. How we were all saved. The freedom Earth was given to live again and for people to love again. I saw it as a sign that we'd all gone too far, and that now is the time to bring back love, hope, and happiness. To understand what it means to be human and understand our frailties, our strengths, our need to protect those we love. To place love and humanity above everything. To embrace the love for our fellow man or woman, irrespective of color or creed. To really ask what it means to be 'of one Earth'. To be together as one as we were to die as one, had you not saved us. For the past two days, I have felt a need to unify the world so that there will be no more war and suffering. People of Earth can look forward to a new age of peace and harmony. A new place that will shine forth the light of humanity."

Sam and Ellie turned and looked at each other, and despite his abilities, infuriatingly, Ashton couldn't read a single indication that passed between them.

Chapter 9

I stare at Sam, caught in the moment, and then I jolt back and telepathically ask my husband, 'What the *fuck*?'

'Sounds like Ashton is aiming for the Nobel Peace Prize,' quips Sam straight back into my mind. Our interactions are faster than Earth time and hardly register a nano-second of time. Ashton isn't even aware of our mental discussion.

'Peace Prize! He wants world domination through his unique form of peace-driven unification. He's like those money-grabbing preachers on the God-on-demand channels. You can't believe him, Sam. He gives me the creeps.'

'Ellie, you're too judgmental. Give the guy a chance. What if he does want peace? What if this is a new phase in Earth's development? Do you know it's not? What does his Balance Shift say?'

I quickly scan Ashton's Balance.

'In Equilibrium,' I say.

'There you are. He's in Equilibrium because of this change he wants to make to Earth. There must be a reason greater than what we understand. Maybe you should discuss this with Aby-od before we close our minds to Ashton's proposition.'

I can hear doubt creep into Sam's mental voice, and I know he believes I am too skeptical and mistrusting. With the background I've got, with all and sundry lying to me, including my husband, is it any wonder?

'Okay, you carry on talking to him. Find out more about his plans. I'm going to speak to Aby-od.'

I smile affably at Ashton, and he looks a tad confused. I can see he expects me to be impressed. I'm not. I'm wary and deeply suspicious, but I don't show him that.

"Ashton, you must excuse me. I have a matter that requires my urgent attention."

"Oh, I'm sorry. Anything I can help you with?"

"No. Above your clearance level, I'm afraid," I say with a whisper of a grin, and commence my shimmer into Kudamun.

Ashton's startled expression dips into displeasure as the Downing Street office fades out and Kudamun overlays it with a solid definition.

I target the Observation Room as I detect Aby-od is there.

Coming out of shimmer, Aby-od walks over to me.

"What's wrong? I thought you were taking out Al Nadir?"

"We will be. But Sam needed to clear a few things with Prime Minister Ashton first. We got talking, and Ashton started telling us about his grand plan. He thinks he can create global unity and peace. He believes he's the one to unite mankind. He's turning a bit weird. And there's that thing about his Balance Shift."

Aby-od looks at me. "What thing about his Balance Shift?"

"It's in almost constant Equilibrium."

Aby-od's eyebrows rise, and he wrinkles up his face. "Impossible. No human can remain in Equilibrium."

"Well, he has. Now do you get why my hackles are up? Something's weird about him. Look."

I flick over to my right and instruct the Observation Screen to bring up the latest visuals on Ashton, Sam, and me. Instantly, the visuals depict what has just happened. I turn the air around with my finger and the visual goes backwards.

"Global harmony and everlasting peace? How do you propose to do that?"

I push my hand forward into the visual and suddenly Aby-od and I are back in the Downing Street private office. Aby-od gazes intently at Ashton as he speaks and listens to every word.

Then he drags his hand away from inside the visual and we pop out of the office reality and back into the confines of the beautiful, crystal Observation Room.

"What do you think?" I ask.

"You want my considered opinion on this?"

"Yes, that's why I'm here. Have you seen this before on planets? Is this normal behavior? Could it be a side effect of the Therab ejecting too much white light into the world? And why hasn't his Balance changed? And why is the Earth's Balance Shift firmly in the white light part of the Balance when I know there are many Al Nadir soldiers still wreaking havoc on the Earth?"

"Many questions, Ellie. What do you think the answers are?"

"Don't be cryptic, Aby-od. I have to get Sam and take down Al Nadir. I haven't got time for your musings. Yes or no? Should I believe Ashton or not? And is there a problem with Ashton's and Earth's Balance Shift not moving much from the light scale?"

Aby-od searches my face and shakes his head. "Why are you so full of animosity for Ashton?"

"That isn't what we're talking about," I snap back.

"Indulge an old, feeble man."

Ellie smiles. "You're neither old, well not by Kudamaz terms, nor are you feeble. But if you want an answer it's because he always comes over like the consummate showman putting on the show that we need to see. He's in control, working the strings and manipulating everything."

"I don't see that, Ellie. He's a powerful man doing a difficult job. How else is he supposed to act?"

I snort in reply to Aby-od's reasoning. "Well what about all this world unification, global peace, light of humanity stuff? He sounds a bit odd."

"Actually, Ellie, he doesn't. To answer your initial question. Yes, I have seen this kind of transition on other planets that have gone through a time of great trauma, like Earth has done with Al Nadir. When they are at the peak of their turnaround, the moment when everyone is tired of pain, suffering, and death, sometimes there is a genuine pull back from war, and people search for unity, harmony, and peace. I know you won't like this, but often these movements are started by a single voice calling out to galvanize others into action."

I stare at Aby-od. I didn't like what he said. About that, he was right.

"And you really believe that Ashton could be that voice for Earth?"

"It's possible. Stay with him. Hear him out. Don't be too quick to consider him insane. Earth is experiencing a new time. They were in darkness but the Therab has catapulted them into light. Maybe it was a little quick, and maybe this harmony drive is somehow connected to the effects of the Therab. I don't know. The Therab is still an unknown for all of us. But what I don't want you to do is to cast him aside and block him from this development. What does Sam think about Ashton?"

"He thinks I should give him a chance and not be judgmental."

"He's right."

"You don't think it's all a bit strange?"

"Strange like a human suddenly being reconstituted? Or Sam and Dumuzi being melded together so that Sam still retains his and Dumuzi's memories as one?"

I shake my head at Aby-od. I didn't take him for someone who could be ironic. I thought he was above all that. But I can't deny that his point is a poignant one. How can I judge when so many things have changed so very quickly? What seems impossible can turn possible in the blink of an eye.

As I think about everything, a rational sense starts to take over. Ashton might be the deliverer of world peace, and that's why he's exerting goodness. He might be part of a plan from the Ancient Ones. My databanks tell me of similar occurrences on other planets. A time of turning. After so much bad, perhaps this is the way for good to take control.

"Ellie, help him. Don't judge him."

"When you say help, what do you mean?"

"Listen to him. Give him encouragement. You'll know what to do. You're the Protector of Earth. If someone wants peace and global harmony and to put an end to war and hate, he needs your support all the way. Give it to him. You may just be helping Earth on a new path toward enlightenment."

I listen to Aby-od. It could be true. It is still too early to make a decision. I have to roll with Ashton and see where he is going with this global peace for humanity then cast judgement when enough intel has been captured.

"Okay, Aby-od. I'll take your advice."

"Good."

"But I'm going to watch Ashton like a bloody hawk. If he puts a foot wrong, he's mine."

Aby-od laughs and his eyes twinkle with a knowledge of what I'm capable of. "Of course. Then he's only got himself to blame."

As long as we're not the ones who'll be blamed if we've read this all wrong, I think.

I invoke a shimmer back to Downing Street to give my begrudging support to a man who could be leading his people into a new future of light.

Chapter 10

29 March 2017

Xiao Chang struggled toward the restroom at Sharm El-Sheik International Airport. His heart pulped with a viciousness that tore at his arteries and his legs were sticks on fire. Every movement hurt. He pushed at the door and it felt like he was pushing at concrete. His strength, the little that he had, now deserted him completely. It was as though his musculature hadn't been grafted onto his skeleton, and all he had was blood, bone, and nerve, and those endings were shooting through signals to his brain, lighting it up like a Christmas tree.

What had happened? Why was he so weak?

With a final thrust, the door to the restroom edged open and he collapsed inside.

Breathing out hard, he grabbed the first wash basin and steadied himself. His lungs strained. Dizziness washed over him. His young, delicate hands curled around the ceramic edge.

Was this a heart attack? Could boys of his age *get* heart attacks?

He tried to rationalize what was happening to him. Always a logical boy, he knew he mustn't panic, as panic was always the killer not the symptom. But the drilling through his lungs and the blazing pain, like corkscrews had been plunged into his body by unseen hands, was too much. Panic was setting in fast.

Gripping tighter, he pulled himself up to full height. It was then that he looked in the mirror. Maybe it was the pain. The disorientation. The fear. But it was the first time he looked.

He felt his face pale and the floor rose up to meet him. Or had it slipped from under him? He didn't know. He couldn't tell.

The effect was the same. He crashed into a heap.

Before unconsciousness hit, one last thought registered: the reflection he saw in the mirror.

A brilliant, shining, white light.

Chapter 11

President Al Hutchinson knew what he'd found. He'd held it in his hands, shaking. The secret. The Holy Grail of science and as sought after as the Higgs Boson. A kind of energy alchemy. And he'd found it, tucked underneath the shelf that was in Treeborne's private safe.

Weirdness had surrounded Treeborne and finding papers claiming a breakthrough in such a previously unobtainable energy source was sure to result in confiscation of said materials. President or not, the papers would be taken from Hutchinson, and he'd never see them again. He couldn't let that happen.

Hutchinson hid the papers amongst his own files and placed them in his briefcase. He then consulted the one man with whom he had an affinity, the one man who, like himself, had seen so much over the last few days. He had also witnessed the supreme power of Ellie Noor and knew how close Armageddon had really been.

Hutchinson called the one man he could trust: British Prime Minster Richard Ashton.

The president's heart had been full of anticipation when he'd made the call. On a locked down, quantum-encrypted HoloLink line, Hutchinson explained to Ashton the documents he'd discovered.

Far from advising Hutchinson to stay well clear, Ashton listened quietly. As Hutchinson stared into Ashton's eyes he could see a reflection of his own enlightened eyes. He recalled the strange power that had controlled Treeborne, and how he'd had witnessed a black, shining giant kidnap the former president from the Pentagon just three days earlier.

The promise of what the find held for both countries was too good an opportunity to surrender up to the authorities, despite Hutchinson's initial momentary misgivings.

"You know this may have origins from…elsewhere," Hutchinson said in a lowered voice and his eyes hooded, as if that solitary word was sufficient for the PM to finish the story.

It was.

"Yes, I am aware. No more talk now. We'll meet tonight. I'll come to you."

That night, Ashton arrived. His plane touched down on a private strip near Camp David, and Ashton was ushered with speed into an armor-plated black Cadillac SUV.

Minutes later, the two men greeted each other with manly hugs. They shared in the knowledge that they were lucky to be alive. Ellie Noor, that strange wife of MI6 Agent Sam Noor, was the reason they were here. No one could explain it. Sam had told Ashton something about Ellie being a 'Kudamaz-human hybrid' but they were words without true meaning. He couldn't understand it. He could only revel in the fact that she'd arrived when she did.

Hutchinson led Ashton through the cavernous study, a hive full of books and journals dating back to the first settlers. Spread out on the desk were pages marked with the White House crest. They all featured the same scrawly writing. Ashton recognized the erratic scribble as Treeborne's handwriting.

With just a cursory glance, he knew that the complex mathematical equations, which even a top Cambridge professor would find hard to produce, had not originated from the mind of the former mad president.

"Where did you say you'd found these?" asked Ashton. Although Hutchinson had referenced Treeborne's belongings during their HoloLink call, he hadn't specified.

"In his personal safe in his private lounge in the White House," said Hutchinson, picking up one of the papers. It was a full page of equations with just a few words interspersed amongst the mathematical hieroglyphics.

Those same words he'd seen when opening the safe had been branded onto his brain and remained with him.

'The Pathway to Low Energy Nuclear Reactions'.

"Treeborne didn't write these," said Ashton, as his eyes roamed over the leaves of scientific wonder.

"I know that," said Hutchinson. "But if we retype them, no one will know where they're from. We can say it's long-term research. It fooled them before with the compound."

"But it won't again. They're not stupid," said Ashton, realizing where he intended to take the conversation. "They'll sniff out Treeborne's smell on this. It's only been three days since…"

"So, what are we going to do?" asked Hutchinson.

"My dear friend, I think I have the ideal solution," said Ashton, "and it will be good for all of us."

Chapter 12

In my mind, I focus on Taman Negara in Malaysia. Previously a national park, now it houses one of Al Nadir's largest South East Asian bases and, if crippled, the rest of Al Nadir's South East Asia network will start to fall.

I seek out to connect my soul force with my quantum energy self already in Taman Negara, and I feel the tremendous pull of my quantum self as Sam and I race through the Reality Gap and into the strange Malaysian jungle.

I can smell the freshness of the forest rain as lush vegetation materializes around me. There must have been a heavy storm just before Sam and I arrived, for I can still sense the static in the air and the uneasy stillness in all the creatures around me. As I sense the vibrations, I know it is not the storm but Al Nadir's presence in the rainforest that has so disturbed the wild creatures around me.

A common jay butterfly hangs upside down on a leaf and I feel its resonance. Its sensation of slow pulses translates within my Kudamaz databanks, and a question comes through.

'Is it safe?'

'It will be soon, my little one,' I answer with immediacy and gentle reassurance.

The butterfly detaches from the leaf and flies off down the wooded path. It is strange how the resonance within flora and fauna is their universal method to communicate. Yet humans, although deemed to be of higher intelligence, cannot grasp this simple but powerful language. It would appear that by having the power of speech, the connection to their internal resonance and the resonance of others died out over twenty millennia ago. As Protector, I have the connection, but this is not a capability of all Kudamaz.

Sam arrives and does not sense what I am feeling. He moves with caution, looking wary.

I sense the dark resonances ahead of me and know Al Nadir's camp is not far.

"They're just beyond that clump of trees," I say, pointing.

Sam walks in the indicated direction. In the far distance, I can hear talking. Sam hears it too. He catches the scent and, like a tiger padding around its potential prey, he gears up for the attack.

I step behind his stride, but the forest grabs my attention. I stand motionless in the clearing and look up at the massive trees. Some of the colossal trunks have been standing for an eternity. My databanks tell me the rainforest had been evolving for some one hundred and thirty million years.

I feel the clamor of beautiful light resonances as the trees and vines recognize my presence. Concern about the human infiltrators of Al Nadir has rippled through their world. I calm them with a resonance note of authority, telling them I'm here to handle the problem, and all the forest is subdued again.

Sam turns to me and urges me to speed up.

"Why don't we shimmer?" I ask, but Sam shakes his head.

"No, I want to approach them normally. I want them to try to take us out and know they can't. That realization should be enough to have them surrender."

I look with doubt at my husband. "These people have been indoctrinated to fight to the death," I reply. "I don't think me turning up in silver pants and matching bodycon top is really going to cut it with them. Not to mention you in your pale blue Armani. They'll think we've drifted off a film set somewhere and are game for ransom demands."

"They're going to have a bit of a shock then, aren't they?" says Sam, grinning.

But there is no humor in his eyes. He has a bloodlust unbecoming of a Kudamaz, and I know his human side is dictating this engagement. Sam is reliving his MI6 days, only now with superhuman powers and a fortifying knowledge of immortality.

My role as Protector is to ensure Balance. No one must be hurt or killed if they surrender. Neither should they be harmed if their Balance Shift is redeemable by my white light. It is my duty to read every single person's Balance Shift to ensure innocents aren't killed in the cross-fire. Our rules of engagement don't allow for collateral damage of any kind.

Sam and I stride forward into the clearing and are amazed by the enormity of the operation. Jumping out from the rainforest are gigantic concrete walls at least a hundred meters high and encased in a heavy, stainless-steel meshing. The massive walls veer off at angles going deep into the forest beyond. It appears to be in the shape of either a pentagon or an octagon.

There is a hive of activity in front of the massive construction. I watch as helicopters arrive on the helipad at the top. Trucks come in and out. People armed with powerful weapons mill around the entrance and further inside. Mysterious technologies are wheeled around the area. People shout. I hear children laughing. I see them playing in the courtyard in front of the building. Mothers appear in long skirts with gun belts draped around their waists and semi-automatics hanging from their shoulders. There is music. I can smell fragrant cooking.

I look at Sam, and in my mind, I say, 'There are families here. Children. Not terrorists. This is their home. I don't know if I can do this.'

Sam's face stiffens and his jaw hardens in the way I remember it did when he stormed into the kitchen just eight days before and shattered my world.

'Ellie, these people are Al Nadir. They are borne of the same regime that almost ripped you apart, and certainly would have done if Aby-od hadn't whisked you away. You owe them nothing.'

I shake my head. This wasn't my mission. I wasn't a compartmentalized, cold government assassin. I was the Protector of Earth.

'Sam, I can't do this. They're human. It's my duty to protect them before harming them.'

'For fuck's sake, you're here because of them. Al Nadir tipped the Balance and made Earth dark and evil. If they'd been making cupcakes instead of blowing up innocent people then you'd never have been called. Don't you get that?'

Sam now shouts in my mind and I feel his frustration.

So caught up am I in our mind discussion, I fail to realize that we are still walking forward. In full view of the open gate, Sam and I stop. A child with a round face and large, dark, olive-shaped eyes glances around at us. I place my finger to my lips and drop down to her height, smiling.

The girl suddenly screams, shouts for her mother, and points in our direction.

The men and women milling around are all at once alert to danger. Like the flip of a switch, they snatch up their guns from holsters, pockets, waistbands, and bags, and aim all their hardware directly at Sam and me.

The sound of concurrent, consecutive firing fills the air, and I understand Sam's words. These people, whose outward appearances look so homely and gentle, have been irrevocably changed by the evil of Al Nadir's constant violent doctrine.

Even a child, not the one I first saw but another of no more than ten who'd been playing on her computer game, picks up a gun she can barely carry and fires with the rest of the inhabitants of the camp. Her steely eyes are cold and impassive to what she is doing.

The pain of how these people have been willfully destroyed by Al Nadir tears into me. I scream with fury and run into the hail of bullets, my mind blasting each one to dust before they hit me.

Sam storms in alongside me. Some of the people turn and run as they see the bullets exploding before their eyes. I can see their confusion and deep fear. This experience is nothing like they have ever lived before. I can see them trying to rationalize what they are seeing with their inner beliefs. Despite being Al Nadir, these people, I know, have some form of belief. I read their Balance Shifts, and many are still just veering into the dark. It has been their sheer desperation for survival that's allowed Al Nadir to take over their humanity.

I shoot white light out of my palms. The people, their faces frightened as the light absorbs their bodies, stand catatonic, too petrified to move. Almost immediately, their Balance Shifts migrate away from the dark.

Sam watches, knowing what I've done, and he smiles at my mercy. His Harmon gun delivers a stun wave to hold these people fixed to the spot.

More Al Nadir operatives stream out of the massive concrete structure. Again, they try to shoot and look amazed when I obliterate their bullets, guns, and rifles. I scan the Balance Shifts of this new batch of Al Nadir's acolytes and realize swiftly that they are of a different mindset. Cold, hard, and dark, they want to destroy Sam and me at any cost. They don't run when they see what I do to their weapons. Their eyes glow with defiance and burning anger.

With a yell, at least forty of these operatives rage toward Sam and me, their knives, machetes, and cleavers swinging with deadly intent.

I recall the sadistic attitudes of those Al Nadir thugs who tried to rape me just four days before. In their eyes flickered the same burning anger and a need to violate and destroy me. I remember hands upon me. Inside me. I was so helpless. I could do nothing but await what was to come.

It is my duty to remain emotionless, but the fury of what they've done to me, what they were planning to do and what they've clearly done to others, overwhelms me. I can't hold myself back.

With a roar of retribution, I fling myself into the on-coming Al Nadir operatives. My hands tear into their weak human flesh. My fingers slice through their muscles and nerves until my grip encases their bones. With a savage force, I rip back, and their arms, legs, and heads disconnect and fly away, spraying me with geysers of blood.

I wipe their blood away from my eyes and it slips down my face.

I am now the warrior Sabena thought I was.

But a warrior for good. Not evil.

I catch Sam's eye as he's blasting operatives with his Harmon gun, now set to annihilate. I can see horror at first in his eyes, but then he nods, understanding completely, and leaps into the fray with me. He pockets the Harmon gun and joins me in hand to hand combat. He follows my destructive path, dismembering and mutilating the constant stream of operatives coming out of the concrete building.

I make an effort to scan each Balance Shift before I tear these Al Nadir soldiers apart. Hardly any of the new stream coming out of the concrete building are worthy of redemption. Those who choose to run and not fight, I save. Those who choose to attack, I eviscerate and strangle with their own intestines.

Sam looks back at me as I plough through the charging idiots. I see a brief smile; a sense of comradery he didn't consider he'd ever feel with me. I'm by his side, fighting the same war he'd been fighting, whilst he shielded me to this savage truth with lies.

Sam and I storm forward, smashing bodies and ripping limbs, and still, these pathetic, dark humans of Al Nadir seem to think they can assault us. Another set of terrorists on the right-hand side of the action set off a barrage of shoulder-held RPGs. I concentrate on the structure of the grenades for a second whilst they're airborne, and they explode in midflight. The terrorists pick up their machine guns, but in a blink, I'm standing over them. I grab the still-firing automatics and fling them, still with the human scum attached, across to the other side of the forecourt. They slam into the concrete walls and crumple in a heap.

A woman who looks a bit like Sabena charges at me with a curved Sinbad-style knife. My hand thrusts out through her chest and she falls down. Horror and confusion flash in her eyes.

The stream of Al Nadir soldiers has now abated. Operatives hang back inside the confines of the enormous building and keep to the shadows.

I scan the structure for humans, using their resonance patterns as indicators, and confirm that there are twenty-two thousand three hundred and one more operatives inside the building. I tell this to Sam.

"You take the ground. I'll shimmer to the first floor," he replies.

"Or we could just do this," I say, and I focus on the molecular structure of the building. Sam sees cracks forming.

"No, Ellie!" he shouts. "You have to review each person's Balance Shift. You can't just blanket kill."

I shrug, annoyed. "Saves time. They're all evil as fuck anyway."

"You're the Protector, Ellie. You have to do things by the book."

I glare at Sam, not wanting to accept his words, and then I shimmer abruptly inside. My focus now is fixed on obliterating, but I pull back on each kill, scanning each operative's Balance Shift.

By the end, only five out of the twenty-two thousand three hundred and one are redeemable.

But, as Sam tells me, five redeemable lives means good, white light increases across the world. If I'd collapsed the structure by molecular disintegration, then they'd have died and that potential would have been lost.

I know that too many innocents have already died in this unforgiving war.

Saving their lives makes my purpose as Protector starkly defined.

Chapter 13

Xiao Chang sat in his seat. His mother, Lei Huan Huan Chang, known as Lei, rested next to him, and his father, Chen, had the seat across the aisle, facing him. After finding Xiao collapsed in the gents' restroom at Sharm El Sheikh Airport, his parents wanted to keep a close eye on their son.

Chen Chang was a stocky man with wide shoulders, strong legs, and a muscular body. He had a constant surly expression on his face as if someone somewhere had denied him everything he'd ever wanted. His eyes were black and held an inner pain.

Lei was the complete opposite of her husband. Slight, graciously framed, and bearing a small height, she had a kind word to say to anything. She was the balancing factor in the family. Although small and thin, she was powerful. Descended from a long line of wealthy merchants from Hong Kong Island, such was her presence of being, that she commanded attention through her almost regal deportment. Her kind attitude was tempered by her eyes, dark and intensely intelligent. One glance showed she did not suffer fools. And if someone posed a threat to her family, she would fight them without consideration for her own safety. Lei would hurt them with every ounce of energy. With every bloodied nail, she would tear into them and leave her mark. Indelible. Unforgiving. It would tell all those who watched that her family meant everything to her. Nothing would harm them. Ever.

Xiao fidgeted in his seat. He grabbed at magazines, flicked through them and, finding them boring, disposed of them to the floor. He dived into his bag, dragged out his smartphone and headphones, and started flicking through screens until he found a game app. His father looked sideways at him, and then nudged his wife's shoulder. She smiled, pleased that their son had returned to a normal boy again.

"Is it good, darling?" asked Lei, watching her son slip back into game-obsessed normality.

Xiao nodded but didn't speak or raise his head.

"Pleased to see you're feeling better, my son," said Chen, standing up and heading over to him. "You gave us all a hell of a fright with your bathroom antics back there."

Chen knocked his son's shoulder lightheartedly, but once again, Xiao gave no reaction. His face remained firmly fixed on the game, ignoring all around him.

"Son, Xiao, can you stop that a minute? We need to speak to you." Chen's voice graveled with annoyance and his hand shot out to the smartphone, snatching it from Xiao's hand and clicking the off switch.

Xiao screamed out, incensed. "What is wrong with you?"

"Son, I was about to ask you the same question."

"What do you mean? There's nothing wrong with me. But there's something wrong with you. Why the hell did you do that? I was playing that game. Bloody idiot!"

Chen rose up. His bulky frame bulked up further as he listened to the insouciance in his son's spoilt voice. He'd given Xiao all he hadn't had himself as a boy. Unlike his wife, born of money, power, and influence, he'd had to toil for every Yuan he could get.

Chen had left school at fourteen to work in a textile factory. It didn't take him very long to work out that it was the garments that held the value. When he wasn't working, he'd read up about fashion and design. Through books, he taught himself dressmaking. With a few others from his town, he set up a garment business, and through his cousin in London, he found outlets in markets and discount stores. Chen was way ahead of all the Primarks and TK Maxxs, a real pioneer of discount runway fashion.

Through persistent hard work, Chen's venture took off in a big way. His three-man band expanded to several hundred, and his designs and quality products attracted the big names in high street fashion. But what differentiated him was his fashion-forward, almost prescient ability to know what was going to be hot before it took flame on the runway. The fashion cognoscenti called him 'The One' in recognition of Chen's mystical talent that seemed to mop up designers' thoughts and turn them into successful diffusion lines of his own creation.

There had been talk of a spy network run by Chen as the spymaster who preyed on other fashion designers, but nothing had been proven. Chen's lawyers chewed up any lawsuits and threatened to ruin anyone who pursued further action.

Chen had been at the top of his game when he'd met Lei.

She'd sat in the front row of the fashion show with all the other VIPs. Her bright, sharp eyes had roamed over all the designs. Before the show started, she'd withdrawn her Smythson notepad from her Hermes bag and kept it in her lap. Unlike the others around her, she'd written detailed notes in the pad as each model appeared at the head of the runway and sauntered down it. Chen had been in the wings, watching his creations take the stage. Lei had turned her head toward the next model and her eyes met his. That was all it took.

Chen knew no one else could come close to Lei. She was the one he wanted, the only one who could exceed his expectations of a woman. The stunning models, the debutantes, and all the colorful clingers paled to insignificance when she was around, her glory was so bright.

The day of their marriage, which came several months later after that meeting of eyes, Chen saw a woman of intelligence, beauty, and resolve. He blessed God for having delivered to him such a prize.

Now, in the airport, he looked back at Xiao, stabbing at the on button like a demented pigeon pecking at a plastic wrapper wondering why it wasn't delivering nourishment, and considered that perhaps his prize had come at a price.

He'd tried to understand Xiao, but it was clear from his son's early beginnings that he was a mummy's boy. Chen's work had kept him away for a great slice of Xiao's life and that parental bonding between father and son had never really happened.

Xiao was selfish and distant. Chen knew his son regarded him as little more than a deliverer of discipline. Chen recognized his role in this development, and how much he was really to blame for how Xiao had turned out. But had he not focused on his business empire, the luxuries that Xiao had taken for granted all his life wouldn't have been quite so forthcoming.

A trade-off in any situation has consequences, mused Chen. How you deal with those consequences determines what is really in your heart.

Xiao snatched a look at his father and his contempt surfaced.

Chen looked away, preferring not to engage with neither his son nor the certain question that had risen inside him.

What was really in his heart?

Chapter 14

Ashton rifled through the papers on Hutchinson's desk, looking at each one in turn. *It would work.* There was enough written there to speed through test developments. Culham Research Center in Oxford was the right option. Their work in photonic energy, low resonance projections, quantum engineering and the like would serve as a suitable precursor to all this. It would deliver the right backstory.

Ashton collected all the pages together in one bundle. He tapped them swiftly on the table to straighten them and took them in his hand. Hutchinson stared anxiously at the British PM. Ashton exuded a cool attitude. Since all the business with Sam and Ellie and virtual Armageddon, he'd constantly displayed an unfazed demeanor.

Hutchinson, however, was perturbed and at odds with himself. He knew the papers were not Treeborne's work, but he couldn't deny the unmitigated economic opportunity they presented.

Ashton picked up on Hutchinson's indecision, turning it to his advantage.

"Al, old friend, you know you can't keep them here."

Ashton's eyes were piercing and alert. No hint of warmth reflected within his hazel orbs. Hutchinson stared back at the pages in Ashton's hand.

"Don't you think I know that? It's why I called you."

"You want me to take them."

Hutchinson nodded but did not speak. His face was drawn and his mouth downturned. Despite his success in politics, Hutchinson was a habitual worrier. He was also fickle and easily influenced. As presidential material went, Hutchinson, although better than Treeborne, was not cut out to take the Oval Office. Ashton had read him the moment he'd met him months ago at an official occasion. He was malleable and really quite pathetic, a perfect instrument for using and abusing.

"Al, I know what needs to be done. Just leave it to me."

The PM gathered up the papers and made to drop them into his briefcase, but a hand descended on top of his, and the president spoke.

"What about…my side…you know?"

And there it was. Ashton felt it coming. Human greed could always be counted upon.

"Your side?" repeated Ashton, slightly amused by how predictable Hutchinson was becoming.

"Yes, erm…my side."

Hutchinson was uncomfortable talking about money. Ashton smiled, relishing in the president's inadequacy, his lack of strength to voice his true desire. A man without conviction in himself is a man who is lost. *And by the nose, I will lead him.*

"You'll be recompensed well."

Hutchinson acknowledged, lowering his head. But any other flicker of gratitude failed to show.

"But first, we need to get these things out of here, away from you. Agreed?"

Hutchinson nodded dumbly. Ashton was taking charge, handling everything, and he was glad. The PM could take the glory for the discovery and handle all the regulatory rigmarole. He'd just take the profits when they came. That's the kind of equation Hutchinson liked. Getting it all for doing a sweet FA. It was the very reason he had entered politics in the first place.

Ashton stuck the papers firmly into his briefcase.

"I think it's time to say au revoir," he said, standing up.

"You have to go so soon?" said Hutchinson, his disappointment visible. He'd wanted to delve into Ashton's confident mind again. He had questions about Al Nadir and how to deal with their implants in the White House staff, of which there were still many, far more than Hutchinson would have thought possible given their rigorous security checks.

"We'll talk again, my friend. I know you have Al Nadir still on your mind. I'm instituting a cleansing process through my ranks. You should do the same. Remember, old friend, you're the leader. You need to demonstrate strength and give no mercy to traitors. Let everyone see it in you. You have to be ruthless now. It's the only stand to take."

Ashton's full and round lips straightened to a sharp line. Hutchinson was suddenly reminded of the snakes he used to chase as a kid out of his parents' garden back in their Florida homestead. A slit splitting across an anguine face, before opening to reveal venomous fangs. He shivered. Why should that memory pop into his head?

"Yes, yes, I-I w-w-will," replied Hutchinson. His nervous stutter returned for the first time since the day presidency was thrust upon him.

"I'm sure you'll know what to do. Accept no excuses, take no prisoners. Where Al Nadir is concerned, that's my motto. Until the next time, my good friend."

Ashton threw his arms open in a gesture of warmth and kindness. His action belied any suspicions Hutchinson may have had.

Holding the president close, Ashton said, "Be strong, my friend. It's what you must be."

Ashton released Hutchinson, who had become unexpectedly emotional in the PM's embrace. Ashton's words had touched him, and tears formed in the corners of his eyes. Realizing what he was revealing to the PM, Hutchinson dabbed his eyes with an old, school-monographed handkerchief.

"Huh, allergies," he muttered.

"It's been quite a ride, hasn't it, old friend?" said Ashton. "It's okay to let go. I often do."

That was all Hutchinson needed. "Oh my God, I thought it was just me feeling like this. I thought that there was something wrong with me. But you saying that, well, well…"

Hutchinson gave into the tears, too choked up to continue.

"I know. You keep thinking you were so close to total annihilation, to absolute death, and yet you survived. You were saved. Allowed to breathe again. To live again. To love again."

Hutchinson couldn't believe what Ashton was saying. These were the words in his head at that very moment.

"Richard, you're so right. We were saved. We must do good and show that we were worth saving."

Ashton turned around. This conversation was better than the last. It all aligned with what had gone before and he could see it would power all that was ahead.

"Al, have I your confidence?" asked Ashton, almost in a whisper.

Chapter 15

Sam radios into the Special Forces waiting in the Chinooks above us, giving them a cleanup code. I watch as the massive helicopters land in the forecourt, and out pour the best of the best. The men leap out and duck to avoid the rotor blades still turning fast. I stand there, my arms folded. The survivors of our takedown are in a heap on the ground. Sam took them out of the stasis seconds before the helicopters landed. They still don't move. In their eyes, I can see the horrors they've witnessed, which are still in replay mode.

As I promised Sam, there were no dead bodies. I zapped all with my rainbow light and obliterated their hideous, torn carcasses. It was perhaps better that way, as I know that the guys arriving now, tough as they are, would have been traumatized if they'd seen those terrorists' remains.

I glance at one of the soldiers and smile. "What time is it?"

"Six fifty-five, ma'am," replies the young member of the Special Air Services.

It's taken just fifteen minutes to clear the entire Al Nadir base of all their people. The base housed twenty-two thousand four hundred and fourteen people. Out of all those, I found only thirty-seven redeemable.

The SAS soldier looks around the forecourt at the lack of bodies, and I know he's about to ask a question.

"Is that *all* the hostiles?" he asks, pointing to the small clump of Asian people, mostly from Indonesia and the Philippines, who sit huddled on the ground. The soldiers are ring-tying and readying them for transportation on the second chopper.

"Yep, that's it," I say, and I don't initiate any further explanation. The SAS guy doesn't have time to pursue as his CO steps up to me, salutes, and confirms he is ready to receive the prisoners on board.

"Thank you," I say.

I don't salute back. I'm not bound by Earthly conventions. I stand, dispassionate and removed from the scene, as the soldiers haul the prisoners away. The girl with the semi-automatic Glock almost as big as she is glares at me as she passes. I read her Balance Shift and it is in the light zone but only just. The bitter hatred for me in her face shows that she is on the brink of darkness.

I turn away. Such innocence taken by Al Nadir's evil.

Sam arrives after a final sweep of the building, despite me telling him there are no more hostiles in there. Ever the alpha-male, Sam has to do things his way.

"Darling, we're all clear back there."

"I know," I clip tartly.

"Time, I think, to let the boys clear up," says Sam, and he nods toward the soldiers pushing the hostiles into the Chinook. "We've got more work to do, haven't we?"

I don't answer. My mind is still on that little girl pumping out so much hatred. I tried to change her, but human will is greater than my power. The darkness that lurks within the human heart thrives on the injustices received. It festers like a disease and consumes from within. Knowing this, I wonder just how much good I can really bring to these wretched souls and others like them who have been pawns of abuse and manipulation in Al Nadir's master plan.

Chapter 16

Hutchinson's eyes widened at such a strange and somewhat hurtful question. Surely the PM knew that whatever was said in secret could be trusted with him? He was a sound man, and not one to tell tales out of school.

"Richard, after what we've been through, I didn't expect that." Hutchinson's voice was made stronger through his indigence.

"Apologies, Al, but what I'm about to tell you will have ramifications on the world."

Ashton headed back to the comfy sofa in front of the president's impressive oak desk, talking as he walked. Hutchinson stepped back and walked in time with Ashton, his face expectant and fascinated.

"That good you spoke of, which we must do, well, it's already in train. The world has experienced unimaginable evil with Al Nadir. Now it's time for us to deliver unbelievable good."

The president sat on a chair to the left of the PM. Huddling closer, he listened, mesmerized by Ashton's voice.

"There is a movement that I've started. It's called Freedom Earth. The name originates from the freedom Earth was given when God delivered to us salvation in the form of Ellie Noor. She is a force for good, and Freedom Earth will be the same. Imagine, Al, a world free of war where everyone is united, irrespective of religion, color, or creed. In the eyes of Freedom Earth, there will only be one color. The color of humanity. And only one way. The way of right."

Hutchinson was flabbergasted. Uniting the world. Was this even possible? Was Ashton mad?

Ashton read the confusion and disbelief rippling across Hutchinson's body. The president flopped back in his chair and stared at the prime minister, absorbing what he'd said. Ashton didn't look mad. He actually looked very sane and measured. But what he suggested, it just couldn't be done. Could it?

Silence screamed between the two world leaders.

Ashton waited, allowing the president time to consider the impossible task he had set before revealing how he could ensure the project's success.

"Despite your misgivings," Ashton said, knowing Hutchinson certainly didn't have a poker face when it came to emotions, "it will be quite straightforward."

The PM's last line was too much for Hutchinson, who spluttered and shook his head vigorously. "Richard, man, I've been listening, but God, I don't see how you say it's gonna be easy when it's never really been attempted before. I mean what you're suggesting, that level of unprecedented peace, it's failed even the greatest peacemakers of our time."

"I know, and you're right. But then they didn't have what we have now."

Hutchinson looked puzzled. The PM was talking in riddles. Clearly, something was amiss upstairs.

"So what do we have now?" said Hutchinson, humoring Ashton. On his question, he lunged and grabbed the bottle of Jack Daniels, pouring a heavy measure in the high ball glass. The mysterious talk bemused his brain and he was in need of a drink.

"Al Nadir," Ashton replied, and he moved over to the table to partake in a tipple of Tennessee's finest.

Hutchinson had taken a long gulp, but on hearing Ashton's response, he started to cough. Associating the name of Al Nadir with world peace was like associating the Third Reich with knitting. It was ludicrous. Incomprehensible. Hutchinson was now unsure of Ashton's game. It wasn't going the way he expected.

The PM, seeing the bemusement on the president's face, smiled. He was absolutely loving this.

"Sorry, old friend, let me elucidate. Al Nadir, as you know, brought over seventy-five percent of the world's terror regimes, crime syndicates, and rogue nations under one banner, Al Nadir. We know where most, if not all, of these people are now that we have control of their terrorist network. Thanks to Ellie taking out Salim and Sabena, our joint special forces were able to enter and establish control of these bases. As you know, Sam and Ellie are working through each country where Al Nadir had command bases. They've secured appropriate assets, captured those who allowed themselves to be captured, and neutralized the rest."

Hutchinson did know this. It had been a very bloody affair, but they were actions that, with the demise of Al Nadir's leaders, had helped to break the stranglehold Al Nadir had on the world. But he still couldn't see how all that intelligence could deliver world peace.

Ashton could see that the president still hadn't had the epiphany moment. His mind wasn't sharp enough to join the dots Ashton had laid out.

"My friend, if I say the words 'make an example', isn't that enough?"

Ashton looked at Hutchinson but even after that clue, nothing registered. Goodness, the man was a neurological sloth, thought Ashton.

"Al, you're the first to hear this. I will be working with a number of key world leaders to agree that every Al Nadir operative, minnow or whale, will be executed on the grounds of treason. All countries, irrespective of their stance on capital punishment, still retain the death penalty for treason. It fits perfectly. And what's more, it shows to the world that all of us have zero tolerance for terrorists, and if we take this stand, it shows we have the strength to achieve much more. People will believe in us. They'll fear us. But they'll respect us for taking this hard line. Do you see?"

Hutchinson heard the words. Although they sounded quite horrific, they also sounded right. Al Nadir had been a blight on humanity and the only way forward was a ruthless purge. Ashton was right. Absolutely right.

"Of course I see and, what's more, I completely agree. Zero tolerance. The only way to be. What do you need from me? You know I shall support you in Freedom Earth. The US will be your greatest ally. I'll make sure of that."

Ashton bowed his head, feigning humility and gratitude. This was so easy. If all the other leaders were as trusting as this imbecile, he'd be done quicker than expected.

"At this stage, the movement is only words on paper. But good, true people have pledged their support. They've given their backing to make it happen. If perhaps the US and UK could, in the near future, sign an accord agreeing to work together as founding countries of Freedom Earth, we could turn those words into actions."

Hutchinson scanned down his appointments on his desk diary then picked up his phone and pressed a number. Ashton watched him cautiously, sipping at his whiskey.

"Nate, good evening. We need to shift my schedule tomorrow morning. Something's come up that I need to handle…Yeah, yeah, it's all okay…I'll let you know…Shortly. Got to go."

The president's voice was officious and clipped, a charade of command

and control. The real Hutchinson was the one in the chair stumbling over his words.

Nate Van de Mart, thought Ashton, the president's chief of staff, was the US equivalent of his own Cabinet secretary, Martyn Redfern. Van de Mart was the president's faithful terrier snapping at the heels of the Cabinet, keeping all those secretaries in order. Ashton had a lot of time for Nate. He'd met him a few times whilst President Looney Tunes had been in office, and he liked him.

He graduated *magna cum laude* in Law at Harvard, had a good family pedigree, a beautiful wife, two kids, a Labrador, and a penchant for BDSM prostitutes. The last aspect of Nate's life, although it would never see the light of day on his resume, was, in fact, the feature that most impressed Ashton. And it was the reason why he liked the chief of staff so much. A man with vices was a man who could be controlled.

Ashton wondered whether Hutchinson was aware of Nate's sexual proclivities. He kept it very tight. He didn't go to dungeons, didn't have a secret pier d'terre, and didn't have a regular girl. He just did his work diligently and kept the Cabinet in good and tidy order.

Ashton's own private intelligence network had almost drawn a blank. Almost. But with his dark connections, slithers of something emerged. A Mayfair club owner with a line in 'recreational specialties' recalled to Ashton's intelligence operative that Nate had dropped in with colleagues for a drink before heading back to DC. He'd slipped him a note asking about 'private dining facilities'. The owner understood immediately.

Under some unknown pretense, the owner had taken Nate to the back of the club. Ashton's intel guy had followed soon after. He'd watched as Nate passed a mangle of mirrors, embedded LEDs depicting dark, swirling galaxies, and plush velvet that adorned the walls, following like a puppy behind the club proprietor. The intel guy observed the club owner as he pressed one of the shattered mirrors stuck on the wall, and it opened. It was a door that led into a claustrophobic, velvet-lined corridor with virtually no lighting, save for red-bulbed wall lights. The corridor twisted upwards and merged into a narrow staircase. Nate, so Ashton was told by his intel guy, followed up in silence. The air singed with frisson and expectation. But also uneasiness. The confusion on Nate's face showed he didn't know where all of this was leading. But Ashton's intel guy could see he had hope.

When the owner came to a small archway covered by a heavy, maroon curtain, Nate, it was said, held his breath. The owner drew back the curtain and Nate looked in. Behind him, Ashton's intel guy looked in too. His eyes fell on the whips and chains hung up on the scarlet wall. He watched Nate moisten his lips and saw his eyes enlarge like saucers. The intel guy looked up to where Nate stared and saw a voluptuous leather-clad dominatrix of Amazonian proportions sliding out of the shadows, her long fingers outstretched toward her next victim. The smile on Nate's face showed the intel guy that his hopes had been answered.

Funnily enough, so had the hopes of the PM.

With his dark side discovered by Ashton, and this knowledge made apparent to Nate through the PM's channels, the chief of staff knew he was owned. No White House secret could be kept from Ashton. Nate was his man in the White House. And that's why he had so much time for him.

But even Nate didn't know about the energy source. That was more than secret. To anyone apart from Hutchinson and himself, it just didn't exist.

"Richard, this may be presumptuous of me," started the president, "and tell me now if I'm stepping over the line." Ashton moved closer and put a hand on Hutchinson's knee, a show of solidarity. Two leaders facing the world together. "But I would like to show my support to Freedom Earth. You've heard I've cleared my morning schedule. So how about it, old friend? Let's show the world what we stand for. Let's show them the birth of Freedom Earth."

Listening, Ashton turned. Each mouthful spouted from the president was a gift. He knew Hutchinson was impressionable, gullible even, but this, this reaction, it was beyond expectation. Maybe all the years of being in Treeborne's company had dulled any smidgen of intellect.

The psyche assessment he'd undertaken on the president showed his need to compensate, to restore what his predecessor had taken, and to give back to the world. Freedom Earth's philosophy underlined his ideology. It was understandable then why Hutchinson had reacted so passionately. With such vigor, he had supported the partnership that Ashton had only softly alluded to in passing.

"Thank you, Al. I really appreciate that. Together we'll stand and together we'll be the peacemakers."

Neither Hutchinson nor Ashton realized what had been said.

But just three days before, those same words had been delivered by a man embracing Armageddon with open arms.

Chapter 17

Chen settled into the in-flight movie. Lei fixed herself firmly amongst the pages of a historic romance, and their son, Xiao, slept peacefully, stretched out on a full bed. After the argument, the Chang family had resolved their differences and took advantage of the luxuries first-class air travel provided.

Chen glanced down at his son. He seemed small when wrapped in the woolen blanket the airline had supplied, much smaller than his attitude, which, when awake, made him appear taller. He was a kind boy, but Chen knew he'd spoilt him too much. He had a slightly pompous streak, a sense of entitlement that Chen recognized could only be found in those children of the very rich. He'd never know what it means for a father to say no. He'd never appreciate the stomach-churning anxiety of not knowing where his next paycheck would come from. Perhaps he'd been wrong to treat the boy as a prince, wanting for nothing. But he was his only boy. He gave him the life he'd never had. It was as though he could live his childhood again through Xiao. Something came alive inside Chen, a realization of youth again. His millions could actually turn back time and take him to a place of plenty, where hunger never touched him and poverty never imprisoned him.

With a sudden and rapid abruptness, his son moved. Xiao sat bolt upright, his back straight as if he'd been pulled up by his shoulders. The blanket fell away from him, and he stared with a cold concentration around the cabin. His eyes were enlarged and bulging, created by a terror Chen could neither see nor hear. Xiao moved his head with a slow sweep, taking in all the passengers. Chen placed a hand on his son's arm but Xiao did not respond. Engrossed in the act of the search, he did not recognize the comforting gesture.

Chen looked into his son's eyes. Dull, almost lifeless orbs stared back.

Chen shivered. It was as though his son was empty, that his body was a mere vessel and none of Xiao existed.

Xiao's eyes glazed over as he swept the cabin. Everywhere had turned white. No color. Just white. Xiao wanted to close his eyes. The light was vicious. Too bright. It burned him. He so wanted to turn away. But something forced him to look. A slow outline. A definition of grey slipped into the whiteness. Things emerged, brought into shape by the darker hues that insinuated into the white. People's faces rose up and darkened at a swift pace. Weird and elongated, their faces grew sinister, their mouths twisted into smiles, but their eyes were without pupils. In their eye sockets, large, black pools reflected the horrors they'd inflicted on others. Xiao could see their darkness. All around him, monsters masquerading as humans. As he watched, they mutated. Their skin dripped down their faces, showing black skeletal bone. Their mouths widened with a laugh that deafened him, and bony fingers extended to caress his skin.

"Xiao, Son, are you okay?" Chen reached out toward his son, but Xiao screamed and backed into the space between the chair beds.

Lei dropped her book and dove over to her son. "Baby, what's wrong?"

Xiao pulled his blanket around him, his eyes now bulbous and red with tears. He tried to close them and still couldn't. Around him, color seeped back in. The horrific faces and maniacal laughter slipped away, and normality enshrouded him again. Xiao hung his head and shook with formidable persistence. His hands rose to shield the memories of the shocking visions.

"It was horrible. They were all around me. They were so dark, so dark..."

"Just a bad dream, Son. Don't worry. We're here. Everything is okay, isn't it, love?" Chen looked at his wife, who now fretted over her trembling son.

Lei smoothed her son's hair and kissed his forehead. "Come on, darling. You're alright."

"But, Mum, there were monsters everywhere." Xiao shivered. The blanket wrapped around his body failed to give him warmth.

Xiao didn't raise his head from his cupped hands. Fresh in his mind were the ghouls with no eyes, just black pools. And reflected in those ebony mirrors were victims in pain, crying, beaten down by the agonies brought upon them. With arms outstretched, they called for salvation, but no one saved them.

Inside, Xiao could feel it. The burning torment of injustice. Lives sold to fuel the coffers of the corrupt. Their last vestige of hope, so palpable. Xiao wept, great sobbing throes that wrecked him as he lived their plight within a moment's glance.

"Son, don't be frightened. There's no monsters here. They've all gone now."

Chen placed a comforting hand upon his son. Xiao looked up, startled by Chen's touch, and screamed.

The black pools of pain and suffering were back. But this time, they were on his father's face.

Gone? I don't think so, Dad.

Chapter 18

Al Nadir's game plan of housing their bases in the most barren and inhospitable places on Earth and hiding beneath their own satellite-image-masking technologies prevented most opportunities for ground or air force attacks.

If a base can't be seen, no intelligence surveillance can be gained.

Now Al Nadir's cloaked advantage has failed. I don't use surveillance methods existing on the universal plane. In my mind, I can see where their bases are across the world. I only need to concentrate on their energy resonance, and their dark vibrations fill me with pain and anger. It becomes a beacon to me, and I can home in on that beacon to uncover any Al Nadir base that so far has been hidden. I start to shimmer and Sam picks up on my shimmer trail.

"Amazon rainforest?" he asks, checking the destination point.

"Yes."

"So amazing."

Sam's voice is tinged with resentment. But I'm not having it, him begrudging my capabilities. I would love to be able to pass up my powers to be human again.

"What's your problem?"

"There isn't a problem."

"Do you think I'm stupid?

"I'm fine. Let's go."

"We're not going anywhere until you tell me why you're so mad at me."

I take a seat on the sofa and cross my arms. Sam shuffles his feet and won't look in my eyes.

"Is it because I know where the bases are?" I venture.

Sam sighs heavily. He brings his eyes to look at me. "It isn't just that, but that is part of it."

I realize so much has been invested, time, money, technology and, most of all, lives into discovering where those bases are. Those bases I can see so clearly in my mind. Sam is feeling bitter about my sudden and immediate clarity.

"It isn't my fault they were hidden from your surveillance abilities."

"I know that, darling. It's just..." Sam stops speaking. He sits down. Sadness creeps across his face.

"And you're thinking why now?"

The frustration Sam feels inside him suddenly explodes.

"Hell, yes! What we have now, our powers, your powers, we could have saved so many lives if we'd only had them six years ago. Why did Kudamun wait until mankind faced a precipice? All that death, destruction, and suffering we've had for so many years could have been avoided if Aby-od had powered you up. Then you could have taken out Al Nadir before they ever got started, before they hit those thirty cities."

"Sam, sweetness, you know things don't work that way."

"But why don't they work that way? From where I sit, it would make a lot more sense for the Universe."

Sam's voice rises. He's not shouting, but his argument is delivered with power. He's been thinking about this for a while. It's true. From a single standpoint, what Sam has said is absolutely correct, but it's not how the Universe works.

"I don't know why, darling. I didn't write the rule book. Only the Ancient Ones know that. I'm just part of the mechanism, an enabler to ensure the rules are followed and the Balance is maintained."

"The *fucking* Balance! Everything comes down to it."

"Of course."

"But why?"

"Sam, I'm not sure this conversation is very productive. We have work to do taking down Al Nadir."

Sam bristles. His eyes darken and his mouth trembles. "When I was human, when I watched people abuse others, I wondered why we were really here. What is life about? Now I'm Kudamaz, despite having all this universal knowledge and supreme power and strength, I know even less. Life is even more of a conundrum than it's ever been. I may know the mechanics of life, but I still don't know why they exist."

Tears form in Sam's eyes. I turn toward him and pull him close to me. He keeps his hands on the sofa and doesn't embrace me. His body shakes with emotion. His tears well and start to drip down his face. As they leave his eyes, they sparkle. I hold his head and bring his lips to mine. Sam closes his eyes as he falls into the kiss.

"Life for you, me, and every species in the Universe is about making choices, and as a result of those choices, you create experiences. Some good, some bad. But we own those choices and those experiences embed within us to form our lives. No one makes them for us. We've been given free will to make those choices. We grow and develop that way, and the energy that comes out of those experiences flows back and forth creating and maintaining the Universe so that it can continue, and we can continue. One needs the other to survive. Our existence is symbiotic with the Universe."

"I feel like we're all hamsters running in a giant celestial wheel. What happens if the hamster jumps off?"

"Where to? Where would this existential hamster go?"

Sam shrugs. "Somewhere he doesn't have to run blindly just to stay alive."

"There is nowhere else. We're all on that hamster wheel."

"What about the Ancient Ones? They have other places outside the Universe."

I shake my head. It's not a good line to go down. Not for a Kudamaz anyway.

"You know we can't speak about those." I slam my words out, fast and hard.

Sam nods, resigned to the fact, but I see that flash of anger in his eyes.

"But it does all feel wrong," adds Sam. "I mean, those poor people who were harnessed by Al Nadir were at their mercy because of their poverty. If they'd been educated and had a decent standard of living, they wouldn't have been quite so quick to jump aboard Al Nadir's train."

"Sam, there's one point two billion people in the world living on less than fifty cents a day, and their homes are slums without sanitation, fresh drinking water, or even a safe place to lay their heads. Al Nadir only harnessed around five percent of those people and gave them an opportunity for a real life."

"A very savage one."

"That may be so but, right or wrong, those people were given a new view of life."

Sam stands up, glaring at me. "It sounds like you're saying Al Nadir were right to go into those slums and take those people. You know Al Douri just went in and bought them like they were guns? He barely considered they were human. To him, they were just implements of war."

"I'm not saying I agree with what Al Douri did. I'm just saying his choice gave a new experience to those people that they'd never otherwise have had."

"But they're probably going to die as a result," said Sam grimly.

"Yes, they will once we get going and stop this crazy conversation we're having."

"You think this is crazy? What I think is crazy is why we didn't have a good, rich person harness the human resource in those slums for something of value to humanity instead of turning them into killing machines."

"I can't answer that, Sam. I don't know why things happen the way they do. But it ensures Balance."

"Well, I don't know about everything being Balanced on this planet. It seems like everything is skewed and pretty fucked up!"

"Sam, you know that's not true. We've seen the Balance Shift and it is well balanced, giving strength to planet Earth and mankind."

"So you think that Al Nadir had to exist to enable this Balance to come about?"

From his tone of voice, Sam is clearly not buying anything I've said. When I think about the logic, it is actually quite insane, but only when I look at Earth in isolation from the Universe. The fact is, Earth does not operate in isolation, and neither does the Balance. Everything is connected and interconnected.

"I don't think that. But that, as you say, is how it's all played out."

Sam scowls and looks away. Then he fires me with a line that seethes with antagonism.

"You're the Protector now. Can't you improve all this? What's the point of you if you can't change anything?"

"Thanks. Nice to know I'm wanted!"

"No, darling, sorry. I don't mean you per se, but your role as the Protector. Can't you change humanity to be kinder to each other? That stuff that Ashton is planning, isn't that right in your purview too?"

"To be honest, Sam, I still don't exactly get what Ashton is planning, but goodness is something that we all want for Earth, as long as there is a Balance. A swing too much to the white light is just as dangerous as a swing to the dark. On no account must Earth become polarized. That's all I care about."

Sam starts to shimmer without indicating anything to me.

"Where are you going?" I snap with annoyance.

"To take out Al Nadir in the Amazon rainforest, as we should have done before starting this thing we've gotten into."

"You started it, Sam, not me. I'm quite happy to get on and decapitate Al Nadir. It was you who wanted to talk about the meaning of life."

Sam doesn't respond.

"Did you hear me?" I stare with pointed insistence at my husband.

"Yes, I did. I'm sorry. I guess I'm trying to get things clear in my mind. Come on. Let's take down some bastards. That'll help me get my perspective right."

I smile while listening to my husband. Just the kind of response I expected. I walk over and hold him tight. No alpha shimmer this time. We're going into that hell hole together.

I initiate shimmer and Silent Waters is overwritten with massive vegetation, flowing waters, tweeting and twittering, and mystical echoes of animals who call the Amazon rainforest home.

Chapter 19

Lei stared out the window and wondered if this was a penance for all the money and position she had but hadn't earned on her own.

The request for a doctor rung out across the Tannoy, stretching through first, business, and then coach. One doctor, a Scotsman hailing from Perth and traveling business, piped up and offered the air stewardess assistance. With gratitude, she took the doctor to the front of the plane where Lei and Chen crouched over a small, shaking, and screaming figure. The air around the young boy tinged with fearful inevitability.

The doctor pulled the boy's hands from his face and intoned a calming sentiment. "It's alright, laddie. Easy now you go. Nae problem. All's okay."

Xiao simmered slightly and his screams waned. He nodded his head, taking the doctor's words into his being

"There you go. All okay now."

The soothing refrain rested his confused and terrified mind. Xiao discerned an uncomfortable feeling in his arm but felt no pain.

The doctor administered a light sedative to quell the boy's hysterics. Lei stood immobile, a tower of angst over her beloved child. Watching, hands splayed star-like, she was ready to act, to do something, anything, to save her son.

Xiao raised his eyelids upward, prepared for the horrors again. The cabin slipped and shivered into view amidst a halo of light and, at the center, reality emerged. People all around, staring, pointing, talking like animations from his games, following actions decreed by a master gamer, the one who wrote the software, designed the interface, and set the rules. Empty of meaning. Only existence.

"He looks much better. Thank you, doctor."

His mother's voice. He remembered. Such love. The halo of light evened out and dissipated to the very corners of his peripheral vision. People moved back. Those vacuous vessels of silent searching departed, leaving him with the one of kind words, the one filled with love.

A hand touched his head. He turned. A soul of pain. Regret. Unrequited recognition of the immoralities of a life in the shadows, feeding off others. But no longer absent omen orbs or black mirrored tunnels leading to deathless torment. His father stared back, concern etched into the creases around his normal eyes.

The boy pitied his lack of light. Chen touched him. Xiao cried. His father would never know that lightness, a happiness that radiates from the soul through the good done to others.

Xiao lifted his hand to his father's crinkled brow.

"I'm so sorry, Father!" The boy collapsed into Lei. Her breasts formed a support for his head, and he nestled, finally peaceful.

Lei scowled at Chen and then at the doctor, her accusation evident in the cold force of her stare. "What is this? What is wrong with our son? What did you do to him? What was in that drug?"

Lei pelted out her delivery sub-automatic style. Both parents glared at the doctor, who, in defense, showed the empty phial.

"Just a light sedative. But it should nae have knocked him oot."

"So it's your fault!" Chen shouted, moving his heavy bulk toward the troubled Scotsman.

Lei sliced down her exquisitely manicured hand in the decreasing space between her husband and the doctor.

"Enough!" She inhaled and glowered at her husband then pointed to the doctor. "This man tried to help our son. It is obvious Xiao has problems and when we land he must be admitted immediately to hospital."

Chen remained still. He could not acknowledge that the great Chen Chang, fashion meister, The One, no less, and loved by the world, had malfunctioning off-spring.

"You understand, Chen? Our boy has problems. He needs specialist help."

Clipped and authoritative, Lei's breeding stormed ahead of her voice. Chen looked at his wife. With reluctance, he nodded.

Lei turned to the doctor who held her son's wrist, checking his pulse rate. "Doctor?"

"Doctor Hamish McGregor."

"Well, Doctor McGregor, when we land, I need you to accompany us to the hospital. You need to inform the clinicians there of the symptoms befalling my son, Xiao. Neither my husband nor I are medical people and therefore I am looking to you to ensure that his condition is communicated correctly to the doctors when he is admitted. No room for error, Doctor McGregor."

Eyes, diamond-hard, shot into the doctor.

"Of course, I will do everything I can for the wee boy."

"Thank you, doctor, because, just remember, that wee boy is *my* wee boy. Answers must be found. Xiao is my life. You understand, doctor? My life."

Lei squeezed the doctor's hand with such targeted fierceness that he winced. Lei ignored him and reiterated her plea.

"Xiao is my reason for living. Nothing is more important. Do not fail me."

The doctor stared into the mother's eyes. Determination and courage lit her from within. He could see her relentless pursuit of her son's wellbeing. It was typical of a mother's stance when faced with such a situation. What was not typical, however, was the unsettling way she delivered her last words. Do not fail me. A threat rather than a statement.

The doctor looked at the boy, now slumped back in the chair bed. His screams echoed an insanity. He pulled his hand away from Lei as she released her hold. What, in a boy so young, had driven him to such an outburst? And what of the darkness in others had he spoken of? He glanced down at the boy, his screams still resounding in his head, and the doctor wondered, did he really want to find out?

Chapter 20

There are moments in history that are seminal. Man's first walk on the moon. Martin Luther King's 'I have a dream' speech. The concurrent bombing of thirty major cities. And, of course, Malta exploding in seconds.

The last two of these moments were delivered to the world by Al Nadir, a terrorist collective corporation that, until recently, had the world trembling under its mighty thumb. However, that morning was a turning point. Another of those seminal moments written into the annals of history.

US President Al Hutchinson and British Prime Minister Richard Ashton, along with various suited officials, gathered on the lawn in front of the White House to pledge joint allegiance to the formation of Freedom Earth. It was a peace movement that would eradicate terrorism and unite the faiths of the world under the banner of humanity.

The US and the UK were the front-runners in the movement. But Ashton intended to work through country after country, starting first with the G8 pack, to secure their allegiance and commitment to Freedom Earth. And with that public acknowledgment, they would sign up to a condition that all Al Nadir operatives, whatever their crimes, would be publicly executed.

Ashton was fully aware of the potential backlash from human rights lobbyists. He'd already developed an uncompromising attack statement to dissuade the troublemakers before they could even consider taking his policy to The Hague.

"Those of you out there who feel that we are being unjust or harsh to Al Nadir, hear this. Al Nadir's reign of terror annihilated millions of people worldwide and destroyed many more through grief and suffering. Death defined our world and it underlined every action they took. We are now in a position to remove that terror completely. Our advances in technological capability deliver power to us. Now Salim Al Douri is dead, Al Nadir are no longer the threat they once were. But make no mistake, they are *still* a considerable threat and it is our duty to our peoples to keep them safe.

"If anyone issues any protest about the hard line we are taking, they will themselves be immediately regarded as Al Nadir collaborators and sympathizers. Thus they will face similar charges and imprisonment leading to eventual execution.

"Both President Hutchinson and I know that this is the only redress we have. Our goal through Freedom Earth is to unite the world and bring good, love, and charity back to restore peace to a planet where once all that lived was war."

Ashton stopped speaking. He looked into the camera. His face was strong and determined. He drew energy from the hundreds of millions of viewers who would, by now, be glued to the broadcast. The cameraman glanced to the side at the head of communications for the White House. In turn, he stared quizzically at the communications director for Number 10. All three men shrugged, not knowing what was happening.

It seemed that the PM had gone completely off script. The bemused heads of communication turned to question the US president without words. But Hutchinson held his position stoically and did not entertain eye contact. He alone knew that Ashton had certainly not gone off script. Far from it. He was, in fact, more 'on script' than he'd ever been. This was what they'd agreed. The empathic moment. The calm minute of peace. A time to remember all the souls who had streamed to heaven, and all the hell Al Nadir had wrought on Earth. The pause was orchestrated to get people to absorb the last words. *Restore peace to a planet where once all that lived was war.*

The president had said to Ashton that initiating a silence in the middle of a state address being broadcast worldwide was a risky and somewhat courageous tactic for a politician. Wrong execution and Ashton would be seen as cheesy or overly dramatic. Or, even worse, a statesman who had forgotten his lines, whose mind had wandered or who was blatantly insincere and false.

Ashton could not be dissuaded. It was to be. The silence had to happen. He was adamant about that. It was the only route to securing that empathic connection he needed with the world. He hadn't even had time to practice. He didn't need to. He had conviction. Total, unwavering conviction. And absolute self-belief.

Ashton's face stared out from TVs, laptops, mobiles, and devices across the world. The eyes of the viewers, as if caught in a tractor beam, snapped into the PM's stare. A hypnotic, time-absorbing delivery captured them and held them transfixed. That pause. A captured moment absorbing the sorrow, pain, and suffering of those millions who had died.

And, in unison, the world believed.

"My friends, that silence honored our dearly departed, the ones who have been taken from us too soon. They are the reason why Freedom Earth has to work. We must make it work. And we must always remember those who have been taken by Al Nadir's actions. We must never, never shy away from the necessary actions that need to be done to eradicate Al Nadir from Earth completely."

Ashton turned to cue up Hutchinson, who smoothly took the frame. No smiling, no insensitive indications. Just pure conviction. Like Ashton.

"Freedom Earth is our new tomorrow. It is the place that we, as the peoples of Earth, can create. Today marks day one of our new world. The United States of America has joined with the United Kingdom to make this new world happen. Al Nadir wiped out so many. But, in doing so, they provided us with the canvas to paint a masterpiece that will be our glorious tomorrow. Free of war, terror, and hate. A place where only peace, security, and love will reside. My friends, I give you America's commitment and unwavering support to Britain and to Prime Minister Ashton on this day that will forever be known as Freedom Earth Day."

Like a slick double act, Ashton picked up the baton of breathtaking delivery from Hutchinson and continued his own speech.

"In recognition of what Freedom Earth stands for and to show the world that we will not tolerate an organization like Al Nadir to choke the life from us ever again, we will be commencing with the public executions of Al Nadir operatives. Starting with a man, Dr. Hans Stein-Muller, who created an insidiously evil device. The nano-bomb. A man responsible for death and destruction on a scale virtually inconceivable. With utter disregard for life, Dr. Stein-Muller's creation enabled Al Nadir to kill indiscriminately, mothers, children, the elderly, and almost anyone who was in the vicinity of the blast zone.

"At nine a.m. tomorrow morning, Dr. Stein-Muller will be the first in the wave of Al Nadir's top lieutenants to face execution. Simultaneously, in the UK at two p.m. tomorrow, Mr. Pedro Russo, the third in command in Al Nadir after Salim Al Douri and Sabena Sanantoni, will face execution for his part in the devastation of Malta and the genocide of the Maltese people.

"Following their executions, every single Al Nadir operative will be executed over a specific period of time. Once the world is cleansed of their evil, we will build again afresh and pure. A world where humanity has, at last, a real home."

The 'Ashton and Hutchinson show' was seen by millions around the globe. It was mid-afternoon in Europe. The president of France, Cyrille Marcie, was informed by his political aide of the broadcast. He turned on the television and watched. Like all the other viewers, he was snapped and trapped in Ashton's piercing, powerful stare, and he was touched by the empathic moment. President Marcie's country had suffered terribly. Paris had been one of the cities amongst the thirty that were hit when Al Nadir revealed their existence. Of course, it hadn't been one bomb, but in fact over a dozen spread across the city, killing thousands in one hateful day. President Marcie had watched as Al Nadir proceeded to decimate his country. Horrific killings, money extorted through kidnapping, and fear, drugs, and prostitution saturated the streets. Before he'd heard the end of the broadcast, the French president picked up the phone and called the US president's office, and he pledged his support to Freedom Earth.

President Marcie's action was not in isolation. During that broadcast, forty-eight heads of state across the world rang into President Hutchinson's office and stated their unconditional support to the Freedom Earth movement. Each one, without exception, had been moved to respond by that 'empathic moment'. Ravaged by the work of Al Nadir, each country's head of state recognized the need to support and commit to such a vision. A singular notion.

Al Nadir, in creating unified terrorism, had, as a by-product, produced a unity in all the countries that had fallen under the yolk of its barbaric actions.

By their insane evil, they had unwittingly drawn the blueprint for world peace.

And Ashton knew this.

He smiled, watching the messages flowing in from those heads of state.

"President Hutchinson and I are pleased to confirm the full support from forty-eight of the world leaders showing right now on your screen."

Simultaneously across the world, the names of the united countries flashed up on people's screens. In real time, everyone would witness the immediate sign up to Freedom Earth.

Tomorrow, the executions. Next the unification of religion. Nothing could stop Freedom Earth, and nothing could stop Ashton. He would achieve what Salim Al Douri had only dreamed.

And all under the banner of good.

Chapter 21

Lei gripped hold of the bed frame. Her son, Xiao, lay outstretched and immobile. Eyes closed. Mouth silent. The hideous diatribe of the macabre was now abated by the strong sedative administered by the hospital doctor.

Xiao slept peacefully. A light smile touched the sides of his lips and his lids flickered momentarily. Lei looked down. Was her son dreaming? She hoped he was. She hoped he'd escaped to a wonderful place with sights of love and warmth, of sweet candy floss visions to soothe his tortured mind.

Lei struggled to understand. There had been no warning, no sign. Xiao had been his usual predictable and highly precocious self. Throughout their holiday, he'd shouted, argued, and questioned the way a teenager does. He stuck to his phone, prodding, swiping, and typing on the screen with a regularity that bordered on the unhealthy. When he'd not been catching up with all his friends on Facebook, Snapchat, Instagram, or whatever channel kids were into, Xiao had stuck his headphones on and vanished into his own world. He'd picked at his food, complained that he wanted a Big Mac and had a tantrum every time Lei or Chen refused to acquiesce to his wishes.

On the plane, in the depths of his trauma, Lei had seen something in his eyes. More than terror, his eyes had an aged wisdom tinged with sadness. Windows to the soul, eyes are said to be, and if this was true, Lei knew Xiao had somehow acquired a very old soul indeed. An ancient force that appeared to pity humans. What she saw in his dark orbs told of a tiredness, an apathy toward a world that had forsaken its morality in a favor of following a path to greed and avarice. The aged soul was both horrified and sorrowful. Lei could see in Xiao's eyes there existed a wretched inference. The acknowledgement of what was to be. That somehow, what Xiao had inside him had resigned humanity to a horrendous fate. A terrible end, which by the sheer act of viewing could burn out the sight and render mute the observer.

Lei stared at her son asleep on the hospital bed. He smiled still. Looking at him, he seemed normal, but Lei knew Xiao's suffering originated from only one cause: possession. A transformation inspired by the dark arts. But who would reap such a manifestation upon her son? Any illness found on the mortal plane, she was certain, couldn't deliver such a speedy reaction.

In her mind, Lei narrowed the timeframe of change. At morning breakfast, he'd been his mischievous self. He'd wanted a bacon sandwich and vocalized his need loudly. His outburst had disturbed other residents. Chen reprimanded him. His stern retort to his son's insolence sent Xiao scampering away out of the restaurant and in the direction of the pool. Annoyed with her husband, Lei left the breakfast table and bounded after her son, ignoring Chen's suggestion that she should "forget the little devil and eat your pancakes."

Lei found Xiao lying on a sun lounger, earphones in place and eyes shut.

"Xiao, come back and finish your breakfast. You've eaten nothing."

"Neither have you," snapped Xiao, not moving.

"That's not the point, darling. Please come back inside. Be a good boy."

"I don't want to. Not interested. Dad's a bully. You know he is. You're always on his side."

"Darling, that's not true."

"It is, Mom. I'm not coming back until he apologizes."

"Darling, you were in the wrong. You shouldn't have shouted like that. You did offend that nice Egyptian family."

"I don't care. I don't care about anything. I just want you all to leave me alone."

Xiao shot out of his lounger, grabbed his snorkel, and pelted down the steps toward the beach. Lei remembered watching him go. She walked after him. He ran to the sand, stopped, removed his T-shirt, and leaped into the sea. Lei arrived at the edge of the seashore. She picked up his T-shirt and watched her son. Xiao splashed about, the waves encircling him, getting higher. One second her son could be seen, the next he was gone, sucked into the encapsulating aquamarine, sparkling and shining.

Lei stayed for a few minutes more to see her son rise up, laughing and waving, and then he dove down into the frothy foam. She turned away, reassured that he was safe. Lei wandered across to the refreshment beach bar and chose Laban, a salted yogurt drink she'd come to love, and sat on a chair lounger, shielded comfortably by an enormous umbrella from the sun's burning glare.

The heat and the light lapping of the sea had a soporific effect on Lei and her lids drooped as slumber greeted her. She couldn't recall whether what she'd seen had been a dream or reality.

Xiao had stepped out of the water, his body dry, his snorkel nowhere to be seen. He had a light glowing aura around him, but as he approached, it faded. Drowsy and confused, Lei tried to stand and found she had no energy. Her son reached out and touched her, and her world slipped away to a void of silence.

Lei remembered waking up to Xiao lying on a sun lounger next to her, earphones fixed and humming some tune. She turned and noticed Chen, who held a fruit plate and hot croissants.

"Xiao came over and apologized. He said I should bring you something as you hadn't eaten. Maybe I misjudged the boy. I'm sorry, darling." Chen bent down and kissed Lei.

Lei rolled on her side and looked at Xiao. He opened one eye and smiled, a beautiful pure smile radiating love. Lei lent in to kiss his forehead.

"Thank you, darling."

Could that have been the moment of transformation?

She had been so very grateful for her son's change of heart, she hadn't thought any more about the weird vision, placing it firmly in the realms of her dreamscape.

Lei shuddered, remembering back to the plane. Had her son been somehow cursed? In his flight seat, he'd behaved like a rabid, frightened animal. Dr. McGregor had quelled his mania, but he had no way of determining the cause of his psychosis. The air stewardess had called ahead, ensuring an ambulance was on standby the moment they landed.

Xiao had come out of slumber just as the plane had made its descent. He turned his face away from Lei and sobbed great heaving throes of sorrow into the small flight pillow. Lei had watched her son and shivered. His small shoulders seemed crushed into the leather seat. It appeared to swallow him into its tan suppleness.

A lump erupted in her throat. Her little boy. Her poor little boy. He was slipping away to another place, a place to which she couldn't follow. Her heart skipped hard, its beat resounding in her ears, caused her body to vibrate with a quickening tempo. She breathed, deep and long, and forced her heart to slow, and prayed for her panic to subside.

The plane's landing gear had dropped, which was always a moment of concern for Lei. She would normally brush her hand against her necklace and pray for a safe landing. This time, however, landing barely registered on her personal radar. Her mind was affixed on her son, her energies focused on his well-being. She had no time for existential musings of what might be. Instead, her mind was focused on what was happening, fused into a reality she couldn't comprehend. But nevertheless, she had to find a way, for her son. She had to solve the puzzle of this cruel conundrum into which God had dropped her.

After landing, Chen had lifted his son into his strong arms. Plane staff fretted and Dr. McGregor, true to his word, accompanied Xiao every step to the ambulance. He gave instructions to ground staff as Chen carried Xiao out through the docking tunnel and positioned him into the wheelchair. Ground staff escorted Xiao, Chen, Lei, and Dr. McGregor into the lift and down to the waiting ambulance.

Chen had spoken briefly to the ground staff supervisor, who'd asked where to deliver their luggage. He gave a card to the supervisor with their London address and the supervisor stated that, "all was in hand, sir." Chen climbed into the ambulance and sat beside a fragile and fraught Lei, and both stared down at their son.

Xiao had stirred suddenly, his expression confused, and he'd thrashed his head back and forth. With his eyes glazed, Xiao opened his mouth wide and out from the depths of his shaking body came a stomach-churning scream. Lei turned away to hide her tears and the pain on her face. Chen held her hand. His grip tightened with reassurance. She turned back to watch Dr. McGregor insert yet another needle into her child.

Xiao's eyes closed and the screaming ceased, and he was sucked back into the world of dreams.

Their lives had been idyllic. But everything needs to be balanced, thought Lei. Perhaps this was the balancing factor. This thing that had taken over their precious son was in Nature's control. If that was so, Lei realized, to get her Xiao back, she'd challenge Nature itself. No force could be greater than the love she had for her son.

Chapter 22

After Sam's deep discussion about the meaning of life, I'm a bit off kilter. As we come out of shimmer, I can't seem to channel my energies properly. I usually don't have to think about my power and it just comes, but it seems my strength of conviction to take out Al Nadir has waned, and with it has gone my ability to focus the powerhouse inside me.

I listen to the harmonies of the leaves and plants. Like in Taman Negara, the wildlife is perturbed by Al Nadir's intrusion and I have to calm it.

"All will be well, my little ones. Give me chance to clear this mess." I vibrate this in my mind and the message is received around me.

Sam is already ahead. We're both expecting to see another structure like the one we saw in Malaysia, but when I focus on the dark resonance that is Al Nadir's base camp, I see that there is only a tall wall about eight feet high. There is no imposing structure or large-scale operation. I can nevertheless feel the overwhelming dark resonance of perhaps hundreds of thousands of people.

I turn to gain his impression. He looks thoughtful then glances downward and points.

"Underground?"

I look to the ground and realize the resonance I detect is emanating upward. I concentrate on seeing whatever is beneath the forest floor. The power I employ is SearchSighting. It has two levels. One level is connecting with the energy resonance within a person, so I see through their eyes. The second level is through a fixed connection, via a phone, for example, so I can see the person on the phone. I see their expressions and demeanor, but I can also see the environment around me. SearchSight was the first power I recognized when my powers as the Protector were bestowed upon me.

I'm now learning more about my abilities and just how powerful I really am.

I zap my energy downward and target the nearest person, and then I leap from human to human. In complex detail, I see what is beneath our feet. It is a massive warren of glass and stainless-steel corridors, rooms filled with technology of all kinds, living quarters with beds, kitchens, sofas, and TVs, prison cells, and some with devices of torture I'd rather not dwell on. There are medical areas that look like hospital wards, huge conference rooms, laboratories, and clean room areas housing Al Nadir's emerging technologies, hangers with automated vehicles and drones. And of course, there are rows upon rows of weapon stores filled to the brim with the worst ordnance Al Douri's money could buy.

As their underground world opens up in front of my mind, I'm deeply enthralled by Al Nadir's feat of engineering. Their underground city stretches far into the jungle.

For a split second, my acknowledgement of what's around me falters slightly. SearchSighting in this way requires a lot of energy and takes attention from my immediate senses.

Sam shouts his warning, but it's too late; the bullets have already ripped into me before I sense them. I turn and stare at the tall, swarthy operative buried beneath the fronds of the ferns growing up from the forest floor. He stands, still firing, but his eyes widen as he sees I do not fall. The bullets enter my body and are absorbed into my energy field. Holes in my flesh pop up where the bullets hit. Blood streams as my skin is ruptured, but then the particles of light that form me realign and coalesce, closing the holes. The blood sparkles to nothing.

This process happens in under an Earth minute and whilst I'm striding forward, closing in on the Al Nadir operative.

Sam's body similarly reacts. We Kudamaz are impervious to Earthly weapons. Nevertheless, the process is jolting and an unnecessary stimulus for my body to receive.

In a panic, the operative carries on firing. With a warrior roar, I charge against him, grabbing the gun with one hand and, with a flick of my wrist, breaking it in two as if it were a party twiglet. My other hand goes straight through his throat, ripping it out and covering me in blood. His eyes widen at the point of impact, and his life begins to fade as blood streams out of his body.

I realize I didn't view his Balance Shift before I killed him.

He's in transition now with his soul about to leave. Quickly, I view his Balance, and it confirms what I already knew. A human full of utter darkness and hatred, and a need to kill others for material glory.

"Are you okay?"

Sam approaches me and touches my shoulder. I flinch and then nod.

"I didn't read the guy's Shift before I killed him. It's the first time I've done that."

"He was shooting us to hell with that M4 Carbine. I don't think reviewing his Balance Shift was all that necessary. He was a mean fucker. You only had to look at him."

I shook my head. "It's not that, Sam. It's the fact I didn't bother at all. I had time when I was walking to him, but I didn't. I just wanted him to die. I didn't think about whether he was at all redeemable. I'd made my decision, and that was it."

"So what's wrong with making your decision? These people are evil, Ellie. They kill first. It's what they've been trained to do. Maybe in another life, they could have been doctors, teachers, nurses, people who save others, but in this life, they destroy others. It's what it is. You're cleaning up mankind's shit. Accept that and just hoover them."

Sam grins at me and pulls my arm to encourage me forward. I shrug, unable to believe that's all I am, some celestial bloody vacuum cleaner!

I have to believe that somewhere, in all those people underneath my feet, there are a few with still-redeemable souls and Balance Shifts just veering to the dark but still able to be brought back to the light.

"Come on, darling," Sam says gently.

I look at him and his face hardens.

"Behind you."

Out of the jungle pour Al Nadir operatives. But not just a few. Our visitation has been observed and Al Nadir has unleashed their Amazon-based army upon us.

"Here we go, sweetness."

Sam nods and storms ahead. He takes his Harmon gun and stun blasts everyone who's charging at him. The blast radiates out and catches each soldier within five hundred yards.

I link to Sam's mind and relay back the Balance Shift of each stunned Al Nadir soldier, so he knows whether to blast them to smithereens or keep them in stasis.

Ever the multi-tasker, I view the Balances of those soldiers in front of me. In a super-nano second, I decide whether to blast them with my lethal rainbow light or bring them back from the darkness with my white light energies.

The screams of the soldiers align with the squawks of the toucans and macaws flying around the tops of the trees. Black spider monkeys climb down to investigate the howls of the humans on the forest floor. A jaguar pads forward inquisitively, but I instruct her to stay back as I don't want her hurt. Her Balance Shift is so light and full of wonder. Despite being a predatory creature, she clearly kills to eat, not for a greater gain. She is also pregnant and as there are so few of her kind, I have to protect her. She heeds my warning, turns, and slips back into the jungle's thick undergrowth.

As I'm fighting, I send out a message on a resonance frequency that I know will be received by the flora and fauna of the forest, advising them to leave for a while. Again, Al Nadir's incursion into their world has caused too much disquiet and disturbed their rhythm of life. A beautiful red and black tarantula drops down from a silver bark in front of me.

'Thank you, Protector, for the warning, I will make sure my family know,' the arachnid says in my mind, and scuttles around the bark and up the tree.

I smile. As Ellie, I used to be quite freaked by spiders, but my universal knowledge now tells me, despite how they are portrayed, they are one of the most connected and intelligent creatures on Earth.

Sam and I zip through the stunned soldiers, picking them off and blasting them with light that enhances or destroys, according to their Balance Shifts.

Over the course of almost thirty minutes, Sam and I take down the stream of forty-eight thousand two hundred and eight soldiers. Only two thousand one hundred and thirty are redeemable. We collect them and place them in stasis in a group, where they will stay until we're finished with what will greet us in the world below.

"Well, I suppose we better start underneath now."

Out of the eyeline of the captured prisoners, I commence shimmer mode, and Sam hooks onto my shimmer trail, knowing that I have the layout of the underground base.

The grey concrete, stainless-steel, and thickened glass that I'd seen through the eyes of the Al Nadir operatives comes into focus around us, and we're standing in an enormous room with a 3D, augmented reality operations schematic floating above a Smart Table. Banks of computer monitors hang above with row upon row of people staring at data, graphs, visuals, sat recon images, and biometric data showing an outline of the human body. This is one of Al Nadir's control rooms and it's a hive of activity.

Eyes turn in synch toward us as Sam and I emerge from nowhere. Although scared at first, their training soon takes over. We see the savage bloodlust that has been drilled into them through Al Nadir's brutal indoctrination and brainwashing.

"Ready?" I look at my husband, and he nods.

"Oh, yeah. I was born ready for this, darling."

Sam grins and takes out his Harmon gun in the very second that bullets start flying.

Chapter 23

Ashton stared at his phone. The support for Freedom Earth had swelled to one hundred and forty world leaders and heads of state. Almost every country had pledged allegiance.

The world was following Ashton's word.

It was blind. Feverish. With a passion that had little sense, except the need to avenge those who had died at the hands of Al Nadir.

Ashton doubted they even read the pledges they were signing up to. Their need for revenge and determination to show strength in the eyes of their own people had been so great, they'd have signed up to anything.

Political engineering. Ashton was the master of it.

He grinned as he realized how advanced he already was. And they hadn't even begun. Just wait until they get a load of this, thought Ashton, tapping the papers Hutchinson had given him.

Scanning through the contents, Ashton knew it wasn't cold fusion. It was something else. God knows what. He'd let his band of top nuclear scientists at Culham figure that one out. He didn't care, as long as it made him rich.

Freedom Earth. It had such a beautiful ring to it. If a leader didn't immediately sign up, they'd be singled out and ostracized by the international community. For they were, by not signing, agreeing to the notion that Al Nadir was right and freeing earth from their tyranny was not the correct course of action.

It was not only unpatriotic to refuse to pledge allegiance to Freedom Earth, but it was also an admission of treason.

The UN listed one hundred and ninety-three countries and two UN observing countries. Ashton had received support from over three-quarters of the world. Freedom Earth was a reality and tomorrow it would be recognized as the only way forward.

"Excuse me, sir. Would you like a drink? Something to eat?"

The air stewardess stared at Ashton, a little nervous but anxious to discharge her duty.

Ashton flicked his eyes up to hers. Wide, dark brown plates filled with hesitation and fear met his. He half smiled, attempting to put the young girl at ease.

"Just a cognac, thanks, and leave the bottle."

As she turned her head toward the galley, Ashton took in her curvy figure. The voluptuous breasts, tight waist, and bouncy bottom made his lips tingle. He imagined cornering her at the back of the plane, slipping his lips down and nestling them between her breasts and…

His phone screamed, shaking him out of his mental enjoyment of her hourglass body.

"Yes?" snapped Ashton.

"Richard, it's Al. Is it possible to do something dramatic for tomorrow's execution? Could Sam and Ellie Noor help us?"

Ashton listened to Hutchinson's utter dependency on him. He couldn't organize even a state execution without guidance.

The prime minister smirked and took a long swig of the cognac that Miss Hourglass had placed in front of him.

"What had you in mind, Al?"

"Some kind of presentation, a stage maybe, or a platform. Something that would really look the part on live TV."

Ashton considered the request. *Look the part on live TV.* Only Kudamaz technology would do. He hoped the super couple were at their London flat and not off-worlding.

"Okay, I see. Al, let me contact Sam and Ellie, and I'll see if they can help."

Ashton could picture Hutchinson nodding furiously as he listened to his old friend's suggestion.

"Please ask them to be quick though, whatever they chose. We don't have much time."

"Leave it to me. I'll call you later when it's all arranged."

The US president thanked Ashton and exited the line swiftly.

Ashton dialed Sam's phone. Eight hundred miles away and thirty-two thousand feet down in his Silent Waters apartment, Sam Noor came on the line with an extremely acerbic, "What?"

By this, Ashton knew he'd caught Sam at an inopportune time. He raised an eyebrow and smiled.

"Oh, Sam, I hope I'm not interrupting anything?"

Chapter 24

Sam and I have just got back from two days of taking down Al Nadir across the globe. From the seventy-five million battle force Al Nadir had, we've annihilated just over fifty-six million. I didn't want to destroy that many humans, but their hearts were black to the core. Too much damage by Al Nadir had already been done. Sam was right. I was cleaning up mankind's shit.

Although I attempt to look inside myself, nothing is there. I am blank.

I don't feel anything.

By the time we'd reached the last base, one of three in Australia, I was just an instrument of justice, meting out the appropriate measure of retribution to those who fought me and those who didn't.

Throughout this take-down, my emotions had been in check through the Protector's shield. I'd done my job, something that I had literally been created to do.

In the end, I managed to save nineteen million people from being obliterated. They were taken by ground forces in the various countries and incarcerated inside gigantic warehouses with the twenty-four-hour armed guard.

After the purging of Al Nadir's created evil, the Balance Shift indicator for Earth shows hardly any movement from the white light zone. There should have been an effect but barely anything shows. I can only construe from this inactivity that the tens of millions Sam and I wiped out were already regarded as needing to be dispensed with by the Balance. If what we'd done in destroying that many humans was wrong, the Balance would have shifted the other way into the dark.

But it didn't.

And now I could put Al Nadir behind me. I could relax and enjoy life again.

So Sam and I were back doing what we started. In bed.

Of course, we weren't tired. That wasn't possible.

We just wanted to play.

With each other.

I watch as Sam pulls away to answer the phone. He puts it on speaker, and as Ashton speaks, I can almost hear the salacious sarcasm in his voice. If I didn't know any better, I'd think that Ashton had bugged the flat.

As I said, we were into serious playtime. After all the death and destruction we have wrought on Al Nadir, we were indulging in some rather rigorous horizontal jogging a few moments ago. It seems, once again, Ashton's innuendo is right on the button.

I snuggle into Sam and make a winding motion with my finger, but Sam ignores me and carries on talking. Annoyed, I slip out of bed and try to move away, but Sam grabs my arm forcefully and pulls me back to him. I drape my arms around his chest and start to nibble his ear. This, I know, will cause instant arousal. It'll be 'bye bye Ashton' before very long.

"So what's the issue, Ashton?" Sam snaps, feeling a twinge in his groin. Now, I can see, he desperately wants to get the pontificating PM off the line.

"Sam, I'll be brief. I'm sure you've got your hands full."

I can't help myself. I let out a little giggle and hope the PM doesn't hear.

"Somewhat," says Sam, pushing a dead flat tone into his voice.

"Right, well, you know we're planning to execute Hans Stein-Muller in the US and Pedro Russo in the UK at the O2. Arrangements have already been made from the White House side, but the president and I feel we need something dramatic, theatrical, if you will, to make a spectacle of those bastards on live TV. I'm looking for your help, suggestions, ideas. The stage design perhaps."

I crawl away from Sam and mouth, "Don't get involved."

Sam puts his hand up, his palm facing me. It's a 'shut up' gesture I remember from human Sam. I huff and move my legs underneath me to sit cross-legged then I stare at the phone.

"I take it this execution is going to be a public display of strength from our country and the US?" says Sam.

"Absolutely! We need to strike hard. Remember our motto. Accept no excuses, take no prisoners."

The PM's voice is chilling. I find myself instantly SearchSighting Ashton.

He plops into my mind with vivid clarity, leering and lounging in his government-sanctioned private plane, his official mode of air transport if BA flights aren't appropriate. His face is sharp with cold eyes that dart continuously over to the shapely air stewardess like they are on yoyo threads. I can see the stewardess doesn't notice the PM's interrogation.

Ashton's head of security sits in a seat opposite the PM. He has stunning, ice-blue eyes, and clearly, the stewardess is taken with him. As she serves his drink, she laughs and flirts. By the head of security's posturing, I can tell he isn't really interested; he's just being polite.

I watch Ashton flinch and his lips curl back in a travesty of a smile. The PM is jealous of his head of security! I can't believe it. His behavior is so childish.

"Well, sir, I believe that's your motto, not ours. But I understand what you mean. You want to show to the world that Al Nadir's reign is completely over and will never return."

"That's right, Sam. They're gone, and they'll never be brought back by any means." I watch Ashton's hand form a tight fist. His knuckles turn white. "There's a DNR stamped right across Al Nadir."

I can see this is a man who knows the definition of pain. Violence flows through his veins. He can't be trusted.

I try to re-read his Balance Shift. The color around and inside him drains, and he rises up from the white background like an expensive, embossed motif on premium writing paper. The dark color quickly defines him, but then the white light influence begins to shape him. The dark and the light come together in absolute harmony. The counter, which only I can see, hovers in front of the PM, flashing an impossible readout. It shows an absolutely aligned Equilibrium of light and dark. What makes it more impossible is the fact that his Balance Shift hasn't changed since I last viewed it a few days before. Just by the nature of the way in which humans interact with other bodies in the Universe, taking and giving energies of dark and light, no one's Balance Shift will remain the same for more than a nano-second. Constant Equilibrium goes against all the universal laws laid down by Kudamun.

Then again, Sam becoming a blended Kudamaz/Human hybrid was never in the Kudamaz book of how the Universe works either. Maybe some things are left unexplained, even to the Protector of Earth.

Sam gives me a quizzical look. He obviously wonders why I remain so quiet. Sam doesn't have my powers, despite being Kudamaz. He isn't the Protector. He doesn't know I am SearchSighting the PM. It is an amazing gift. I can see in my mind someone afar, and yet I can still recognize all that is happening around me.

"So what can you do for tomorrow?" asks Ashton.

I witness via SearchSight his alcoholic dependency as he knocks back one cognac and pours another. What is it with all these politicians and their obsession with alcohol?

"You're after theatrical, right?" says my husband, and he beckons me to hand over the notepad by his bedside. Well, it looks like a notepad. But with Kudamaz technology, looks are, of course, deceiving.

I hand it to Sam. On opening, a multidimensional grid appears and hangs in the air, floating above the bed.

"Leave this to Ellie and me. We'll sort it from here, sir."

I grimace as I hear my husband continue to address the PM so respectfully. Sam shrugs, clearly saying, 'why not?' But I know why not. For one, the man doesn't deserve our respect. He should be respecting us. And two, I don't trust him.

In my SearchSight vision, Ashton returns to full color, no longer showing his Balance Shift of complete Equilibrium. He is now looming in my mind in high definition. I can see him make an upward thrust with his arm in response to Sam. From that movement, I realize that a lot is depending upon tomorrow, and what a dramatic performance Team Ashton/Hutchinson can show to the world.

"Thank you, Sam, and please thank your dear wife too."

I watch Ashton's eyebrows rise lasciviously as he mentions me. I shudder. His glass arrives at his mouth and he swigs the contents back in one hit.

"Well, you can thank her yourself. She's here," says Sam, and he beckons me closer.

I stop SearchSighting Ashton and he pops out of my head. For some reason, I have to concentrate on SearchSighting. Although I can see around me and do things, the moment I speak to the person I'm SearchSighting, the connection is gone, and I can't do it any longer. Or I haven't found a way to maintain speaking to and SearchSighting the same person. I wish I had, for I would love to see Ashton's face when I speak to him.

"Hello, Ashton." I never refer to him as sir. "Don't worry, we'll give you a good show for tomorrow. Just relax and enjoy the rest of your cognac. Oh, and don't get too worked up about Mr. Security getting it on with Miss Hourglass. I believe he bats for the other side!"

Sam's mouth drops. The look of disdain he shoots me makes me realize my impulsive behavior may have been somewhat rash. But I've done it for a reason. I want to get a reaction from Ashton.

I hear Ashton laugh a cold, hollow laugh. He doesn't reveal any concern for the invasion of his privacy nor the blatant abuse of my powers against him.

"Good intel, darling." His smoothly delivered endearment makes me feel unclean like I am some whore he's just screwed. "That's an interesting ability you have. Do be careful dropping in. You never know what you might see. I wouldn't want to shock your innocent mind."

"Who said I was innocent?" I say with silky breathlessness, playing Ashton's game.

Sam stares at me. His eyebrows knit together with annoyance, and his mouth turns down at the corners. Ashton laughs again, this time a little more heartily. I can tell he is enjoying this line.

"Ashton, a word of warning," I purr. "You don't know me and you'll never know me. So don't presume or second guess anything about who I am. Live by these rules and we'll do just fine."

It is all too much for Sam. He shuts off the multidimensional modeler, lifts himself off the bed, and glares at me. I breathe in as my eyes dance across his gorgeous, naked body that would leave a Greek god in the shade. Being half Kudamaz has accentuated what wonders Sam already had and makes his physique literally mouthwatering. To say he is a distracting influence is an understatement. I can barely remember what I've just said to Ashton.

The sound of my faster breathing has a desired effect on the PM.

"Never is a long day, sweetheart."

I hear him breathing deeper and I know from an almost imperceptible smack of his tongue that he is licking his full lips. The thought makes me squirm.

"Longest day you'll never see," I hit back. "Anyway, must go for now. We'll be back once we've finished your stage for tomorrow. It'll be done tonight. Bye, Ashton."

I don't wait for his response. I shut off the connection. Looking up at Sam, I expect him to blast me for my untoward behavior. But instead, he just grins and grabs me off the bed.

"You're a naughty one, aren't you?" I smile as his hands creep around me.

"What was that really all about?" says Sam, kissing behind my ear.

"Just being Agent Provocateur, darling. Sometimes people need a little push to reveal what they really are. Surely, as Mr. Super Spy, you should know that?"

The glint in Sam's eye shows me that he does.

Chapter 25

Lei's hands circulated around the coffee mug; its contents now long cold. Her fingers interlaced and she held it still. Her ebony eyes fixed to a point on the table. Surroundings unnoticed. Time not recognized.

Her mind was caught up in her son. His screams shattered her bones and poisoned her blood. Two lives inextricably connected; a supernatural confluence to make one soul.

Unaware of movement, of Chen's hand as it rested on her shoulder, the deep timbre of his voice, now far away, was merely a faint echo from a distant place.

"Come on, love. You can't stay here like this."

Chen had watched his wife descend from hysterical crying to emotionless stone. Her body had stilled to become barely alive. Her eyes, unblinking, were rooted to a spot that existed in her mind alone.

He'd placed a comforting arm around her, but immutable resistance had greeted his show of love. He'd spoken words of reason, of pain, of devotion for over three hours, just words, words, and all were sucked into Lei's vortex of silence. A black hole absorbing his emotions and increasing her negative energy, feeding her pain and speeding her forward to entropic destruction.

"Lei, you must stop this!" Chen shook his wife hard. He angled himself across her sight line and stared into her eyes. A flicker of anger reflected. "You must stop this, for our son."

'Our son' rippled through Lei, stroking her with a soothing reassurance.

He was still theirs. Not lost completely.

Her eyes blinked, and she looked at Chen and nodded. She pulled her hands away from the mug and rested them, palms down, in front of her. The remains of something sticky on the table from a previous diner infiltrated her awareness. Slowly, her perception inveigled its way in again.

Lei stood. Chen rushed to her side to steady her elevation. She was stiff from a three hour long immobility and weak from draining emotions. She placed a hand on the edge of the table and the other into the crook of her husband's elbow then issued a listless smile to Chen and squeezed his arm a little.

"Come on, my love," said Chen. "Let's see this through together. Let's go back to Xiao. They're taking him off the sedative. He needs you there when he comes around."

She raised her hand, sweeping away the remaining tears. Touching her face, she realized her mascara had dripped down. Lei reached into her handbag and took out her powder compact. In the mirror, a wretched face stared back. She breathed in and out deeply. With each action, greater fortitude settled inside her. She tidied her face, reapplied her makeup, and nodded. She was ready.

Strength was what she had to show for Xiao's sake. She had to demonstrate the reserve her family had always seen in her. However broken she was inside, her external casing must be unbreakable; her son must see her this way.

Lei walked with Chen into the hospital room where Xiao slept. Again, he looked so peaceful that one could easily believe all was well. A normal child asleep. The doctor had already reduced the sedative, and Xiao stirred beneath the sheets. Lei grabbed his hand. Her heart quickened and she prayed for salvation for her son, that somehow this madness would leave him and normality would restore itself.

Xiao flicked his eyes open wide, not as gradually as expected after being under such a heavy sedative. His intense stare clamped onto Lei and burned into her.

"Mother, the light, I feel it."

Lei instantly thought that Xiao referenced the tunnel of death and that he was going toward the light.

"Darling, you're not dying. You're a young boy. Remember, my darling, you love to swim, you love your games, your football. It's all waiting for you."

Lei wanted to overwrite Xiao's mind with everything that he treasured, giving him a reason to live. As material as it may seem, she knew Xiao valued these things and that they could, perhaps, bring him back.

"They are things, Mother. Just things. They break and last not forever. But I have the light. Do you understand? The light is wonderful."

Lei brushed his cheek. She could see his serenity, his utter peace. She was so pleased to see him looking so gentle. "Oh, darling, I love you. Your dad loves you too. Chen?" Lei engaged her husband, and he came forward.

At his movement, Xiao turned his head to his father. Serenity bled from his face and horror possessed him.

"Father, I pity you. The darkness in you. It will eat me. Devour me alive. Stay away from me. Stay away!"

Xiao's voice screamed as his inconsolable body shook. Tremors ripped through him and forced violent convulsions as if shooting him with a huge electric current. His head tipped back and his eyeballs rolled revealing bloodshot whiteness. His mouth drooped open. Saliva dribbled at the sides. His motor functions had gone.

Lei watched the seizure take her son over. Doctors attempted to stabilize him, but as they worked, he fell limp on the bed, his body static. Lei, dizzy from the suddenness of silence, held onto the bed frame and stared at Xiao.

A hurt drove up inside her. Before she could employ a filter, she yelled, unrestrained, "What have you done to my son? Why couldn't you save him? What kind of bloody doctors are you?"

Chen came to her side and Lei collapsed in his arms. His hand smoothed down her hair, and he hushed at her to control her outburst. She pushed away and turned to face the doctors. Her eyes glared, mad with a fury that her husband had tried to repress.

"I want answers right now. What is wrong with my son? You've had him for hours now. You must have some prognosis. I want to hear it because what I just saw is not right. I want you to tell me what you're going to do to make it right."

Whilst the other doctors attended to Xiao, the lead neurologist replied to Lei's demands.

"Mrs. Chang, we do not know what is wrong with Xiao. What you have witnessed was some form of seizure. His brain has gone into a vegetative state, a coma, if you will, and is now unresponsive. As you can see, my colleagues are intubating him to maintain his basic functions. But in this state, we can do nothing. I'm sorry, Mrs. Chang, but all we can do now is monitor him and hope for the best."

"But how did this happen? He was speaking just now. How can he have had a seizure? How can he be in a coma?" Lei suddenly shook with despair. "Will his brain be damaged?"

The consultant straightened up. He tensed and applied his professional persona before responding. "From what I have witnessed, and going by his life signs, I'd say the current position isn't a favorable one. After a seizure of this magnitude, brain damage may be a possible outcome. But Mrs. Chang, please be assured, we'll do all we can. I've seen many cases of patients suffering from unresponsive wakeful syndrome, or persistent vegetative state. And sometimes, a sudden trigger, internal or external, pushes them out again, and they have eventually recovered. Have hope. Have faith. All is not lost."

Lei stared at her son, tears falling silently down her face.

"Hope and faith are all I have left," she whispered, and bent down to lay a kiss on her son's motionless forehead.

Chapter 26

The plane navigated through the clouds with effortless ease. Unfortunately, Ashton's personal journey through his thoughts was much more turbulent.

He'd responded to Ellie's brief goodbye only to realize that she'd abruptly gone. Irked, he'd gone to find the stewardess, only to discover she was upfront with the captain. Returning to his seat, Ashton thought back to Ellie's reference to his cognac, his security guard, and the shapely stewardess. No question about it, Ellie could 'see' everything that transpired in his plane in real time.

What did the Company call it? Remote viewing. An amazing capability. But did she have to be connected in some way, like by phone, or could she do it independent of any connection? Ashton would have loved to understand the operational parameters for how the viewing worked, but he doubted he ever would.

Such a power made him very uneasy. Could she read his mind as well? Would she know his plans? Did she already know? Should he continue?

Deep inside him, something triggered. A strong overwhelming reassurance flooded him, and he cursed himself for being so weak, for being so quick to want to fold. What was he thinking?

Renewed with a strength of absolute conviction, he smirked. If she wanted to play dirty, he could play dirtier. He was, after all, in politics, the birthplace of dirty tricks.

He thought about Ellie, and his hand grazed momentarily over his awakening arousal. Ashton slipped down into his seat, pulling the table over the top of his lap, giving cover to his further grazing.

Closing his eyes, he could see Ellie, feisty and fabulous, and so confrontational. He'd heard through the mission reports that she'd never broken under torture. Neither MI6 nor Al Nadir could break her. Unbreakable, beautiful, and strange Ellie Noor. He realized now why Maide, the former head of MI6, had been obsessed to destruction with her.

Ashton remembered her standing in the war Cabinet a few days ago, radiant, with warrior eyes eating up everything around her. He'd been terrified but also drawn to her. She was powerful, unquestionably, but deep inside, almost buried, he'd sensed a vulnerability. Like a child in the dark afraid of the monsters that lurk, Ellie was lost and running blind. The powers that would save others were her own monsters, for by their creation they had taken away her right to be human. And now she was that little girl lost in the dark, desperate to find the light.

Knowing this, Ashton realized that Ellie was not a being of unimaginable power. She was, in fact, someone who could shatter easily.

It was all a question of wavelength, and finding the one Ellie was really on.

Chapter 27

I lean against the beautiful crystal wall and watch my husband. We have retired to our quarters in Kudamun to work on the challenge Ashton has set.

"He wants dramatic," I say, staring at Sam's flow of creations.

Sam looks across at me, frowns, swipes his hand through the air, and the holographic model that floats between Sam and me vanishes.

"You try," he mutters, and shoves the MD Modeler in my hands.

Sam's childish retort is to be expected. He's been playing with the MD Modeler for what seems like an eternity. With flashes of brilliance and flurries of panache, my husband has sketched out design after design, but nothing seems to click. The exuberant structure I know Ashton and Hutchinson want is infuriatingly far from being fashioned.

I snatch up the MD Modeler and descend into the corridors of ancient history for inspiration. Who were the ones that reveled in architectural wonder? The Greeks, the Pharaohs, the Romans. Embedded in the crystals surrounding me, the knowledge facets spring to life. On connection, they explode into vivid light and color in front of me. Suddenly, I'm in the Coliseum in Rome, standing next to the emperor and looking down on the gladiators. Thumbs up and a soul walks free. Life was so cheap at that time, determined by a flick of the opposable thumb.

The Coliseum is awash with movement, cheers, and screams, and words of fawning to the emperor. Praise be to the one who presides over all. His poise and position brings me back to Ashton. He has adopted regal tendencies as a man who must be listened to and obeyed. The one who refuses will be subjected to the will of a man who cannot be read. Not even with my powers can I establish the true nature of his purpose.

Of course, the requirement of the stage is for world effect. The power of

Freedom Earth writ large. But what will this power really deliver if left untethered and allowed to drift away from an institutionalized morality? Where will the compass needle point if the ultimate power delivers a new direction?

I watch the scene around me. I take in the structures. The lions carved on each side of the emperor's throne are magnificent. Their roars, caught in time, are a signature statement, the prelude to the attack. A serendipitous scene. I can't waver from this design. I'm constructing death. There could be no better manifestation than the pounce of a lion, jaws open, blood-stained teeth, spittle dangling, and tongue swiping, anticipating impact. Savoring torn flesh. That sumptuous satisfaction as claw and maw descend to wipe its victim to oblivion.

The technology, our Kudamaz know-how, will be employed to make the execution painless, but the build-up has to be the very example of showmanship. That is the brief from Ashton.

Tension amongst the public is high over the executions and it is imperative that both leaders are seen as humane. This remit doesn't preclude the opportunity for them to play the psychological torture card. Preparation for this humane execution will not be pleasant. Moments before the lion strikes, the fear of looking death in the face will be the traitor's punishment. They will know it is the end. No reprieve from a bleeding-heart liberal, no terrorist brotherhood there to create a diversion for escape, no opportunity to plead ignorant or insane. No chance at all except to face an on-coming fate. An unknown delivery but a certain final outcome.

My lion's strike will be a Harmon wave, and the fear will be generated through the application of a simple hood. The prisoner's imagination will do the rest.

Sam watches as I use the light matrix on the MD Modeler, my hands and mind working in unison to fashion the stage design inspired by my journey to ancient times. The lion heads takes position on both ends of the stage, and behind them are the steps to the traitor's elevated demise.

"A Harmon grid, do you think?" I ask Sam.

He nods. The Harmon grid is totally painless but dramatic. With the elaborate lion stage, it will make a spectacular visual statement.

"What about Freedom Earth? Ashton is going to want the title of his new brainchild there."

I consider Sam's suggestion. Looking at the design, there doesn't seem to be a natural place to insert the words.

"Try it right in front, if you make the stage really high."

I imagine the words carved into the stage front. My hands whisk through the air, and the MD Modeler emblazons 'Freedom Earth' on the stage fascia. With a flick of my hand, the light-based design starts to solidify into a crystal structure that mutates into wood as I select the material on the MD Modeler's design console. I leave the Harmon wave grid columns as impressive chunks of crystal with a wooden carved pinecone on top. I use pinewood for the stage base, the lions, and the steps.

The model hangs in space, a scaled version of what is to come.

"Like it?" I ask, examining Sam's face.

Sam has been watching me, and appreciation is in his eyes, but I could sense he is also a tad jealous. "You know it's a brilliant design, sweetness. It has the wow factor for the killer event."

I'd become so engrossed into the design that I'd forgotten its purpose. A misplaced thought driven by obsession. What is wrong with me? What do I have to prove? Have I been touched by Ashton's megalomania? I shudder.

"I'm not altogether happy about this."

Sam turns his head and gives a ponderous glance. "With the design? It's fabulous."

"No, Sam, not the design. It's what Ashton and Hutchinson have asked for, and that's what they've got. No, it's the fact we're doing this at all. Public executions? It's the stuff of centuries past. I know Al Nadir have been terrible. But this…" I gesture to the model floating in the air in front of us. "It makes an exhibition of their death. I'm not sure this is right. What is Earth becoming when death is entertainment? Are the inhabitants barbarians? Are we? It makes us no better than the Roman emperors who ruled over life and death."

"But if this was as wrong as you say, wouldn't we have seen a Balance Shift to the dark?"

I know Sam's comment is correct, and that is what worries me more. The Balance Shift on Earth has moved only minutely since I brought it to Equilibrium four days ago. If Ashton and his activities with Freedom Earth are so damaging, would there not have been a significant movement to the dark? Every way I turn in my mind, I reach the same conclusion. What Ashton is doing is deemed good at a universal level, otherwise, the Balance would have shifted.

Resigned to this, I nod to my husband.

"Yes, I suppose you're right. We'd better take the MD Modeler to the Manufacture Pod and get this design made for tomorrow's event."

Sam and I take the design to the Manufacture Pod. It appears to be a large cube of crystal about two meters high. But as we all know, Kudamaz technology is deceptive.

I lock the MD Modeler device into the top of the Manufacture Pod. Pale blue and purple lights start to erupt on the top side of the cube. The crystal that forms the cube has sentient properties, just like all the other crystal structures in Kudamun. It acknowledges the docking activity and begins to read the data stream from the MD Modeler. Lights inside the crystal flash a continuous purple, and I hear the single word, 'Ready', reverberate in my mind.

Sam nods subconsciously, and it's clear he's heard the word too.

"Time to go, eh?"

"You shimmer first, and I'll follow with the Pod. Ashton's cleared the stadium of staff, hasn't he?"

The last thing I want is someone seeing me materialize and freak out.

"Yes. He'll be waiting there, but no one else. Let's go."

Sam's usual alpha-male shimmer dominates the room, and I wait for him to leave. The O2 Stadium leaps into my mind. I hold onto the Pod and, around me, I feel the cool air that signifies London in late March. The sun is out but a bracing wind warns that winter hasn't released its hold quite yet. Spring still has to wait a few more days.

Sam is standing to the side talking to Ashton. I give an affable nod and concentrate on my work. I position the Pod so that its output is balanced on either side to make the stage. With the MD Modeler still docked into the Pod, I press a button on the console.

A loud harmonic sound makes Ashton turn and stare. The Pod lights up with a purple, flashing light, and then, from the front of the Pod, an elongated cone extends outward. From the cone, crystals fly out and start to arrange themselves into a stage. These crystals are self-replicating, sentient nanocrystals that initiate and self-organize. They mutate into different materials beyond crystal to meet the defined design requirements contained in the MD Modeler's data flow.

Ashton watches open-mouthed as the nanocrystals build up the design of the stage in a matter of minutes. I love making that man at a loss for words.

"Wow, Ellie, Sam, will you never stop surprising me?" Ashton is thoroughly blown away by our Manufacture Pod. I can see the money signs in his eyes.

"Sorry, Ashton, not for sale or license."

"Would be wonderful though," he mutters, looking with abject desire at the Pod.

"Yes, but not for a millennium or so yet. This is for our use. You have neither the ability nor the understanding of how to use it. And, as humans, you'd abuse it totally."

I really enjoy telling it plain to Ashton. Although supposedly a friend, I'm always a little uneasy around him. I still can't pinpoint why.

"Sir, we hope that you like the stage," says Sam.

"Wonderful! Exactly what I wanted."

"Good. Well, Ashton, we gotta go to DC now and deliver Hutchinson's stage."

"Yes, of course. I'll leave you to it."

I watch Ashton wander away to the side, and although out of earshot, I used my telepathic communication with my husband.

'Sam, do you think I should speak to Aby-od? I'm still not comfortable about things.'

'If you're concerned, talk to him.'

I consider maybe I'm a touch paranoid about the whole 'Balance Shift not moving much' thing. The world has gone through a dramatic and rapid transformation following the deaths of Al Douri and his faithful bitch, Sabena. The light I expelled into the world via the Therab's multiplying effect has changed the dark/light structure. Across the globe, people who were on the cusp of darkness have been forcibly swung back into the light. Their soul forces have been realigned, enabling them to follow new paths filled with love, happiness, and good opportunity.

Has this sudden transformation affected the overall Shift status so that Earth's default position now veered naturally toward the white light? Was this why I've experienced so little change in the past few days?

'I'm telling you, sweetness, speak to Aby-od,' Sam repeats. 'We don't want your grey cells agonizing over this. Too many more important things to think about.'

I am about to advise Sam that there aren't many more important things than a planet's Balance Shift going AWOL. But looking at his concerned face, I didn't want to provoke an argument or cause him further anxiety.

'It's not that it's particularly bothering me, it's just my knowledge in this area isn't as proficient as Aby-od's. I don't know whether Earth's current lack of Balance Shift is just a normal state after additional white light energy is released into a world. That's what I need to chat with him about.'

'Really, darling, you shouldn't be worried. The fact Earth is in the light constantly means that Earth is promoting and driving good. I mean, everything here is good, isn't it?'

I stare at my husband, at Ashton, and then at the execution stage we've been complicit in designing.

Good? I'm not so sure.

Chapter 28

What separates humans from any other species is their ability to think and use their intelligence in a more abstract way than just searching for food or a mate. Humans can make complex decisions in multidimensional environments in a split second. They have evolved to appreciate art in a variety of forms. They can imagine the most amazing concepts and create unbounded love.

Unfortunately, they can also manifest irrefutable hate.

Prime Minster Ashton had incited such hatred in his broadcast the day before. President Hutchinson had fallen into step, and forty-two other world leaders that had pledged their allegiance to Freedom Earth had acknowledged the need for justice beyond a cell. They all wanted blood. Al Nadir's blood.

Hans Stein-Muller, the genius creator of the insidious nano-bomb was the first to fall. Stein-Muller, when he'd been caught, would have believed he would spend the rest of his days in jail. But the world had changed in a week.

From his holding cell in the bowels of Langley, Stein-Muller had been taken to the RFK Stadium in Washington D.C. The venue seated over forty-five thousand spectators, but that day, only a small entourage linked to the president was present. Stein-Muller arrived in an armored truck, flanked by four armor-plated Humvees, two on either side. His arrival was received by tough, tooled to the gills, military stars, who had been chosen for the role after showing their worth in the theatre against Al Nadir.

The military mighty giants opened the back of the truck and jumped inside. Stein-Muller was at the top, hooded, handcuffed, and chained in a bright orange jumpsuit. The army sergeants pulled him to his feet. He reluctantly stood up.

"Move," said one of the sergeants, and he prodded Stein-Muller in the back, who grunted and shuffled forward. "And no monkey business," added the sergeant, cocking his gun.

Stein-Muller hobbled toward the back of the truck and two army officers grabbed his arms and yanked him down the steps. Once on terra firma, he was marched into the stadium by the officers. He had to be guided as they refused to take the hood from his head.

Stein-Muller couldn't see anything around him, but he could hear the boots of the army officers as they stepped on the tiled floor inside the stadium entrance. The cavernous hall echoed their footsteps as the party strode forward. Stein-Muller could smell their sweat. It melded with the essence of cotton candy, popcorn, and take away hot dogs that floated in the air. From those smells, he sensed he was in a stadium. The officers pushed him and he felt the air on his face. More doors had opened in front of him. A further prod to walk. The boots rang out hard on the tiles, and Stein-Muller knew he was in one of the tunnels leading onto the pitch.

Suddenly, he was cold. Fear flashed through him. He'd been told nothing, just herded out of his cell and clamped in irons with a hood placed on his head. Something was happening. And his instinct told him it wasn't good.

His defense lawyer had said, "Don't worry. You'll be in jail for a while, but Al Nadir wasn't just you. They've got bigger fish to catch. You'll be free within ten years."

With every hard nudge in his back, Stein-Muller realized his lawyer's faith in the system was misplaced.

Heavy hands pushed him in a specific direction. Underneath his feet was grass. His conjecture had been right; he was in a stadium. Why the hell was that?

Stein-Muller's stumbling entrance was watched by President Hutchinson, Frank Weitz, defense secretary, and Dave Reiner, chairman to the joint chiefs of staff, along with other four-star generals demanding retribution for all the deaths that Stein-Muller's little bombs had caused to their troops.

They had already taken their seats in front of an elaborately constructed stage in the center of the pitch. On seeing the scene, their heads bowed in respect, not for the accused, but for the people who had created the platform. The speed at which it had been produced demanded recognition.

The stage was massive and spread across the entire width of the pitch. Its ornamental carvings befitted more of a Roman gathering than a modern one. Created in smooth pinewood, the construction had two staircases made in the shape of lions on either side leading up to the main floor. Unlike a theatre stage, where the height from the stage to the ground is just a few feet, the height of this one was well over ten feet. On top of the stage were two hefty, crystal pillars about fifteen feet wide with carved pine cones on the top. Between the pillars stretched a thick, wire lattice frame. In each corner, a solid, metal bar with a cuffed end protruded. Halfway up the middle of the stage in front, the words 'Freedom Earth' in a huge, bold typeface had been carved.

The president and his men waited patiently for the accused to arrive.

Stein-Muller stopped walking. The sergeants had reached the staircase and were going up, pulling him step by step, whilst the other sergeants behind pushed him hard upwards. With their push and pull action, Stein-Muller ascended the stairs. His bare feet touched the wood and he knew something terrible was about to happen.

The hood stuck to his face. He breathed in and out quickly and the fabric trapped in his mouth. He wanted to gag. Sweating hard, he tried to swallow his fear.

The steps seemed to be taking forever. Where was he going?

Roughly, he was grabbed. The shackles around his feet were removed and his handcuffs were unlocked. Guns were cocked again and audibly conveyed to him a message: don't try anything.

Stein-Muller stood there, still hooded. He was disconcerted. What was happening?

He felt something being placed over him and belted around his waist. Nothing made any sense.

"What are you doing?" he asked the darkness.

"Quiet," said a hard voice. "You have no right to speak. Another word and I'll rip your fucking tongue out. Understand?"

Stein-Muller understood. He waited. And, as he waited, he felt a pressure around his chest and his feet unexpectedly lifted off the wood stage. Something was hoisting him up. What the *hell* was happening?

His legs and arms were pulled to the sides, and he was spread-eagled against a metal frame that dug into his back. Something metal was strapped around his wrists and ankles. It felt to Stein-Muller like a thick iron cuff. This wasn't good. None of this was good.

Stein-Muller was, of course, quite correct. None of what was about to happen to him was good. However, the VIP spectators watching with great intent could be forgiven for enjoying the show so far. Stein-Muller, murderer of the many, was about get his comeuppance.

Outside the stadium, a huge crowd had gathered but no one from the public was allowed entry. Messages put out deliberately by the president's men on many social media platforms soon had the public execution of Stein-Muller trending like crazy throughout the world. People had arrived from across the state to watch his demise.

These were the same people that had, just a few days before, been terrorized by Al Nadir. They were a public worn down by horrific terrorism and uncompromising national security measures. Their lives had been led in a totally controlled way. No one was free. Always, the specter of a sudden attack or vicious government retaliation flickered in their peripheral vision, just on the cusp of possible realization. It was an uneasiness that both sides had imposed on them. They never believed there would ever be peace or that those who had wrought so much evil would be brought to book.

They couldn't arrive at the stadium fast enough.

When they arrived, the doors were bolted and heavily-armed military patrolled directly in front of the stadium entrance. But the public did get access to huge, super-high-definition screens positioned around the entrance. The screens started out blank. The crowd muttered with discontent. Was this what they'd driven miles to see?

Then a fuzzy picture sharpened, showing a recent explosion at a shopping mall. Emergency service personnel carried out the charred bodies of women and children. The innocent victims of Al Nadir. A booming voiceover started as more images depicting barbaric terrorism took over the screens.

"These deaths were the result of evil technologies created by one man, Dr. Hans Stein-Muller."

The images on screen displayed photos of a young Stein-Muller at school, and then at university. They depicted a young man who had a warped fascination with science and how it could be used to command and control others. The images displayed Stein-Muller's love of the high life, gambling, women, excessive drinking, and, later in his career, drugs.

"A conventional career wasn't going to give Stein-Muller the lifestyle he craved. When Al Nadir came knocking, he answered their call without hesitation," continued the voiceover. "Stein-Muller was paid more money than most of us would see in an entire lifetime to destroy innocent lives. Instead of putting his incredible scientific brain to good use, he used it to upgrade the suicide bomber. No wires, no explosives, and no failure."

On screen, image after image showed explosions and the carnage that followed. The crowds watched dumb, open-mouthed, sucked into the show that was being put on for their benefit.

Each word had been drafted to extract as much vitriol from the public as possible. After ten minutes of consecutive images of devastation delivered by Stein-Muller's hand, the public desperately wanted to rip him apart. Mothers screamed for justice as the images of horrifically burned little children flew up onto the screens. The rest of the expanding crowd called for immediate and uncompromising retribution.

President Hutchinson could hear the calls and screams from outside the gates. The microphones on the screens had captured their bitter vengeance and transported their echoes around the stadium.

The hate was palpable.

The president and his men felt it. But most of all, Stein-Muller could feel it soaking into his skin. Hanging there in the contraption of *whatever the hell it was,* Stein-Muller sensed the atmosphere. It was like the hate itself was radioactive and creating a cancer that ate voraciously at his insides. Stein-Muller breathed long and fast. He listened to the voices.

"Kill the bastard! Kill the animal! Kill the fucker!"

It was clear to Stein-Muller that there would be no long jail sentence. No opportunity to write his memoirs, or take up painting, or read all the books he hadn't had time to but had been looking forward to reading whilst in jail. No, whatever the future, his ended here. He breathed deep. *Get on with it,* he wanted to say, but somehow couldn't. He couldn't encourage those around him to spur on his own death.

He didn't need to. Someone was speeding up the action anyway.

President Hutchinson stood up and ascended the stairs to the stage. He had in his hand a trailing microphone. He looked like a singer who was about to deliver a song to bring the house down. He took his position directly in front of the wire frame. Stein-Muller's arms and legs stuck out behind him, reflecting a weird take on the Ano Domini Man.

The TV cameras came from either side and focused on the president. They were not only beaming images outside the stadium to the waiting crowds but also around the world. Suddenly, the screens filled with pictures of the president standing in front of a suspended Stein-Muller. The crowd howled and whooped with vicious delight; their sadistic need sated by the display. The man they hated with all their hearts was about to be executed.

At the same time in London at the O2 Stadium, the same set up was being broadcast and flashed up on screens. The only difference was that Pedro Russo was the man in the iron cuffs. The people of Britain had been shown similar images of Russo's evil terrorist activities, which had culminated in the destruction of Malta and the five hundred and seventy eight thousand lives gone in an instant. Baying for Russo's blood did not adequately describe the atmosphere at the stadium gates. The public were on the verge of anarchy against a pathetic government that had been unable to stop the slaughter. If they had managed to grab Russo, he would have been shredded to pieces.

Prime Minster Ashton copied the president's movements, his position mapped out clearly on the stage. The TV cameras zoomed in on Ashton and he began. In the US, the crowds watched.

"The time for talking is over," said Ashton.

Hutchinson continued, "The time for terror is done."

Ashton took up the words. "No more will one organization, one country, or one man rule our lives with death and destruction."

Hutchinson followed. "We will not bow down to terrorism in any form."

Ashton continued. "We will stand tall as a proud country, a proud land, a proud world."

"For we have a new chance, a new beginning to bring goodness back to a place where once only darkness lived."

"We will eradicate evil and deliver the light."

Ashton and Hutchinson, in synch, announced, "Together, our nations form the new way."

The two leaders placed their right hands in their jacket pockets and retrieved a small device. The cameras didn't dwell long on the devices, just long enough for viewers to see that the instrument was oval and gunmetal in color. It had a single button at the top, which appeared to be in the form of a prism. The two men turned and aimed the device at their respective prisoners:

"We are Freedom Earth," they both said, and pressed the prism button down, shouting in unison. "And today we cleanse our house of evil."

In London and Washington DC, Ashton and Hutchinson left their stages and took their seats back in the front row. They watched and waited.

A crackle was heard, soft at first, but then it grew in fierceness. Stein-Muller and Russo, still with hoods over their heads, could hear the cracks and sparks.

The audiences outside the stadiums stared, dumbstruck, at what was to happen. Sparks of brilliant blue shot out simultaneously from the corners of the metal frame toward the prisoners. The sparks were like long bolts of lightning snaking toward their outstretched arms and legs.

The president and Ashton looked smugly toward the cameras that were circling the VIP guests, but one camera in each country remained stationary on the prisoner.

Another crack and the blue lightning illuminated the frame.

Neither Stein-Muller nor Russo had time to scream.

The massive charge zapped into them, frying every nerve and catapulting them into hell. Their bodies glowed momentarily with a blue aura. There was no jangling of limbs reminiscent of electrocution. No movement from the prisoners at all. In seconds, it was all over.

Despite the gruesome spread-eagling to begin with, the actual process of execution was most humane. Neither Stein-Muller nor Russo felt any physical pain for longer than a few seconds. The pain they would have felt would have been psychological. Strung up, suspended, in the dark, hearing the chanting voices of the public wanting them dead, and then hearing the crackle of electricity, they would have been aware that death was close.

The public stared at the screen and realized that was it.

But as they watched, they knew they'd been cheated. This was not the execution they'd been promised. This swift, humane killing didn't even begin to measure up to the pain, suffering, torment, and torture that those Al Nadir chiefs had put their victims through. This wasn't justice; this made a mockery of it.

A man who'd been looking at the transmission called out in a small voice, "It's not enough. It's not enough." Others turned to look at the man, who became more vocal. "This is not justice. They should feel pain."

Another man nodded and agreed and started to shout, "This isn't justice."

A woman whose family had been wiped out in an Al Nadir bombing at a West London shopping mall only months before screamed, "Give them pain. Give them pain."

On the other side of the waters, the crowd outside RFK felt the same way. Taking up the initiative from their UK counterparts, they screamed violently, "Give them pain. Make them pay. Justice through pain. Justice through pain."

Ashton watched the crowds across the continents and smiled. They had turned into a baying rabble.

Amidst the loud calls for justice, the man who started it all backed away and left the crowd. Walking quickly, he headed for his car. A smile landed on his face for a moment and then like starburst from a firework, instantly faded. He listened to the public and their calls.

"Give them pain. Make them pay."

What a good idea, the man thought.

Chapter 29

Temenos could feel the hatred. With concern, he flashed up the Balance Shift counter. The numbers, red and alert, bounced before him. It was the same minuscule change as before. The Ruler of Etima returned to view the first executions of Al Nadir chiefs in the Observation Room. His hand touched the screen, and the O2 Stadium in London manifested around him. The crowd's screams were redolent of lynch mobs; fury was in their eyes, and their chanting was a mantra of the macabre.

"Give them pain. Make them suffer."

The words sparked him, initiated his senses and replenished his being. The souls of this burgeoning thong were ebony. He could feel their life forces and he could feel their minds, almost to the point of manipulation. Temenos wondered. Was it possible to influence a human's free will? An experiment perhaps to learn if Aswa-da had been right in this hypothesis.

Temenos observed a young man, well-educated and casually dressed with expensive flair. The perfect specimen. Temenos concentrated on the young man's mind. It was just dark enough to surrender to him. Filled as it was with wanton thoughts of sex, gruesome computer game tactics, and anxiety over exams, it proved an easy mind to infiltrate. Temenos dropped a single thought amongst the detritus of twenty-first-century living: "Kill them all. They're all traitors, so kill them all!"

A grave Antediluvian law had been broken. Never influence free will. Instant execution awaited him. He remembered how Aswa-da had manipulated the US president, placing knowledge of quantum mechanics in his tiny, pathetic brain. No alarm had sounded. No observation had been captured. Just like now. Aswa-da had taught him how to blind Kudamun's sensors. He'd followed Aswa-da's instructions and once again they did not fail him.

The young man, his mouth drawing back, his face stern and vicious, began to scream the words Temenos had planted.

"Kill them all. They're all traitors, so kill them all."

Temenos watched his handiwork take shape, and then morph into a greater purpose. Those loaded words infested others around the young man. Temenos recognized the tightness in their faces. Glacial coldness in their eyes. Accepting of the darkness that flowed now within them. The words touched their tongues and their souls crumpled in defeat.

"Kill them all. They're all traitors, so kill them all."

It started a slow, mumbled cry that mutated into a baying call. Loud and defiant. The throng had found their vocation. Found their voice. They unleashed rage for complete righteousness. Words took form. A reality crystalized. Two executions were not enough. Al Nadir needed to be wiped out. The single voice of over ten thousand standing outside the O2 Stadium blasted around the world and found its home on the screens of people watching on their myriad devices.

It was a call for justice.

People listened. Sounds inveigled their way in, weaving a path of thoughts to necessitate such action. Amongst the words, they heard the screams. They remembered the pain. Millions had suffered. Lives had been destroyed for Al Nadir's greed and domination.

There was no other way.

On their tongues, the words were a source of comfort. A justified retribution.

"Kill them all. They're all traitors, so kill them all."

All nationalities, young and old, joined a chorus to herald the final outcome for all Al Nadir terrorists.

Temenos sensed the growing swell of loathing. He smiled.

The young man who he'd initially instilled the hate chant took out his phone and posted on social media. Someone had started a #KillThemAll hashtag, and within minutes, it was trending in hundreds of millions. Within the swirling mists of green and blue, there was a planet lost in a frenzy of fanatical hatred. Outside RFK Stadium in DC, the crowd yelled with bloodthirsty conviction, echoing the world's plea.

Back in London, cameras skipped from the crowd outside to Ashton inside. In DC, the cameramen did the same. The screens split, showing Ashton and Hutchinson side by side. Their faces beamed. With heads nodding in time to the rhythm of vengeful words, Ashton grabbed his mic.

Once again, showmanship style took over his performance.

"Hear those words!" screamed Ashton. "I will give you what you want. I will make them pay. I vow, here and now, every single Al Nadir terrorist will be executed. I promise you, they will pay with their lives for their crimes. They will *all* die!"

An insanity took over the crowd. They'd heard Ashton's pledge and, like a trigger, the people's emotions fired. Their fervent desire was the need to kill.

In honor of the man who would make their emotion a reality, they cried out his name.

"Ashton, Ashton. Kill them all. Ashton, Ashton. Kill them all."

Inside the stadium, the PM basked in the glory of his making. The carrion call shook the air as the demand for Al Nadir's flesh flooded the waves of sound and broadcast.

A camera thrust forward to capture his reaction. Ashton turned to face it and patted down the air, making a play for quiet. Outside the stadium, the massive screens displayed his wish and the masses halted their cries.

"Thank you, my friends. Thank you. I will not fail you. I have made my promise, and unlike others in the past, when I make a pledge, I stick to it. There will be no U-turns. I will not shy away from responsibility. I will not back down. What you want, you shall get. You have stood by me. I will stand by you. Mr. President, will you agree to do the same?"

The gigantic screens showed Hutchinson taking the mic. His face, a block of steadfast assurance, stared into the camera and hollered, "I do!"

The screams of the US contingent drowned out the riotous British mob.

Like a weird transatlantic wedding vow, Hutchinson repeated, looking deep into the camera, "I do. I do."

On both sides of the Atlantic, the hordes went wild. Two world leaders were giving them, the people, exactly what they had always wanted. Brutal payback.

"I will stand by you, Prime Minister Ashton, in every action. I promise the United States will do the same and execute every single Al Nadir terrorist. They will pay. They will suffer. As members of Freedom Earth, no one will ever touch our land, and no one will harm our peoples. We are one. We are together. We are Freedom Earth."

Temenos listened and was amused. He noticed a small girl with inquiring, blue eyes and long, blonde hair in pigtails. She was no older than three and perched high on the shoulders of her father. Temenos focused on her. So very easy. Her mind malleable and very open. The thought took only a second to seed before actions defined the moment.

"We are one. We are together. We are Freedom Earth," she cried.

With the help of Temenos, the girl's small voice carried across the group. Temenos waited. It wouldn't take long. Temenos had raised the girl's timbre and the resonance of her genteel voice slipped into the crowd's ears. Words repeated, forceful but of pure origin. They touched those around her. A woman standing to the right of the girl's father took up the chant. The girl's father joined in, and then the guy to the left of him began. Four more, seven, ten, twenty. It went on, growing in momentum, increasing the strength of words with every repeat.

Temenos gazed, his skin flushed with feeling, and he absorbed the vindictive energy waves that encircled him.

A steady camera zoomed in on Ashton to capture his reaction to mass adoration. Ashton raised a fist and thumped the air in triumph as the impressionable, gullible souls screamed.

"We are Freedom Earth! We are Freedom Earth!"

He snatched the mic, and akin to an ancient demi-god, he stood, formidable and mighty, and soaked up the veneration from the crowd.

"From the mouth of babes, the truth is spoken."

On Ashton's words, people screamed, and the girl who started it was raised high by her father. A crane camera decided it was time to target her for an up close and personal shot.

Ashton could see the screen in front of him filled with the face of the small child.

He looked into the camera, smiled, and asked, "Little girl, what's your name?"

"Melanie."

"Well, Melanie, what do you want?"

"I want the bad people to go away forever."

"What else do you want, Melanie?"

"I want peace. I want all of us to be Freedom Earth."

Ashton turned to the camera. "What do you say? Let's give Melanie what she wants. Let's take away all those bad people forever. Let's be a world of peace. Let's all be Freedom Earth!"

Decibel levels of the screaming horde outside the doors of the stadium reached heavy metal concert levels as they signaled their compliance to Melanie's request.

Screens flipped to show the US reaction. Across the waters in RFK

Stadium, Hutchinson echoed the same. With a fist raised, pumping the air, the DC mob yelled, "We are one. We are together. We are Freedom Earth."

Temenos stepped back and withdrew his hand from the Re in Kudamun. Around him, the crowds, the screens, and the stadium doors vanished. Back in the Observation Room, he reflected.

Such success, he'd not expected. The speed of conversion had been incredible. Fickle and stupid were the humans who inhabited Earth. Aswa-da had always impressed upon him this fact, and with his own eyes, Temenos realized the veracity of his words.

Their cloying, needing ways. Their presumption that they should be saved. That they were even worthy of saving. Peoples of a world content to let their fellow man suffer and die of starvation while they look away and gorged, submerged in a reality of avarice and hedonistic extravagance. With a greed unending and a want never sated, black were the hearts of the populace, and blacker still would they become before his actions were known.

Temenos noticed a flicker of something to his left. He acknowledged the entrance. A figure concealed in the shadows came forth.

"The time is soon. The words have been spoken," declared Temenos.

The figure nodded and slipped further back into a place he knew well. The dark.

Chapter 30

It is April 2. The first public executions since April 2, 1868 have just taken place, and Ashton is riding the wave of the people's adoration for him and their revenge for Al Nadir.

The PM has invited Sam and me to private discussions concerning a matter that will affect and change the world. He added on the phone that it would "Change the world *for good.*"

As I wait in the Morning Room at Chequers, Ashton's official country retreat, I muse over the syntax of Ashton's last sentence. Like human Ellie before, words always find a way to captivate me. *For good.* Its significance on first hearing was clear. But further investigation into what Ashton really said shows that the words are ambiguous and shrouded in a mist that makes the real meaning difficult to interpret. Change the world to be a good place? Or initiate a change that Earth will never recover from, forever trapped in a design fabricated by a man of questionable values?

The PM joins Sam and me, and we retire to the beautiful garden terrace. We sit in white Victorian garden chairs with delicately carved backs and plumped-up flowery cushions. I reach over and grab Sam's hand so that our arms dangle over the sides of the chairs, making a V sign in front of Ashton, a conscious inference that we, the Kudamaz, will be the victors. I'm not really sure why I did it. But it certainly feels good. Ashton unnerves me and such signs, small as they are, seek to undermine his intrinsic presence. He has a level of power beyond his office. I can't fathom it and reprimand myself for such a deficit.

Sam turns his head, eyes twinkling. He squeezes my hand with reassurance, and then lets it go. I smile. It's enough to feel a momentary touch, skin to skin. Sam will always be mine. Brought alive by my love.

I notice Ashton watching us in his peripheral vision, despite his focus on his phone. With haste, I pull my hand back completely and attach my sights on the PM. My gaze burns through the image he projects for the cameras, the manufactured mask he wears to secure his popularity. And secure it, he has. In the UK and across the world, Ashton is idolized and loved. After taking a hardline stance against Al Nadir, culminating in those unforgettable transatlantic executions, Richard Ashton is a man who can do no wrong. Through his movement, Freedom Earth, he's galvanized a gullible world to jump at his behest.

It strikes me, looking at Ashton, that the world domination Salim Al Douri had sought is now in Ashton's grasp, and he's never had to raise a gun to achieve it.

"All set?" asks Ashton, as he slips his phone back into his pocket and swings his head to peer at me and then Sam. It is a strange, quizzical look that verges on sardonic. I try not to notice his increasing resemblance to Salim and commence the meeting.

"Absolutely, Ashton. What is all this about?" I lean forward, and Ashton moves with me, licking his lips, and sneering in his salacious and disconcerting way. I force myself not to notice.

Sam, it seems, has noticed and he glances back at me, eyebrows raised, then snarls, "Out with it, sir. We haven't got all day to hang around."

Ashton straightens, smoothing his hands over his immaculate, tailored trousers, and sighs. It is a little, despondent utterance, and I realize it is just to intrigue us. I don't take the bait.

"Right, well…" says Ashton, and then pauses, eventually of the opinion that his maneuvers can't work on the Kudamaz. "Religion. I want to unify it."

"Why?" I ask, stone-faced. The proposition is outlandish, to say the least.

"Why? Do you even have to ask that question? Ellie, my dearest, religion is the bane of mankind's life. To bring all the world together as Freedom Earth, one has to bring their hearts and minds together too. Religion rules their hearts and minds, and thus I have to bring religion together to bring the people as one."

I think about Ashton's response. Unification of religion. A bizarre and incomprehensible notion. Religion is intrinsically divisive, borne out of centuries of animosity that cannot be healed overnight. Hostility rages inside people, manifesting perceptions of what they think they see, founded on what they *have* to believe rather than *what* they believe.

Religion has always equaled manipulation. As Kudamaz, I can now see it is a tool to control great swathes of the populace. It is a structured process by which mankind can be held to account and support the Kudamaz Elders' job of keeping the Balance of light and dark. Wars fought over territory descend into wars over religion. Further breakdowns in culture, hatred, and distrust of others not following the same path fuels a constant tension and gives suitable play to both the Houses of Giznu and Etima to gain dominance.

Aby-od's predecessor, Lord Dimkur, had changed the Balance of dark to light through his use of the Therab, an energy multiplier. Dimkur had used the Therab to increase the light energy in moments of darkness on Earth. I had myself deployed the power of the Therab only a few Earth days ago to restore a light balance. Even when I'd used it, I hadn't fully comprehended its function. Only now do I appreciate the way in which the Therab's power operates.

Light energy spewed out from the Therab imbues into the fabric of a human soul and gives a sense of hope, joy, and faith. This white light, which cannot be seen by humans, attacks dark souls, turning them lighter. I must stress, a dark soul doesn't necessarily mean an evil person. It is often one who cannot see the way clearly. They have before them multiple paths. Indecision or fear clouds their judgment. Feelings of having been overlooked for promotion, or not reaching their full potential, or even not finding the right partner in love grey the light of their souls. Darkness taints their lives. Jealousy, envy, and self-pity take hold, and they are unable to determine a path back to the light.

The Therab, by furnishing them with light energy directly to their souls, gives them back the power of hope, faith, and joy. It acts as a confirmation that they *can* achieve. That the best is yet to come. But also to be at peace with what they already have. A satisfied soul is one that will not open the door and let in the dark. It will be happy in its own lot. The power of this position is unending. Once belief is restored and satisfaction instilled, a person naturally achieves. Good begets good.

When I was human, I always had the feeling that attraction of energy was the way things worked. Now, as Kudamaz, I know with one hundred percent certainty that this is the mechanism by which the Universe ebbs and flows and keeps my fellow Kudamaz in their cosmic bureaucratic jobs.

Restoration of a person's belief without the application of the Therab is extremely difficult. Religion and psychology are used by humans with middling success. In the absence of a cosmic superweapon, love is the most powerful device to turn a person's Balance.

What humans fail to realize is the tipping point between love and hate, the transition to which is obsession. Obsessive love turns to hate if unrequited. Obsessive behavior against another is a behavioral mode that greys the soul.

Religions of all kind breed obsessive behaviors. 'Our way is the right way'. 'There is only one God, our God'. By this notion, others are ostracized automatically, made to feel inferior, or worse still, by lack of understanding or poor interpretation, they are demonized as the 'evil ones'.

In the Observation Room on Kudamun, I have watched this behavior. I know it has endured for years. One set of humans killing another for not believing what they believed. Their politics wound into tenets of what they believe so that any other way is faced with torture and imprisonment. The need to fulfill by association, to be recognized as one of the crowd, to do what the masses do only spurs the spread of this grey inveigling of the soul.

With such a discordant foundation built on suspicion, lies, and confrontation, I cannot conceive a moment when religious leaders will lay down their metaphorical staffs and hold the hands of a sworn enemy of a millennium or more.

Ashton, however, appears intent on persuading me differently.

Chapter 31

It is said that the air stills around you when something incredible is revealed. Time itself seems to slow to allow the words to be absorbed and the assimilation of their meaning to be made clear. Ashton's intention 'to unify religions' has a similar effect.

I look at Sam. His acceptance of the PM's wishes is evident. He nods, deep in thought, and smiles while Ashton sets out his grand plan.

"So I need you chaps on board to provide the icing. Are you in?"

"Icing?" I snap. I didn't appreciate his description of our involvement, like top billing at a theatrical event.

"Yes. Final proof that there is more to this life and this universal reality than we as humans could ever have imagined. You are proof of God's absolute existence, that something else watches over us and that we are genuinely accountable for our actions, good or bad."

Ashton's eyes burn with a fervent passion. The passion isn't targeted at me but for his unification objective.

"Ellie, Sam, I want to show the world we can be one. Through Freedom Earth, much has already been achieved, but true global harmony needs beliefs to be aligned. They need a single common message, something that connects and binds them. You are that connection. You make all this possible."

Ashton smiles. It is soft, not his usual leering, salacious smirk and I wonder whether I'd got Ashton all wrong. In that brief moment, I witness a man who has an ideal, a desire to make peace a complete reality. Such is the energy of his focus, his face shines. I read his Balance Shift, and once again perfect Equilibrium displays. Why does this always happen? Is Ashton really a guiding light, a force for good? Or does he have another agenda? The only way I'm going to discover the truth is to remain complicit in this engagement he's scheming.

If we're central to his unification plan, central I will make us.

I glance at Sam and ask to his mind, 'What do you think about this?'

Sam responds instantly, 'It's an amazing idea. We have to help him. Even if we just manage to unify the big religions, that'd be enough to harmonize the populace of Earth.'

'You don't think he's up to something else? I mean, can he be trusted? Is he really that good?'

'Darling, there'd have been a swing to the dark if what Ashton had been doing was bad, but it's strong in the white zone. Humanity's light shines and it's all for good, darling. You have visual proof through the Shift Indicator.'

Our silent exchange causes no raised eyebrows from the prime minister. Delivered in our usual way, at a speed faster than Earth time, our telepathic discourse lasts a mere fraction of a second from Ashton's perspective.

He continues his statement about how the world of religion needs us.

"So you see, my dear friends, you are crucial in ensuring Freedom Earth unleashes humanity's light, enabling it to shine bright."

Sam takes a sharp intake of breath, hearing his telepathic words repeated by Ashton.

'Could he hear us?' Sam's question crashes loudly into my mind. Urgency and worry flicker amongst the syllables.

'Impossible,' I respond. But doubt slips into me, dragging its coat tails of disquiet. 'He'd have to be Kudamaz to intercept. But he has no resonance. No, darling. It has to be a freakish coincidence.'

Sam's face masks his concern, and he looks closely at the PM.

"It's clear I've been wittering on too long," says Ashton. "As usual, I've said too much. Now I'd like your views. Will you help me bring back the world to its harmonious former Eden? A place where the peoples of Earth lived as one, irrespective of color or creed, where all are truly equal before the eyes of God. Under Freedom Earth, all will live in peace, free of evil, suffering, prejudice, and pain. All I need is your support to make my vision a reality."

I don't jump on an answer immediately. I know Ashton is not finished.

Always one to gild the lily, he continues, "Or perhaps you'd like the world to dissolve into the dark swamp of evil? People hating each other for where they come from, for what they believe in. Perhaps, that is how you want Earth to be. Make a better sport for the Kudamaz, eh?"

I listen to Ashton and I realize that although he's baiting me, there is more veracity in his words than I care to acknowledge. The Kudamaz are caught up in ensuring Equilibrium exists throughout the Universe. But on some level, some twisted perspective becoming of Ashton, all they are doing is playing a game. A sport for those with nothing better to do.

Why not tip the odds and make Earth a favorite?

"Ashton, you've fought your corner well. I'm sure Sam and I can weigh up your argument and consider our options accordingly."

I sneak a glance at my husband to ensure he is still of the same mind to stall further activity until a better understanding is secured of the real objectives of religious unification, beyond these outlined by the PM. Sam gives a brief nod of encouragement and then unexpectedly interrupts my flow. I sit back, a little irritated.

"Yes, Ellie's right. I agree we have to consider our position before we make a final decision."

Ashton's eyebrows knit with frustration, and I can see he wants confirmation, not protraction.

"What would you need us to do if we were to agree to our involvement in this unification plan?" I ask forcefully, jumping in to take command, and I shoot a sly grin at Sam.

"Actually, very little. Just your appearance at an opportune moment. We need you to cement the decision for the religious leader engaged to pursue the tenets of unification under the banner of Freedom Earth. I would want you to explain your engagement on Earth to a sufficient level to secure commitment to the cause, but not to be at the detriment of your own operations. Reference Freedom Earth, the path of goodness, the realization that peace and harmony are close. That sort of thing."

"You mean give it a theatrical, theological spin?"

Ashton laughs at my utterance but doesn't show a sneer or smirk, and those moistened lips that he always seems to be licking when in conversation with me stay demurely dry.

"Yes. If that's what gets results. Reveal enough to show them they're part of something bigger."

"We're all part of something bigger, Ashton. Don't think you know all the answers." I thrash out my retort as if my words are a whip. I relish in the acerbic tingle.

"I never said I did. Ellie, why are you so confrontational with me? I'm only trying to make the world a better place. As Protector of Earth, you should want that too."

Ashton's face is humble, penitent even, with not an ounce of his usual sardonic arrogance and lascivious gameplay. Either he is a bloody good actor or somewhere down the road, I'd read Ashton completely wrong.

"Of course I want that, but the world already is a better place."

"And universal peace and harmony through the unification of religion will elevate it to another level of consciousness. Mankind will finally evolve. Do you understand? By traveling this path together, we can obliterate a future that would still see millions suffering just because they had the wrong birthplace. Freedom Earth will be our new Eden. Please stand with me Ellie, Sam. Together we can make this happen."

I shiver. His voice saturates me. My being. I can feel a warmth inside as if he touches my soul force. Drifting, dream-like, I glance at Sam. But the room has dissolved. Around me, I see the pitiful faces of people caught up in wars borne of religion. The same terrible existence they'll endure centuries from now if I don't act, put my differences with Ashton aside, and agree to help him with this unification.

"Ellie, you know it is your duty as Protector of Earth to do this for mankind. They're depending upon you. They need peace. But you and Sam are the only ones who could deliver such an end."

Ashton's voice I can hear, but I can't see his body. Around me are still the visions of torture and religious persecution of innocents labeled as evil by warped social perspectives and media indoctrination. I have the chance to stop it all. To lift humanity to its next level of consciousness. To enable humans to experience the joy of oneness, connected peace, and everlasting joy.

I'm enraptured by this revelation, this incredible opportunity to literally enable human evolution. I stare back at Ashton. His eyes glaze over and he seems to sway. Or is that me?

Lightheaded and unsteady, I try to grip reality. But it trips like a treacherous adulterer away from me.

Before I can stop, a force that I can't fight or comprehend, nor even want to fight, rips the words out of my mouth.

"We'll stand by you, Ashton."

Chapter 32

Ashton watched, amused if not delighted, by Ellie's reaction. His trigger words had stormed her recalcitrant gates, bursting them wide open with a battering ram of truth. He'd reasoned that her conditioning to 'protect' must be hard-coded into her being. That was why, as human Ellie, she'd never broken under torture, and whatever her physiology was now, the need to protect humanity was still there and existed as the primary reason for her being. Go against that and she was going against her reason for creation. He just had to push her to experience the pull of such conditioning.

His carefully couched phrases and mention of the word 'duty' shifted Ellie's mind. No different to assets or hostiles he'd manipulated to betray their countries or their causes back in the days when he was a British Intelligence agent. He'd drilled her to the point of her conditioned state and flicked the 'humanity needs you' switch.

"Are you sure, Ellie?" questioned Sam, his tone dubious.

Ashton tried to hold down a scowl that was building across his face. "I think Ellie's of her own mind."

Ellie paused and flicked a look between suspicious Sam and serene Ashton. "Yes. Absolutely, yes. This is momentous. We'll both support you. If there's any chance of Earth being a united, harmonious place, this is it."

Ellie reached out over the arm of the chair and gripped Sam's hand, and then, in a gesture that Ashton was momentarily overwhelmed by, Ellie reached out and grabbed the PM's hand, holding it tight. In unison, displaying clear solidarity, Ellie raised both hands upward and shook them with strength.

"Peace on Earth, Ashton. If you think you can do it, who am I to stand in your way?"

Ashton's benevolent grin set off a chorus of smiles from Sam and Ellie. His grin hid his immense relief at securing the Kudamaz couple's collusion in his grand unification scheme. Without them, Ashton knew he'd never be able to execute one step.

Now he'd impregnated Ellie with the notion that, through religious unification, peace and mankind's natural evolution would take place. His 'baby', it seemed, was weeks away from being born.

Chapter 33

A positivity had immersed Lei. She believed without hesitation or doubt that Xiao would regain consciousness. It was just a temporary blip. That was all. Just a little inconsequential irrelevance in a life otherwise charmed.

Her initial pain of witnessing her son fall into a coma was over-ridden by a strength of conviction that he'd wake soon. The fact his descent into a coma had followed so quickly without warning suggested her son's state of brain inactivity would be in abeyance with a similar speed of expedition.

"How could this possibly be lasting?" Lei chirped with inappropriate merriment to Chen. "It happened so suddenly. He's a fit boy, healthy and strong. This will soon be over. Xiao will be back with us, you'll see."

The mother's power was in her self-assurance that things would get better, that her child would recover and that all was not lost to her. But that self-assurance had to stand battle with trickles of self-doubt as the hours tumbled into days and then to weeks.

Lei held Xiao's hand throughout, talking to him like he was there with her in the room. Her grip was strong and tender. Her manicured hand encased Xiao's small fingers, those fingers so often glued to a phone or game-station console. Fingers that pronounced his rudeness at his parents, teachers, and anyone who wielded authority. Fingers that covered his face from sights unknown but terrifying.

Lei pushed her will into Xiao. She forced his body to accept her desire for him to live. Her own life-force, she imagined flowing into Xiao. A physical manifestation of her love, it slipped through her hands into his small slithers of skin and bone.

In her heart, Lei prayed.

By birth, she was a Buddhist and belief in the never-ending circle of life had been drilled into her. Death is the beginning. We are all connected. Our energies are eternal, imbuing life into another form. But for all that formative indoctrination, Lei couldn't accept Xiao's position. She couldn't accept he was dying.

Something had happened, something beyond her understanding but not beyond her comprehension. A power inside her son caused his condition. A power, ancient and wise, but unthinking and desperate in its assertion to exist. Her son was but a vessel, a container for its being. A container that leaked and couldn't hold that which it possessed.

Lei couldn't speak of this to her husband. Chen, a pragmatic soul and grounded in the reality of a concrete world of certainty, would never countenance such metaphysical musings. He wasn't a spiritual person, having adopted a position of agnostic years before they met. And no amount of discussion by her in subsequent years could convince him to reverse this thinking.

"When you're born, you're already on a downward path. Just got to grab as much as you can before you hit the bottom."

That was Chen's doctrine. He'd cited it many times. Lei, on hearing it for the first time, asked him what he meant by 'grab as much as you can'.

"Money, position, power. You know, the stuff that makes life livable."

"Is that your only consideration? Material things?"

Lei's question brought a snarl from Chen as he remembered the years of nothing, of struggling and trading off between buying food or fuel. Never both.

Lei dialed back on her judgmental attitude. Chen hadn't been blessed with any spoon, let alone a silver one, and certainly not the platinum one she'd been brought up on. Material things affirmed his status. No, in fact, more than that, they gave him definition. They outlined him and gave him a purpose to succeed.

Lei didn't know much about Chen's business dealings in the early years. The truth was, she didn't want to know. Chen, despite his faults, was the man she loved and would always love.

The lives of two men mattered more than her own: Xiao and Chen. Her world began and ended with them.

Chen was difficult, brash, and often downright rude, as infuriating as he was brilliant, and lovely as he was loathsome. Countless times, she'd packed her bags, "That's it, we're over!" almost forming on her beautiful lips. Then she'd stop and glance at Chen, a hulk of a man made minute by emotion. How quickly he crumbled. Arms up, she'd encircle him. Feeling love, his recklessness quelled. Forgiveness in his quiet rumble. A stealthy love, he delivered upon her before she knew. In her cells, Chen existed, part of her in him, and him in her. A spiritual bonding that ascended the physics of ecstasy.

Lei recognized an age-old love. It was this acknowledgment rather than his multimillionaire status in the fashionista world that attracted her. It drew her to Chen with unaccustomed abandonment of protocol, and threw their lives together as one.

She could never leave Chen, and he could never leave her.

Forged together through something unexplained, Lei gained explanation from such an unknown. It was an explanation that more existed between heaven and Earth than what could be perceived by human senses. That ancient powers infiltrate the mortal plane. And perhaps her son had encountered one such power.

"I can see the darkness in others," her son had said. He'd issued sorrow and pity for Chen. Lei knew these were not the actions of a young boy.

His ailment was not biological. The doctors, consultants, and a stream of ego-driven clinicians prodded, poked, and examined, but every one of them had failed. Their words, derived from a reliance on a science, couldn't deliver the truth.

Only a truth in her heart created her absolute positivity. A truth to keep her, day after day, grasping Xiao's hand and willing him back to life. A truth hidden by confused and confounded paths those doctors had taken. Lei could see they wouldn't find the answers they sought, for the places they searched held nothing but more questions.

What they searched for, she already knew.

Xiao would wake. Alive, renewed, and with a greater strength, he would return the grasp of his mother's hand.

And all would be well.

Chapter 34

In Kudamun, as on Earth, the force of change rippled through, turning over Antediluvian laws, ageless practices, and bureaucratic protocols during one convening of the High Council. The Therab had been removed from Earth. The elders recognized the device was too dangerous even to leave in a time lock, but they also knew, like Aby-od's ancestors, that they couldn't destroy it as it would have caused an immense extinction level explosion throughout the Universe. Life would be wiped out everywhere. Their only choice was to return it back to a moment when such an explosion could potentially be used in a positive way. The elders carefully took the Therab back in time to moments just after the Universe had been created. A controlled detonation of the Therab was arranged and the energies from the explosion were naturally sucked into the on-going explosions and reactions brought about by the Universe's creation.

Aby-od knew that Aswa-da's actions would deliver ramifications so far-reaching that the Kudamaz would never return to their old ways. For one thing, now humans, at least a handful of them, were aware of there being forces in existence beyond comprehension, and that they watched the Earth constantly, counting every act of good and bad, dark and light. That knowledge alone meant that Kudamun and its interactions with humans would never be the same again.

Of course, the revelation that humans could be reconstituted using stored Kudamaz life-forces also indicated a new era for Kudamun, and the way in which it regarded humans.

Aby-od recalled the moment after Sam Noor's reconstitution. He remembered his absolute joy at achieving such an incredible feat, but also his utter confusion. Sam had melded with Dumuzi's life force, he hadn't been overpowered by it. This showed Aby-od the human will to live was far stronger than even the Kudamaz one. Humans were truly amazing. They might not be so advanced as other species across the Universe, and they certainly could display relentless evil, as well as stunning good, but one thing was undeniable: a human's need to survive whatever the odds.

That sense of spirit, coupled with the love that forever connected Selema and Dumuzi and Sam and Ellie, changed the very laws of what was possible. It had delivered Sam into the form he now had. A true Kudamaz-human hybrid.

Following Aswa-da's disappearance, Aby-od had placed searches on him. His own resonance signature, like a human voice, would reveal where he was. If he tried to shimmer to any planet or into Kudamun, his resonance signature would trigger an alarm. Under the Grand Order of Kudamun, he would undergo an immediate full body transference. This process would lock Aswa-da's ability to shimmer, and he would be transferred to a holding cell in Kudamun. Once inside the cell, harmonic bars would activate, destabilizing his cellular structure and making shimmering impossible, as he would not be fully locked into Kudamun's plane of reality.

Aby-od had instigated the searches himself. The machinations and betrayal by Aswa-da, and his absolute exploitation of their Antediluvian laws, Aby-od took personally. It was an affront to his leadership and an abuse of the power Aswa-da had as Leader of the opposition.

The House of Etima represented dark energy, but that did not mean the Leader had to be evil. Dark energy was not about destroying things. It wasn't about total dominance and control. A percentage of dark energy could be used to manifest a want, a desire, or a drive to do something. When balanced with white light energy, dark energy could deliver transformational change for a person, a country, or even a world. It was all down to application and, of course, Balance Shift.

No, Aswa-da didn't do what he'd done for the House of Etima; he'd done it for himself, and for his insane plan to rule Kudamun and change the light/dark balance in the Universe forever.

Despite being rigorous and exacting in his process of the search, Aswa-da had so far eluded him. Aby-od knew he could only be still on Earth. Anywhere else, and the alarms would have sounded throughout Kudamun. But where would he go? A seven-foot-tall giant of a man resembling someone from a civilization thousands of years ago would protrude slightly out of the social fabric that was modern day Earth.

If he hid in any of the big cities, if a human saw him, they'd think their drink or food had been spiked. Of course, Aswa-da could be clever and reside amongst the winos and druggies, where seeing a seven-foot giant was an everyday occurrence.

The other place Aswa-da may be hiding was in the uninhabited parts of Earth. The jungles and the deserts, too barren and too remote to support life, could offer excellent cover for a criminal cosmic bureaucrat hiding out.

Then Aby-od remembered most of those inhospitable places were, in fact, inhabited, or they had been, by Al Nadir's armies before the crackdown initiated by Ellie and Sam Noor.

And what a crackdown that had been.

Aby-od recalled looking at Sam and Ellie from the Observation Screen when they arrived back in the fray. A visceral deluge took over. Ellie, her arms flying, legs kicking, cutting down, taking out, zapping with rainbow light, obliterating weapons, splintering bullets, severing limbs, speeding in a blink, a cataclysmic eruption of a Kudamaz power wrought on the evil of Al Nadir.

Sam in a similar flow.

The humans couldn't catch his movement. Speed beyond their perception gave him an advantage. Strikes delivered and Harmon guns fired. With Sam alongside Ellie, their combined might was totally invincible and more effective than the most elite Special Forces of any nation on Earth.

The ground was reduced to mangled bodies in seconds, and then to twinkling, lethal rainbow light the next. In the space of a few Earth minutes, an entire Al Nadir base was cleared of all hostiles. Ellie's battle force was monstrous, but undeniably driven by surging goodness. Aby-od dared not even rest a single thought on what if that battle force was driven by surging evil.

At Ellie's core, pure light existed. She was a being comprised to protect the Earth, and who could only deliver justice borne out of total goodness, not sanctimony or emotive manipulation. A force for good, her path rested in and was directed by the power of the white light.

Aby-od switched to another memory like a human would change a TV channel. Allied forces in the area had pulled back on Sam and Ellie's entry. Into the lion's den strode the Kudamaz couple as Al Nadir turned on their heaviest artillery against them. Laser guided-gizmos grilled and glowed before disintegrating to dust.

In fear, many ran. Sam shot his Harmon gun to paralyze the fleeing figures. The harmonic penetrated their bodies, their muscles contracted, and the vibration blocked their nervous system. Unable to move, with their bodies incapacitated, through terrified eyes, they witnessed their more courageous and stupid colleagues be eviscerated and destroyed.

No army. Just two people.

Confusion catapulted through their minds, tangible enough for Aby-od to touch. He turned away from the Observation Screen as it depicted a gory descent into humanity's retribution for the years of Al Nadir's evil control.

A retribution at the hands of Sam and Ellie.

Those still alive were rounded up and stunned momentarily with Sam's Harmon gun. Their bodies, immobile but heavy with the weight of what they'd seen, waited for the armed forces to return. The authorities shackled them, and lead them one by one into massive lorries.

Aby-od recalled how the Observation Screen showed Ellie standing with Sam by her side, arms folded and resolute, with not an ounce of emotion showing in her face. She'd emerged from the base, where she'd wrought carnage on the terrorists and watched the survivors as they were hauled away.

Aby-od wondered. Was this her revenge? Was this act her need to decimate Al Nadir for the pain they'd subjected her to? Did personal emotion infiltrate? Or did the Protector answer to a pure need to eradicate evil?

From the scenes, at first only savagery persisted, driven by a singular want: absolute retribution. But Aby-od observed more. He saw a measured subtlety in how Ellie discharged her power. Only those who made an immediate threat, through weapons or fierce assault, were obliterated. Those who demonstrated weakness and an inability to fight were left unharmed, if albeit paralyzed for a short period by a Harmon gun. Aby-od knew Ellie was reviewing all the hostiles' Balance Shifts at lightning speed. That continual monitoring was providing the determinant for her actions.

Despite how dark things looked on the Observation Screen, Ellie's mission was driven by goodness and light. She saved lives before she took them.

Sam was also guided by her knowledge, as he chose to zap hostiles into paralysis rather than oblivion.

Renewed with assurance at this stance, Aby-od left the Observation Room. Over the coming Earth days following Sam and Ellie's crackdown on Al Nadir, he'd returned to view their progress. He wanted to ensure that those lines of engagement inherent in a planetary Protector were not crossed.

With gratitude, his observations confirmed Ellie's reconstitution as the Protector had been total and encompassing. A complete success.

Absorbed in his quiet hubris, Aby-od failed to detect a watcher. Flush to the wall and in the shadows of the Observation Room, the watcher's eyes glinted as anticipation floated through him. Everything was as it should be.

The pieces were connecting. The rise would be unstoppable.

Chapter 35

Sweat mingled with musty sandalwood struck his nostrils. A practical scent for practical people. Scientists, who lived their lives in labs, testing and validating. Ashton reasoned that their daily activities gave them no need for expensive perfumes. Their existence, dull and predictable, required nothing more than cheap, mass-produced deodorant. *Clive Christian* was a different world. His world. And those around the chamber had no place in it. They were there only to do his bidding and make his discovery legitimate.

An hour had passed since Ashton had arrived. The boffins had been experimenting for over a month. Every time, the results had been the same. There was a perfect and continuous level of energy generated into the collector from the collision of a single photon in a chamber housing a specifically engineered crystal.

When the scientists had commenced the experiments, they could not comprehend how their prime minister had come by such knowledge. They had followed the typed instructions and complex equations, but all had misgivings. The equations themselves held little relevance to current day physics. In fact, they held little relevance to science at all. They were more the work of Hollywood filmmakers. The levels and densities being worked at appeared impossible. The chemical configurations to create the crystal structures were absurd. They didn't exist in nature. Still, the scientists rolled their sleeves up and set about the experiments, firm in the conceited notion that the instructions were pure science fiction.

It took a day for the crystal to generate. On opening the clean room to inspect their work, their conceit evaporated. The weird crystal sat in the center of the dish, taunting them to finish the experiment. The crystal was maroon in color and fifteen centimeters high with facets of different lengths. Some of its surfaces seemed to shine while other parts were muted. When one looked at it, there was an inner twinkling, like starlight had somehow been trapped within the planes of its construction. The scientists stared. It was unlike anything they had seen. They muttered amongst themselves that the physical laws of nature had been broken by the thing's creation. Some were afraid to continue but realized they had no option.

Following the instructions, a material was constructed to make a chamber to house the crystal. The metal they'd made, they had never heard of nor touched before. They didn't even know what to call it. It was like gold only with a heavier density. The molecules were in a different configuration. In lieu of any chemical name, the scientists called it Gold Plus.

The chamber was forged out of the Gold Plus material and the weird crystal placed inside. The chamber was thirty centimeters in height and half a meter in length. It looked like a rectangular pipe. Finally, a collection box with sensors was attached to the end of the chamber to collect the energy that would come out of the experiment. All that was left was for the scientists to position the gun and fire a single photon down the chamber to the weird crystal.

Ashton knew everyone in the room was desperate to ask where the technology originated from, but all scientists were silent. They had been forced to sign the Official Secrets Act before they could even touch a single leaf describing the new energy source.

Ashton glanced at his Phillippe Piaget watch and tapped its face. His chief scientist noticed the signal and recognized it was time to speed up proceedings. He told one of his boffins to "Get on with it!" and the egg head fired the photon gun. The particle of light streamed down the chamber. Hitting the crystal, it appeared to be absorbed, and then the light refracted at a strange angle, causing it to shine a brilliant cobalt blue. As the light was emitted, it winked in and out like it was a sewing thread hidden by fabric. The energy wavelength vibrations were caught and locked into the collector, which then channeled the energy directly into the generator.

Heads turned, including Ashton's, toward a grid-work of lights on the tech plate spread out across the wall. The lights blinked out initially to signify the traditional power shut down. One of the scientists rerouted the power distribution, pushing the 50,000 square meters of sci-tech space to rely wholly on the new energy source. Ashton, Redfern, and the scientists all watched nervously as the grid-work lit up.

A whole quadrant of the military research lab was powered by the new crystal-based energy.

The experiment had been a success. The quadrant was far larger than any other previous experimental area. Ashton nodded with calm authority. Around him, scientists cheered and congratulated each other.

"So it works? That's great! No time must be wasted. I need existing power plants to be retrofitted to accept the new energy source and scaled up immediately." Ashton's measured voice carved up their celebratory stance.

Redfern pulled the PM to one side. Having witnessed the new energy source in full glory, he knew matters would soon snowball. Scientific experiments, even those as massive as the one just carried out, were still contained. But when this new energy source was unleashed on the world, things would change. The UK's place on the world stage would literally be under the spotlight. And he couldn't see OPEC members, Russia, China, Uzbekistan, or any other country with oil, natural gas, or shale sitting by and watching happily this new positioning.

Had Ashton thought all this through? Redfern glanced at the PM, who looked back with his characteristic one eyebrow raised.

"Prime Minister, sir, could I speak with you privately?"

Ashton nodded and turned to the scientists still encasing him. "Hear what the man said." Ashton gestured toward the door.

The scientists, although thinking how incredibly rude the PM was, refrained from speaking and headed silently through the door that Redfern had opened for them.

Ashton stared back at Redfern as the last scientist slipped back into career oblivion, the stardust of his recent achievement falling from him as he walked away.

"Okay, decks are cleared. What did you want to say?" Ashton's annoyance at cutting short the demo was evident, but Redfern ignored him.

"They're not going to sit by and allow the UK predominance in the energy market." Redfern eyed the PM as he spoke.

Ashton shook his head. "What can they do? I'm prime minister of the United Kingdom. I'm the one championing this new energy. Even if they wanted to, they wouldn't dare. No one has the balls to do it."

Ashton's arrogance suggested naivety to geopolitics, and particularly the energy sector. Redfern, however, wasn't convinced. A lot of words could be used to describe the PM, but naivety wasn't one of them. What Redfern didn't know was Ashton was arrogant because he had cause to be. Besides MI5 and MI6 at his disposal, despite their services being for 'God, Queen, and Country', Ashton also had his own network of spies, analysts, bullies, and assassins. A private, carefully constructed global network of people in influential positions fed Ashton's intelligence machine. He had learned from Al Douri the essential lesson of having eyes and ears everywhere. If he knew what was going on, what actions were soon to be taken, he could take measures himself proactively and counter the risk.

Remove the threat.

"But, Prime Minister, what if they do challenge you?"

Redfern's voice was reassured. But his inference placed in Ashton's mind a situation of such game-changing proportions that only certain war with the offending countries would redress the barbarity made. With the US as staunch allies, Ashton was suspect of any recriminations from countries uncomfortable with the UK wielding such power. Still, it would be imprudent of him to not galvanize the full weight of his intel machine into keeping him safe.

"Redfern, my friend, you always err on the side of caution."

"I know the darkness that is in others. Once this goes live, the Sheikhs, the Oligarchs, and anyone else whose continued wealth relies on the pursuit of traditional energy sources will place a price on your head. You will be a target despite your position. Make no mistake, sir, you will be a marked man."

Ashton took a moment to consider Redfern's words. His response was quiet. No drama. Not even anger. But his delivery chilled his Cabinet secretary.

"And I will *mark* the man who even attempts to do what you infer. Make no mistake about that!"

Redfern stared into the PM's eyes. He saw in them a man who knew his worth. A man with no limits.

And he knew it was no casual threat.

Chapter 36

Chen moved the Liberty drapes and stared from the bedroom window of his luxurious London townhouse. He watched Lei get into their car and head for the hospital as she'd done every day since Xiao had dropped into a deep coma.

The daily journey had become a ritual. It was something Lei lived to do. Perhaps it gave her meaning. All Chen knew was that he couldn't do it.

His son's eyes had scared him. They had touched him in a way he didn't want to accept. It was as though his son could see inside him. What was in his heart. What was in his soul. As much as Chen had kept his past buried from his family, he knew that Xiao had seen all his dark and terrible secrets.

Growing up dirt poor brings about a different type of morality. It's easy to talk about doing the right thing and maintaining one's integrity when you live a comfortable life, have food security, and don't need to think about where the next paycheck will come from. He'd lived on the other side, where scruples and standards were a luxury he just couldn't afford.

During his early years, slogging in the textile factory for endless hours, he didn't see the sun for almost a year.

A slave by any other name.

He rose at four, started work at five, and left at nine at night. Sixteen hours a day with hardly any time to take a break. With the rest of the boys and girls in that factory, he worked the looms and other textile machines until he couldn't open his eyes. Many had fallen asleep while working the machines and suffered life-changing injuries.

None were compensated. In fact, the factory owner docked their final week's pay as their accident had left them with an inconvenience. Chen shuddered. Such coldness. Such evil against those who had nothing.

Is it any wonder this treatment would shape him into a person who'd take a darker road in life?

Days before his fifteenth birthday, the factory owner discovered some of the work was sub-standard and took his anger out on a young girl of no more than sixteen whom Chen had befriended over the year. The owner slipped his belt off and Chen could see he meant business. The girl cowered into a corner and the factory kids stopped working and looked on, knowing what was to happen.

"Eyes back on your work, scum!" yelled the owner.

The factory kids leapt back into what they were doing, too terrified to disobey.

Chen kept one eye on the owner as he tried to continue his work.

The owner cracked the length of his belt on the floor like a whip. He stood towering over the young girl. He was a huge-boned man, all muscle, no fat, with menacing eyes and lips curled into a snarl.

Crack! Crack!

The sound of leather on concrete, Chen would never forget.

The girl whimpered, backing further into the corner of the factory. But there was nowhere for her to go.

"Strip!" the owner bellowed. He was still advancing.

The girl, now crying, shook her head.

"Impudent little rat. I said strip!"

The girl shivered but didn't acquiesce.

Chen heard the leather belt slice through the air and hit down with a hard slap on her soft skin. The girl screamed. Chen stopped what he was doing and focused his full attention on the unfolding scene. The owner grabbed the girl's flimsy cotton dress and tore it down. It pooled at her feet revealing her young naked body. The girl placed one arm across her breasts and a hand down to cover between her legs.

The owner leered and licked his lips. He flicked the belt down and targeted it across her naked body. The belt bit into her supple, young skin with a vicious whoosh, bringing a red welt diagonally across her torso, and the girl fell. Seeing her buttocks on show, the owner sneered and brought the belt down hard against her fleshy peaches.

On the floor, the girl tried to shield herself with her arms. The owner started to laugh as he brought his belt down with increasing speed across the girl's body. Chen could see from the bulge in his ill-fitting trousers that the torment was arousing him.

Chen knew what the owner would do next.

As the owner advanced on the trembling girl, now hunched on the floor. Chen picked up the scissors by his loom, and slowly and silently left his station. Any sound of his movement was lost in the sounds of the whirring and swooshing of the textile machinery. Standing behind the owner, Chen could hear as he unzipped his flies. The owner pinned the girl to the floor, one massive hand across her throat, the other fumbling at his button.

Chen watched, unsure of what he was doing. And then he saw the girl's face. The desperation in her eyes. The pain and shame.

All for getting a few wrong weaves in a fabric.

At that moment, everything became clear. The burning injustice of life. It was time to make the change.

Chen grasped a tight hold on the scissors, for fear he would drop them. He bent down just behind the owner, screamed with rage and thrust the scissors deep into the owner's back. The man was alerted by the scream, but by that time, the scissors had already buried into his heart. The girl cried as the owner vomited blood over her stomach. Chen pulled the man off the girl and onto his back. With her feet, the girl pushed away from the owner. On her face, Chen saw relief and abhorrence. Chen snatched some fabric from the floor and wrapped it around the girl's shaking body. She huddled in the corner and didn't move.

Chen stood up and looked around. The factory kids were catatonic. They'd halted working and were now just staring at him. Chen took a cloth from his work area and pulled out the scissors. He wiped the handle and both blades. Without a look back at his fellow factory kids, Chen placed the scissors in the tray with the other tools. Chen then dug in his pocket for a box of matches. He sparked up a match and burned the cloth until it was black and charred.

The factory kids around him were silent, mesmerized by his calculating actions. Even the girl he saved remained in the corner, unmoving and unspeaking.

Chen walked into the small dingy side office. Papers were everywhere. The place was untidy, but Chen knew exactly what he was looking for. He skirted around the old wooden desk and pulled at the bottom drawer. It was unlocked. A large money box lay inside. Chen reached in and lifted it out. It was also unlocked. The owner hadn't shut it after handling the takings that day. Chen stuck his hand in and took out all the money, far more money than he'd ever seen in his life. He divided it into halves. One half, he pocketed.

The remainder, he took back out to the factory floor.

"This is your money. You have earned it," Chen called to his fellow workers.

The kids crowded around and snatched at the money he left on the side. He pulled out a wedge of cash and gave it to the girl who'd been assaulted.

Her face lit up as she smiled. Chen held her small, trembling hand in his, and then swiped a side look at the dead factory owner. Time to leave.

His anger had abated, but it was by no means gone. Much more would befall others before Chen would feel a balance of true justice in his life.

Chapter 37

A light breeze touched the man's hand. He enjoyed its presence. Coming from a land of continual blasting heat, the coolness of the air was a comforting stroke. He relaxed back in a cushioned outdoor chair and nodded subconsciously. The arrangements were to his liking. He sipped at his cocktail. The sprawling private residence cloistered away behind high, metal gates in an exclusive lane in fund manager land just seventeen miles out of London served as an ideal safe house for discussing international relations. Far from the spotlight of the press.

A flicker moved to his right. His eye caught it and followed it as the luxuriously landscaped garden lit up with a cavalcade of color. Proud, strutting peacocks emerged from behind bushes and trees.

Ashton had certainly thought of everything. Perhaps this meeting would be more magnanimous than he first supposed.

"Your Highness, the prime minister is five minutes away. He gives his apologizes for his tardiness."

The man, luxuriating in the magnificence of his surroundings, dismissed the PM's lateness. "It is of no consequence. I have more time to enjoy this." Prince Khalifa, heir to the Kingdom of Saudi Arabia, gestured to the verdant green. "But perhaps the PM may benefit from my suggestion. A helicopter is faster than a car every time."

A supercilious smirk denoted his position in the forthcoming power battle.

"I shall inform him, Your Highness." The prince's manservant departed, leaving the prince alone to his thoughts. Alone, that is, but for the fourteen strong bodyguards of dubious military backgrounds, six of whom carried close protection detail with explicit orders to shoot first and ask questions later. The prince's men were a formidable force.

Safety did not even raise in his consciousness, for the prince didn't have to belittle his brain with such trifling considerations. Someone was always paid to do these tasks.

His mind was attuned to greater matters, like the one facing him that day: maintaining his kingdom's energy supremacy.

The overtures Ashton had made were disruptive and unsettling. Al Mukhabarat Al A'amah or General Intelligence Directorate (GID), Saudi Arabia's external intelligence agency, had investigated the initial claims. But British Intelligence had locked down all back channels usually used in such matters. His GID assets inside MI5, MI6, and CIA had been silenced. Even Mossad, who always delivered, proved useless this time. Such actions had annoyed the prince. However, he knew affability was the way forward. Until this meeting, all he had was whispering. The talk of the excited. And he knew talk was dangerous if it had no substance.

"Your Highness, my apologies!"

The prince swung his head around to meet the originator of the voice. A clipped, if slightly effeminate, timbre announced Ashton had arrived. The prince did not rise from his seat. He regarded the PM with distaste as he took in the number of his entourage, which spanned to over twenty – many more than his enforcer team. Even more were milling in from a side entrance.

Ashton smiled with smooth efficiency. His diplomatic bomb was delivered without hardly a word said. His people stood attentive and primed; their Sigs nestled comfortably in their side holsters. They took their positions around the PM.

The prince watched. He'd dealt with other PMs in the past, but none had shown this degree of posturing. Like the preening birds he'd witnessed around the gardens, Ashton was a political peacock. But what did his father always say about peacocks? "The weight of their vanity makes them easy to catch."

The PM placed a hand out to the prince, who still remained seated. Ashton understood the little game being played. He carried on smiling and made a slight bow. But as he came out of the bow, he exclaimed, "Your Highness is unwell?"

Both sides froze. Each entourage, alert to the atmosphere, were on point.

Birdsong stopped. The peacocks turned to stare at the patio. The breeze that had so welcomed the prince vanished. A heaviness took over. The skies darkened.

"Unwell?" muttered the prince, after a few seconds of contemplation.

"Why yes, Your Highness. Your strength to stand seems to have departed from you. You must, therefore, be unwell. Shall I call a physician to attend to your needs?" Ashton, now at full height again, stared down at Prince Khalifa. At the edge of his mouth, a shadow of a smirk emerged. "Jensen, get Dr. Chambers here at once." Ashton's eyes never left the prince's as he instructed his confidante. The prince matched Ashton's glare.

"No, no, that will not be necessary. The journey, you understand, it tired me. But I am quite recovered now." With abject reluctance, the prince pressed down on the sides of the chair and urged his portly frame to stand upright. He was a man in his late forties. But with the many indulgences and vices his body had been subjected to, his body told a much older age.

Prince Khalifa's hand outstretched to Ashton, and the PM received it warmly. He shook it and touched firmly the prince's elbow in parallel. The strength Ashton imparted gave the prince cause to wince. His security detail sharpened their stance, and made to move forward in the direction of the British PM. Ashton noted their gesture. He pulled back, released the prince from his grasp, and indicated for them both to take the patio chairs.

"Please sit, Your Highness. I see you are still quite fatigued after your journey. Would you care for some more refreshing cocktail? A meal perhaps?" Ashton fussed in front of the prince in a show of caring and benevolence. The prince nodded. Ashton ignored the anger in the prince's black eyes and delivered the refreshments order to a waiting servant. He turned to face the prince again.

Ashton could see Khalifa seething.

"Now, Your Highness, we can return to matters both our countries need addressing."

The prince raised an eyebrow. "Both our countries?"

"Why yes. The new energy source we have..." The PM searched for the most apt word. "...discovered will need to be regarded within the current global energy mix, alongside oil, gas, nuclear, renewables, shale and so forth. The abundance of the new energy will impact the markets." Ashton waited for the prince to ingest this information.

"Impact the markets, you say."

"It could destabilize them completely." Ashton dropped the words like grenades.

"That, Prime Minister, is very bold talk for an energy source no one knows anything about, except you."

"Bold talk but nevertheless true, Your Highness. Would you like to see the recording of our last demonstration a day ago?"

Without waiting for the answer, Ashton beckoned Jensen over with the tablet.

He placed it in front of Prince Khalifa and pressed play. In silence, the prince watched and listened to the PM's Chief Scientific Advisor's commentary.

"Impressive, Prime Minister. But can it be repeated? Is this experiment you have done sustainable?"

"It is. Would you like to witness it for yourself, Your Highness?"

"I would indeed like to witness it. Only then can I be a true believer in this new energy source." Prince Khalifa stared at Ashton. His cynicism was apparent as he stood without his previous hesitancy and issued a command to the British Prime Minister. "I wish you to take me, right now, to this place of experiment. Allow me to see this new energy source."

Ashton stood and bowed his head in acceptance to the command.

"Of course, Your Highness. I will take you there right now."

Ashton flicked a look toward Jensen, who spoke hurriedly into his phone, advising the recipient that 'a further demo would be required'. Ashton had already primed the lab to expect this call, so it caused no concern. In fact, it was exactly what Ashton wanted.

Further into the grounds came the sound of rotor wash. The prince turned in the direction of the noise, surprise on his face.

"A helicopter, Prime Minister?"

"Of course." Ashton strode forward. "Please follow me, Your Highness."

With some contempt, the prince moved down the steps of the patio to the side lawn where the helicopter waited. His close security stayed tight by his side.

Ashton's helicopter, an Airbus H155 Dauphin, brought a slight exclamation of delight from the prince. It was his favorite way to travel short distances. As he settled into the cream leather seats, with his closest guards ensconced behind him, he wondered how a British prime minister had the financial means to afford such opulence. The prince saw the smirk on Ashton's face, and he sat with a fixed look of disparagement.

Ashton sat beside him and patted his arm, the gentle tap a further sign of his unabashed attitude to mock certain protocols.

"Time to make you into a believer, Your Highness."

Chapter 38

Prince Khalifa was a man who could not be terrified. The very notion of the emotion was anathema to him. He'd never had a need to acknowledge the reaction, although his regime had instilled terror into the hearts of the populace. His world had been cushioned by blatantly immoral levels of wealth created by the continual flow of black gold that ran in the seams of his beloved land.

He observed the experiment, supplemented by further commentary from Ashton's Chief Scientific Advisor. That quickening of the heart, that perspiration on the ridge of his forehead, that clammy palm, all registered his terror. It was a terror that, until then, he'd never known.

The lights on the control board lit up, and with those LEDs illuminating, the future of his great country started to darken. Assured, was his position. A place of supremacy. Perched high on a hill stacked in billions, with never-ending global investments. He had the type of wealth only the mega-rich can even visualize. Beyond the realm of the everyday man was Khalifa, and his type were encased safely in their financial citadel. Above the law. Magnificent and mighty.

A deeper look would pronounce a slightly skewed perspective. The billions that rested heavily within those global tax havens were subject to fluctuations. The profits born of the petrol and natural gas supplied to an ever greedy and wanton world could wax and wane. Entrants to the energy market, renewables and nuclear, presented threats. They could impinge upon the kingdom's profitability and damage its future economic standing.

When wind and solar had burst onto the energy market, Prince Khalifa showed little concern. High operating costs, variability in securing reasonable kilowattage, and negative reports on the effects on wildlife created protest votes against large-scale wind farms. It all but killed the renewables market. Big 'green deals' from governments started fizzling out, companies in supply chains went bankrupt and suddenly, renewables were not the panacea of new energy.

Khalifa's intelligence sources validated what he already knew: renewables had no real legs. Shale gas was different; it had potential. It could harm the kingdom. But judicious veiled investments ensured that profits were maintained.

These new energy sources, however dramatic, had not attacked the mainstay of the kingdom's economic control, the automobile market. With just over a billion cars worldwide and rising, the demand for gasoline was strong. The hybrid and electric substitutes took the headlines and served for great publicity to bolster the climate change debate, and make environmentalists 'feel better'. But figures couldn't lie. Only two point five percent of cars didn't use gasoline.

Car manufacturers had invested billions in their oil powered engines. None were about to sit back and let that investment dwindle. His kingdom and the car industry had mutual vested interests. None wanted the demise of a technology that had served them and lined their pockets for over a century. Or so it was understood.

The words on the commentary flipped his comprehension. Retrofit a car in a day with the new engine. Car manufacturers supported in redesigning to incorporate the energy capsule engine. Filling stations changed to photon light source providers. A car would apparently run on light.

Prince Khalifa had a glimpse of what could be. He saw a twisted reality where this new energy source undermined his country's leadership. His family's power would falter, giving opportunity to hostile factions, coup d'état possibilities. The rise of the suppressed. They would bay for blood. His blood. Peasants taking over. A revolution. Changing his life. Taking his life. That thought delivered to him this unkown state; he now felt terrified.

"So, Your Highness, what do you think? Pretty amazing, eh?"

Ashton, his stance firm and pointed, observed the prince. They both held their cards tight, and like a poker game, no one was showing their hand. Ashton waited. Khalifa, measured in his response, smiled, a gracious slow expression with a touch of insouciance.

"As I said before, Prime Minister, it is an impressive display. But can this source be readily found? How sustainable is it?"

A nod fell from Ashton in recognition. It was what he expected. The words confirmed it. Khalifa was concerned. Ashton turned toward the prince with a smirk of arrogance. The expression infuriated Khalifa, but he maintained his cold diffidence.

"One could ask the question, how sustainable is air?"

Bemusement fixed upon the prince's face. Science was never of interest to him, except, of course, practical biology.

Ashton absorbed the prince's inadequacy. "Allow me to explain, Your Highness. The world around us is defined in atomic terms, electrons, neutrons, and protons. Beyond the atomic world is the quantum one, made up of quarks. They come in different types or flavors: up, down, strange, charm, top, and bottom. They have different properties including spin. The angle of spin can make them a wave or a particle."

Science talk. Ashton could see the prince's eyes glazing over. He obviously wanted the abbreviated, executive summary. Not like he'd ever gain enrolment into the Institute of Physics. Ashton watched him fidget, uncomfortable and desperate to understand how all this quantum stuff created the energy he'd just seen. Ashton enjoyed the prince's discomfort. Reaching your knowledge ceiling, old chap!

"I don't want to bore you, Your Highness, so I'll get to the point. We've found a way to harness the energy of quantum spin through the use of specially crafted crystals and complex metallurgic processes."

The prince listened with intent, but Ashton noticed the signs of stress on his face as Khalifa's brain tried and failed to grasp what had just been said. Discomfort mounted, and he ventured forth. The placement of his words were artificially authoritative.

"This spin, from the quark, well, is it really that vigorous enough to produce the energy I have seen?"

"Your Highness, this is not just one quark, but a chain reaction bringing in the energy from trillions upon trillions of quark spin everywhere. The source of the energy is virtually limitless."

Their eyes locked. Ashton's were calm and cool. He was in a position reassured by incredible science. The prince's were pained and ponderous. Khalifa squirmed a little as he spoke.

"Limitless supply?"

Stalbridge listened and smirked. He observed the gravity of the words on the prince. Khalifa brought his hand up to his mouth and smoothed the ends of his mustache in contemplation. But he couldn't hide his anxiety. Black gold and natural gas had strengthened the prince's country's influence in geopolitics. The West had turned a blind eye to their flagrant abuses of human rights, their dubious political and religious affiliations and their continual pomposity and vanity on the world stage.

That would change. Eyes would see again.

Stalbridge witnessed revelation taking over the prince. Oil supply equaled global power. Without the need to keep the kingdom sweet, their misdemeanors would reveal themselves, and they'd have to answer for their crimes. The political dynamic was a fragile one, as fragile as a rose in the garden of the safe house so admired by the prince. Shake it with vigor and petals fall. The PM was agitating the branch, and soon the petals would descend.

Khalifa wriggled again in his seat. It was apparent to Stalbridge that Khalifa wasn't used to squirming or feeling uncomfortable, but that seemed to be the only movement he could muster. A dangerous game now stood before Khalifa. And the players weren't all known.

"Your Highness, you look weary. Perhaps I have bored you. For that, I apologize. Come let us eat and talk about the future of our great lands together." Ashton placed his hand out in front of him, allowing Prince Khalifa to join him. A magnanimous gesture, it was the inference of equality. But reading Khalifa, Stalbridge knew the prince had interpreted it otherwise.

"Prime Minister, what are you going to do with this new source of energy?"

The two leaders walked toward the exit from the laboratory. Scientists stood on command. Ashton barely cast them a glance. Stalbridge behind thanked them in his usual, flippant way, and continued a few steps back, but close enough to hear Ashton's response. He sneered as he listened; a checkmate if ever played.

"The question really is, Your Highness, what are *you* going to do?"

Chapter 39

Evolutionary leaps in any planet's development are seen with a mix of joy and caution. Hearing about Ashton's new energy source fills me with both.

"What do you think about this energy stuff?" I ask Sam. He just shrugs in his typically non-committal way.

We're in the Knowledge Suite, and I've just pulled up the background on Quantum Force. Complex calculations bounce up in 3D in the middle of the room.

"Ashton's turned his research papers over to us for verification. He did so in good faith. But he didn't have to do so."

Sam's words niggle me. Once again, I'm seen as the one distrusting of Ashton, a great man doing a difficult job, or so Aby-od and Sam say.

"He's only sharing everything because he wants our help and support. You know Ashton. He's not really a sharing kind of guy."

Sam smiles and shakes his head, finally agreeing with me.

"No, I guess not."

"Where do you think he got this energy knowledge from?"

I stare hard at Sam and motion to all the papers we can see floating in front of us.

"It's all here. Ashton says it's from decades of research. There's a whole stack of papers referenced as Oxford, but they link back to research done in Fermilab and CERN. They detail work in low resonance energy projections, quantum mechanics, photonics, quantum spin and harmonic energies.

I nod hurriedly. I know I'm not making my concerns clear to Sam.

"Yes, I know he has a bona fide backstory. But is there one definitive research paper that details exactly how this quantum energy was discovered?"

Sam looks at me, bemused. "Why do you distrust Ashton so much? You've got the Observation Screen to look at if you don't believe his story. Watch it, see the path of discovery for this new energy. Check up on Ashton. Validate for yourself what he says to be true."

I screw my face up, twitch my nose, and rub my eyes absently. They're all idiosyncrasies I had when I was human, and they have remained embedded within me. I just can't shake them, despite knowing that hard-coded behaviors shouldn't still exist within my Kudamaz framework.

"Observation Room. Yeah, you know, I think I will."

Without warning, I shimmer into the Observation Room.

"Oh, that's just great," I hear Sam announce, annoyed, as my shimmer pulls me into the Observation Room.

I stare at the screen. The sentient crystals around it detect my presence, and the screen blinks into life.

"Run Quantum Force energy development trail from the beginning until now."

On screen, I watch scientists in mid-1950s garb investigate the quantum world. Through experimentation, they seek to understand more about the energy that exists in the sub-atomic domain. Knowledge streams directly via the sentient crystals to my knowledge banks, giving me an immediate understanding of the different paths scientists were taking at the time. The knowledge link identifies the small number of routes that would eventually lead to the Fonda/Dearing/Ashton seminal paper, 'The Pathway to Low Energy Nuclear Reactions'. The nuclear in question is rephrased as spin energy from quantum elements known as quarks.

I watch the Observation Screen and see an image for a few seconds that concerns me. For a mere couple of Earth seconds, I think I see President Hutchinson sitting with Ashton, and then the picture disintegrates. The date is March 30.

The image quickly turns to static and then I see a stream of experiments. A press conference after one of the later experiments goes successfully and quantum spin energy is harnessed for the first time. Then there are images of Ashton talking to scientists, laughing with them, signing personal checks to support the research, and watching demonstrations in laboratories.

I see all three leaders of quantum energy: PM Ashton and Oxford Professors, Fonda and Dearing. I note that they all keep tight-lipped about the actual science being employed. However, they do big up the fact that the UK is facing an energy renaissance, not seen since the days of North Sea oil.

I look at the papers and actual timelined events. It all should feel right. So why doesn't it?

And why was Ashton with Hutchinson?

I call out, pushing the Observation Screen to show me the feed again,

"Revert back to March 30 this earth year, and query on President Hutchinson, PM Ashton, and new quantum energy source."

My query is targeted and precise. That couple of seconds of feed unnerve me.

Maybe it is a glitch in the query process, although that has never happened before. Or maybe Hutchinson has some involvement in this new energy.

Either way, my exact search term should reveal the truth.

The Observation Screen jolts like it's caught between reveal and hide, and this indecision causes mega-interference across the systems.

Static eventually dissipates, showing a view of Hutchinson welcoming Ashton to Camp David. I watch them as they talk about Al Nadir. Ashton opens up the discussion with, "I know you still have Al Nadir on your mind…" Both leaders become emotional, hugging each other.

Suddenly, I feel I'm being watched. I spin around quickly, but no one is there. And then I see the air sparkle. The hackles rise at the back of my neck, and I hold myself ready to strike the incoming Kudamaz.

But it's Sam. He notices my tense posture and warring stance.

"Everything okay?"

He puts his arms out to embrace me.

"Yes. No. I don't know. I felt a presence here seconds before you arrived."

"You must have caught my resonance. It does happen, Ellie. It's not a problem and nothing you should be concerned about."

Sam's arms enfold around me and I try to believe in his logic.

"But there's something up with the Observation Screen. Look."

I reset and query on Ashton, Hutchinson, quantum energy and March 30, and the screen brings up a smooth picture of Hutchinson greeting Ashton, walking with him to his private office in Camp David, pouring a drink and talking about ridding Al Nadir implants from their ranks.

No interference or static flickers at all.

"I can't see anything wrong, Ellie," says Sam, watching the prime minister and president's meeting.

"No, I know you can't. And you know what else you can't see?"

"What?" snaps Sam, clearly a bit fed up with my constant examination of everything Ashton.

"Any reason why the Observation Screen would bring up that sequence of events under a query about quantum energy. Neither Ashton nor Hutchinson mention it once."

Sam's face stiffens and his eyes darken. Although his thoughts remain closed to me, I know he wants to seek the truth as much as I do.

Chapter 40

Often is the way of the weather to reflect the mood of the moment. Had the weather portrayed the mood of Prince Khalifa, a rush of storm clouds would have gathered and rain in torrents would have descended.

As it was, the weather did not home in on the troubled mind of the Saudi Prince. The sun beat its powerful rays upon the heads of the prince, PM and their entourages, as they vacated the laboratory.

Ashton was aware, following his loaded question, that the prince's pause of consideration had plunged into an obstinate silence. He strode forth, just edging a little ahead of Ashton. The PM smirked with amusement. He adored gameplay and could hold his position all day. He doubted, however, that Prince Khalifa could remain silent for much longer, given his natural obsession to command and control. Ashton was a master of the tactical move; all he needed to do was wait.

Jensen gave Ashton a sideways glance. Ashton nodded with virtually imperceptible swiftness. The slightly raised eyebrow denoted his derision of the prince. Jensen had seen the maneuver before and he had no hesitation in knowing his friend would win.

Ashton heard the small intake of breath from Khalifa, the prelude before the spoken word.

"Prime Minister, is there something you want?" Khalifa stopped, turned and stared with anger at the PM.

Ashton's trademark smirk grew wider. "World peace would be nice."

Jensen had to bite his lip from laughing. Ashton was playing the crown prince like a two-bit gambler. His obvious mockery was out to rile the prince, forcing him to become more furious, lose his concentration and make rash decisions without being fully aware of the facts. Ashton was an expert in such techniques.

"Prime Minister, I think we both know what I mean."

Khalifa's eyes had narrowed, and his intent stare struck Ashton as desperate.

Ashton led the prince away to the side out of earshot of his people and the prince's.

"Your Highness, it would be unfortunate if matters forced us to reassess the viability of some external energy sources. It is in my purview to divert such reassessment and continue on well-established paths of engagement. There would, of course, have to be a consideration apportioned to reflect such a decision, and commensurate to the concomitant degree of risk for the other party, if such a reassessment, and the actions thereof, were to take place."

Khalifa, schooled in Eton and Cambridge, was well versed with the labyrinthine construct of sentences delivered by legal scholars. He also knew when one of those scholars was delivering to him a shafting.

He smiled but no joy could be found in his eyes.

"How much?" The prince's voice was deep and dead of emotion. His two words were said almost in a whisper for fear his entourage would hear.

Ashton took out his phone, punched in a set of numbers on his calculator and showed them to the prince. Five billion pounds sterling.

Khalifa had to steady himself not to collapse.

"And if I agree to these t-t-terms?" the prince quavered.

"Our well-established paths of engagement will remain, well…established." Ashton made the pun of the words and smiled with complete satisfaction.

"I will have to reflect on this. Not a decision to be made quickly. I'm sure you would agree."

"Oh, quite, Your Highness. I do understand. In the meantime, we will continue our roll-out plan." Ashton spoke with brisk assurance.

Khalifa broke protocol and held onto Ashton's elbow. "Roll out plan?" The prince's voice carried forth his confusion.

"Yes, Your Highness. Didn't I say? We will roll out to car manufacturers and power plants. We're intending to start immediately with the conversion process."

"I didn't realize…I thought…What about the legislation? Regulations? I don't understand. How can this be done so quickly?"

"It's hardly quick, Your Highness. We have been working on this for many decades. Only now has that solid research paid dividends. And as for the legislation, an inconspicuous little Bill went through Parliament last week. Actually, it swept through. Didn't it, Jensen?"

Ashton looked at his confidante. Jensen nodded, the smugness showing with clarity on this face.

Khalifa swallowed and appeared to wince before speaking. "What Bill?"

"The '*Transmission, Distribution and Resource Supply through Advanced Technology Bill*'. Haven't you heard of it? Can't say I really liked the title. A bit wordy. Of course, who reads Bills these days? Yes, it went through without a glance. House of Lords just rubber stamped it as usual. You see, very few people these days want to rock my boat. They're all after keeping safe their comfortable, easy, but infinitely unimportant little lives. Once one looks above the parapet, well, it's no longer peace in the mind's eye. Reality has displayed herself…" Ashton glanced at a young political aide with a shapely ass standing by the lab's entrance. He licked his lips, considering she'd be his next conquest. "Exposed herself, if you will. No going back. But all the time you keep your head down, well, it could be wine and roses outside. Nothing's there to dissuade you from this thought. Do you see what I mean?" Ashton swung a look back at the prince, who, despite his darker pigment, had paled in the last few minutes.

"Yes," mumbled the prince. Ashton's words and blasé manner had left him bewildered, and he couldn't return back a level of coherent engagement.

"Everyone wants to keep the status quo, don't they? The last thing we need is for that tree to be shaken. Goodness knows what might fall out. And where those leaves might end up. Incarcerated. In someone's natural history collection."

Ashton fixed the prince with a dark, deep stare.

Khalifa's neck hairs bristled, and he shivered. The PM was unlike any other head of state. His maneuvers were comparable to a Mafia boss or a Russian crime lord. At that moment, the prince considered that leaving with his life would be a gift.

"Your Highness, I would advise that it would be most favorable if you could find a way to accelerate your reflections. After all, one does look to maintain the level of comfort so afforded by our current engagements. Doesn't one?"

The prince remained silent. He stared at the ground. A Saudi royal being hustled by the British prime minister, it was unthinkable. He could never let this be known. His family would tear him to shreds. Khalifa raised his head and glared with fury at Ashton.

"Yes, Prime Minister, one does. I have reflected, and your terms are…agreeable."

"Excellent, Your Highness. Here are the details already set up." Ashton flicked his fingers and Jensen supplied to his waiting hand, a tablet.

Khalifa gasped. Somehow the tablet already had his private and usually hidden Swiss bank account details pre-loaded with the PM's personal account details. The sum of five billion pounds was also already inputted in the amount field.

Ashton smiled. Arrogance exuded from him as he watched the prince almost drop the tablet with shock.

"Arranged thus so your transaction would be as painless as possible."

The prince typed in his code, overcame the biometrics with a swift retinal and thumb scan, and handed the tablet back to Ashton, who was still smiling with superior hubris.

As painless as possible, thought the prince, as he watched the PM. When my GID catch up with you, they will redefine for you the meaning of pain.

Chapter 41

Inside the luxurious surrounds of the Dauphin, a place where even the rotor wash held a cadence suggesting opulence and aloofness, Prime Minister Ashton nestled his taut backside into the ecru soft leather armchair. Only Stalbridge traveled with him. The prince declined his offer of a jaunt back to London, stating that 'he'd had his fill of British hospitality and had to return to his homeland'. Following that statement, Ashton watched him duck his head and disappear into the bowels of his custom-made Brabus Maybach, a car kept in London for his visits, and head off in the direction of White Waltham airstrip, where his private jet waited on standby.

"He's going to be gunning for your blood, Rich. You know that?" Stalbridge poured a Jack Daniels and knocked it back, neat. His brow furrowed with concern when Ashton didn't respond. "Rich, did you hear me?"

Ashton swung his head around from the large portrait windows of the Dauphin and sneered, waving a hand away, nonchalant to his fingertips. Absolute confidence radiated from his being. Stalbridge stared at his friend, amazed by his casual dismissiveness of the obviously dangerous situation he had placed himself in.

"Of course I did. No doubt his GID boys will be spinning into overdrive, searching every part of my life, reviewing the best time to take me, dump me in one of their godforsaken holes somewhere, and torture the fuck out of me. Or they may choose to tap two in here." He knocked the side of his head with his forefinger. "Either way, as you say, old chap, they're certainly gunning for me!"

"Doesn't that worry you, Rich?" asked Stalbridge. His expression was a display of genuine alarm.

Ashton shrugged and shook his head. "No. Why should I be worried?"

The PM looked sideways at his friend, his eyes laughing, his mouth relishing the taste of the whiskey. He really was a man without fear.

"Rich, you must be joking? You've just hustled a Saudi prince out of five billion sterling."

"Not hustled, Jen, old man, just put forward an insurance proposition with a large upfront premium."

Stalbridge howled, and hit the JD bottle again, pouring two fingers. "God, you take the biscuit, Rich. Next you'll be saying it's a donation to Freedom bloody Earth."

"Now, I hadn't thought of that one." The PM laughed hard.

"But, however you dress it up, it doesn't mean they're not gonna get you." Stalbridge maneuvered the conversation back to highlight the apparent risk.

"They can try," said Ashton. "But I doubt they'll get very far." The PM eyed Stalbridge with a knowing, mischievous look that his confidante recognized.

"What did you do?"

"Got to have insurance, you know. They've got theirs in place, and I've got mine."

Ashton took out his phone, opened an app Stalbridge had never seen, and touched a button. The nanodot RF antennae that he'd placed with surreptitious adroitness on Khalifa's jacket started transmitting. Instantly, the gravelly Arabic tones of Prince Khalifa burst from the small device.

"He doesn't sound very happy, does he?" Ashton smirked as he sipped his drink and listened to the diatribe streaming from his phone.

"Would you after losing five billion? How did you do this?"

"Hold on," Ashton interrupted Stalbridge, waving a finger in the air. "I need to hear this. He's talking directly to Mustafa Al Khamazi, director general of the GID."

"You understand this?"

Stalbridge was becoming more astounded at his friend's abilities by the second. He didn't know about Ashton's MI6 background and his learning of many languages, including Arabic, as part of his job. They'd been friends since Eton but Stalbridge remembered they were so much more. Thinking back, he blushed. Rich had protected him, cossetted him, and when he needed him the most, loved him. He wasn't ashamed. It was a rite of passage thing. A friendly shoulder to cry on, a warm body to nestle into, made those early years bearable. As a grown man, women were now his game. But Rich would always give him that slight tingle of anticipation. He couldn't help himself around him. He knew if the invitation was made, he'd jump. But it never was.

He'd left the UK and worked in New York in banking. Communication dwindled, and new lives and loves took over. And then he heard Rich was in politics. A gentle leap from lawyer to politician. All were actors, playing out their scenes; only the audience changed. Then he was PM, and suddenly Rich reached out to him to be his political advisor. It was a great offer that he felt he couldn't refuse. He couldn't even if he wanted, such was the tremendous pull of his charismatic friend.

So began the architecting in secret of a concept to unify people across the world, a concept Ashton eventually penned as Freedom Earth, at the end of March.

"Yes, I do," Ashton muttered harshly, still listening and nodding quickly. "The little shit! So that's his plan."

"What plan? What's happening, Rich? Can you tell me?"

Annoyed that Ashton ignored him, Stalbridge remembered there is nothing worse than sitting in a crowded room where everyone is talking in a language you can't understand or speak. Isolating but at the same time awkward, the inadequacy foisted by the situation is demeaning. Constantly, your eyes watch to see if a coherent word will fall from lips of twisted confusion. Could they be laughing at you? Talking about you? Your clothes? Hair? Humiliation soaks in, but moving is not an option. Trapped, you're left to endure a garbling ridicule until a sign is made to leave and the ordeal is over.

"Jen, shut up a second. Let me listen. You're always yapping, noisy bugger!"

Stalbridge's face deepened with a smattering of rose, and he remained in silence.

Ashton placed the phone on the rosewood side table and brought out a notepad from his inside pocket. He scribbled words, partly in English, partly in Arabic, as he paid attention to the voice now shouting from the phone.

"Are you going to tell me what on Earth they're saying?"

Stalbridge couldn't hide his testiness with Ashton. He wanted to, as he wasn't that upset, but he couldn't help acknowledging the hurt that Ashton caused him. He wanted to be part of it all. But his friend didn't recognize his need.

The PM peered up from his note-taking. "Everything alright, Jen? You look a bit peaky."

"I'm okay. Just feeling left out, that's all."

"Left out? Oh, I see. Sorry, seconds count, Jen, old thing. Had to hear what that shit was going to do. I knew he'd act when he was in the car. His anger was boiling over. He had to take back control otherwise he'd burst. GID were his first port. I knew that absolutely. And it would be him, not one his lackeys, to set things up. He had to be back in control, back in the driving seat, taking his own steps to ruin my life."

"And now what happens?" asked Stalbridge. Perturbation rose within him as he considered what he was to be party to, and where 'ears on a Saudi prince' would lead to.

"Now we wait, Jen, my old man."

"Wait for what?"

Stalbridge bewildered, Ashton lucid, the two men were worlds apart, but with memories of a night time shared to bind them.

"A peacock, Jen, caught in a trap of its own reflective glory."

Chapter 42

Temenos watched Ellie run the queries. Her investigations were too close to the truth. His predecessor Lord Aswa-da had schooled him on the unthinkable for a Kudamaz, shielding views from the Observation Screen.

For the Observation Screen to work, the resonance of the time stream of the targeted planet had to align with the resonance wave of the Observation Screen. Without this symbiotic resonance linkage, errors would be broadcast in live view and playback. If the Observation Screen detected a difference in the resonance frequency, it would deliver the broadcast with interference. If that same observed moment was watched in playback mode, the difference in resonance frequency would render the observed moment as void. This void status would signal to the Universe that the event never happened, and thus the Universe would delete the event from the Observation Screen databanks to avoid a time-space anomaly.

Temenos knew all he had to do was use the device Lord Aswa-da had built before he disappeared just over six Earth weeks before.

Temenos looked down at the device in his hand. It was a small, tear-shaped, pale blue crystal with a raised, small ruby at its base. Its function was similar to a Harmon gun in that it sent out a specific harmonic frequency, but this was to disrupt, not destroy. The resonance that was sent out differed from the one linked to Earth on the Observation Screen by a few points in frequency. More specifically, it targeted the observed feed from Earth on the mention of any query relating to Prime Minister Richard Ashton, US President Al Hutchinson and quantum energy prior to April 1 of that Earth year.

He'd been about to install the disrupter device within the light energy network of the Observation Screen, but Ellie had shimmered in and suddenly started to piece together a jigsaw he never believed she could put together.

Her appearance had required him to work fast. He'd slipped into sub-shimmer, which enabled him to vanish from the Observation Room but stay within the connection range. He'd headed to the very back of the large Observation Room, slipped into the dark shadows between the crystal columns, and waited.

Watching as Ellie came out of shimmer, Temenos noticed that she'd been so single-mindedly focused on querying the relationship Ashton had with quantum energy, she hadn't detected Temenos' sub-shimmer in the shadows. Her failure to detect him had given Temenos the immediate opportunity to trigger the disrupter device and send a different frequency resonance at the observed feed.

His timing, however, in synchronizing the trigger had been a tad too late. Ellie had, unfortunately, grabbed a glimpse of something she never should have seen.

He stayed in sub-shimmer long enough to watch Sam and Ellie shimmer out of the Observation Room. He didn't like the stern look on Sam's face, but there wasn't anything he could do.

Coming out of sub-shimmer, he felt a deep reverberation just outside Kudamun's plane, and he recognized the return of the Revered One.

"My Lord, I have done your bidding. All is as it should be."

Temenos' voice shook a little as he stared into the air that had started to mutate. It looked like something had gored out the atmosphere in the Observation Room. Gradually, a dark void emerged, floating.

Temenos peered in and gasped as two eyes rimmed in red glared back at him.

"All is not as it should be. The Protector is a persistent investigator. She is a risk to everything."

"But, my Lord, there is no risk. Humans are welcoming all the changes. The Chosen One is now in their hearts. We cannot fail."

Temenos waited for a response. It boomed within his mind.

"For your sake, I hope you are right!"

Chapter 43

Khalifa's hand throbbed. Where his fingertips had touched Ashton's tablet, the heat of fury seared him. Blood pumped from his furious heart and surged into his arteries. He wished his hand was devoid of all its internal makeup. With no blood, bone or muscle, it wouldn't have moved to authorize the transaction. It wouldn't have been used to abuse, and to take from him that which was his by a sideshow swindler with power, a combination afforded by position and circumstance.

Claims made by the PM had been verified by the GID. The new energy company 'Quantum Force' was legitimate. The new Bill the PM referenced had swept through Parliament. Jaguar Land Rover in Coventry and Nissan in Gateshead were about to start a pilot run on the new capsule energy fueled by the quantum energy. Brown sites bought up by Quantum Force were in stages of redevelopment to be made into quantum-energy-driven power stations. Even existing power generation sites were in discussion to bring the quantum energy online as a backup power source to renewable technologies.

All of Ashton's claims checked out. Khalifa wished they hadn't. He wished they'd been a veil of lies and deceit. But Khalifa heard his GID confirm all he'd seen and heard, and he hated to hear the truth. It was so much better to take down an enemy if he's a lying cheat. Better on the conscience.

Ashton held the power, literally and metaphorically. In fact, considered Khalifa, the two delivered the same objective.

Ashton could destroy his world.

The prince had never had to fight for anything in his life, but he knew that was changing. His place of persistent calm and serenity would soon be splintered into pieces. Ashton was an enemy like none encountered before. In the past, there had been political maneuverers and bad judgment calls. Friends had tried to take too much or stepped over a line one too many times.

That line had invariably widened as his habits of drugs, drink or women took greater hold of him. He'd needed support and a backstory. Often just a plain cover-up. Excuses for his excesses. The auto-erotic asphyxiation going a little too far. The drug-fueled orgies with those freshly flown in underage virgins. And, dare he forget, the game of Russian roulette that took out a diplomat's son.

His confidantes and associates had cleaned his shit until he shined radiant again. And then hands would flop out, waiting, expecting, and they'd come back again and again, caught like a planet orbiting a sun, their greed insatiable. But still, they were all containable within his enormous mountain of wealth.

More importantly, they had never threatened to fracture the mountain by disturbing its foundation. World dependency on his oil and natural gas was the bedrock of his fortune. If a cost-efficient, viable alternative was launched on the automobile and energy markets, sales of his country's commodities would shrink. It may not be by a great amount at first. But over time, power and control and ultimately wealth would begin to erode.

Ashton's new quantum power signaled the death strike for his country, one that he knew mustn't happen. If he could be sure that the five billion would stop the development of this power from becoming commercialized, then he could rest easy with such an investment. The problem was he couldn't be sure. He'd been coerced into parting with that money. He'd looked into Ashton's condescending, smarmy face and saw the eyes of a traitor.

His lips said one action, but his eyes took a different course.

The money paid was just for Ashton's amusement. That was why, British PM or not, he had to be taken down.

Khalifa spoke with hurried brusque words to Mustafa Al Khamazi, director general of the GID and his friend. He confided in what had happened but took a more patriotic stance.

"My friend, I have sacrificed that which is mine to preserve the future of our great kingdom. But the money is of no importance. What concerns me is that the claims this man made are true. His new source threatens to destabilize markets that have been relatively stable and flowed profits with unerring regularity. We cannot wait for what may happen. We must take action now. Have you gained access to his diary?"

A strong, gruff tone drilled into Khalifa's earpiece. "Everything has now been accessed. We know his every movement. We will engage at an opportune moment." Mustafa did not deliver any prefix of 'Your Highness'. This was a black call with no adherence to royal protocol.

"In the city?" suggested Khalifa.

"I would prefer not to say. But the city may not be the best place of engagement. We will review options accordingly."

"You will keep me informed when it is done."

"Of course."

Mustafa rang off and Khalifa stared out from his Maybach. He remembered Ashton's insolence and solid self-assurance. His smug, mocking mouth. His devious, twinkling eyes. Ashton fancied himself as a playboy on the side.

Khalifa wondered how much of a playboy he'd be without a head.

Chapter 44

The private chambers of the Leader of Kudamun and Head of the House of Giznu are much different to our humble quarters. Our living area, although massive by Earthly proportions, is small compared to Aby-od's place of residence.

As I step over the threshold, the first thing that strikes me is the enormous stretch of ice-blue crystal that indicates no natural end to the room. The expanse of glistening ice blue is broken up intermittently by beautiful columns of crystal with intricately carved creatures from across the Universe. Staircases leading upward to higher rooms are made of the same crystal, and archways fronting other rooms branch off from the cavernous hallway. Peering through, I can make out all manner of Kudamaz technologies in the rooms beyond.

Light radiates from the Reality Gap above and catches the sides of the crystals. The light refracts, and rainbows bounce across the walls and floor. The rooms are sparse of furniture, except for the soft, blue, fluffy sofas I personally love. I know that Aby-od configures his internal décor as he needs it through the Manufacture Pod, as all the Kudamaz do.

In one of the rooms, I see row after row of crystals from golf ball to tennis ball sizes in an array of colors. I scan my databanks, but no intelligence exists on their application, only the inferring statement of 'Overseer of the Universe'.

I'm puzzled.

"Aby-od, what are they for?"

Aby-od turns around and sees me pointing to the crystals. Sam goes to pick up one.

"Leave them, Sam."

I notice Aby-od's tone is uncharacteristically hard and authoritative. Sam pulls his hand away quickly.

"What are they?" asks Sam, as intrigued as I am.

"They represent my responsibility as Leader of Kudamun to keep the Balance throughout the Universe. Each one of these crystals denotes a galaxy. The color of the crystal signifies the level of development of the galaxy, and the size of the crystal symbolizes the scale of star systems within that galaxy."

Aby-od picks up a viridian crystal, and instantly in front of us, a strange elongated galaxy pops into existence in the center of his quarters.

I recognize the galaxy immediately as Mas-Ki-Ya, one of the furthest galaxies in the Universe, and a big one with one point two billion stars. Just over half of those stars have planets that have generated life of some kind.

I watch as Aby-od draws his hand through the revolving galaxy and touches one of the areas of shining dots inside it. The shining dots come forward as if enlarged by an invisible zoom. The configuration in front of me changes, showing planets in orbit around a mighty star. Aby-od touches one of the planets then brings his fingers together so their tips are touching, and pulls back. This action zooms in and gives the planet a clear definition. I observe a mass of green and purple clouds and flashes of brilliant gold lightning.

Sam nods and his eyes grow large with amazement at what he's being shown.

We both recognize that this scene we're seeing isn't a visual representation or model of the planet; this is a real-time view of the planet right now.

"Can you zoom in deeper? See what's happening on the planet?"

"No, Sam. This is as far as I can go without using the Observation Room. But I can still see a planet's Balance Shift through this process."

Aby-od circles his hand in the air, and the Balance Shift indicator that I've come to know bursts into being, then flickers and moves its counter gauge toward the light side.

"So you can see any planet from afar and read their Balance Shifts? Wow! I knew you had a heavy responsibility, but I didn't realize your remit covered so much."

Aby-od smiles serenely. It's obvious he wants to avoid unnecessary adoration from me.

"Aby od, this is absolutely incredible. I can't believe you do all this, that you manage all of these galaxies." I indicate to the rows of crystals stacked high.

Aby-od laughs. "If it were only these, I'd be a happy Kudamaz. Try this lot."

Aby-od slams at a seven-pointed star embedded into the crystal, and the wall behind the shelves starts to disintegrate. I step back in awe and watch the sudden appearance of a staggering number of crystals perched on shelves. The shelves, like Aby-od's quarters, seem to run deep into the wall recess, travelling to a vanishing point far into the distance.

Sam whistles. I turn back to stare at Aby-od. I have mind-blowing powers, but this is at a different level.

"How do you know if their Balances have shifted? Isn't that something that needs to be addressed?"

Aby-od smiles and looks slightly smug as he answers my question.

"The crystals are all sentient and always monitoring their respective galaxies. The intelligence from the monitoring connects directly into my databanks. They can alert me if something needs High Council engagement or intervention."

"So the Universe is on cruise control," mutters Sam.

I shoot him a disparaging look.

"Sam has actually got a good take on how the Universe is managed and overseen," replies Aby-od. "But think of it more as the auto pilot on your Earthly aeroplanes. The crystals make little adjustments and alert me when an issue needs my involvement."

"You can make it sound as normal as you like but, Aby-od, you are overseeing the whole *fucking* Universe. It's absolutely amazing. You're awesome!"

I realize I'm falling fast into idol-worship territory, but I can't help myself. My role as Protector of Earth is confined to Earth only, and that's hard enough. Aby-od's workload is the entire Universe.

Aby-od looks at me with a twinkle in his eye. I know he's pleased to have demonstrated his role in Kudamun. Ever the modest one, Aby-od would never have proffered such a demo of his own volition.

I should have known. But although my databanks are well-stocked with universal knowledge, context is sometimes missing. Being told he's the Overseer of the Universe and actually seeing it for myself are two very different things.

"Ellie, Sam, did you want to have a chat about something?"

After witnessing Aby-od's universal overseeing, I have virtually forgotten about the reason behind our visit.

I pull myself together and concentrate.

"Could the Observation Screen hide an event that happened on Earth?"

The smile vanishes from Aby-od's face. "What do you mean, Ellie?"

"Is it possible for something to happen on Earth but for the Observation Screen not to show it? Or show something different?"

Aby-od shakes his head, but I can see he's pondering my words.

"What you claim is impossible. Have you experienced this?"

"Yes, I think I have."

"You think you have? Explain." Aby-od's tone is clipped and cold. This is a very different Aby-od to the fatherly guy I thought I knew. He is clearly worried about what this glitch infers for Kudamun.

"I queried on Ashton's involvement with quantum energy. I wanted to check all he was doing was legit and wasn't going to bite us on the proverbial ass."

Sam arches an eyebrow.

"And was he?" asks Aby-od.

"The query brought up the feed from March 30 this Earth year showing Ashton in Camp David with President Hutchinson. But it lasted a mere Earth second or two. The feed then went into static interference. I queried again to include quantum energy and it brought up Ashton and the president on the same day. I watched the entire feed. We both did."

I indicate to Sam, who nods his head.

"But never once do they mention anything about quantum energy," I continue. "I've queried many times, always including quantum energy, but it brings up the same feed sequence. Why is this happening, Aby-od? Why is a feed coming up on a query that's irrelevant to the content it contains?"

Aby-od's face is grave as he listens to me. I know he's running through possibilities.

"When did you first see the two Earth seconds of feed that subsequently vanished?"

"It only showed the very first time when I ran a query on the full development of quantum energy on Earth from the beginnings of the research path. The feed showed the late 1950s Earth and steadily broadcast the various progression of the research, arriving at the present day with the emergence of Quantum Force. The clip about Ashton and Hutchinson came up within that initial query. It stayed on screen for two Earth seconds. There was no sound and hardly any time to take in what else was on screen until static interference took over. When I queried again, those two seconds had disappeared."

I look at Sam for back up. I know I sound pretty crazy in making such an allegation against infallible Kudamaz technology.

"I didn't witness Ellie's initial query on the quantum development path, but I certainly saw her query on Ashton, Hutchinson, quantum energy and March 30, and the Observation Screen brought up a feed that did not contain anything about quantum energy at all."

Aby-od fixes me with a cold stare then moves away from us, looking into the distance of his quarters.

I say nothing. I desperately want to connect and speak to Sam in my mind, but Aby-od would hear immediately.

I pull Sam over to me and whisper in his ear. It's illogical; Aby-od can surely hear my vocal conversation as clearly as he can hear one in my mind.

"Do you think he believes us?"

"Of course he does. Why should he think we lie?"

"I don't know. That look he gave me. I've never seen Aby-od look so cold and hard."

"Darling, he's worried."

At that moment, Aby-od turns back to look at us.

"I'm going to check on the Observation Screen light circuitry and internal operations. I need an independent witness. Sam, as you are a senior elder of the High Council, would you mind accompanying me? Ellie, for your own protection, you can't be involved in this investigation. I suggest you go back to your quarters or return back to your home on Earth. The choice is yours."

I stare, dumbfounded at what is happening.

"Are you saying that you think I'm lying?"

Aby-od's eyes flash darkly. "No. But you have made a serious accusation regarding the operational conduct of the Observation Screen. The implications suggest foul play, either by our house or Etima. Under the Order of Kudamun, anyone making such accusations must have real, physical evidence, otherwise, they can be sentenced to death for incitement to mistrust and thus, treason. You know how the Antediluvian laws work, Ellie. I don't need to tell you this."

I stand still, unable to speak. Sam's face is now stricken. I can see he's having trouble comprehending what's just happened. This has to be some kind of misunderstanding on Aby-od's part. I'm just talking about a couple of Earth seconds I may or may not have seen.

"Aby-od, for fuck's sake, what are you saying?" says Sam. "Ellie could be sentenced to death because of some little glitch in the Observation Screen? This is insane!"

He storms over to Aby-od, grasping his arms roughly. Aby-od maintains his stance.

"If Ellie continues to make this serious accusation, I have no choice as Leader of Kudamun but to report this to the High Council and commence a full investigation."

"And if she retracts the accusation?"

I feel as if I'm not in the room. Aby-od and Sam are one on one. Sam is holding back his anger, but I can see it's simmering just beneath the surface. That hatred of Aby-od inside him is in danger of being reignited.

"Then we leave things as they are," answers Aby-od, keeping his watch on Sam. I am completely ignored.

"I didn't see it," I call out. "It was a mistake. I'm sorry."

Sam releases the grip he has on Aby-od and looks around at me.

"Ellie, are you sure you want to say that?" Sam stares at me, questioning my judgement.

"Eyes play tricks. There's too much bloody crystal everywhere here. It makes for optical illusions. I'm sorry, Aby-od. I took up your time unnecessarily. Sam, let's go."

Aby-od nods, and his soft smile returns. "A wise choice."

Sam is still furious, but joins me as I start to invoke shimmer. He picks up my trail to Silent Waters. As our London waterside apartment filters into view, wiping out the icy-blue crystal of Kudamun, I breathe deeply and then explode with seething vitriol.

"Fucking hell! I thought they'd changed. This bloody obsession with those Antediluvian rules."

"I didn't realize you were making a serious accusation. I would never have taken it to Aby-od. Well, now we know what we have to do."

"And what's that?" I reply, unsure of my own mind, and still shaken.

"Confront Ashton. We need to get the truth from the donkey's mouth."

More like the serpent's mouth, I think. But I refrain from any further accusations.

Now I know just how damaging they can be.

Chapter 45

It was such a great feeling knowing he was soon going to be really sticking it to those towel heads and Ruskies simultaneously.

Energy supremacy my ass! The war hadn't even begun, and he was already making plans to finish them both in one swipe. That's what Quantum Force would do.

Kill the competition.

Ashton smirked and sat back at his glass and titanium dining table in his exclusive penthouse apartment on Vauxhall Bridge Road. He savored his fine Bardolino wine and Chateaubriand meal

He leisurely took in the accompaniment he'd acquired as his dessert; she was a lithe, young political researcher who'd caught his eye in one of the dreary meetings. Ashton couldn't quite remember her name. Roberta? Rowena? Robyna? God knows! He wasn't really big on names, and anyway, he didn't intend for her lips to be talking.

After Katzy's death, Ashton had purposely gone into sexual freefall. Every night (and sometimes during the day) he was with someone different. He rationalized away his actions. A coping mechanism. Just a way to handle the bottomless pain of losing the one person he actually loved. He knew he was burying beneath those meaningless shags with handsome guys and gorgeous girls the torment of those minutes. When time had stopped. When realization had hit. And he had known those ripped out eyes had belonged to the woman he'd loved.

Ashton never took his conquests back to Number 10. Instead, they were shielded away within a place very few knew about with the exception of his constant close protection outside the front door. Ashton was free to enjoy himself.

He picked up the glass, took a gulp of wine, and then stared at the researcher as she ate. Ashton looked at her lips smacking down over the fork and pulling back the delicious meat. She liked to eat. Her figure told him she obviously didn't eat that often and this was a bit of a luxury. Her pale blue eyes widened as the meat hit her taste buds and she entered food heaven.

"Mmmm. This food is so good, sir."

"Well, eat up. You need to build your strength, darling," Ashton murmured, bending forth and stabbing at a piece of meat. "You're going to need it."

Listening to the prime minister, the researcher giggled and knocked back a large amount of wine, draining her glass.

Ashton moved forward with the bottle.

"Need to fill you up again, don't we?"

Ashton smirked and licked his lips as his eyes caught sight of her luscious legs through the glass table.

The researcher, no more than twenty-two, thrust forward with her glass to receive her top up. Ashton eyed her ample breasts, which, in her tight-fitting Karen Millen number, were only accentuated further.

"Are you trying to get me tipsy, sir?" the researcher slurred, then she snickered into her glass.

"Call me Rich because I am!"

Ashton laughed at his own lame joke, and the blonde-haired researcher with a stunning heart-shaped face laughed too.

"Okay, Rich."

Ashton's eyebrow leapt up. Takes orders quickly. That's good.

He finished off his steak and slugged back his wine. Ashton was quite eager to plough into his dessert.

"Rich, could you get me reassigned?" The researcher mumbled the words and held down a slight hiccup.

"You don't like working with Prickly Perkins then?"

Ashton knew Janice Perkins, the energy secretary, was a punctilious and difficult individual. She probably worked the poor researcher to the bone. Ashton gazed at her as she sat drinking her wine. Her lips turned a trace of crimson as the wine touched them.

But what lovely bones to be working on.

"Oh my God, Rich. You know she's called that?" The researcher spluttered her wine out of her mouth, laughing hard.

"Of course." Ashton smirked. "I started it!"

Ashton's eyes sparkled with the thought of mischievous playtime. The researcher picked up on the vibe, and suddenly realized she'd stepped way out of her depth.

"Erm…maybe I should…"

Ashton lasered into her eyes with ruthless desire.

"If you say go, I won't be happy," Ashton growled, staring at her with dark intent.

The researcher breathed faster as Ashton stood up, grabbed her in a tight hold, and dropped his lips onto hers. He pressed her body onto his and held her hands behind her back. He lifted her onto the table. Plates, cutlery, and glasses tumbled in a shattering heap on the floor as Ashton pushed her down, his mouth on her lips, her neck, and down to her breasts. He yanked at her dress impatiently and heard a rip.

"I'll buy you a new one," he muttered coldly and snaked his hand up the researcher's thigh.

The researcher panted and breathed heavy. Ashton didn't care whether she wanted sex or not. She was in his apartment at night and that gave him the absolute right to do whatever the hell he liked.

He pushed her legs apart, maneuvered his trousers down and got ready for action.

"Oh fuck! Sorry, Ashton. We'll come, erm, back later."

Ashton heard Ellie's voice, almost laughing behind him, and immediately his ardor was deflated. He pulled his trousers up and helped the researcher put her dress back on. Embarrassed, she looked away from Sam and Ellie, ran into the bedroom, and closed the door.

"Great *fucking* timing!" snarled Ashton, tidying himself around the waist.

Sam and Ellie had impish expressions on their faces. Ashton thought they looked like school kids who'd seen the math teacher making out with the head teacher. Ellie's eyes carried a wicked gleam in them, and Sam enjoyed the moment of his humiliation.

"What do you want?" snapped Ashton.

"The truth," Ellie ventured.

This time, the smiles had dissipated. Her face was determined and indomitable.

"What's the connection between you, Hutchinson, and Quantum Force?"

Chapter 46

As I say the words, I analyze Ashton. I examine every nuance in his face, his posture, his movements. I'm checking for signs of lying. I clock a look at Sam, and I can see he's doing the exact same thing. Rigorously.

Ashton straightens himself and stands tall. His eyes do not waiver, nor change shape or expression.

His glare is unflinching and rock solid.

"As a close friend and ally of the UK, President Hutchinson has a private investment arrangement in Quantum Force. Other than that, he plays no part."

I flick a sideways look at Sam. He nods, indicating that he accepts Ashton's words.

I hate it. I desperately wanted Ashton to have lied, especially after catching him inflagrante delicto, so I could have ripped into him. Not literally, of course. That may be a step too far. But I would have done it verbally.

Now I have nothing on him.

Every indication and nuance I read from Ashton told me he just didn't lie.

"And Hutchinson has really played no other part besides being an investor?" I press, staring deep into Ashton's handsome, smug face.

He holds my stare with a strength I didn't know humans possessed and cuts me down with a scythe-sharp, "No!"

I look at Sam and he circles Ashton, who turns back over his shoulder, peeved by Sam's movements. In parallel, I walk to the other side of the PM. We're like predators circling our prey. At least that's how I want Ashton to feel.

He pushes his height again, throws back his shoulders and strides past us into the lounge, goes to the drinks trolley, grabs a whiskey, pours far too much, and sits down on the sofa.

He gulps most of the drink down before whipping his head up to Sam and me.

"Do you want to tell me what the *hell* this is all about?"

'We can't tell him a thing,' I shout in Sam's mind.

'Yes, I know, but he deserves an explanation.'

'No, he doesn't. The perverted prick, he doesn't deserve a fucking thing! Just because we rained on his little parade. Tell him it's above his pay grade. That'll kill him.'

'Ellie, you're being nasty.'

'Nasty? Look at what he was doing just now. That's nasty!'

'I didn't see her trying to get away.'

'Oh, that's it, the man's view. Don't be an idiot, Sam. She was trapped. She couldn't say no. Power and money, sweetheart, it works just like a rufie.'

Sam refrains from any further exchange in my mind. Instead, he focuses back on Ashton's question.

"I'm really sorry, Prime Minister, but you don't have the clearance to receive such intelligence."

I feel the giggle inside me rising up. Looking at Ashton's face flushing a shade of pink only exacerbates it further. I force myself to be stern and grip hold of Sam's hand to steady my emotions.

"Thank you for your cooperation," I murmur, pulling my lips together.

Ashton stares at me and then at Sam. He shrugs and breathes out, bitterly annoyed by the game being played on him, then sits back.

"Pop over to Chequers tomorrow. I'll run through the investments in Quantum Force. It'll put your mind at rest that I'm being a good boy."

I flash a look toward the bedroom and smile.

"Ashton, I never thought you were anything less."

Chapter 47

Religious unification has been put on the back burner in favor of Ashton's current focus, Quantum Force. The energy experiment is blossoming rapidly into a fully-fledged industry.

With Sam's interest in all things engineering and technology, my husband leapt into the fray to help Ashton and give the PM his wholehearted support.

I just don't feel the same way.

I see that the new energy is fabulous for mankind relinquishing their dependence on fossil fuels. But it is also fabulous for Ashton as an initial private investor. Having signed all those initial seed-funding checks, he's been tipped to be a very wealthy guy indeed.

After confronting Ashton in his penthouse, he'd suggested we attend one of the investment discussions with Jensen Stalbridge, Ashton's investment partner and confidante. It wasn't really a discussion but more of a closed, top-secret meeting at Ashton's country retreat, Chequers.

Sam and I sit in the morning room at the back of the mansion. It's all plush, plump sofas and heavy drapes adorning French windows that open out onto the patio and an immaculate garden stretching beyond.

"Ellie, my dear, you know everything I'm doing is for the good of Mother Earth? I know what a temperamental old girl she can be. I just want to give her and mankind the best shot at survival and maybe an evolutionary leap ahead. You're not wanting me to back down on that, are you?"

Ashton's eyes twinkle with mischievous goading.

I scowl and sigh. "Of course not. But all this new energy, well, it's going to be good for you."

"Yes. Good for mankind."

Ashton smirks, glancing up and down my body.

I inwardly shudder.

"And good for you personally." I fix Ashton with a deep, stern stare from my stunning and unnaturally-blue eyes. I pump up my internal energies so that my eyes look as if they are actually glowing.

I watch as Ashton notices and swallows. His smirk also drops a fraction. "I'm not quite understanding what you mean, Ellie, my dear."

"I mean, Ashton, you're going to be extremely rich. You are the principal investor, are you not?"

Ashton's smug face lightens up on hearing my accusation. I don't like that response.

"As Stalbridge here can verify, I've already signed away a large percentage of my predicted profits to worthy causes. At the moment, I'm the principal investor. However, UK PLC will take the lion's share of investment and, of course, the returns now that we are moving into the implementation phase. I've also secured a few overseas investors, just to add a bit of color."

I see Sam nod, accepting Ashton's position. I seethe. Doesn't anyone get this guy? He's doing it all for himself.

"But you," I say, increasing my voice, "as prime minister will gain financially from the investment in Quantum Force?"

Ashton steals a look at Stalbridge, who opens his mouth, ready to back up the PM.

"I assure you Prime Minister Ashton has been completely transparent in these energy dealings. All transactions have been documented. The probity of his undertakings is without question."

I bristle at the piousness of Stalbridge's approach. *Without question.* Yeah right!

"That may be," I respond. "But you did get that new energy Bill through Parliament pretty damn sharpish, didn't you Ashton?"

My glowing eyes laser into the PM. He holds his nerve against me and does not flinch. He merely licks his bottom lip in his usual salacious way.

"I'm just ensuring that the right legislation is in place to support the UK in the development of this new energy source."

Ashton's smooth response fills me like treacle; it's thick, sweet, and more than one mouthful makes you want to puke.

"So you're saying you're not going to personally benefit from Quantum Force?"

"I don't think that's what the prime minister said, Ellie," remarks Sam.

I shoot him a look that could explode something, preferably Ashton's head.

"With the greatest respect, Sam, that's *exactly* what Ashton has said."

I'm aware of Ashton regarding our little interaction with some mirth.

"Something funny Ashton?" I snap.

"Oh no, not at all. It's good to see a husband and wife at work. I just need to have a danger sign somewhere nearby."

I glower, and Ashton, knowing he's poked me, begins to smirk.

I notice Stalbridge starts to grin too. Oh, that's something I'm not having. I'm not having us being turned into a game for jokes and ridicule.

"Stalbridge, can you leave us now?"

Stalbridge's merriment holds initially on his face, and then he realizes the meaning of my words. His mouth drops into a flat line.

"Leave?" he repeats incredulously.

"Yes, leave now!" I instruct sharply, glaring with ire at Stalbridge. He turns back to look at Ashton who imperceptibly nods. Stalbridge leans forward, gathers his papers into his briefcase and leaves wordlessly.

I push myself forward and glare with uncontrolled menace at Ashton.

"Okay, here it is. We're watching you. If you screw around with Quantum Force, if it doesn't work or if it's been stolen from another country, we'll know all about it. Sam has been given clearance to guide and support you, but if I feel for one second that we're not being told the truth, that's it. You're on your own – for everything. Including that religious unification thing. Understand me?"

Ashton stares. His smirk becomes a smile that hardens on his face. His head tilts slightly to one side and he regards me with curiosity.

"You don't like me very much, do you, Ellie?"

The directness of his statement stuns me completely.

Sam jumps in to defend my position, but I remain silent, at least until I know Ashton's game.

"Prime Minister, of course Ellie likes you. Why would you think such a thing? We see you as a twenty-first-century peacemaker and an innovator of mankind. Freedom Earth, religious unification, Quantum Force, they're all such incredible developments. We have acknowledged what you are doing, and what it could mean for the evolution of humans."

Ashton's sickly smile spreads as he listens to my husband's words.

I want to scream inside Sam's head, 'Stop it'. But I refrain from doing so. As much as I hate to admit it, I know Sam is right.

Ashton may not be a nice person. No, scratch that. Ashton is *definitely* not a nice person. But what he's trying to achieve with the world has universal ramifications that could help mankind. I do not have the right to let my personal feelings dictate or jeopardize the relationship. I must be more open with Ashton, and give him the latitude he needs to get the job done.

I push a smile at Ashton. It's not easy when I really wanted to smite his smug face. I summon up a benevolent vibration within me, which hopefully Ashton could pick up on, and believe in my own positivity.

"What you are doing for Earth and mankind is absolutely wonderful. As with your political addresses, emotional standing and personal preferences do not enter into the discussion. Sam and I are behind you and we want to see you achieve success. It will bring an evolutionary leap for mankind as a whole. That, Ashton, is our first, last, and only consideration in this engagement."

Ashton straightens his back as he listens, and his customary smirk slips into a sneer. He arches his eyebrow and moistens his lips. His stare is cold, his demeanor unyielding.

"Well, well, it seems I have a worthy advocate in you. I am so pleased you're both behind me in my humble endeavors."

I heard Ashton say advocate, but what resounds in my mind is adversary.

Ashton turns his head sideways to look at me. The sunlight streaming in through the French windows catches his eyes and it glints, and inexplicably I'm transported back to six weeks prior, standing in front of Salim Al Douri, the most evil man on Earth.

I'm aware of both Sam and Ashton talking, but that glint has captured me. My soul-force pulls me back to that moment with Salim, when he taunted me, not knowing of what I was capable.

I feel a cloud cross my soul, encasing my internal energies of white light, and I allow the darkness to flood me. I want to kill Salim for no reason other than to feel his absolute pain. And to let him know he's suffering for my enjoyment.

I jolt suddenly.

My databanks and the strangeness that just happened are incompatible. I didn't feel that way. I didn't let my soul become dark for revenge. Yes, I'd tortured Salim, but only to get confirmation that he'd not hidden the quantum bomb anywhere else.

Everything I'd done was with a sense of duty, just like a soldier, to bring the Balance back to Equilibrium and protect Earth from destruction.

I still feel that flickering darkness. I shiver, not with abhorrence but with expectation.

Ashton watches me and I get a sense of knowing from him, as if he's aware of what I'm feeling. It's an irrational thought. But as he arches that bloody eyebrow so sardonically, I can't help but conclude I'm right.

Chapter 48

It was a day just like any other. Nothing held an indication of what was to happen. Ashton stood in front of the mirror and straightened his tie, a smug perpetual sneer on his face. He grabbed his phone and scrolled down the diary appointments. He had a visit to a London academy who had been doing interesting fund-raising things to support Team GB's Paralympians. He would deliver the usual guff about being 'a shining light in the educational community'. Then a spot of luncheon at his Mayfair club, 'Inferno'. Then off to Birmingham to talk to a bunch of dodos masquerading as industrialists.

Still, it was his job as PM to do the dutiful tasks of office, at least until such a time those tasks darkened into shadow, as his true vocation came into effect.

The door to his bedroom pushed aside and a haughty, breathy voice sounded loud.

"I'm going to be late tonight, Daddy darling. So don't fret and don't send in your bloody awful agents. They scared the shit out of my friend last time!"

Abigail, his eldest daughter with her nineteenth birthday approaching, stood in the doorway. Her forever-glued phone was in one hand and strands of strawberry-pink streaked hair twirled in the other. Her face was disdainful and unapproachable. She had a complete lack of interest in anything not in her mind-space, which was principally sex, cannabis, and getting totally rat-arsed on any liquor she could lay her hands on.

Ashton glanced at his daughter. His apathy of her life was apparent. His response merely showed his obsession to maintain a familial high-standing in the public's eye.

"Just make sure you stay away from the paps. Don't want your bloody exploits splashed across the dailies and headlining on those dreadful reality mags."

Abigail sashayed into the bedroom and dropped her arms around Ashton's neck. She smirked, licking her lips and purred.

"Don't worry, Daddy darling. Whatever I get up to will be behind closed doors."

Ashton pulled down Abigail's arms, and held her wrists tight with one hand, gripping her chin with the other.

"Remember who I am, darling daughter of mine!"

"How could I fucking forget!" Abigail knocked down Ashton's hand from her chin and pulled away from his hold.

Dismayed and disgusted, Ashton released her. She was the product of his marriage with Natasha, her mother, a woman who had intentionally developed Abigail to be a spoilt, entitled brat, as an act of sheer spite against him. Abigail, realizing she was totally unloved and a just a pawn in her parent's power games, had run totally off the rails. She screwed anything that moved and took so many chemicals, a major pharmaceutical was considering her body to be the first ever walking lab.

Her mother had long stopped caring what Abigail did. In turn, Ashton used his wayward daughter as a vehicle to derive sympathy. Given his holier-than-thou righteousness and his mission to strive for peace and justice, those around Ashton thought he was a man who, although burdened with a terrible daughter, acted with considerable fortitude and grace.

Abigail turned and shook her ass in rebellion at her father before leaving the room. Ashton stared at his daughter's guileless, exhibitionist outburst. He considered having her abducted and rendered to a cell for a week or two. He only ceased such a consideration as he realized, knowing how perverted and sick his daughter had become, that the experience would probably excite her, rather than frighten her into behavioral modification.

He could, of course, have her popped. Clean and smooth. No fuss. A bullet to the mangled mess she deemed to call a brain.

Natasha, that bitch of a mother, would wail. But he could put the event down to Al Nadir stragglers taking their vengeance. It would go a long way to assist his world profile. Daughter assassinated by terrorists. Hmmm, it was certainly something to cogitate on, should she get too much to handle…

The door banged hard and Ashton knew she'd left the house. Good riddance.

Another shadow floated in the doorway. Could he not be left in peace to finish dressing?

"Yes, what is it, Natasha?" snapped Ashton, pulling on his jacket. He flicked a look at his Philippe Piaget watch and sighed loudly.

"Rich, don't antagonize Abigail. You know she's a delicate soul."

Ashton's wife leaned her slim body against the door frame. Her lips wrapped into a heart-shaped downward pout and her eyes froze over with ice-tipped loathing.

"Delicate soul! Our daughter? Exactly what reality are you in, darling?"

"Unfortunately, the same one as you."

"No one's asking you to remain. There's a perfectly good knife in the kitchen with your name on it."

"I wouldn't want to deprive you of your calling!"

"Talking of which, aren't you going shopping today? Harvey Nicks has still got a gown or two remaining that isn't hanging in your wardrobe."

"What a good idea! Anything to relieve my eyes of having to absorb any more of your cell structure than is absolutely necessary." Natasha snarled a smile at Ashton and slipped into her dressing room.

Her rapid departure meant Ashton's quip, "Ditto," was lost to her ears.

Ashton returned back to the mirror and smiled; thankful he didn't have to rely on Natasha for servicing of any kind.

He closed the door and headed to his private office. Cumberford, his Parliamentary Private Secretary (PPS), leaped up from his desk when Ashton strode through into the office.

"Good morning, sir. Are you ready for your excursion into the educational jungle?" Cumberford's jowls jangled as he laughed.

Ashton nodded but looked a little solemn. "Come, come, my good man," he replied. "We should recognize the value of education."

Cumberford listened and laughed harder, realizing the irony. "Oh, sir, I do recognize the value of education. But what these people deliver can hardly be regarded as attendant to educational standing."

"Cumberford, we must be magnanimous. These people deliver an educational diet concomitant to their needs. And all is relative, remember that."

Ashton appeared to be stern, but the mischievous twinkle told Cumberford that the PM invested no truth in a single word. Cumberford turned toward his desk to avoid further mirth and scanned the PM's diary. His main concern was to make sure that Ashton was where he needed to be at every hour of the day.

His phone buzzed, and he answered crisply.

"Yes, I'll advise him." Cumberford called over to Ashton, who busied himself in front of his desk with his back to his PPS. "Sir, your driver is ready. Protection on standby."

Ashton flicked through some papers with a nonchalant gesture. Just an ordinary day like any other. No attention needed.

"Right, Cumberford, I'll be lunching at Inferno. An entrepreneur wants to chat about augmented reality in politics and I thought I'd give it go."

Cumberford recalled the file on the tech entrepreneur. Ex-model with a body to worship.

"Hmmm, sounds interesting. Good choice. Enjoy 'giving it a go!'"

Ashton sneered, his tongue lightly touching his bottom lip. "Don't worry. I will."

The PM left Cumberford to consider his lunch-time antics, the customary smug grin still on his face.

Chapter 49

Ashton slid into the back of the Jaguar. The car carried a twenty-first century version of armor-plating, with its body and windscreen super-coated in nanotech material, making it impervious to all bullets.

Ashton exchanged pleasantries with his driver and first line bodyguard then settled into the leather seat. He sat back, closed his eyes and thought about the path he was carving. A soft breeze touched his face and Ashton's eyes opened, alert and suspecting. Paul Dawes, his director of communications, slid in beside him, clasping a leather folder.

"Morning, Prime Minister. Pleased the rain's held off. Shall we run through your itinerary for this morning?"

Dawes was a serious fellow with a squashed body and an oval face displaying dark, piggy eyes and lumpy, dry, peeling lips. He looked like at one time he was tall, but he'd rubbed a giant up the wrong way, who had taken vengeance on Dawes by pressing his whole body downwards.

Ashton flicked a look to the side, out of the darkened windows and up the street, as Dawes sat back and belted up.

"Yep, right. So what's happening with this academy then? Why all the brouhaha?" said Ashton, smoothing his hands down his thighs, feigning enthusiasm.

Dawes unzipped his leather folder and took out his tablet. He swiped the screen and immediately in front of him floated the key events of the day in a suspended version of his online diary. The HoloTab was gaining popularity amongst techy early adopters. Ashton preferred to just look at his phone, as he wasn't that bothered about learning all the haptic controls the HoloTab demanded. Encrpted sat HoloLink was a different matter. He used that all the time, but HoloTab wasn't his thing. He couldn't be bothered to learn all those bloody haptic commands. He had people like Dawes and Cumberford for that. However, Dawes, on the other hand, loved the new gadget and had spent hours perfecting his presentation capabilities in it.

"So you'll be meeting with Mike Hyde." Dawes moved his hand in an upward motion and a picture of Hyde standing in front of the academy popped up against the diary entry. "Hyde is the principal and founder of the London Sports Academy. He's melded general education with sports science and entrepreneurial business studies."

Dawes flipped his hand over and an outline of the curriculum displayed, followed by various photographs of school kids, events and Mike Hyde at the Paralympic games. Ashton nodded, taking in all the data delivered. Dawes continued, his tempo increasing as he got more enthused about the topic of discussion.

"So Hyde wanted to give the kids a focus, and he's used fund raising for sports, and particularly the Paralympic games to help kids develop entrepreneurial skills. He supported the kids' development of a gaming app called Sports2Go, which sold like wildfire, raising well over fifty thousand pounds for Team GB in the Paralympics."

At this point, Dawes swirled his hand around. Press articles and YouTube HoloVids came up and instantly started to play. Ashton was immersed in the moment. Within the confines of his car, scaled down kids were projected in hologram form, jumping up and down with excitement in their sports hall as they watched Team GB Paralympians win on their wall TV screen.

"Yes, right, seen enough," snapped Ashton. Dawes swiped through the air and the holo-scene vanished. "A shining light in the educational community. So what's the dirt, Dawes? What aren't you showing? Did Hyde whip the money away for a sojourn to the Caribbean? Or been naughty with the girls or boys?"

Ashton grinned broadly, but Dawes responded stony-faced.

"No, Prime Minister. Every penny they made from Sporst2Go went straight into the pot to fund the Paralympian efforts in Team GB. And your other suggestion…well, Mr. Hyde is a decent human being who is beyond reproach."

Ashton nodded, enjoying Dawes' obvious discomfort on the subject.

"Goody bloody two-shoes then! Well, that's all fine. Anything else I should be aware of? Any skeletons lurking in Hyde's cupboard? That sort of thing."

Ashton stared at Dawes, eyebrows raised. Dawes shook his head with some vehemence.

"Prime Minister, Hyde runs a school academy, not a nightclub. What were you expecting?"

"Not sure," pondered Ashton. "But I wanted to check. You know, my reputation and all that. Can't take the risk."

"I appreciate that, but the academy, I assure you, is whiter than white. That is the reason we are taking you there."

Dawes' voice was indignant with just a smattering of hurt. Ashton had implied he hadn't done his job properly, that his scrutiny and probity of the academy had been slapdash in its execution. The PM noticed a slight tremble in his comms man's bottom lip, redolent of a young boy who'd been told off for a misdemeanor his brother had done.

"Listen, Dawes, I'm not suggesting that you've been anything other than super thorough."

Dawes' cheeks inflamed, and a whisper of a smile touched his dry, scabby mouth. "Thank you, Prime Minister."

"Listen, old chap, why don't you relax a bit for the rest of the journey? You've earned some downtime!" Ashton grinned again sideways at Dawes, who looked surprised by the PM's generosity. Ashton was a man who usually grilled and worked his people mercilessly.

"That is very kind of you. I will avail myself of the offer."

Dawes took out his headphones and cued up on his tablet an episode of some procedural crime drama. Ashton watched him and was thankful he didn't HoloVid the ghastly episode.

Ashton opened his briefcase, removed his phone, and fixed wireless earplugs into his ears. He tapped on an album. Soft music filtered into his mind. Inwardly, he was preparing. Just like he'd been taught decades ago. He knew it would happen that day. What wasn't clear was when. Ashton had weighed up possibilities and he knew it had to be en route, either that morning going to the academy or during the trip to Birmingham. Inferno wasn't in his diary, so unless the GID was suddenly psychic, he doubted they'd attempt anything at lunchtime.

Despite knowing and taking measures, the uncertainty of the maneuver still dangled scythe-like above him. He looked around at Dawes, who was still engrossed in the episode.

Ashton moved in his seat and his Kevlar Slimline vest rubbed underneath his shirt. He'd worn a three-piece Ermenegildo Zegna affair. The waistcoat detracted the eye from any potential bulge from the vest. Working out at all hours in his home gym had served him well. His toned, slim body nestled comfortably into the sharp Zegna tailoring. The cut of the trousers flared a little at the ankle and was tight at the thighs, accentuating his firm buttocks and cinched in waist. By any model agency's standard, he was in very good shape, and ironically, even better than when he'd been an MI6 operative. Back then, he'd been more wiry with less muscle than he had now.

His Sig sat in his inside pocket. A small berretta strapped to the bottom of his leg was hidden by the unique tailoring of his trousers. He'd never lost his martial arts, having kept up his black belt karate training with one of Japan's champions, a man who'd represented and won gold for his country in the Olympics. His Krav Maga was also up to scratch, having enjoyed a sparring round with a particularly gorgeous Mossad agent called Erin just two days ago. Erin had put Ashton through his paces on the mat and in her bed.

Ashton was confident he could match and block any assault, but just in case his judgment was awry, he had his personal security back up on standby.

Ashton's mind unexpectedly wandered back to Erin, the agent he'd taken a tumble with earlier in the week. Her body erupted into his thoughts, her skin under his touch, taut and soft, nipples erect and playful. She sighed and writhed as his lips engulfed hers. His hands meandered down her body, resting between her legs. He'd ridden her hard for hours. His libido was not dented by his age. Indeed, Erin, half his age, had struggled to maintain his pace toward the end of their assignation.

"Prime Minister, we're here."

Dawes nudged him, and his bodyguard looked over his shoulder, checking on the PM. Ashton rubbed his eyes and yawned.

"Late night, difficult meeting," muttered Ashton, wanting to appear vulnerable. He waited for his bodyguard to open the car door. He heard a scream of cars braking, as his close protection screeched to a halt outside the entrance to the academy.

Ashton emerged from his Jaguar and looked up. Principal Mike Hyde stood under the overhang on the roof that spelled out the name 'London Sports Academy'. When he spied the PM, he did a tiny leap and hurried toward Ashton to greet him.

"It is a pleasure, Prime Minister, to welcome you to our humble seat of learning," said Hyde, his East London accent breaking through despite the hours of elocution lessons to bury his background.

Ashton smiled with fake warmth, carrying out his prime ministerial duties to the letter.

"Oh, Mr. Hyde, the pleasure is all mine. I'm delighted to visit an educational institution that upholds the patriotic values in equal measure to its educational ones. Remind me, just how much did your Sports2Go raise for our great Paralympians?"

"Fifty thousand pounds, Prime Minister," said Hyde, beaming, his face a catalog of pride and patriotism.

"My goodness, fifty thousand pounds. Well, isn't that truly marvelous." Ashton looked around to his entourage soliciting their dutiful nods.

Hyde reversed a little and swept his hand toward the entrance of the academy.

"This way, Prime Minister."

Chapter 50

Ashton walked and talked with Hyde. Despite his preconceptions, he found himself getting quite intrigued by Hyde's story. Hyde was a guy who'd dragged himself out the dirt and squalor that he was born into to become a self-made millionaire. He started off by selling sportswear deemed imperfect by their manufacturers. Hyde was smart and noticed that the clothes had often been rejected for something as minor as a seam not quite straight, or even the washing instructions being sewn in back to front. In manufacturing terms, they wouldn't pass muster to be sold at the exorbitant branded sportswear prices, but by the people where Hyde lived, they were equivalent to Haute Couture at a tenth of the price.

Before long, Hyde had progressed into retailing gym equipment and bicycles, and he launched his own brand of sportswear, BuzzSport. It became a notable brand in its own right, creating affordable gym systems and high impact sportswear. Hyde later moved on to real estate, buying up disused warehouses, the usual domain of vagrants and druggies, and turning them into community gyms. BuzzGyms were open to residents of housing estates for a very nominal fee, again at a fraction of the big-name gyms. However, potential members did have to prove they lived on the housing estates and were not affluent individuals just wanting to take advantage of the favorable low rates.

Hyde created sports classes to help kids' interests grow outside of just becoming a gang member. Hyde always considered his motto 'building up the body builds up the soul'. Respect for oneself and one another was always Hyde's ambition. When the opportunity came to develop an educational enterprise that melded his ideology into reality, Hyde ran into the venture at full tilt. He used his faith in the underdog, along with his love of sport, business, and education, and molded a structure that became the London Sports Academy or the Buzz Academy, as the locals knew it.

Ashton listened to this incredible background and wondered why Hyde hadn't been knighted or, at the very minimum, awarded a national award from the Queen. It seemed that lately, it was the least deserving, attention-seeking parasites that were nationally recognized.

Ashton pulled Dawes to one side and whispered, "Make sure Hyde is mentioned in the Queen's birthday honors. He more than deserves it!"

Hyde didn't hear the quick instruction, as he was so excited to show the PM the room where Sports2Go gaming application was created, and introduce Aaron, the thirteen-year-old boy who first had the idea.

"Aaron, well done. Wonderful achievement!" The PM shook the boy's hand with warm affection.

"Thank you, sir," said Aaron, with considerable assurance, given his youth. "I'm pleased we made so much money for Team GB and for our Paralympians."

The boy may have been well-schooled in what to say, and Ashton was sure this was the case, however, it couldn't be denied the strength of character behind the boy's delivery.

"Impressive boy," Ashton said to Hyde, as they turned away to finish the final leg of the academy tour.

Hyde nodded. "You'd never think just two years ago that boy was in one of the roughest gangs and was a serial juvenile delinquent engaging in many a heinous crime. Between our focus on sport and education, together with our firm doctrine, the boy evolved into something quite different. Our chief advantage is the fact that the boys and girls board here. They have excellent dormitory quarters, and we impose a regime of cleanliness, tidiness, and self-respect."

"A bit like the army then?" said Ashton.

"Yes, I suppose so, with a much greater emphasis on sport and business. Well, actually, we're about developing the entrepreneurial capability and business insight in the young."

"How do their parents react?" asked Ashton, genuinely interested in Hyde's take on reconditioning the generation Y unreachables.

"Very well actually. They see their children at half term and most are happy with that. We have a strict policy that doesn't permit parents to access their children until the holidays. You see, sir, for many of these children, it is their parents who are to blame for their delinquency and disrespect."

Ashton could certainly see that point. But although it did feel a little to him like a social experiment, he was still fascinated by Hyde's ability to develop such a venture.

"Who pays for all of this? I mean, apart from the education costs, you have the boarding and accommodation. That must be quite a sum."

"Prime Minister, it is quite a sum. I am the major contributor. However, I have a board of wealthy philanthropic investors who care deeply about how Britain's young can be turned around. Now we can see this venture working, there are plans to take this model to all major UK cities in their most deprived boroughs and give the disenfranchised a chance to prove themselves."

Ashton was completely awestruck. Such a mission should be better recognized. He made a mental note to arrange a meeting with Hyde at Number 10 and discuss further engagements with him allied to Freedom Earth and the indoctrination of the young into its tenets.

Hyde swung around, animatedly talking, and Ashton suddenly discerned something delicate about him despite all the power pumping and bodybuilding prowess. The turn of his hand, the hold of his gait, even his careful deportment in his address of others. Beyond the East London twang, something lurked that Ashton understood.

The prime minister considered the worth of his new discovery. He swept a side glance at Hyde, who was in full and florid flow describing the next steps with Team GB's Paralympians. His tall muscular frame, azure blue eyes, and sculptured face caused a dryness at the back of Ashton's throat, and a trace of a tingle down his back. Hyde looked back at the PM and smiled.

Click!

Ashton held Hyde's gaze for a second longer than necessary and turned away to discuss a matter of peripheral importance with Dawes.

The end of the tour had arrived. Ashton thanked Hyde and shook his hand. Drawing his hand from Hyde, Ashton let his fingers brush against the principal's tips. Hyde's eyes dilated. Electric frisson from the unexpected softness of the PM's touch shot through him. Hyde collected himself, his eyes questioning whether he'd read the PM's signal correctly.

A knowing smile flickered on Ashton and he lowered his eyelids down purposefully for a second. On opening, his eyes burned directly into Hyde, and there could be no misinterpretation.

"Excuse me, Prime Minister, before you go, I'd like to share with you something I'm working on that could support your Freedom Earth movement. However, it is quite secret. If I could so be indulged?"

Hyde stared at the PM. His lips moistened a little and his beautiful azure eyes were now plates of enchanting blue, wide and expecting.

Ashton nodded, and turned to his first bodyguard, who looked perturbed and confused by this development. The directive was that the PM must never leave their sights. However, it was common knowledge too that to go against the wishes of the PM was career suicide. His word was law.

"I don't believe I'll be needing your services for the next few minutes. We're only going into Mr. Hyde's office. You're right outside the door."

"Prime Minister, sir, it hasn't been recced. I don't think-" protested the first bodyguard.

Ashton interjected, cutting the man down with sharp, biting authority. "Don't think. Thinking is my job. Wait here. I won't be long."

Hyde opened the door and beckoned the PM into his office. Ashton strode in and Hyde closed the door as he'd passed the threshold, separating cleanly the PM from his close protection and associated entourage.

Ashton spun round.

"Right, well, what do you want to show me?" asked the PM, with a small laugh in his voice. He knew very well what was going to happen.

Hyde's lips were upon him before he could breathe out. Instinctively, Ashton's arms encircled Hyde, his hands reaching up to caress the back of his neck. For a second or so, Ashton's world was sucked into returning, with ferocity, the kiss he'd received.

A familiar click brought his senses back online.

A second click confirmed his unfortunate position as a dupe.

Someone pulled Ashton away from Hyde and his hands were dragged back and tied.

Ashton breathed, slow and determined, forcing down anxiety, panic and, most of all, anger. He had to focus on exactly what was around him, and what he could use to alleviate his situation.

Hyde stood in front, grinning sardonically at Ashton.

Ashton concentrated, his mind absorbing every ounce of stimuli. He refused to enter into an anger state, for anger clouded judgment.

"Get him out the back, quickly," hissed Hyde.

The two unspeaking men who, through their immense height and broad chests, resembled real giants, hauled Ashton over to the fire door at the back of the office.

Ashton looked from side to side and could see two Glock 43's with Silencerco Osprey silencers trained at his head. He stared at Hyde, refusing to show rage. He could see his position seemed to irk Hyde.

"Why?" Ashton asked, his eyes calm, showing no panic at all.

Hyde walked toward the PM, taking in his incapacity, smiling, and savoring every second.

"I was passed over," stated Hyde. He attempted an equal level of calm and coldness in a bid to match Ashton's. But the flame of rage flared brightly in his eyes and revealed his hurt. "This country never recognized me. Not even when Team GB Paralympians achieved their brilliance in the Olympics and all the training time was funded by me with Sports2Go and beyond. Even then, I was shunned. Never accepted. Always regarded as an outcast because I never went to the right school. Never had the right background. Never had the right breeding to warrant recognition. This country, or rather your establishment, didn't want to see a boy from a council estate and coming from a broken home achieving so much. I've given my all for this country and got nothing. Not a single ounce of recognition. That's why, Prime Minister."

The irony hit Ashton, and he laughed hard.

Hyde watched and bristled, believing the PM was laughing at him. "What's so funny, Prime Minister?" he snapped.

"This is. You are. Only a few minutes ago, I'd instructed my director of communications to ensure you were recommended for a Queen's Honor. Shows how wrong my judgment was."

Hyde stared at Ashton and could see the verisimilitude caught in his eyes. In his voice, the tone of truth rang clear. Such a knowledge startled Hyde, for his actions were based on the ignorance and indifference he'd received up to that point. What could he do now? He'd played his hand, revealed everything. Ashton's assertion that he deserved honoring changed everything.

He'd betrayed the very man who had finally acknowledged him.

Irony indeed.

Ashton raised an eyebrow, seemingly asking, "What next?"

There would be no 'next' for Hyde. His life was over. The money settling in his off-shore account from Prince Khalifa would remain, gathering cobwebs of interest, until some bright sleuthing soul discovered the hoard.

He turned to the two giants and gestured for them to lower their guns and release the PM.

"Enough, boys. It's over." His voice shuddered with desolation and remorse.

Ashton grinned, flicking a sideswipe at the two giants. Their expressions were solid, and Ashton noticed the immutable stance of authority. Despite Hyde's belief, he was no longer in command. They worked for Khalifa, not

Hyde. If he turned, their instructions from Khalifa were to take him out. The grip tightening around Ashton's arms affirmed him of this new dynamic.

Hyde didn't know. He didn't have time to see.

The giant's trigger finger sprung back, and Hyde fell to the floor, his body seeping crimson as the bullet drilled into his heart. Shock and pain flashed through his face. His body trembled as life dribbled out of his mouth with his final words.

"I never meant to harm you. I just wanted...to be remembered."

Ashton expected the scene and remained impervious, despite how he'd momentarily lusted after Hyde, his sudden death didn't affect him at all. With rapid efficiency, his training kicked and he used the moment. With one of the guns pointed momentarily away from him, he stamped hard on the first giant's foot whilst he drove his balled fists up into his scrotum with savage force. Stunned and gasping, the first giant dropped back, losing his balance. The second giant, who'd just killed Hyde, brought his gun round to face Ashton. But the PM spun around behind the first giant and used him as a battering ram, pushing his massive bulk against the second oaf. The second giant, trigger-happy, blasted his gun and shot into the top of the first giant's shoulder, who instinctively howled.

Ashton hit the floor and rolled away as his close protection blasted away the office door.

His protection entered, firing at the two giants. With several slugs a piece slamming into them, limbs shattered, and torsos turned to wells of pumping blood. They crashed to the floor and jangled as the high-velocity bullets that kept on coming chewed their bodies into dog food.

Ashton's primary bodyguard ran to him and raised him off the floor. The PM pushed him away and moved over to search the bodies of the giants. No ID; their fingertips were burnt off by acid. Not a word was spoken between the two, so no way to determine nationality. All to be expected, thought Ashton.

"Sir, leave that to the specialists," said his primary bodyguard. But he held his tongue after Ashton glared at him with customary vehemence.

Dawes entered; his face frozen by the scene before him. Ashton smirked slightly, witnessing Dawes seeing a dead body for the first time. He turned his head away in time, thus failing to observe the sight of his director of communications hurling up his breakfast over his primary bodyguard.

"I'm sorry. I'm sorry," whined Dawes, and he vacated the area to find a restroom and clean himself up.

"Sir, you must leave now," said the sick-sodden bodyguard. He indicated to his close protection colleagues to remove the PM immediately.

"Check outside. They were leaving from there." Ashton pointed to the fire door at the back. "There may be more out there. Get them. Get them alive!"

Ashton was hustled out of the office, into the corridor amidst screaming children and teachers, and into the waiting Jaguar. He heard further gunshots and realized that the giants must have had other colleagues.

He hoped they were still alive; he'd really enjoy *talking* to them.

Chapter 51

A half-light drifted across London, dipping the ancient city into shadow, befitting of what it harbored, for deep, many tens of meters down underneath the Thames, was a bunker where any vestige of mercy was left at the threshold.

Incarcerated in this bunker was the last surviving member of the quartet who had tried, unsuccessfully, to abduct the British prime minister, Richard Ashton. The perpetrator of the foiled kidnap attempt was slumped naked in a metal chair, surrounded by bits of what used to be attached to him, scattered on the floor.

Ashton and aforementioned victim of the thwarted kidnapping stood by a metal trolley replete with implements to encourage talking. He wiped his blood-soaked hands. He'd slipped a bit on the last *encouragement.* Too much lubrication.

Ashton turned back to the immobile lump.

"Not going to give the girls a party anymore, are you?"

He sneered at the gushing pool where the prisoner's testicles and penis once rested.

"Hey, fucker! I'm speaking to you. Answer me!" Ashton pulled the man's head back, but nothing registered. His remaining eye was swollen shut. Ashton grabbed the man's ear and yelled, "The party's over big boy. That goes for your Khalifa too. Thank you for your enlightening information. Better than an encyclopedia, you've been, old chap. Most informative. So sorry I have to say goodbye. Just as we were getting on so well."

Ashton reached into his pocket for his Sig. The prisoner still hadn't moved. Was he even alive? He indicated to one of the interrogators to check his pulse.

The interrogator nodded. Ashton smirked, pointed and fired into the seated mound of flesh that was barely recognizable as human. The bullets hit into the man with a gentle thud, as if Ashton was shooting into a thick pillow. The prisoner's body heaved up and shuddered under the force of the bullets' velocity.

Ashton laughed, thoroughly enjoying the opportunity to empty his magazine into the GID agent's lifeless torso.

The magazine finished. Ashton returned his gun back to his pocket, slapped his hands together, rubbed them, and looked round at his interrogators.

"Fun's over here. Where to next? The Saudi Embassy?"

"Sir, the embassy is sovereign foreign land. We can't touch anyone on it."

Ashton eyed the interrogator. A stupid man. He didn't understand the true nature of world domination. By its definition, there were no boundaries, no lines. Just a freedom to take, command, and control. That was the power bestowed by his Freedom Earth.

"I can touch anyone I like. If I suspect them of treason, of being terrorists, making hostile overtures toward any country under Freedom Earth, including this great country, I can instruct the Freedom Earth army to remove those individuals and render them to a cell where they will wait for summary execution. As the Kingdom of Saudi Arabia is one of the many countries under Freedom Earth jurisdiction, I have absolute right to do what needs to be done to protect and serve all the countries under Freedom Earth from terrorist activity of any kind."

Ashton's serene delivery belied his fury at being queried by his interrogator, an underling with no understanding of the new political landscape he had spent time tilling.

Before he could target any further anger at his interrogator, his cleanup team arrived.

"Good timing, guys. Oh, and when you're finished, put his ashes into a vase for me."

Chapter 52

Ashton arrived unannounced. He was at Prince Khalifa's Knightsbridge penthouse. His intelligence had advised him on the prince's location that evening. Ashton, accompanied by his close protection, entered the penthouse elevator and ascended. Cradled in his arms was an ornate mock-Ming vase. Along with the vase, the PM carried his habitual smirk of derision.

The elevator doors opened. The prince's protection greeted Ashton and his entourage and instructed them to follow into an expansive shining hall of white and mirrors with art deco floors and furniture.

After a walk of such length it almost seemed impossible in a so-called apartment, Ashton emerged into an even larger and more grandiose room. The interior décor was rich with vibrant reds and golds. Luxurious fabrics clothed chairs and sofas, and massive woven rugs depicting Arabia of old adorned the marble floors. Around him, there idled artifacts from Louis XIV.

Amongst this finery perched, like a peacock, sat Prince Khalifa.

Ashton glanced around and nodded with some appreciation. Khalifa eyed the vase and swallowed, and sighed slightly louder than he meant to. The silence in the room reverberated his sigh.

"Prince Khalifa, Your Highness." Ashton made the first move. He couldn't be bothered with the silent game-playing of before. For the mess he'd made, Ashton was eager to rub the prince's nose in it. Make him eat his own shit.

"Prime Minister, what a pleasant surprise. To what do I owe this visit?" Prince Khalifa didn't offer any of the usual hospitalities. He could barely hold down his loathing. His abject frustration that the man before him wasn't dead had to be reined in.

"I just wanted to return your property."

Ashton proffered the mock-Ming vase toward the prince. Khalifa didn't move. He stared at Ashton and then at the vase. Finally, he shook his head and backed into the sofa, sickened.

"That is not my property." Khalifa's tongue was clipped and cold.

"Oh but, Your Highness, I think you'll find it is."

Ashton's smug assurance forced Khalifa to react. He stood up and thrust his hand, palm upward, toward the PM, revulsion reflected in his eyes.

"Prime Minister, I tell you again, that is not my property."

"And I tell you, Your Highness, it is your property. You know how I know it is your property? Because it told me so. Vases, amazing things. In their design, they speak the words of their owners. Oh, and this one, this vase, it *screamed* your name so clearly, there was no doubt. Absolutely, it is your property. And I'd hate to deprive you of your property, so thus, your Highness, I have returned it. Back to your safe keeping, if you will."

Khalifa didn't speak. He stretched out and took the vase. His hands showed a hint of a tremble. A sallowness saturated his skin. In danger of fainting, his close protection moved in preparation to catch the prince. Against their better judgment, he remained perpendicular.

"Good. Well, I'm pleased that is all cleared up, Your Highness. I hate these misunderstandings. As a country under Freedom Earth, we must all stand together. Mustn't we?"

Virtually inert, the prince's nod was barely a response.

"I do hope that no more of your vases find their way into my hands. One must keep one's property under firm lock and key. Don't you agree, Your Highness?"

A single impassive nod.

"Right. Well, I have to depart. I'll leave you in peace. Oh, by the way, Your Highness, you'll be interested, as I do remember your excitement regarding our new energy source, to know that we'll be starting the conversion of the existing power stations this coming Monday. Super news, isn't it? Well, goodnight, Your Highness. Sleep well."

Ashton turned away and left with his close protection now in diamond formation for fear of reprisal, should anyone dare.

In his magnificent lounge, Prince Khalifa, still somewhat comatose by the interaction, suddenly came alive. He looked down at the vase and a burning anger drove through him. He threw the vase against the wall in front of his credenza. It smashed, scattering the ashes of his GID agent across his priceless Louis XIV antiques.

On the walk back to the elevator, Ashton heard the crash and shot a sideways smirk to his primary bodyguard.

"Do you think all is not well in the Palace of Versailles?"

Chapter 53

Lei recognized Chen's reluctance to join her daily visit to Xiao's bedside. Seeing her husband sitting in his favorite armchair in their drawing room, not wanting to face their son, brought her distress.

She knew that the darkness Xiao had spoken of perturbed Chen. On hearing his son's allegations, his face had drained, and a far-off look had taken him, as if he was transported back into the past. Lei had seen his hands grip the sides of the armchair and his features turn rigid.

Lost at a point in time, decades past, Chen stared ahead and did not engage with Lei.

Lei sat peacefully opposite him, her back pulled straight, knees together and hands clasped. She didn't try to force Chen into conversation. Her husband seemed to be made of marble. His eyes didn't blink, or at least she hadn't seen them close.

"He spoke of darkness."

Chen's voice broke the silence.

Amongst the sumptuous surroundings of cream, gold and deep rich crimson, there was a waft of something misplaced within the confines of such luxury.

A waft of desperation, redolent of those who have nothing.

Lei looked at her husband. She did not know his past. They'd met when he'd had the world at his feet. The fashion cognoscenti had already nicknamed him 'The One.' His ability to predict what people wanted and his tendency to set fire to the runway with his incredible creations was legendary. Despite having a diffusion line, celebrities clamored to be in Chen Chang's gang. Being seen with a Chang bag, shoes and, of course, in the stunning clothes was all they wanted.

When Lei welcomed him into her life, she'd known very little about his early years. It was plain to see that life had been tough. She wasn't so naïve as to believe you could come from the wrong side of the tracks and be a fashion mogul overnight.

Sacrifices had obviously been made.

The truth was that Lei never wanted to know. Perhaps she'd been wrong in adopting that position, but that was her decision. She'd heard the rumors. There were tales of a spy network preying on young designers, followed by intimidation and bullying. Not to mention the whispers of how Chen really got his start-up money. Running errands for the Chinese mob.

But rumors were little more than expressions of probability, someone else's take on what may or may not have happened.

"He said I had a darkness in me."

Lei listened but said nothing. She could feel that her husband wanted to talk. He had to get out whatever was eating at him inside. She wanted to encourage him but stopped herself. Lei didn't want to lead him. He had to reveal it in his own words and in his own time.

Lei considered the words of her son. She believed Xiao's reference to the darkness in Chen signaled an understanding of energies. Her son didn't have such knowledge. In her spiritual readings, she'd learned about the universal balance between dark and light energies. She'd read about beings from in between worlds who were involved in balancing energies. As crazy as it sounded, Lei firmly believed an ancient being of great power was inside her son, and that power could detect dark or light energy inside others.

Lei didn't pretend to understand the workings of the world. But thinking about things like the balance of light and dark, and Xiao's place within this mystical machinery, made her feel calmer.

Death was a mortal requirement. If Xiao really had an ancient force inside him, perhaps he now lived under a different set of rules. Perhaps death was not an option. This thought gave Lei a strange reassurance and the vital strength she needed to grow stronger as each day passed.

"He said my darkness would eat him. Devour him alive."

Chen's voice, usually so booming and embedded with undeniable power, was shaken and broken.

"Xiao pitied me. He really pitied me. Me? Chen Chang. The One. Lei, my darling, why would he do that?"

Lei regarded her husband, taking in his deep concern. She stared deep into his ebony eyes.

Composed and with a solid tone of determination, she answered, "You tell me."

Chapter 54

Chen remembered the first time Lei's eyes had fixed on him. The world had fallen away. Nothing mattered, only getting her in his arms.

It was one of those moments that come few and far between.

Undoubtedly, it was love at first sight.

It was an over-riding power of Earth shattering love, hope and goodness. Chen had believed his past sins had been overwritten. The energies of goodness and the joy of being in that ecstatic state of love had cancelled out the evils in his past.

Of course, now Chen knew he'd been completely wrong. Evil never leaves you. As the good times roll, it becomes buried, under years of Bentleys, private jets, and five-carat flawless diamonds.

But it never ever goes away.

Chen knew his son had somehow shoveled through the years and uncovered his evil. It was a pain so immediate and overwhelming that Xiao had been sent into shock. He was responsible for Xiao's seizure. His life was causing Xiao's death. Only a confession could save Xiao now.

Chen stared back at Lei, the woman whom he loved body and soul, and the woman he knew he could lose on his next words. But they were words, for the sake of his sanity, that he had to say.

"I killed a man."

Chen watched Lei's reaction.

She didn't move. Her eyes widened, and a mist of sadness drifted over them, but not a veneer of sadness, the kind that produces tears after a sentimental movie, this was the pain filled sadness of betrayal.

Chen shifted uncomfortably and moved his bulk forward on the seat to lean in Lei's direction. His unassailable wife remained speechless.

"I guess you're wondering why I'm telling you now."

Chen breathed deeply. Why didn't she say something? Anything. Swear at him. Shout at him. Chen rubbed his hands on the wide arms of the chair. It was time. He had to tell the truth and live with the consequences.

"It's Xiao, his condition, it's why he says he can see darkness in me. He says it because it's true, Lei."

Lei tilted her head ever so slightly to the left as if considering her next move. Chen waited for a response but when none came, he continued.

"I killed a man when I was fifteen to protect a young girl from being assaulted and raped by an ignorant, filthy pig. I stole his money and left. But the police were quickly on my track. Mob bosses had heard what I'd done. They bought off the police and recruited me. I became their instrument to do whatever was necessary."

Chen kept his eyes on Lei. He didn't waver or avoid eye contact. Although ashamed of his past, Lei deserved to see his steady delivery. He owed her that much.

Lei's face softened, her mouth loosened, and her jaw slackened.

"You did a good thing. You saved that girl," Lei said finally.

"And I lost myself," admitted Chen.

"You didn't know. You believed what you were doing was right."

Lei stood up with unexpected speed and walked across to Chen. She knelt down beside him and took his hand in hers, then pressed it to her soft lips.

"Chen, I never for one second thought life had been easy for you. I always knew your rags-to-riches story was just that: a story. Working in a textile factory one minute and having a production line of designer knockoffs the next, it's just not possible. The money and connections had to come from somewhere, and Chinese banks have never had much of a knack for lending to teenage waifs. I may have been brought up in a world of wealth and entitlement but I'm not blind to life. I knew what I was getting when I met you. And I welcomed it with open arms."

Chen was truly astonished. All this time and she'd known it was all lies.

"Why? Why did you stay with me, knowing what I might be?"

"I love you, Chen. I knew the darkness within your soul needed my light, my happiness and positivity. Like yin and yang. My darling, we define each other, and in doing so, we define our existence together."

Chen felt the words touch him deep within. A woman, white in heart and soul, had happily wanted to embrace him and heal his darkness.

"I'm sorry I lied to you."

"You didn't lie. You just selectively recalled events."

At the edge of Lei's mouth, Chen detected a slight pulling as if a flicker of something more than a stern flat of her lips was imminent.

Chen placed his hands down to encase her face, radiating love.

"I am blessed with you, my darling," said Chen, bending down to kiss his wife.

Their lips met, and Chen felt a surging force of light filling his void of darkness. Whilst in the embrace, Chen could see that Lei's question remained unanswered. It surfaced on her lips, but Chen jumped ahead.

"What do you think has happened to our son?"

"You want my feelings, my intuition as a mother?"

Lei pulled away from Chen and stared forward. She was remembering Xiao during the happy times. When life had been perfect.

Chen nodded.

"Whatever I say, please don't think me mad."

"Gone on," said Chen softly.

"You know I've always been a spiritual person."

"I do."

"The Universe is such a wondrous place. I know there is so much left undiscovered or not understood, even in this age, where technology dominates our lives. We live online, permanently connected but inextricably isolated and alone at the same time. All of us search for meaning. We wait and yearn for a glimpse of something that tells us there is a reason, a reason for everything. I think, somehow, in Egypt, Xiao found part of that reason. I don't know how, but I feel Xiao encountered a force, an ancient power connected to our existence. And it's still inside him."

Chen heard Lei talking but her words were like a verbal conundrum. He couldn't make any sense of what she'd said. Chen interpreted Lei's words in the only way he could.

His son was possessed.

Lei shook her head on Chen's new assertion.

"No, Chen. I'm sure the force isn't malevolent. More the opposite. I think it detects good and bad in us."

Chen considered Lei and the implications of what she'd said. Chen recalled that Xiao went into a seizure after telling him to, 'Stay away'. Was it possible his darkness was so damaging and destructive Xiao had been torn down by it?

"Oh my God, Lei. He saw me. He saw the secrets I'd hidden from you.

He saw my darkness." Chen's lips trembled, his ebony eyes filled with tears and his austere face crumbled.

"Oh God, Lei. Have I caused his coma?"

Lei leapt up, shaking her head, and held Chen tightly.

"No, darling, no. You must never think that! What's happened to Xiao is beyond our comprehension, but I have faith that because it is metaphysical and not biological in nature that he will get through this. He will return back to us."

Lei smiled at Chen.

He struggled to return the smile. How could he, a down-to-Earth man, even contemplate words such as metaphysical? He didn't believe in God, heaven, or hell.

He only believed in himself.

But now, this thing with Xiao, it really meant rethinking everything he thought he knew. Chen worked his massive arms around Lei's slender body and they held each other close, as each tried to understand, and believe in the impossible.

Chapter 55

Religion is a funny thing, considered Ashton, as he sat alone in his office. The perfect oxymoron. Across the world, religion had been used to impart evil, whilst in the same instant also used as an instrument of good to guide the shallow people of Earth. It is a faith-taker and faith-creator. Blood is spilled in the name of religion. Lives are broken for a good that seems fleeting and fake, all for a being who would not reveal themself, nor give assurance to a forsaken world. A world longing to understand, to experience that moment of existence, of irrefutable proof. Something undeniable. They wait for a moment that will define all pasts, presents, and futures. To cast a shadow over scripture, blast open the good book, whichever faith is followed, and give an exquisite truth. A truth that no prayer, psalm or verse could ever hope to encapsulate in the jumble of words and meanings. Words written by interpreting intellectuals but failing even to meet a fraction of the immensity of true revelation.

Ashton knew he could offer the world that revelation they desperately sought. It would be the desired carrot to drive the faiths to unite. It seemed impossible. But tell him a couple of months ago that the Universe was overseen by a bunch of cosmic bureaucrats, who counted up every act of good and bad that was done to keep the energies in balance – a cosmic spirit level, if you will – and he would've said, impossible. It would appear impossible was the new possible.

Could he dangle the truth in front of them without revealing it? How much could he tell them? And would they believe him?

The red aura in the sky would be his starting point. It was the opening bat from which he would deliver his strike. The world remembered the strange red glow. Many considered Armageddon was close. The churches, mosques, synagogues, and temples became crammed full with bodies that evening. The devout and the sudden believers mixed amongst the throngs, to listen to the ranting of some and the soothing words of others. One common denominator brought the world together: fear.

Even when the red light vanished, the rantings, the sermons, the words of love, joy, and salvation, all continued through the night. People stayed, determined, although soaked in a blissful ignorance, to understand what was happening. Community brought them through, shoulder to shoulder against a common foe. A war-time camaraderie. It gave them hope. It didn't matter if it was false or true; the collective consciousness of the gathered swell made it bearable. You were not alone. That was the sentiment, and this would be the carrot that Ashton would suspend in front of the religious leaders of the world. Proof, undisputable by any means, that Earth is not alone.

Chapter 56

Given the enormity of the task and the need for gravitas and credibility, Cabinet Secretary Redfern had been tasked to set up the meeting.

Redfern commenced by contacting the Primate of All England, the Archbishop of Canterbury, Most Reverend Gregory Forster.

Ashton had not confided in Redfern as to the rationale behind the meetings, only that they were, 'of great importance to humanity and must be undertaken immediately'.

Ashton made it clear to Redfern he wanted meetings with every religious leader residing in the UK, Redfern did not question this statement. Redfern considered probing further but then he drew back. The PM displayed a closed expression, eyes dark and cold. The Cabinet secretary knew better than to pursue a line of investigation that already had an inherent blockage.

Redfern contacted Most Reverend Gregory Foster, but instead, on his private line, someone else picked up the phone. Redfern knew it had to be his senior personal assistant. Redfern breathed in, annoyed he wasn't speaking directly to the archbishop. Redfern considered that dealing with the Senior PA was somewhat beneath him, but he continued to set the date. The PA immediately obliged with two dates. Both were some way into the future. Dutifully, the dates were conveyed to Ashton, who scowled. Displeasure ate away at his handsome features.

"Sooner, Redfern, sooner! Today. Tomorrow at the latest. What is wrong with you, man?"

Redfern took the admonishment without reaction, but inside he bristled. I'm not your bloody diary secretary, he thought, and punched in another call to the senior PA to the archbishop.

"Those dates aren't any good. The PM wants it to be this afternoon or tomorrow."

"You've got to understand, Mr. Redfern, the archbishop is a very busy man. He has his diary filled up months in advance."

"And you think the PM of the UK is any less busy? My good man, make this happen. I would not want to be the one to say you refused the prime minister's request. It wouldn't do your boss any good either."

Redfern's caustic inflection hit home with the senior PA. He snuffled and took a deep breath a few times as if he'd been on a long run. He sounded a little asthmatic. Redfern waited with patient authority.

"Erm, well, no, I'd not want to cross the PM. Let me see what I can do," muttered the senior PA. "I'll call you back."

"No. Check your master's schedule now. I'll wait. I need to return to the PM with a definitive date and time." Redfern was well-versed in the PA runaround routine, and he wasn't going to be at the mercy of some little upstart playing telephone tag with him.

"Oh, right. Okay. Well, the archbishop could see the PM tonight at 7 p.m. for dinner."

Redfern scanned the PM's schedule on his diary secretary's screen. Only a delegation from the Norwegian Embassy. He could rearrange that with little harm done.

"Tonight is excellent! The PM will see the archbishop at Number 10 at 7 p.m."

Redfern replaced the phone before the senior PA could squawk out the request for the meeting to be held at Lambeth Palace.

He buzzed through to the PM. "Prime Minister, sir, the archbishop will be able to meet with you here tonight at 7 p.m. I'll arrange for private dining accordingly."

Ashton smiled as he listened. "Super job, Redfern. House points all round!"

"Sir, may I inquire as to the urgency?" Redfern's toe once again descended into the murky top-secret waters.

"You may, and all will be revealed very soon, but not quite now."

Redfern stared at the intercom, sucked in his cheeks, and grimaced as if he'd swallowed a sour cough sweet.

"Of course, sir," he replied with a begrudging air. "As you wish."

The intercom clicked off, and Redfern was left with deafening silence, both in the room and his mind. He was no closer to really knowing what was transpiring with his boss.

Chapter 57

Beyond the door, the prime minister of the UK, Richard Ashton, started to craft the lines he would use for his first of many meetings with the religious leaders.

Ashton considered his opening play: "We are not alone."

It was very cheesy, yet extremely accurate, and it would take him forward at a quicker pace, rather than a pussy-footing, pontificating speech.

Redfern remained until just after 7 p.m. to ensure that all aspects of the meeting were attended to. Of course, he wanted to purloin snippets of discussion, and catch a word or two that would raise the veil on the true objective of the PM. Ashton was wise to the maneuvers of his Cabinet secretary.

When the first course arrived, the PM dismissed Redfern, with a curt, "Shouldn't you be off home now?"

Redfern nodded and stated that he, "Merely wanted to be satisfied in the knowledge that all proceedings were discharged as planned."

"Of course they are. You're behind it, aren't you? Now off you go home. I won't have another word said on the matter." Ashton glared with annoyance, and Redfern took his leave with reluctance.

The Most Reverend Gregory Forster flicked his mop of curly light grey hair this way and that to catch the gestures between the PM and his retiring Cabinet secretary. The archbishop was a middle-aged man, housed in an uncomfortably tall, wiry frame, who resembled more of a shagged-out hippy with a lugubrious gait than a leader of the Church of England. He gobbled down the tuna carpaccio like a man who hadn't seen food before and waited for Ashton to return his attention to their conversation.

"Right, well, where were we, Your Grace?" asked Ashton, as he sat down opposite his dinner guest.

"You were about to say something about understanding the true meaning of everything, which, I must say, is quite astonishing for someone with neither a scientific or religious pedigree." Despite Rev Forster's tramp-like appearance, his responses carried a degree of incisiveness that placed the receiver on an unwelcome footing.

Ashton allowed the archbishop this moment of smugness. The line of his mouth pulled back and little wrinkly streams popped up and ran into the corners, then faded into his skin. He raised an eyebrow.

"You know, Your Grace-"

"Oh, please call me Reverend Gregory."

Ashton nodded but didn't reciprocate with, 'Call me Richard.'

"You know, Reverend Gregory, when I was in school, my master always drilled into me the importance of waiting."

Reverend Gregory shifted his lips upward in a ponderous pout, his hands cupped and thumbs together as he listened.

"Waiting is a skill. And it is a skill very few have. Observing the scene, analyzing the flow, assimilating what isn't being said or done, deciding upon the moment of interjection. For that moment delivers impact, elegant and optimized. It is the very objective of waiting."

"Yes, I see." Reverend Gregory had no idea whatsoever as to the meaning behind the PM's discourse. But he didn't want to reveal that to Ashton.

Ashton smirked. It was obvious to him, the lack of comprehension on the part of the archbishop. His smirk widened, and a supercilious tone tickled in his throat, daring him to verbally swipe the ignorant man before him.

"You see? Well, isn't that wonderful." Ashton stared at Reverend Gregory with a quizzical expression.

The archbishop didn't know how to proceed. He reached out to the wine by way of a diversion and his sleeve brushed against Ashton's glass. The cut crystal goblet toppled over, spilling the remainder of the Chardonnay across the Spanish lace filigree tablecloth. Reverend Gregory jerked back from the table, mortified by his abject clumsiness, and offered to clean up the mess.

Ashton waved away the incident, indicating that the slight accident was in the past and shouldn't be considered further. Grateful, Reverend Gregory attempted to return back to the PM's confounding conversation.

"So Prime Minister, you were saying...about waiting?"

"Ah, yes. Waiting is something that man is poor at. We dive into wars, situations, debates, without knowing the facts, without assessing all the players. Our impatience at having to wait brings forth obsession, greed, and avarice. Death and destruction of others have come through mankind's inability to wait. And so has our need for religion."

Reverend Gregory shuffled, awkward and uncomfortable in his chair. But he chose to listen rather than interrupt.

"Religion has become a prop for mankind's impatience. It's a proxy for what man is waiting for. A crutch to support the masses through their period of slow, silent purgatory. Religion helps man keep alive the reason for their waiting."

"And what reason is that, Prime Minister?" asked the archbishop. The unexpected talk had left him perturbed and uneasy. He was a great orator and could handle himself in a debate, but the line of discussion was disjointed, like drop-in scenes in a dream, and he was unsettled by the lack of sense in the conversation.

"To know the meaning of their existence. To touch enlightenment itself. To know…they are not alone."

The archbishop smiled. He was back on his patch again. This was a line he could handle. He dipped into the usual book of responses and gave his standard delivery.

"None of us are alone. We have God forever at our side."

"Very true, Reverend Gregory. But, with due respect, these are just words."

Ashton looked up. Conceit mixed with pity hit the archbishop, and he stormed, pushing aside the main course of sumptuous pheasant. Anger flashed across his usually benevolent features.

"Not words, Prime Minister! Not when He is with us always."

"With us always? So show Him to me. Where is He? Show Him to me! I want to see Him now."

"Prime Minister, I do not know what the meaning of this insult is, but your affront to me and to the Church is unforgivable. I'm afraid I cannot remain in your presence a second longer."

The archbishop stood up, ready to leave.

Ashton placed his cutlery down, put his elbows on the table, threaded his fingers together and fixed them beneath his chin. He raised his eyes upward to the archbishop and cast him a glance, solid and shattering.

"Sit down!" Ashton's voice, a force that could cut through metal, left the archbishop shaking. Reverend Gregory fell back into his chair. "Unable to wait, that's humans. You're no different, needing to leave for fear you may hear something that dents your absolute faith in a fairy tale that has been propagated for two millennia. Wouldn't you just like to hear, just once in your life, a truth that is backed up by fact? By reality. A physical reality. Not words in a book. Not pictures or stained-glass windows. Reality. Wouldn't you like to see physical proof of God? A proof that shows we are most definitely not alone."

The archbishop heard but couldn't react. His mind had trapped his mouth. Was Ashton mad? What did he mean? What had he found? Physical proof of God? Where could such a find take him? Could he be blessed? Made a Saint? What power he'd have.

"And what are you thinking, Reverend Gregory? Ten to one, your thoughts are less than pure." Ashton pushed back the chair, rose up and walked over to Reverend Gregory, who blushed, as Ashton read his mind was instant clarity.

"Well, I was, erm, wondering at the state of your mind. I mean, to say such a thing, well it implies a certain madness." Reverend Gregory tried to straighten his back, showing confidence, as he sent his retort to the PM.

"A certain madness. Yes, I suppose it does. To the eye that has not seen, madness can be the only hypothesis." Ashton moved behind the Reverend and gripped his shoulders, digging his fingers hard into the shoulder sockets. The archbishop winced and tried again to stand, but the PM held him firmly in the chair.

"You must have had enough of waiting. That laborious, never-ending flow of constant expectation, of wanting so much to believe, to see, to witness for the first time ever. But every time, your hopes have been crushed. They were obliterated to dust by the heavy foot of uncertainty. It vacillates over your faith until you just read the words in your sermons, but read is all you can do. No meaning is held for the words that have betrayed you. The words hold a blank resolution. The bitterness tinged your tongue. You have felt it all your life, from the moment you made the pledge to believe. Little by little, the inadequacies imposed upon you eroded that belief, until your flame of faith is nothing but an ember of insecurity. And you are hollow."

Beneath the PM's hands, the archbishop trembled. The man that held him knew him better than his own soul. He had been stripped bare of the fripperies and fineries of his office. He was nothing more than flesh and bone. Soulless and wanting. And waiting.

"Wouldn't you want to be whole again? I can show you the truth. I can give you enlightenment. Remember March 26?"

A slow nod jiggered the shoulders Ashton held.

That date, the archbishop would never forget. He'd carried on his sermon and his marathon prayer session throughout the night. Canterbury Cathedral had been packed to bursting. People had streamed in, convinced that the end was approaching. He had looked to the heavens and had seen the weird red light emblazoned across the night sky, and he'd searched himself for answers. Searched God for answers. But none had filtered through.

'A judgment,' many of his congregation had screamed. But he couldn't bring himself to believe that rationale. That the end was really nigh without him having touched enlightenment. Without him having all the answers.

"I know why that red light happened," continued Ashton. "I know what it is all about, this thing we call life. I know why we're here, and I'll introduce you to the one who saved us all."

Ashton released his grip and, with smooth precision, massaged the archbishop's shoulders. His soft touch bordered on sensual exhilaration, and the Reverend let out a small sigh, indicating that the experience wasn't new to him. The PM raised his eyebrow in recognition of another little foible uncovered.

"But how do you know all this, Prime Minister? By what means have you come to learn of this evidence?" Reverend Gregory's voice quivered with an unforeseen anticipation.

"That, I cannot reveal. If you want to stop waiting, if you want a full explanation to the meaning of life, if you want to see evidence of God, physically, without exception, like those prophets of the past, then you must agree to what I say next."

The archbishop didn't need to consider. For such a revelation, he would have given everything he possessed to the man who stood behind him.

Ashton paused his slow massage and dug his pointy fingers inward again, affecting a shiver of excitement from the Reverend, an individual who clearly enjoyed pleasure and pain in equal measure.

"Do we have an agreement, Reverend Gregory?"

Ashton spun the chair holding the Reverend around, and the archbishop took a breath before realizing he was facing the PM. Eyes burned into Reverend Gregory. The religious leader couldn't break the connection. He wanted to tear his eyes away. He wanted to leave the room. But still, he couldn't. What the PM offered was so great, so magnificent in its promise, it couldn't be refused.

"We have an agreement, Prime Minister."

The archbishop whispered the words, now scared that, if he increased his voice, somehow he'd be guilty. He feared that by this pact, he was disloyal to the Holy Orders he'd taken. That by a mouthed, almost mute acceptance, nothing could touch him.

He hoped to remain unsullied by this interaction. For he still wanted to be virtuous, despite sacrificing the virtue he knew he must, to learn the truth. To touch enlightenment. To end the wait.

Chapter 58

Moments drop into one's life when everything from that instance on is either redefined, brought into clear focus or decimated completely. There are, however, few moments when all conditions coalesce and play simultaneously. Reverend Gregory Forster was in the midst of one of those moments. His self was redefined, brought into focus and decimated in one fluttering swing of Ashton's words.

"We are not alone. This world is overseen by other beings who work directly for God. I have met them. They keep us in order and keep our world, and the rest of the Universe, in balance. If you put aside your differences, your interpretations, and age-old traditions, and unite with the other faiths across the world, I will introduce you to two beings who can verify my claim. And you will touch the face of God."

The archbishop froze. Inside himself, a voice called out, "Sheer madness."

A second voice piped up, "Believe him. He knows the truth."

Another little voice chirped with a shrill clarity, "Danger lies ahead for you."

And a fourth sounded from nowhere. "Revelation will be the prize."

And more still.

"Follow this man."

"Leave the room now."

"Your destiny in the hands of God himself awaits you."

So many voices, he was drowned in sound. Reverend Gregory couldn't discern the words. They became a blanket of noises, a mental interference stopping him from reaching his own voice. That place of reason.

Growing louder, leading to a booming crescendo of one word 'believe', and the room slipped away from him.

His head followed the path of infinity, his neck malleable, moving from side to side, slightly up. His eyeballs rolled back, and then down, his head flopping as if he had no bone in his neck.

He had to bring himself back. Find his center. Make him whole again. Ashton must have drugged him. Done something. Put him under the influence. He was sinking into himself. He struggled, but the words, like covers, pulled over him. "We are not alone; we are not alone."

"Archbishop? Reverend Gregory, are you unwell? Reverend Gregory, speak to me!"

Ashton's cries broke through Reverend Gregory's stupor. They carried into his consciousness, and like a lifebelt, the archbishop hung onto them. With every syllable uttered, he dragged himself out of the churning tide of contradictory cacophony.

And then he was aided further. Hands were on him, hauling him back. His head fell against the cushioned top of the chair. He opened his eyes to see Ashton's striking orbs staring down at him, genuine concern ground into the creases around his eyes and mouth.

"Reverend Gregory, I do apologize for giving you such a shock. I thought it best to tell you so that you may prepare for the Unification. I see now you are unwell and cannot take such a burden. Perhaps one of your fellow colleagues would be more suited to receive this news, and meet these beings, these emissaries of God himself."

A hand struggled out to attempt to halt the rash decision being made by the PM.

The archbishop wheezed and licked his arid lips. "No, no, I am the one. No one else. I can take this. It is just…" Reverend Gregory took a breath. "So much to absorb. For a man of God to hear that the Lord's emissary is close. Prime Minister, this is astounding and wondrous. But what you ask of me, of all my colleagues in the other faiths, it is difficult. If not impossible. I cannot even believe it could be done."

"Belief is a powerful aid, Reverend Gregory. Did you ever believe you would have the chance to touch God? To actually *touch* enlightenment. To learn the truth. Beyond anything your scriptures to have told you. If you want to, you can achieve this."

"Can I not be introduced to these beings without this need to unify religion?"

"Unfortunately not."

"But how do I know they even exist?"

"Do you doubt *me*? Prime Minister Richard Ashton?"

"No, no, I do not doubt you. But why the need to unify religion? We have had different religions over thousands of years."

"And we've had wars, suffering, segregation, and pain. Don't you want to end all that?"

"Of course, I do." The archbishop was indignant. "But, Prime Minister, it's impossible. The chasm between our faiths is just too wide." Reverend Gregory shook his head, and dizziness took him over again. As the room started to swim, he watched Ashton scowl, and the PM's lids hooded over. With dismay, he touched the archbishop's hand.

"And I thought you were ready. Mankind has been waiting for this for so long. You would have been revered for making a road to enlightenment. Those beings that I could introduce you to, they hold our destiny in their hands. From God, they have been given the authority to judge and decide on our fate. But I can see from your reticence that you're not equipped to represent the Church of England during this momentous, history-making time."

The archbishop could only think of Revelation 20:4. *"I saw thrones on which were seated those who had been given authority to judge."* Could these beings really be those referenced in the Book of Revelation? Was this part of God's End Time? Had he been chosen to play a role at this moment, the final stage?

"Prime Minister, I will agree to work with you. But I must meet these emissaries first." Reverend Gregory breathed deep. His mouth had burst forth words, but he could hardly believe their meaning. He paused for the PM's response.

"I cannot confirm they will be agreeable to a meeting before all religions are unified. It is their will that I am enacting. These beings have carved the tenets of Freedom Earth. They are intrinsic to its future development. Freedom Earth is becoming the overarching ideology of the world. Its movement has been blessed by the emissaries and through this action, Freedom Earth has been blessed by God himself. It is not a religion; it represents the philosophy of life. The way in which life was always meant to be led, in harmony, without prejudice, without hate, showing one color, one creed, one voice. To be bathed in the anointed shower of God's greatness. To live together under the light. That is the very center of Freedom Earth's purpose. That's why I say that religion must be unified, for there cannot be separation. Fractures in the whole will not reveal the full picture. It will be disjointed, its power incoherent and weak. Together, the strength of all religions solidified as one is the true target of God's blessing. The only one: Freedom Earth. Now, Reverend Gregory, do you understand why you are needed? Why your involvement is at the epicenter of this glorious moment?"

A tingling ruffled inside him. Anticipation? Fear? It was a feeling he could not describe. Mastery of words was his forte. But summoning up the combination of letters that represented, to an adequate level, the sensation that coursed through his body was beyond his current capability. Devoid of understanding, but still hoping that Ashton's words held truth, Reverend Gregory took in the prime minister's face. He scrutinized his eyes, those sparkling mirrors in which reflected his own desperation, his want to be part of something unbelievable.

For every second the PM spoke, Reverend Gregory could feel the unveiling of a mystery that, by the weight upon his mind, had clouded his perspective. Clarity of purpose burned fierce in Ashton's eyes, and through this clarity, the archbishop knew his purpose was now found.

His path lay before him and his guide, Ashton, was a man who, like the disciples some two thousand years before, was truly blessed by God.

Chapter 59

I watch the people below hurrying along the wharf. They appear aimless and disconnected, fixated on their phones, unaware of what is around them. I get a sense of their Balance Shifts even seven floors up. They're a seething mass of darkness made up of self-centered impatience and lacking in moral responsibility. As I stare at these humans, who resemble the ants I watch run along the patio in my house in Winchester, I shudder with disgust.

Was this the mankind I sacrificed my humanity for?

Feeling their Balances, sacrifice for them is a totally anathema concept. Saving their own skin is the doctrine humans live by.

Then I notice, amongst the dark mass, pinpricks of brilliant light.

These are the ones that fill me with hope.

I see a priest walking fast through the crowds. He passes a woman with a scarf on her head. Obviously, the woman is a Muslim and the priest is a Catholic.

The Balance Shift on both parties pings at least two points toward the dark.

Religious unification? You must be kidding! Ashton, you have no chance with these humans.

"A penny for them, darling?"

I lean back into Sam as he places his arms around my waist. His head rests on my shoulder and his lips meet my neck.

"I'm just thinking about those guys down there."

"Humans?" says Sam, nibbling gently at my earlobe. Sparks fly up inside me, and I know my sensual light circuitry is being fired up. My energies are building, and I know what happens when I get that sensation.

"Darling, can you stop that?"

I try to halt the buildup as I need to focus on something else, but Sam also has to comply.

"Stop?" Sam's hurt is audible. "Why?"

"I need to talk to you."

"About humans?"

"About everything, Sam. What's going on with Ashton, this unification thing, are you really okay with it?"

I flip around to face Sam. He knows by my intense eyes blazing with questions that playtime's definitely over. Sam doesn't answer at first. I know he's considering his response. He turns toward the window.

"If there's a chance, however small, for us to help bring peace to this world, then we owe it to them." Sam points down at the people scurrying along the wharf far below us. "We owe it to them to at least try."

"You really think Ashton's going to pull it off?"

"Without us, no. With us, he's got one hell of a chance."

"You don't think all this peace malarkey is a bit too early in mankind's development?"

Sam spins to face me. His eyes are burning coals of sudden anger.

"Ellie, you are not God!"

I leap back and stare into his beautiful dark brown eyes flickering with fury. I say nothing.

"You have no right to determine mankind's development path," continues Sam. "What's early? What's not? Who knows? You don't know the grand plan any more than those poor buggers down there. We're only instruments, tools to shape this planet's future. Ashton may, in your eyes, be a cunning, manipulative bastard, but the good he's doing for Earth is undeniable. We have no choice but to help him and play our part to the best of our abilities."

I stare at my husband. The anger that suddenly defines him tells me that he believes what he says with every light particle of his Kudamaz being.

"I understand what you're saying, my darling," I reply. "But look at them. Their religious indoctrination of what they should believe is too great. It flows in all of them like a poison, stopping reason. Even common sense comes second place when religious beliefs are tested. And that's only those who believe in anything at all. You know Earth has just over a billion people who believe in nothing? No God, supreme deity or all-seeing power. In this country, over a third of the population don't believe in anything. They barely believe in themselves. They just let life happen. They're content to just exist, happy as long as there is enough crap on TV to watch, booze to drink and weed to smoke, all to escape the boring, meaningless lives that they themselves have created."

"Ellie, that's all a bit harsh."

"Sam, this planet was almost broken. It was facing dispatch, AKA annihilation by Kudamun. That wasn't just because of Al Nadir. It was down to the lack of hope and faith in people's souls. Invoking the Therab to bring white light to those dark souls was only a temporary measure. Sooner or later, mankind will sink again, and the Balance will drift back to its default position."

"And what's that?" snaps Sam. I know he doesn't like to hear this. His face is stern and upset by our discussion.

"The dark, Sam."

"So what you're saying is Aswa-da was right? All of mankind is rotten to the core."

I hear Sam's voice get a notch louder. I shake my head.

"No, Aswa-da, that little fucker, wasn't right. There are good people here, but I don't think there are enough."

"So maybe mankind needs a catalyst?" Sam's voice is still increasing in volume. A touch of sarcasm is hitting, but I let Sam say what he needs to say. "Oh yes, something like religious unification. A movement like Freedom Earth to push them once and for all out of their bloody default position!"

I cannot deny Sam's ability for flawless logic.

"Give peace a chance, eh?"

"You said it," replies Sam.

"No, you did. And much better than me."

I smile, realizing just how myopic and self-opinionated I've become. Sam is right. It's not my job to determine Earth's future. My role is to protect and help mankind reach their future. When I think about it, it all makes perfect sense. The signals are before me: the constant light positioning of the Balance, Freedom Earth bringing nations together, the purging of Al Nadir's evil on Earth, even the new energy Quantum Force that has the potential to stop wars fought over oil and pipeline dominance.

The signs tell me a change is coming for Earth.

I recall Ashton's words. *Change the world for good.*

Like human Sam, when he was in MI6, I have no choice but to do my job. I have to do my duty and give Ashton one-hundred-percent support.

As I reconcile myself to this notion, a fluttering sense of disquiet wells up within me for a second. But I dismiss it. I see it for what it is, an irrational fear borne of my need to justify my own existence with tales of Ashton's dark mechanics.

I look at Sam, arch an eyebrow, flick my head toward the bedroom, and then turn back, biting my bottom lip. Sam grips my waist tight and brings my body into his. I make a small jump and wrap my legs around him. My arms hang around his neck as his hands cup my ass.

Now our controversial conversation is over, our thoughts can turn to something much more stimulating.

Chapter 60

A great impetus had taken over Reverend Gregory. A natural momentum was created, and with it, a fervent energy to communicate with fellow brethren his newly acquired revelation. Reverend Gregory Forster took it upon himself to make the initial steps with his counterpart in the Catholic Church, the Most Reverend Matthew Knightly, Archbishop of Westminster.

Reverend Gregory's initial reaching out to Archbishop Knightly was at first greeted with cold apathy. Knightly had neither time nor inclination to pursue such fanciful notions as 'uniting the faiths'. Reverend Gregory persisted. Fresh in his mind was the meeting with Ashton's emissaries. He could feel their energies prickling the air around him still.

After his meeting with the PM, he'd been invited back the next day. Nothing had been said as to why. He had agreed without further consideration. The PM's private secretary had escorted him to the prime minister's private office. And there he'd been left, sitting on the sofa. Waiting.

The first five minutes had flown by. Reverend Gregory absorbed the room's details. A tidy bookcase of hardback first editions. A leather-topped desk and leather revolving chair. A credenza filled with ingredients to raise one's spirits. A low-level coffee table with a faint stain where someone had forgotten to use a coaster. An antique globe depicting a world that hadn't quite been fully discovered; 'here be monsters' circled where New Zealand was today. Gregory finished his examination, and looked at his watch, shook his head and wondered why he'd been summoned.

As the five minutes drifted to fifteen minutes, Reverend Gregory fidgeted on the sofa. He stood up, rolled the globe and snatched a furtive glance at the credenza, licking his lips and feeling thirsty. But then, resolute to keep a trusted position, he retired back to the sofa as he heard movement outside the door.

Ashton strolled in with a smug swagger. "Oh, they're not here yet?"

Reverend Gregory jumped to his feet on the PM's entry. His face reddened with a guilt only he knew. The PM noticed and smiled.

"Fancy a drink, Reverend?"

"Oh yes, please. Whiskey. What did you mean, they're not here yet?"

"Sam and Ellie Noor. My emissaries of God. They haven't yet arrived. I thought they'd be here by now."

Ashton poured two fingers of his finest pure malt and handed it to the grateful reverend. Just as Gregory clasped the glass, the air in the room seemed to awaken, like something had stimulated it, and right in front of him, a sparkling aura appeared. Gregory held the glass, transfixed by the sight. Before his eyes, the aura solidified into two shapes. The aura dissipated and what was left were two stunning humanoid forms.

In shock, Gregory's hand failed, and his glass headed for the floor.

The female leaped out with a speed that couldn't be captured by human eyes, and the glass nestled comfortably in her strong hand.

"Hello, Reverend Gregory. Pleased to meet you. I'm Ellie and this is Sam, and this is your glass," announced the female humanoid known as Ellie. She returned the glass to his hand.

Gregory sat back on the sofa. A heaviness washed over him. Numb and inert. His face impassive. His mind running hard to compute what he'd just experienced.

Ellie placed her hand out to touch his knee in a gesture of reassurance, but it caused him to shake.

"Reverend Gregory," began Ashton, "these are the emissaries I told you about. You requested a meeting before starting with my work to unify religion."

Reverend Gregory stared at Ellie and Sam, and then at Ashton.

"How…who…what…?" started Gregory. But he realized he was being unintelligible.

"I know, my friend, so many questions. But all you need to know is Ellie and Sam are our friends, and they have great plans for unifying religion under the banner of Freedom Earth, the banner of humanity itself." Ashton commanded immediate confidence and obedience in Gregory.

The archbishop breathed in, put his hands between his legs and bent forward toward Sam.

"Please, Sam, tell me more. I need to understand."

Sam nodded. If this man was to be brought into the confines of their secret work, he had to know a little more than them just being 'friends.'

"Reverend Gregory, we are from Kudamun, a place between what you understand as heaven and hell. We are responsible for managing the worlds in our care. Ellie and I have Earth in our care."

"Oh my God!"

All that Ashton said the day before slotted into place in his mind. The archbishop looked upon the humanoid forms introduced as Sam and Ellie with a reverent and new understanding. From the sofa where he sat, his legs fell down to the carpet. Before he could consider a more refined trajectory, his knees plopped with a thud to the floor. His arms reached up to the shining couple, his hands clasped together in prayer.

"Oh dear God, thank you for this revelation you have bestowed upon me."

He stumbled across the right words to say, and then lowered himself down to the floor, and prostrated himself in front of Sam, Ellie, and the PM.

The intensity of what the vision meant grew inside him, compounded by a lifetime of teachings, scriptures, and moments of uncertainty. So many times, he had questioned meaning; what was it all for? The pain and suffering of the many. Terrorism and capitalism in equal parts ripping the world to shreds. He wondered on the nature of the God he worshipped. Observing the most heinous of man's crimes, Gregory had escaped to a dark corner, the place in his mind where no light could penetrate, and there, he'd placed doubt on the deity's very existence. Allowance of such a wicked world to persist, giving way to the wretchedness of man, could only mean God himself had indeed turned his back on humanity. Surely, he had given up on his children and left them to run amok, left them shackled with a free will that brought only destruction and death.

Conviction in his faith slipped, and his journey for hope followed a path deep into a whiskey bottle. The transparency of his loss was masked by layers. He had created tautological contrivances and meaningless words like 'Praise the Lord!' and further slipped into an invented landscape. A wait for truth had gnawed on his soul.

Gregory drew a breath and pulled himself up to rest on his knees, his sight elevated to rest on Ellie.

"Why now?" he asked finally.

The question was addressed outward, but Gregory also asked it of himself. He recollected times when he'd needed restoration of his faith, but none had arrived. Had he delved so far into the abyss that an emissary of God was his only safety line? That assurance only made Gregory shiver with wonder. His faith flooded back to him in waves. He was bathed in their absolute munificence and bountiful promise.

Ashton watched Ellie as she shrugged, and muttered, "Why not?"

Her nonchalance was evident and embarrassing to the PM.

Sam smiled ruefully and stepped in.

"What Ellie means is, we care about this planet. Any time is a good time to introduce ourselves. But to answer your exact question, the prime minister here has set the Earth on a path of goodness with the development of Freedom Earth. We can see that unifying religions would be a step to greatness that we, and others like us, recognize as essential to planetary peace and harmony."

Sam's matter of fact delivery, touched with loaded precision, provided Gregory with the information he needed to support the PM's cause.

Ellie stared at her husband and shook her head slightly, as if annoyed that Sam had taken her pitch. She pushed forward and picked Reverend Gregory off the floor and helped him back to sit on the sofa. Gregory couldn't comprehend that he was actually being touched by God's emissary.

"You see, we've monitored a big change in Earth since Al Nadir has been removed," said Ellie. "This chap here, he's doing marvelous things. Aren't you, Rich? But he needed a bit of support, a guiding hand if you will. That's what we're here for."

Ellie sat back on the arm of the sofa and smiled at the PM, Gregory and, lastly, Sam. The PM smirked but Ellie knew he didn't like her disparaging tone. Gregory stiffened, not knowing quite what to do at being in such a close proximity to an angel. Sam glared at Ellie, his eyes telling her to behave. This marital interaction was lost to Gregory, who tried bravely to compute the fact he was in the presence of supreme beings.

Ashton walked over to Gregory. With eyes earnest and sharp, he locked Gregory into them. "You now understand why unification has to take place. And why you must help me on this mission. A mission that will change mankind's place in the Universe and deliver peace and harmony forever more."

"Of course, I…I…I…un-un-der-stand, Prime Minister," stuttered Gregory.

"Thank you, Reverend Gregory," said Ellie. She grasped his hand and held it. Gregory seemed to gain energy from the touch, for he stood up, straight and strong.

"I will be there for you, Prime Minister. I will help you make this unification happen. I cannot believe the incredible moment that I have been a witness to. But I will not fail you. Nor will I fail my God."

"Glad to hear it." Ashton looked at Ellie and Sam and nodded swiftly. It was their signal to depart.

"Reverend Gregory, it was lovely to meet you, but we have to leave now. We will see you again soon. You have our support whenever you need it." Ellie smiled and clutched Sam's hand.

Gregory and the PM watched as the air slipped and slid around Sam and Ellie, and their bodies infused with twinkling lights. Gregory could see the aura of light that surrounded them, and he knew without doubt that they were angels. In his mind was Matthew 17:2. *'And he was transfigured before them, and his face shone like the sun, and his clothes became white as light.'* Such a similar vision before him, Reverend Gregory, a mere mortal on earth, was too great. His body shook suddenly with thorough amazement.

The twinkling lights faded. The supreme beings had gone.

Gregory turned to Ashton. He was the portrait of a man vindicated from the guilt of uncertainty.

"Prime Minister, what you have revealed to me today will stay with me forever. I am your servant and shall do your bidding of whatever you may ask of me."

"Of course, you shall. I didn't expect anything less." The PM issued his customary smirk and placed his hand on Gregory's arm in a reassuring gesture.

A knock on the door shook Gregory back to the present moment.

His personal assistant showed in a portly gentleman in his mid-fifties. Although of somewhat stumpy build, his stature declared to the world his inner power. Dark brown eyes, serious and inquiring, stared out from the Most Reverend Matthew Knightly. He looked at his host, the Most Reverend Gregory. He obviously wondered what on Earth was so important that he was dragged out of the confines of his office.

Gregory opened his mouth to recount the experience he'd just recalled. As Knightly listened, he realized with a growing sense of wonder, of how so very important his visit had now become. He pledged his support on similar terms to that of Gregory to the PM. He must, before any further consultation was made with Rome, meet these 'supreme beings' and marvel with his own eyes at the miracle that had placed the Most Reverend Gregory on the path to religious unification.

"It shall be done."

Gregory smiled with warm satisfaction at his achievement.

Chapter 61

In times of chaos, unholy alliances are forged. Through a common purpose, atheist and faithful follower of God sat side by side. Communist values collided with the imperialist principles to create fellow comrades in arms. Non-believer and believer joined in one single goal.

Ashton must be stopped.

Prince Khalifa Butti Al Faisal, heir to the Al Faisal Saudi Arabian royal fortune, was the current mark of Ashton, the man who'd hustled Khalifa out of five billion pounds.

In anger, Khalifa had arranged through his GID to abduct Ashton. The plan was to then render him to his country where Ashton's life would have been slowly and excruciatingly extracted from him. But that didn't happen. His meticulous plan homing in on Ashton's weakness, his sexual ambivalence, something that Khalifa found repugnant, was to be the noose that would grip tight around the corrupt PM's neck.

Khalifa's GID best black ops guys had set the stage. Mike Hyde, founder of the Buzz Empire, philanthropist, and educational reform champion would be the enticement to entrap Ashton. Hyde's stunning good looks, his penchant for attractive gentlemen, and his bitterness at the establishment's ignorance of his success made him the ideal instrument for luring the PM.

Part of the plan had been executed. Ashton had been captured and held in Hyde's office. But something had happened in those minutes after Hyde closed the door. It had resulted in Hyde's death and the demise of almost all the Egyptian wet workers GID had called in. The remaining mercenary fell into Ashton's clutches, where intelligence had been quite literally ripped from him. Or so Khalifa could suppose, given the inference Ashton made when he'd presented the vase and the ashes it contained.

Khalifa knew Ashton was a man who didn't recognize political boundaries. He had no limits. Khalifa's last run-in with the PM stated he was much more than a preening, posturing politico. His GID found nothing on the man. He was a lawyer, then a journalist, then a politician. Just as they always seemed to be, thought Khalifa with rye retrospection. But none had behaved like Ashton. A breed apart, his arrogance and the sum of not just political power showed that Ashton possessed much more.

Khalifa settled back into the cushion of the luxurious sofa and stared out at the early dawn sneaking across London's rooftops, with the stealth of a tomcat weaving amongst chimneys. Its silent approach, a mask to what lay ahead, was unknown and unforgiving, but relentless in its pursuit to deliver. Movement swayed his eyes away from the glass wall of the penthouse.

A man the size of hill sat down in the chair next to him and grunted, shifting its hulking frame. On top of that enormous body perched a ball, and inside it, a sharp but constrained brain. The hill snorted:

"This PM, it's like he's running his own fiefdom. There're crime lords in Russia with less cajones than Ashton!"

The hill's voice was a deep resonating grumble, like iron machinery turning gradually clicking into gear. Khalifa nodded and shuffled uncomfortably in his seat. Sophisticated eliteness was his usual environment; he wasn't used to rougher characters. The hill moved and revealed its true identity as General Gregor Ivanov, Russian ambassador to the UK and station chief for the GRU. The Glavnoje Razvedyvatel'noje Upravlerije, or GRU, was Russia's external military intelligence equivalent of the CIA or MI6.

Ivanov gripped Khalifa's arm and deepened his stare. With eyes of solid dark blue, piercing and naturally interrogative, he examined rather than looked at a person. He couldn't casually observe, even if he wanted to. Trained to intimidate and elicit information, his stance was rough and brutal, and diametrically opposed to that of Khalifa's slender, aloof deportment. Ivanov gripped Khalifa's knee and the Saudi prince winced instinctively.

"You know, he says to me, 'Gregor, it's time for Russia to step aside and make way for a new energy powerhouse!' And then he smiled. A real snake."

"More like a hyena. He's always smiling."

"But what can we do? He's prime minister. You made a play and it failed. His security is too tight for a simple kidnapping."

"He has to have a vulnerable spot. His family? His wife? Daughters?" said Khalifa.

But Ivanov grimaced and shook his head. "No love lost between Ashton and his wife. He'd be pleased to be rid of her. Same goes for his daughter, Abigail. GRU has her as wayward, an alcoholic and a junkie. We'd be doing the bastard a favor if we got rid of her! The other daughter is just a child. And I'm not in that kind of business. But perhaps..."

Ivanov leaned forward, thinking. He grabbed the vodka bottle and poured a hefty dose, and slug it back almost without breathing.

"No. Too risky."

Khalifa watched as Ivanov tipped a further three-finger measure and knocked it back in one. Ivanov didn't react. Khalifa considered perhaps alcohol made up more of the fluids in his body than water.

"So, it's him," said Khalifa. "We've got to break *him*. He's the one we're after, not his family. There has to be a way."

Ivanov drew forward and grasped Khalifa's knee again in fierce excitement, as a thought popped up like a bubble in champagne. Khalifa shuddered, sensing the brutal power beneath the Russian's hand.

"Comrade, I think I know how we can capture this snake."

Khalifa leaned in to hear the suggestion, and on listening, he smiled.

"It just may just work, but your people must be kept to a minimum. Would your man be compliant with this arrangement?"

"Compliant? Are you joking? We *make* him compliant. This is for Mother Russia!"

"And for my glorious Kingdom of Saudi Arabia!"

Ivanov nodded and poured yet another significant dose of vodka into the two glasses. Khalifa leaned forward and grasped the glass. Ivanov's massive hand gripped around his own. He rose it up and chinked loudly with the prince's.

"Death to the traitorous pig!"

Chapter 62

Ashton permitted himself a moment to relax and contemplate next steps. Alone in his private office in Downing Street, he'd instructed Cumberford to leave and hold back any visitors. He wanted to glimpse quietness amongst the whirring wheel of government. Over the past few days, he'd been a very busy man. All the main denominations of the Christian Church had now been engaged. Through his first believer, Reverend Gregory, the word had been taken out to the rest of the leaders in the Christian faith. Calculated and crafted, these entrees spread through all corners of the Church and the PM rapidly received overtures from other Christian leaders.

Ashton knew that, during this period of reaching out, the specifics of the 'revelation' were omitted. But the official gossip, steeped in loaded expressions of 'life-changing experience' and 'faith affirming truth', brought forth interest. The phrases were cryptic enough to create a fervor of intrigue and a desire to participate in the PM's work.

Then, once they had agreed, Ashton switched on the angelic sightings like a conveyor belt of belief. Methodist, Presbyterian, Baptist, Reform and so many more, all came through Ashton's private office to meet with God's emissaries, Sam and Ellie. Everyone acknowledged the miracle of their arrival. Ashton smirked hard, loving the power his association with the Kudamaz couple bestowed on him. Delivery of the truth had been turned into a sausage factory of salvation. In they came, confused and afraid; out they went, converted and amazed.

Which one would he focus on next, Judaism or Islam? Ashton considered that both religions were going to require careful handling. But once he'd secure their commitment, he'd be in a position of strength. He wanted all faiths, at least the Abrahamic ones, to be united by June 1. After that, he could work through the other religions. The bulk of Christianity, Judaism, and Islam behind him would power his engagement with the rest.

Ashton pressed the button on his phone. "Cumberford, come in here."

Redfern had organized the first religious engagement, but once the archbishop had been nabbed, Ashton saw no need in having his Cabinet secretary undertake the menial task of arranging meetings, and he had reassigned the duty to Cumberford, his PPS.

Cumberford entered on instruction and stood to attention, awaiting Ashton's word.

"Ah, Cumberford, good. Arrange for the Chief Rabbi, Jacob Newton, to meet with me immediately."

"Yes, Prime Minister, immediately," stated Cumberford, and he clicked his heels and left to carry out Ashton's instruction.

Cumberford rang through to the private secretary in the office of Chief Rabbi Newton.

"Chief Rabbi Newton would be grateful of more information. As much as he is honored to receive a private audience with the prime minister, he has many calls on his time."

Cumberford bristled at the suggestion that Rabbi Newton had something more important to do than meeting with the PM. "I'm not sure you understand. The prime minister is not making an invitation that comes with an RSVP. This isn't a choice, but a command."

The voice on the other end spluttered slightly on hearing the arrogance of the prime minister's staff. "Command! I'm not sure that-"

Cumberford ripped through with savage gusto. "You're not sure that your master wouldn't want to attend the PM's meeting, especially given the momentous information that will be imparted?"

Cumberford knew from previous experience of setting up other such meetings that all the religious leaders emerged quite different from the person they went in as. Such a transformation illustrated the gravity of this union, and the reason for any religious leader to accept the PM's invitation.

"Momentous information," repeated the chief rabbi's private secretary. Caution now sounded in his previously pious and condescending voice

"Quite so. Life-changing, I've heard. Certainly, something that your master wouldn't want to miss. Goodness knows what would happen to a chap like you if this opportunity was made forfeit due to inadequate diary planning."

An uncomfortable laugh and then a snort, although derisory in its delivery, held no value in belittling the PM's PPS. Cumberford knew the game was over.

"So shall we say seven tonight at Number 10?"

It was a statement of fact, not an offer.

The chief rabbi's private secretary sighed with resolute weariness. "Seven tonight, of course. I'll clear Chief Rabbi Newton's diary accordingly."

"Much obliged, old chap!"

Ashton stood smirking in the doorway just behind Cumberford's desk. "Bit mulish, was he?"

Cumberford flipped a look back, shaking his head defiantly. He was not about to let the PM see he couldn't handle the making of a simple appointment.

"Yes, I've heard the chief rabbi's boy is a bit of a prickly little upstart. No match for you, eh, Cumberford? Rip him a new one if he didn't comply with you, wouldn't you?"

Ashton's smirk slipped into a wider grin as he weighed up his PPS's capability in the political arena.

"Absolutely, Prime Minister. I put him firmly in his place."

"Thought so. What time is my meeting then?"

"Here at seven tonight."

Ashton's eyebrow raised with admiration and he playfully punched Cumberford's shoulder. "Good man. That's what I like, no hanging around. Get to the action pretty damn quick."

Cumberford blushed, partly from Ashton's contact and partly from the embarrassment that his deeply hidden feelings toward the PM would be revealed unexpectedly.

Ashton did indeed notice but masked his recognition swiftly with a sideways sweep. His habitual smirk was still in play on his face. So, not just Jensen then, old bean. And he basked in Cumberford's secret adoration.

Chapter 63

Seven on the dot and Redfern still remained in the office, hanging around and appearing to look nonchalant. But he sat with silent determination. Ashton still hadn't confided in him as to the rationale behind the religious engagements. Redfern considered confronting Ashton about these meetings, but the moment to enquire proved elusive.

Ashton emerged from his private office. "Any sign of the rabbi?"

"No, Prime Minister. Nothing so far."

"Right, oh well. I'll be in here." Ashton attempted to duck back into his private office.

"Prime Minister?" interjected Redfern.

The PM stopped. "Yes, what is it?"

"Prime Minister, what are all these religious meetings about?"

Ashton stared at Redfern, reading his face. A slight twitch underneath his right eye denoted uncomfortableness. He'd expected Ashton to have advised him of the strategy behind the religious meetings before now. So, as the knowledge hadn't been proffered, Redfern felt awkward and somewhat piqued. The fact that he had to resort to confronting the PM directly triggered further annoyance.

Ashton could also see Redfern's imagined horror of having to deal with a refusal to offer an explanation, an action Redfern knew the PM was perfectly entitled to do.

"Why do you think I'm holding them?" Ashton questioned back to Redfern.

"I'm not sure, Prime Minister. Some kind of interfaith initiative? A way of building bridges?"

Ashton's sturdy eye never blinked as Redfern started his hypothesis. "Go on."

"Well, Prime Minister, could it be that you want to find common ground to bring the religions on the same page?"

Ashton made a slow clap. "Very perceptive, Redfern. I congratulate you."

A ripple of a blush appeared on Redfern's cheeks and then vanished as he composed himself. He gave a short nod in the PM's direction.

"It was the only conclusion, Prime Minister."

"Actually, Redfern, it wasn't. But let's leave that aside. My plan is to unify religion. All religions under one single banner: Freedom Earth. They can still continue with their separate faiths, but all religions must subscribe to the overarching ideology of Freedom Earth."

"And how is that going, Prime Minister? I can't imagine it has been easy."

"It's going very well. Rather smoothly. And I don't foresee any problems tonight either."

Redfern tilted his head. Inquisitive but brooding eyes stared hard at the PM. "How do you do it?"

"Do what?"

"Convince them."

"Ah, that's my little secret. For now, anyway." Ashton touched the side of his nose. "It'll all come out shortly, but-"

Redfern nodded abruptly. "I understand, Prime Minister."

"Listen, be a good chap and show Chief Rabbi Newton in when he arrives. I've got to pop back in and prepare for my guests."

Redfern listened and wondered if he'd misheard. "Guests, Prime Minister?"

A short, slightly rotund individual sauntered into the office and stole Ashton's attention. "Oh, Prime Minister, a delight to see you again," said the man.

Ashton took the outstretched hand and grasped it with warm affection.

"Chief Rabbi Newton, so good of you to make time in your busy schedule. Come, we have much to discuss."

Ashton swiped a look over his shoulder. "You can leave us now, Redfern. I can take things from here."

"Very well, Prime Minister, as you wish," muttered Redfern, standing up. His lower lip thinned and slipped in a scowl. He couldn't hide his disapproval of the PM keeping his cards close. He believed he'd been in the PM's confidence for almost everything. But this situation proved him wrong.

Ashton ushered the rabbi into his private office, smirking.

"So, Prime Minister, what is it you'd like to discuss?"

Ashton approved of Chief Rabbi Newton's forthright approach. He deserved an equally blunt response.

"Religion. I'm unifying all the faiths, starting with the Abrahamic ones, and then the rest."

Ashton examined Rabbi Newton's expression. He didn't expect the facial explosion that followed.

"You're not serious! Unify us with Christianity, Islam, Sikh, Hindu? Oh my word, even Buddhism! Oh dear, oh dear." The rabbi spluttered and laughed until tears dripped down his face. Ashton didn't respond, he let the rabbi continue his targeted ridicule. "Prime Minister, I had expected an entertaining evening, but I hadn't expected stand-up comedy!"

Ashton wandered over to the drinks cabinet, poured two brandies and handed one to the rabbi.

"You know, Rabbi Newton, that was exactly what I expected. Those before you acted the same way. Derisory quips. Mentally-ill innuendo. Oh yes, I've had all those responses. That was until they had seen the truth, until they had witnessed the power of God."

"Witnessed the power of God?" repeated the rabbi, placing his glass down. A look at the PM told him this wasn't a jolly jape. "What do you mean?"

"Haven't you wondered about life? What is it all for? What is God's plan? Haven't you ever thought what it must be like to have the knowledge of God? Not knowledge of the belief that He exists, but actual proof. A knowledge of God that is irrefutable and complete. I can give you that tonight. But you must give me something in return."

Ashton delivered each word with a simple tone. He didn't place emphasis on one word more than another. Their content was sufficient to build the gravity of the message inside the rabbi. As if coming to his own conclusion, the rabbi shook his head.

"No, no. What you say isn't possible. If this was the moment, then it would be the time, but we can't be in the Messianic era. All signs show it isn't yet."

"What if the signs haven't been read correctly? What if you didn't have the knowledge to read them or interpret them until now? Until this moment. Tonight. I can introduce you to God's messenger, his Mal'akh who comes from a world beyond our reality. They watch us. They weigh our acts, good and evil. And we are constantly judged."

Rabbi Newton remembered the words of the Torah. The continued insistence within them alluding to: *"realities far above and beyond our material existence."*

"Beyond our reality?" The rabbi shivered, repeating the PM's words.

"Yes, in a place between what is understood as heaven and hell. But it's beyond our understanding. They live with us but beyond us. That is what I have been told. To know more, you will have to speak to them."

"Them?" whispered the rabbi, as if a higher pitch of sound could break the magic that the PM was weaving.

"Yes, the emissaries, or messengers of God. They're coming here tonight."

"They exist? You know them? You speak to them?" Rabbi Newton grabbed hold of Ashton's arm. "Tonight!" he shouted, as the PM's final word broke through, mapping out a new level of consciousness that he neither expected nor was prepared to receive.

"Of course, tonight. It is God's emissaries who requested the religions to unify. So horrified are they by our constant wars, they want it all to stop. Otherwise, they'll act. Remember when the sky turned red in March?"

The rabbi recalled the terrifying vision. His congregation of believers filled the synagogue that evening. Everyone believing judgement of their sins would be made that night. He'd prayed and read scriptures. He'd tried to keep their spirits up, to uphold their belief in goodness and faith.

He'd claimed, "Whatever the outcome, salvation awaits us, and we should not fear the anger in the skies." But fear had remained in their eyes. And nothing couldn't shift it.

Overcome, still remembering, his throat dried and he choked up.

Ashton laid his hand on top of the rabbi's.

"It's okay to be emotional. It could've been the end for all of us." Ashton watched the rabbi dab tears from his eyes with his hankie.

"Want to know what stopped our destruction?" Ashton shot a glance at the rabbi. His face, now drained, resembled a headstone in the cemetery. "I mediated for mankind. Freedom Earth is the movement *they* wanted, to bring humanity into the next phase of their journey, the next stage of enlightenment. To feel the harmony of true unity, of true love for one another. Join me, Rabbi Newton. Agree that you will support me in unifying religion. Accept their call."

Before the rabbi could answer, something happened. His mouth dropped open and his eyes glazed over with confusion and awe. Behind the PM, the air sparkled with particles of light and reality dissolved in the area inside the particles. Within the light, something was forming.

Ashton smiled as he took in the reaction of the rabbi. Sam and Ellie had arrived. He flicked a look behind him.

"Oh, they're here. Chief Rabbi Jacob Newton, may I introduce Sam and Ellie, emissaries of God."

Chief Rabbi Newton stared, dumbstruck. It was all too much. Here he was, a humble rabbi, being graced with the presence of angels, just like the prophets of old. His body suddenly couldn't hold him. His head swam in a giddy state and he tumbled forward.

Ellie moved to steady him, and he straightened himself in her arms. Eyes of brilliant, unnatural blue looked down at him and the shining face smiled. Rabbi Newton absorbed this vision and slumped again. His befuddled brain failed to compute the experience.

"Goodness, Ashton, get this man a brandy!" quipped Ellie, suppressing a giggle.

Sam shot a disapproving glare, and Ellie feigned ignorance. She slipped to the side and pulled the rabbi up to a seated position.

Sam settled in on the other side of Rabbi Newton and nudged him gently. "Rabbi Newton, have a drink. We've much to talk about."

The smell of the brandy tickled the hairs in Rabbi Newton's nose, and his olfactory system kicked in. His eyes snapped open and he pushed down in the seat, half backing away in alarm, as one of the angels moved the glass to his lips.

"Oy vey! What is happening? Who are you?" Rabbi Newton cast a perplexed look from Ellie to Sam and finally to Ashton. "I mean, what are you? Messengers? More like magicians, sheez!"

Ashton smiled, indicating to his emissaries to deliver their enlightened view to Rabbi Newton.

Sam edged a little into the corner of the sofa to get a better angle in which to address the Rabbi.

"Rabbi Newton, I'm sorry we scared you. That was never meant to be. As the prime minister explained, we and others like us want to guide humanity's next step. It's a move that will place Earth on a path of planetary peace and harmony. Freedom Earth started this evolution in motion. But the completed unification of religion would recognize humanity's elevation to a higher level of consciousness. A place of greater awareness, of understanding, where suffering and pain would be overshadowed for wonder and light."

Rabbi Newton listened and trembled, not knowing whether he should interrupt. The message these 'angels' delivered told of incredible things. But despite what he'd seen, their mind-expanding entrance, could he really believe from just the first sight of their being? As the initial shock started to wear off, Rabbi Newton's analysis quickened. Ashton's theatrics in politics were well known. Maybe, somehow, it was all smoke and mirrors.

He noticed the female. Ellie turned to him and smiled. He couldn't place the reason, but her smile alone comforted him. Until she spoke.

"You don't believe us, do you? You still think we're fake. That this is all smoke and mirrors, created by Ashton to trap you."

Rabbi Newton sipped at his brandy, but Ellie's examination of his inner thoughts caused him to splutter. He couldn't fail to hide his surprise. A good parlor trick if ever he'd seen one.

Ashton remained quiet as he observed Ellie slip into action.

"You broke your left ankle when you were seven. You fell off your bike, and although you went to hospital, the bone never quite aligned, giving you a faint limp you now carry."

Although amazed by the detailed research Ashton had done, the rabbi knew having this information didn't mean she was God's emissary.

"You're right, and so? What does that mean to you?"

"Nothing. But the limp means much to you. All your life, you've tried to walk tall, but that limp has stunted your confidence. Isn't it time you had a confidence booster?" Ellie dropped to the floor and placed her hands around the rabbi's ankle. She rubbed it for a mere few seconds. Heat exuded and the bone clicked into place.

"Stand up," said Ellie.

Rabbi Newton stood with shaky hesitation.

"Now turn your left ankle."

Rabbi Newton acted on Ellie's instruction. The continual ache he'd had throughout his days had vanished. Aligned once again correctly, his ankle was perfect. The knowledge threw him off balance. Awash with sudden uncertainty as to his place in the Universe, and what this 'miracle' meant, he sat down again heavily.

"I d-d-don't understand. How did you do that?" stuttered the rabbi.

"I can't explain. But I need you to believe us."

Dazed by what he'd witnessed, Rabbi Newton nodded.

Ellie slid back beside the rabbi, and Sam jumped into the discussion.

"Rabbi Newton, we are from Kudamun, a place outside of your reality, between what has been described by humans as heaven and hell. But it's much more complex than that. We are responsible for managing the worlds in our care. Ellie and I have Earth in our care, and we want Earth to achieve its new ambition. The path of true enlightenment. Will you help us? Will you help Prime Minister Ashton unify religion?"

Rabbi Newton, still in analysis mode, realized his first conjecture had been correct. Around him were angels from a place beyond human understanding. *Beyond our material existence*, he thought, as the words of the Torah, the Teaching, came back in floods to him. And they had sought him out. Of all the rabbis in the world, he had been chosen. They'd cured him of an affliction that had ailed him all of his life, and made him complete. They had given him the truth and brought alive the words of the Teaching. They'd opened his eyes and his heart to the wondrous Godliness that this truth delivered, and given him the ability to discern meaning of a reality beyond the mortal plane. Overwhelmed by this knowledge, Rabbi Newton sobbed his reply.

"I will be there for you. For all of you. This gift you have given me, I cannot describe…I will be your servant forever. I will be your mouthpiece. I shall stand by you, Prime Minister, in this time of transformation."

Ellie nodded and placed a hand softly on the rabbi. "Thank you. Earth thanks you. We thank you, all of us."

Ashton breathed deep and looked down, hiding a smug smile. Not as difficult as he'd expected. But then, he thought, when you have miracle-making 'angels' on your side, nothing ever will be.

Chapter 64

"I don't expect you to know, but what you're doing is destroying my son. You need to find somewhere but my son, Xiao, is not that place."

Lei sat in the chair beside Xiao. She still found it heart-breaking to look at him. All those tubes, monitors and machines, she knew they were all that kept her son from passing over. But they symbolized a lack of everything. A lack of his movement, his smile, even his sulky voice. She longed to hear his voice.

"Please, help me." Lei slipped down, out of the arm chair and onto the floor. Her hand went up in prayer, and then she took her son's limp, lifeless hand in hers and imagined his body encased in love.

She didn't really know what she was doing. Ever since that frank and revealing exchange with her husband just over a week before, in which Chen had confirmed his son could really see the darkness within him, she'd been obsessed with contacting the force inside of Xiao.

And persuading it to leave.

Every day since May 8, Lei had made the trip from her home in Berkley Square to Cromwell Hospital to pray and plead for her son's freedom. Sometimes Chen joined her, when his fashion empire didn't call on his time, although Lei knew he had more than enough capable lieutenants to enable his time out.

Today, her driver brought her alone.

"Please, I beg you. Whatever you are, I feel you are good. So you must see what you're doing to this fragile child is wrong."

Lei closed her eyes as she felt the tears come again. She held Xiao's hand, but desperation started to seep into Lei's address.

"Why won't you speak to me? Say something. Do something!"

Lei gripped Xiao's hand tighter.

"I know you can hear me."

She hoped she was right.

"Xiao loves life. He loves every part of it."

Lei tried to calm her voice. She breathed, deep and slow, and pushed a soft comforting tone, as she opened up a window on Xiao's life.

"All that trashy junk food, addictive, immersive reality games, loud bass-dominated rock bands, all the sports, cricket, tennis, football, boy is he a big Chelsea supporter, social media stuff, the Snapchating and Instagraming, that's his life. Of course, he's not an easy little boy. He can be precocious and obstinate. And he's often moody and rude. And a darn great handful. But when he laughs, he can light up a room."

Lei remembered all the birthday parties and sleepovers, and times when he just brought all his mates from public school to stay without telling her. 'Mum's really cool, she'll be fine.' That had been his mantra. With her, he could pretty much get away with anything.

"He loves life and now he needs his life back."

Lei waited before continuing. She hoped she'd said enough to provoke a reaction. She hadn't considered what reaction that could be, or whether it would be safe for her son.

Lei suddenly felt reckless. She stared at Xiao's body, still, almost deathly. Whatever was in Xiao hadn't responded to anything. It had all been Xiao-centric. She had to try a different tact.

"I know you entered Xiao in Sharm El Sheikh. I saw my son come out of the water dry and glowing. I don't why you chose my son. Perhaps he was just there, and it was an opportunity for you. What are you? An ancient spirit? Another being from another place? Another world? Why did my son see my husband's darkness? How could he see something unseen? Was that you? Have you given him a power but he's too young to take it? And that's why he got sick? Or are we humans unable to take the power, irrespective of age?"

Lei searched up and down Xiao's immobile body for an indication.

In anguish, Lei lent forward and placed her hands upon Xiao's shoulders. She looked quickly around for any medical staff. Seeing none close by, she gripped hold of her son's shoulders and shook him hard. Tubes bounced up and down, and Xiao's torso shuddered under the force applied by Lei.

Through gritted teeth she hissed, "Tell me! What do you want?"

She still didn't fully comprehend what she thought she believed. A benevolent force inside her son's body.

Lei waited for a reaction.

Nothing.

Only the slow beep beep of the monitors and the deep pumping wheeze of the artificial respirator.

Then Lei stared at the life-signs monitor, and her eyes grew wide in disbelief.

For a second, she thought she could see a single word appear on the monitor screen.

As the heavy beating of her forlorn heart took over, Lei realized she'd either made contact, or else she was really quite insane.

Chapter 65

Ashton's face turned down into a bitter scowl as he listened to his White House spy, Nate Van der Maart, give news of President Hutchinson's intransigence. The president had failed to fully embrace Quantum Force, despite telling Ashton that he was behind him and the revolutionary energy source one hundred percent.

"He seems to think that maybe a more controlled rollout would be more sensible." Van der Maart trembled as he spoke, and Ashton detected the slight warble in his voice. He bit back annoyance at Van der Maart's sudden weakness, a weakness he'd never, up until that point, displayed.

"What are you going to do?"

"I'm not sure. His arguments are pretty sound. Even the science guys here agree."

Ashton could feel a snarl forming inside his throat. He breathed deep, controlling his anger, and channeled it to only grip his burner phone tighter.

"You know, this is the first time your task hasn't been accomplished. Do you remember our discussion?"

Ashton heard Van der Maart's breath quicken and knew he remembered the price of failure.

"I know, I know," stuttered Van der Maart. The assured cadence that he carried in all political discussions had decayed.

"I don't want to institute such measures, but I will if you can't get things back online."

"I understand."

The line suddenly descended into silence. Ashton could almost hear his spy's synapses firing as he imagined those measures.

"Has there been independent testing?" Ashton asked, breaking the cerebral pause.

"Erm, yes, and all was positive for energy generation. But as I say, some channels are advocating a phased rollout. Maybe starting with the Eastern Seaboard cities first, instead of the blanket approach you guys are undertaking."

Ashton considered Van der Maart's words. It was clear their rationale was accurate and in point of fact, their action was absolutely correct, but it wasn't the action he needed.

"Okay, so you tell Hutchinson this. Quantum Force is perhaps the most significant discovery in the history of mankind. All of us leaders have a duty to pioneer this revolutionary energy, enable our peoples to gain the benefits, and feel the true wonder of this incredible power."

Ashton heard Van der Maart intake his breath a few times, and then he breathed slower, as he concentrated on the PM's instructions.

"I understand, sir."

"If you can't do this, it will mean a flight out for me. And for you."

Van der Maart crumbled as the meaning of Ashton's words left no wriggle room for other interpretation.

"I will turn things. I promise you."

"Excellent. And I'll keep your hardware fixations tucked up safe and sound."

"Sir, after this, can I have the materials?"

Ashton smiled. *Bold little fellow.*

"And why should I give you the materials?"

"Well, then I would have done this for you. Quantum Force, it's going to make you, well, very wealthy. And, I thought, maybe, erm, you could reward me."

"Reward you?" said Ashton. "An interesting concept. But no, afraid not!"

"Oh," muttered Van der Maart.

"I will, of course, keep everything for you securely locked away with my impenetrable security. The best money can buy. My gift to you."

Ashton smirked, listening to Van der Maart snuffle and attempt to stand up against the PM's recalcitrance. It wasn't happening.

"Sir, erm, that's very-"

"Generous. Yes, I thought so."

The line again dropped to silence, and for a second, Ashton thought Van der Maart had just left, but he could still hear a slight hiss of his spy's labored breathing. Ashton waited and didn't press engagement.

"So, I'll do what is required."

"Good chap. It needs to happen soon. By the end of this week. Can't delay. Too much to do. Understand?"

Ashton's last word, delivered with an ice-sharp tone smacked against Van der Maart's ear. Encased within it was a brutal intonation of what would follow if he failed.

"Yes, sir. I understand."

Ashton pressed the call off and stood up. If that little White House twat couldn't spin the president, everything would take so much longer. Time, he just didn't have.

Chapter 66

Cumberford reviewed the list. From the Christian faiths, almost all had pledged their allegiance and commitment to the prime minister. The leader of the Russian Orthodox, Bishop Mikhael Litinov, hadn't responded. His PA had said he'd been out of the country but would respond on his return.

He cast his eye over another name on the list, Dr. Adnan Al Shirawi, head of the Muslim Council of Britain. He wasn't exactly the voice of Islam, as the faith didn't have the equivalent of an archbishop or chief rabbi to speak out for all Muslim people in Britain. However, in lieu of such a role, Dr. Al Shirawi was the best possible person to meet with the prime minister. Cumberford realized that he hadn't received a confirmed meeting date from Dr. Al Shirawi either. His deputy had excused his lack of RSVP due to overseas travel.

Annoyed by yet another religious leader giving him the runaround, Cumberford snatched up his phone and stabbed the numbers with building irritation.

"Dr. Al Shirawi does appreciate the prime minister's invitation and he will endeavor to meet with him on his return."

"I should hope so!" snorted Cumberford. "This meeting is of the greatest importance. Continuance of Dr. Al Shirawi's position is predicated on his attendance."

The deputy head took immediate umbrage at Cumberford's insinuation.

"I fail to see how non-attendance would affect Dr. Al Shirawi's position. I find your attitude most impertinent!"

"You can find my attitude any way you wish. The fact remains that failure to attend this meeting will result in a reallocation of power within the Council. And do not question how it will be done, only understand that it will happen if Dr. Al Shirawi doesn't meet with Prime Minister Ashton immediately on his return."

Cumberford's well-honed diplomacy flew out of the window. Throughout the days of the Al Nadir, he'd harbored a soul-eating hatred of Muslims. Al Nadir wasn't a religious terrorist organization. It was, if anything, far removed from any theological ideology except for greed and ultimate domination. But Al Douri had funded those terrible Islamic fundamentalist regimes, just as he'd funded drug lords, prostitution kings, people smugglers, country-wide organized crime syndicates, and secret cells within global intelligence agencies including the CIA, Mossad, Interpol, MI5, and MI6. Al Douri had gone to bed with anyone who could underpin his aim to destabilize global economies to assist his own megalomaniacal goal: holding the world to ransom.

Cumberford realized his hatred was misplaced, but he couldn't hold back on the temptation to paint everyone connected with the Islamic religion in Al Nadir's deathly abyss of black.

A brief sigh sounded, followed by an indignant "Well, I-"

The rest of the sentence failed to form as Cumberford interjected the deputy with a sharp, acidic, "Yes!"

The deputy head sighed again, and by this, Cumberford knew acquiescence was close.

"Right, well, I see. Yes, of course, Dr Al Shirawi will make the meeting with the prime minister."

"On his immediate return?"

"Yes. Absolutely."

"And when might that be? It would be most helpful if it was very soon," said Cumberford, not relinquishing his dogged approach to secure a diary date.

"Then I think I can be very helpful. Dr. Al Shirawi is returning tomorrow."

"Excellent! Tomorrow evening. 8 p.m. Private office at Number 10."

"Dr. Al Shirawi will be delighted."

"Of course he will," replied the self-assured Cumberford. His superciliousness couldn't be disguised.

As Cumberford replaced the receiver, Ashton emerged from his office staring at papers in his hand. He looked up with casual interest.

"How's it going then, old chap?" Ashton sidled round Cumberford's desk and stared at him piercingly with his startling hazel eyes as if they were deep syringes into Cumberford's uncomfortable orbs.

"Extremely well, Prime Minister," said Cumberford, looking away from Ashton's alarming glare to review his notes. "Dr. Al Shirawi, head of the Muslim Council of Britain, is meeting you here tomorrow at eight. He's been in Abu Dhabi on business, apparently."

Ashton smirked derisively. "Always an excuse for that sort. Any luck with the commies?"

Cumberford nodded. "Yep. Just about to chase up on Bishop Mikhael Litinov, leader of the Russian Orthodox Church in the UK. Once he's done, all Christian denominations would have been seen by you. Assuming the Muslims play ball, that'll complete the Abrahamic faiths. Shall I focus on bringing in the Sikh, Buddhist, and Hindu leaders?"

Cumberford's distaste at the thought of such individuals given passage to the inner sanctum of Number 10 was hard to miss. Ashton certainly didn't.

"Look, old chap, I know it's not the cricket we usually play, but we have to be amenable to these types. Keep on going with the religions. Absolutely no let-up! I want them all behind me when the announcement is made in July."

Ashton realized he'd revealed a fraction too much. Cumberford's eyes widened as broad as dinner plates.

"Announcement, Prime Minister? What are you announcing?"

"I'll explain in good time. For now, those meetings with the remaining religious leaders need to happen quickly. You're a good man, Cumberford. You've done well in a short time. Don't disappoint me."

Ashton reversed the inquiry so that Cumberford wasn't asking questions, but Ashton was demanding a certain outcome. He placed pressure on Cumberford to deliver but also pronounced a recognition that he held Cumberford in high regard, and that his conduct as his PPS was sound. But Ashton also made it clear that, should he fail to complete his task, his future prospects could be brought into question. All of this implied praise and threat through a few loaded words. Ashton's ability in subtle subversion was partly his cornerstone of political success.

Of course, the other side of his cornerstone was his own personal intelligence network, which fortified his position as a leader in government. It gave him the dirt on his respectable colleagues and revealed which individuals in all business sectors could enhance his standing, who could be used to influence decisions where and when necessary.

Ashton created his network soon after he'd left British Intelligence. Most of his network was made up of colleagues and associates from other intel agencies whom he'd met over the years. Extracurricular work was always sought after by retired operatives looking to bolster their pension pots. Ashton's new career as a lawyer frequently required surveillance. However, he kept his network in place more to support his political ambitions than to spy on the lives of those he was defending (although sometimes having that intel too paid off.) As a top city lawyer, money was in abundance and added to the sizable nest egg he'd accrued through his tradecraft and blackmail opportunities at countrywide levels.

Leaving to pursue a final career in journalism gave him the political connections he needed to cement his political goals. He used his acquired resources to fund his intel network, and through even more black off-the-books operations, even whilst as a journalist, funds poured in to expand his net even wider. His surveillance operations bore increasing fruit. By the time Ashton was elected Member of Parliament, a foregone conclusion given it had been a solid 'true-blue' Conservative seat almost since Pitt the Younger, his intelligence network covered four continents, and operatives were embedded in the heart of the biggest industry partners, political circles, and influencing institutions.

Over time, Ashton had acquired meaningful information enabling significant fast-tracking of his position from a lowly MP to Cabinet minister, and finally to prime minister in just six years.

It was perhaps the speed of Ashton's ascendency that made everyone cautious of him. Ashton was a formidable individual but still a man who kept his secrets close to him. Much was not known about Ashton, and it was this air of mystery that caused those around him to keep their interactions with him on a civil footing.

Cumberford, on hearing the PM's response, pulled back on any further quizzing as to the whys and wherefores of Ashton's game. Swiftly, he turned to the phone again, renewed with extreme confidence for being PM Ashton's 'good man', and called, on loudspeaker, the personal assistant to Bishop Litinov.

Niceties were in short supply as Cumberford plowed into the unsuspecting PA.

"The invitation by the PM was issued weeks ago. Your lack of a reply has now been taken as a personal affront to the prime minister and a sign of severe disrespect to our country. If Bishop Litinov does not support a meeting, Prime Minister Ashton will escalate this matter. And I have to say that, although both of us know that this isn't a matter for further concern, to other parties, this inaction may be construed as a diplomatic incident."

The PA harrumphed at the inference and muttered quicker than Cumberford knew he could speak.

"Bishop Litinov has been in Moscow for the whole of last week. His return is in two days' time. Please understand, Mr. Cumberford, that our activities should never be regarded as intentional. We respect your prime minister and your country. No disrespect was ever intended. It is just that Bishop Litinov's travel has prevented a fixed diary arrangement. Bishop Litinov is in the country on Thursday evening. His plane touches down at five. He would be pleased to welcome the PM to his office in Chiswick around seven. A traditional Russian feast will be laid on for the prime minister. The very best vodka, Stoli Elit, and our finest Beluga caviar will be offered as a token of thanks to Prime Minister Ashton for his understanding in this unfortunate matter and as an expression of our deep regard and admiration for your Prime Minister Ashton, and all of his great endeavors in creating Freedom Earth."

The PA's fawning gave rise to a begrudging smile on Cumberford's usually po-faced features. Two down, three more to go. Then he was through dealing with all those religious upstarts, posturing prats, and fanatical phonies. Then finally back to doing some serious work, giving hell to the likes of those who couldn't fight back.

Cumberford buzzed through to the PM to inform of the good news, but he'd already heard the discourse.

"I would have preferred the meeting with Litinov here. But if I have travel, that's fine. This is too important to quibble over a meet location. Stoli Elit Vodka and the Beluga always placates one having to travel!"

Cumberford heard the PM's usual smirk reflected in his voice. In auditory terms, it was a cross between a derisory snort and a condescending 'told you so' sigh. Undoubtedly, it was the PM's signature reaction to almost everything, and especially used, thought Cumberford, when matters pertaining to the PM didn't transpire quite as planned.

"You have a done a marvelous job. Now get your finger out and start chatting up the Buddhists. I want a meeting with the Dalai Lama. I'll go and see him, or if he's traveling, he can pop in here."

Cumberford stared at the intercom, his mouth drooping down. "You want to meet the Dalai Lama?"

In the doorway behind Cumberford, Ashton appeared. Cumberford turned around, staggered by the PM's stealth-like footwork that he didn't even sense, let alone hear.

"Of course, Cumberford, and close your mouth. The dumb catching-flies look is not becoming of you."

Cumberford shut his mouth, and his teeth whacked together as they caught in the closure. Ashton grimaced at the sound.

"Is there a problem?" Ashton glowered, and Cumberford crumpled, unable to meet the PM's eye.

"We don't usually engage with him. It's usually the Head of State. I'm not sure whether he'll entertain a meeting." Cumberford shirked back as he spoke.

Ashton nodded. A smug sneer drifted across his face. "You could be right, Cumberford. I'll go and see him. Get his buy-in to things directly."

"Shall I organize your plane, Prime Minister?"

Ashton placed his hand up, palm forward.

"No need. I have other travel arrangements," responded Ashton enigmatically. He delved into his inner pocket to retrieve his phone.

Cumberford stared at the door as it closed, but he was just able to snatch the first few words.

"Sam, hi. A little favor, if you wouldn't mind?"

Chapter 67

"Shut it off!"

I move out from underneath the covers in time to observe silk sheets slide softly down the contoured musculature of an arm. It reaches out to quell the incessant sound emanating from a bedside table. Seconds before, that arm had been wrapped around me. The owner of the arm was, of course, my sweet Sam.

The sheets slip further down my back, and I pull myself up.

"Tell him we're too busy to deal with his shit again!"

Sam flashes a look at me. I know he's taking in my mouthwatering figure and is considering that, maybe, my reaction is the right one, especially as Ashton is 'requesting a favor'.

I take the phone and press it on to speaker.

"Hope I didn't catch you at an awkward moment."

We hear Ashton's schoolboy snigger and Sam growls, "No, Prime Minister. As always, your timing is bloody impeccable."

Ashton ignores Sam's blatant sarcasm; he dives straight into the issue.

"We need to get the Buddhists on our side. The quickest way is to meet with the Dalai Lama in Dharamshala in India."

"Yes, okay. So why do you need us?" snaps Sam.

"I thought you may be able to use your transport system to get me quickly to Dharamshala?"

Sam raises an eyebrow. I thunder into his mind, 'He wants to shimmer with us. No, Sam, that's not on. He's got a plane. He can use that. We're not a fucking celestial taxi service!'

'Okay, okay, I heard you. But let's hear him out. There may be a reason for him wanting to shimmer there.'

'You are too bloody easy with him. He's a freeloader. You know that?'

"Sam, would that be okay?" says Ashton. "I'm sure if I appear to him with you both, he'll know that he has to support me. That connectedness stuff Ellie talks about, well, it's at the center of what Buddhists believe in. It should be an easy ride."

I listen to Ashton and shake my head. 'No way. He's turning us into a freak side-show. Like pulling a rabbit out of a hat, he's pulling us out every time he wants to impress or influence or manipulate. Not having it.'

"Can't you use your plane, sir?"

I home in on his resonance and SearchSight him. In my mind, Ashton bursts in. His mouth flips into a scowl, and he drums his fingers on the top of the desk. He's alone. The curtains in his private office are still drawn. The room has little illumination, save for the brass desk light. I wait for the PM to speak and listen as annoyance rings out in every syllable.

"I could, but I really don't have the time. I have a meeting with the president of the Sikh Council of the UK tonight. It's like I almost need to be in two places at once, and you're the only...people...who can deliver this dual location ability to me."

"Why the hurry? Can't you just take it slower? Go next week."

Ashton screws up his fist. Burning impatience is building up fast. He takes a breath and pauses as if centering his anger and then smiles sweeter than fondant icing.

"Look, yes, you're right. I could wait until next week. But every moment the world is not unified in religion under Freedom Earth is another moment when they are fighting, when there is bloodshed, torture, and death. Every moment wasted on facile matters of societal acceptance, touring schools, factories, going to marginals to boost influence and attraction to our party, even having meetings with my brain-dead Cabinet, all these things, they pale when seen with the eyes of someone who has already seen the truth. Don't you understand, Sam? When you and Ellie revealed to me who you are, what Kudamun is, why goodness and balance are so essential, my life took on a new meaning. I couldn't just go back to being Prime Minister Richard Ashton. This experience has touched my soul. Even if I wasn't in power, even if I was just an everyday chap on the street, I'd be compelled to drive this new beginning for Earth. In my life, I have done things that I'm ashamed of..."

Ashton stops, giving an opportunity for the words to sink into Sam. A flicker of a smirk flashes across his lips, and them solemnity casts across his face again.

Looking at Sam, I can see he is deep in his memories. Ashton hit a home run on the guilt field.

"I know you understand me when I say I want to put things right. Tell me, Sam, if you had your time again, wouldn't you want to make things go differently?"

Ashton's playing my husband. I can see it plainly. But Sam, by his thoughtful expression, can't.

'Sam, don't listen,' I tell him telepathically. 'He's regurgitating the past. A past that had to be. You know it's all predefined. Nothing could have been changed. Don't let him fool you.' I hope my words get through, as goodness knows, I'm shouting in my mind loud enough to be heard in China.

Sam doesn't respond back to me but continues to talk to Ashton.

"Prime Minister, I know better than most that life is predestined, and we follow the script that has been drafted for us all. Whatever you did, whatever we all did, we believed it was right at the time. We can't change a thing."

I notice Ashton's eyes glaze over as he remembers, and memories, clearly visceral and brutal, rip into his consciousness. Ashton submerges completely, caught in a mountain landslide of yesterdays. For a second, I believe Ashton has a shadow of remorse. His eyes, watery and distant, appear fixed on a point in the past. Tears bunch in the corners. Ashton blinks, and a teardrop wanders down his face. I watch with disbelief; nothing can deny he's revealing himself, his vulnerable hidden side. My observation suddenly feels wrong, like I'm violating a personal, intimate place, and having done so, I'm tainted, unclean as a result of my unwarranted inspection.

"Sam, is Ellie with you?"

Ashton asks the question unexpectedly. His face is thoughtful and questioning. Can he detect me SearchSighting him? His air is eerie, and he unnerves me. Sam looks around, indicating for me to speak. I nod.

"Hello, Ashton."

The second I speak, the PM pops out of my mind, and I'm left with just his voice.

"Ellie, my dear, you know that Earth needs a chance at peace. I've been a very bad man in my past, just like Sam."

My eyebrows raise as Sam shrugs with ambivalence. Ashton's honesty is refreshing, if nothing else.

"There's darkness in all of us Ashton," I reply.

"Yes, Ellie. But with Freedom Earth and full religious unification, that darkness will be flattened, making greater room for the glorious light. I can't turn the clock back, and Sam's right, what's done had to be done. But now I have in my grasp the way to create a future filled with love and goodness. And the quicker this is realized, the better it will be for all of humanity."

Sam tips his head to one side and shrugs. Ashton certainly has a strong case.

"Yes, Ashton, I can see that. It's just your urgency…it seems odd," I venture slowly.

"Odd?" he repeats. "What a strange take on our mission. It is, after all, your duty as Protector of Earth to bring peace to humanity, to unleash the light of love and joy. Humanity needs you."

It hits me again. As a few weeks before, that sudden dizziness steals reality from me. Ashton's words are said from far away, as if down a long, long tunnel. Something triggers in me a cavalcade of chaos. Visions of persecution, the incarceration of innocents, their deaths at my hand if I refuse this man who presents a new future of hope and religious unification. I open my mouth. But something inside tells me to hold back. Then the visions pound my mind, more horrific with each wave, more defined, stressing mankind's brutality to others. Awash in the bloodiness of what humanity has become, I feel imaginary bile rise in my throat. I just want the visions to stop.

I find myself crying out, "Yes. Yes, whatever you need. We'll be there."

Sam stares at me. His eyes question me, and, in my mind, he asks, 'Are you okay?'

"I'm okay," I answer on autopilot. "Humanity is my first and last consideration. Nothing must come between my duty as Protector of Earth."

Ashton sighs. "I thought you'd say that."

I stop talking and attempt to SearchSight Ashton to see his expression. But I can't. My strength has been inexplicably drained. I summon up my knowledge banks, but nothing returns. They fail to enlighten me as to what is happening.

"Would we be able to go soon?" asks Ashton. "It's early afternoon in Dharamshala, a perfect time for tea with the Dalai Lama."

Ashton's voice is losing its humility, and his usual sarcasm breaks in.

I look at Sam who still stares at me. He senses my sudden energy loss.

'Are you sure you're okay, darling?' Sam asks me in my mind, with growing persistence. 'Can you travel?'

'I think so.' I know my reply isn't convincing.

'What happened?' says Sam worried.

'I don't know. I think, I…happened?'

'What?' says Sam, baffled by my cryptic response.

'What I mean is, Ashton triggered something within my makeup. I'm Protector of Earth. My duty is to bring peace, keep the Balance and protect mankind. Somehow, he knows what button to press. The visions I had, Sam, they were terrible. And I know they'll happen if I don't comply with Ashton. It's like he's got a remote control, and I'm the channel he's selecting.'

I try to refrain from showing the prickly uncomfortableness I felt.

Sam shakes his head. 'Ellie, darling, that's impossible. He's not Kudamaz. How would he know what to say?'

'I know it's crazy, but it's the only answer. You carry on talking to him. I'm going to speak to Aby-od. Maybe he can shed a greater light on what's happening.'

'Alright, darling. I'll see you later.'

I disintegrate into my signature rainbow sparkle, and just remain caught in Earth's reality to hear my husband quip back with a trace of the acidic to Ashton.

"We'll pick you up at ten hundred hours. Be ready, sir. Bye."

Chapter 68

Lei held Xiao's hand. In her mind she replayed what she'd seen on the monitor.

'Survival.'

It was a single word loaded with ambiguity and speculation. Had she made contact with the force inside Xiao? Or was Xiao himself using the force's power to say he needed to survive?

Then again, had she really seen the word at all?

Had her messed up, stressed-out mind manifested something that simply never happened? Was there really a force inside Xiao or was he just perceptive of her husband's true nature?

Lei found the more she thought, the more she twisted herself into a tornado of turmoil and self-doubt.

Abruptly, she pulled away from Xiao's lifeless hand and stood up.

Seeing him, and feeling that intolerable wracking, wrenching pain only a mother can feel when her child suffers, Lei knew her judgement wasn't just clouded, it was opaque.

Lei headed to the café area where she'd been so many times before. It was the place where her hope and faith had tumbled down into an abyss.

She whipped out her smart phone, stared at it, and the face recognition loaded her screen in seconds. She tapped onto her favorites and selected Chen.

Inside his top-floor office on the corner of Northumberland Avenue, Chen looked down at the caller ID. His throat tightened and dried out like sandpaper, and behind his eyes, pressure built. He felt hollow in the pit of his stomach like someone had carved him out, and his legs shook as nerves overstimulated and his muscles couldn't respond in time.

He gripped at the side of his desk to stop himself from pitching forward.

On the third ring, Chen answered.

"Yes, Lei?"

Chen made a valiant attempt to maintain a position of zero emotion. He knew in less than five minutes he had to be in a board meeting with new investors. It was a place he couldn't show any weakness.

"Chen."

Lei's voice was small. Chen could hear a quivering vibration as she breathed into the phone.

"Is he…?" Chen couldn't bring himself to say it.

"No change," said Lei quickly. She remembered that she'd only promised to call Chen in the case of Xiao's death, or in the slim case of him waking up.

"Then why the call?"

Chen only just controlled the anger he felt coupled with the relief that Xiao was still alive.

"You know our terms. Only call when-"

"I know," interrupted Lei. "But I had to call. I think I've made contact with it."

"It? Who?" said Chen, mystified by his wife's cryptic call.

"The force inside Xiao."

Chen sighed deeply. Oh God, she was back to that again. A week or so ago, even Chen had believed something weird had happened to his son. And during their 'revelation' discussion, he'd tried to conceive the notion that a force had indeed taken over their son.

He'd tried to believe in the impossible.

As the days went on, and Lei's obsession to contact this force had gone from an interest to an absolute fixation, Chen distanced himself again. Taking the simplest route, he submerged himself in work.

He'd seen the whole 'contact the force' thing as a channel for Lei's grief and pain, a new focus to act as an emotional crutch. So he hadn't dissuaded her. But he also hadn't gone out of his way to encourage her either. He wanted Lei to carry on, allowing her to eventually, and somewhat painfully, see the error of her ways.

It was therefore impossible for Chen to believe his wife had made contact with something that didn't actually exist.

"How, Lei?"

Chen glanced at his Audemars Piguet Royal Oak watch, and inwardly cursed himself for answering the phone.

"I asked it what it wanted."

Lei's voice was measured, but Chen could discern a tinge of excitement bubbling just beneath the surface.

"And?" said Chen, trying to play down his annoyance. By now the new investors would be seated in the board room. He had to wrap up this nonsensical conversation quickly.

"It wrote a word on the life-signs monitor."

"It *wrote*?" Chen couldn't dial down his incredulity at his wife's response. "How the hell did it do that?"

"I don't know, but that's not the point. I asked it what it wanted, and it told me."

"And what did it want?" asked Chen tersely, swiping another glance at his watch.

Listening to this madness, he couldn't deny that maybe it was time to consider a psyche evaluation of his wife's state of mind. A few days in an exclusive private clinic somewhere might sort her out, and give him some peace and quiet.

"Survival."

Chen listened and thoughts of having his wife committed vanished. His body went inexplicably ice cold.

"What did you say?"

"It wrote 'Survival', Chen, on the monitor. But whose survival? The force or our son's?"

Chen wasn't listening. The word had catapulted him back into a dream he'd had the night before, a dream that had replayed the very same word. It had taunted him on his deeds of the past. It showed him how he'd used that word to validate the reason for everything he did, forcing him to be inhuman within his own humanity. Driven by a need to survive. At any cost.

Chen knew Lei was not insane. She'd been right all along. Nothing was a coincidence. Everything was connected.

And Xiao was the link.

Chapter 69

Kudamun materializes around me and Aby-od turns his head in my direction as I come out of shimmer.

"Something wrong?"

"Aby-od, I know that, as Protector, I have a duty to protect the Earth, to bring peace to mankind and to keep the Balance Shift. Recently, I have experienced strong visions, horrific in detail, and feelings that if I make the intention to refuse whatever is being asked of me, these visions will become reality. Whilst I experienced these visions, my energies ran down to minimal strength. I was incapacitated. I couldn't even summon the strength to SearchSight."

Aby-od stares at me. His face hardens with worry, and he holds my arm and leads me down to sit on the sofa in his private chambers.

"Ellie, from the description you have given, this is the Pain of Parsu. But Ellie, this is totally impossible. It is your duty to protect Earth and mankind. Hardcoded into every Protector is a type of kill-switch."

"A kill-switch?"

I can't believe I have a lethal trigger within me. This whole Protector thing is like a work in progress.

"Ellie, Protector, you must by now realize that you are a powerhouse of energy. If those energies were to be flipped, to be used for bad, or for your own gain if you turn against your duties as Protector of Earth, you could become a force that could destroy all life. This is why the kill-switch is there. The trigger is a group of words delivered with a specific resonance pattern. But Pain of Parsu can only be triggered by a Kudamaz Elder. This condition can never be triggered randomly. Even if people talk about your duty to protect mankind, without the resonance pattern, this would not invoke the kill-switch. Nothing that people on Earth could do can drain your energy. You must have been mistaken and randomly SearchSighted some poor Earth souls who were going through some kind of living hell. The drained feeling, it must be your imagination."

"Aby-od, that is utter bullshit!" His eyes widen at my vociferous reaction. "Ashton's done it to me. Twice!"

"Impossible, Ellie."

"It's not impossible. I described what happened. You defined it as Pain of Parsu, the Protector's kill-switch to ensure my power is drained and I witness the horrors of humanity if I decline my duty as Protector. You said it. Not me."

Aby-od continues to shake his head, but I grip his arm hard and swing him around.

"Ashton did it. I swear he did, Aby-od. That's why I'm here now."

Aby-od interrogates me with his age-old eyes. "You do speak truth."

"Of course I do," I snap. "What the hell is he, Aby-od? Why can he control me?"

"I don't know. But if it isn't some kind of coincidence, or a weird SearchSight condition, then there may be more to Ashton."

"I told you, Aby-od. I always have done."

I can see Aby-od is holding back. The Balance Shift across Earth is still well balanced, tilting toward the light. Ashton himself is also in Equilibrium, despite this being almost impossible. Under the Order of Kudamun and the Laws of the Ancient Ones, Aby-od can't instruct intervention. There is still nothing to suggest evil doings.

"I suggest you continue with him. Help Ashton all the way with the religious unification plan and his Freedom Earth project. Be his right-hand man." I narrow my eyes, looking grave. "Sorry, his right-hand woman. I can do nothing. The High Council would never sanction intervention on the circumstantial and somewhat fantastical grounds you are purporting."

My jaw drops slightly. Is Kudamun still so bound by protocol and Antediluvian laws, even after everything that's happened?

"You must watch him, analyze, and wait, and we'll see where this takes us."

"Okay, Aby-od. I understand. But let's hope he doesn't take us too far down the rabbit hole."

Aby-od turns his head quizzically; my earthly literary quip is lost on him.

"Got to go now."

"Where are you going, Ellie?"

Remembering Ashton's suggestion of tea with the Dalai Lama, I answer, "The Mad Hatter's tea party!"

And I shimmer out before Aby-od has an opportunity to quiz me further.

Chapter 70

Uneasiness.

That was the feeling running through Ashton. Up to that day, the faiths he'd met with and introduced Sam and Ellie to, had been overwhelmed with absolute joy. They had embraced the opportunity to play a role in bringing enlightenment and continual peace across Earth. Those leaders believed they had been singled out by a divine power, to receive such a calling.

Even if they were skeptical at first, within a few minutes of interacting with his 'emissaries of God', they'd been on their knees, giving thanks for the blessed visitation. The Dalai Lama had even been aware that such a visit was to happen. But this meeting tonight would stretch Ashton's manipulative abilities with religious leaders to its limits.

Ashton swallowed, breathed in, and focused on something that would build his strength for the next meeting. With a flush of exhilaration, he recalled the moments of yesterday's meeting with the Buddhist leader. An extraordinary day, he had learnt just a little more about Sam and Ellie's world of Kudamun.

"Okay, Ashton. You've never experienced this shimmer thing before, so I'm warning you now, you're going to feel extremely disoriented. You may even want to vomit. However, I advise against hurling up over the Dalai Lama. That may scupper future negotiations."

Ellie spoke fast with a sarcastic undertone. Ashton ignored the jibe, nodded, and listened. He was seated on his sofa, all ready to depart from his private office in Downing Street.

Ellie stood in front of him looking down, and Sam, as usual, was by her side. His eyebrows were pinched together with annoyance and he cast a disapproving glance at his wife. Ellie didn't relent.

"I'm just saying, we've got to warn Ashton of what he's letting himself in for. I don't want him to come back and try and sue us for poor delivery of service!"

Ashton smirked. "My days of suing are over, sweetheart!" He enjoyed the slight twitch his 'sweetheart' reference generated in Ellie, and the disparaging look he received as a result. "So let's just get on with it."

"Fine!" snapped Ellie. She explained the process in a matter-of-fact way, as if she was lecturing to a student. "You'll basically be treated in the same way as our clothes or anything else that we carry with us. You'll be encased within our joint energy field and transported in the blink of an eye to Dharamshala. You won't be aware of the travel at all. It will, to you, happen in an instant. It is that immediacy of changing physical locations that could cause nausea and dizziness, as your human brain struggles to process the shift in consciousness. The relay of information from and to the Reality Gap, although instantaneous at the quantum level in your brain, still produces a shudder in your perception field. Thus, you'll have a feeling of sudden, stark displacement. Are you still okay to proceed, Ashton?"

The prime minister listened, absorbing every word. Ellie's explanation, framed up for his benefit in the Earth physics he understood, was very clear.

"I'm more than ready to proceed." Ashton rose from the sofa.

"Okay. Ashton, come over and stand close to me. Sam, please encase us, and commence shimmer."

Sam placed his arms around Ashton's body, and Ellie did the same. Their hands met, and the couple held each other tightly. Ellie puckered her lips and blew a kiss across Ashton's shoulder to Sam, who smiled, appreciating the playfulness of his wife.

Ashton, compressed between them, in a literal Kudamaz sandwich, looked on. Envy pricked at his eyes; he knew his life with Natasha would never be like that.

Ellie started the shimmer in unison with Sam. Ashton's eyelids dropped as he started to blink. The view of his private office impressed on the inside of his lids. When he opened his eyes, everything was different.

Daffodil yellow walls, wooden floors, doors and windows, and sunlight hitting him from all angles.

The shift from the darkness of his office to the sheer lightness of this new place caused his heart to thump harder, racing forward as his brain comprehended the stimuli borne of the new environment.

"Are you okay?"

Ashton nodded, but then had to steady himself, as a wash of dizziness smacked him. He placed a hand on Ellie's shoulder. "Woo, quite a trip!"

Ashton looked from left to right. He was in a Buddhist temple, no denying that. The prayer wheels and soft recitation of *Om Mani Padme Hum* reverberating in the air reinforced the notion that he was indeed in Dharamshala, and in the home of the Dalai Lama.

Sam released his hands from Ellie's grip, and Ashton stepped out of their encasement.

The room around them was empty. Some offerings of fruit, juices, biscuits, and chocolate had been made in front of a statue of a beautiful, jeweled Buddha.

A door opened to the right and a small, bespectacled, elderly gentleman in a crimson cloak, with a round face and shaven head, walked in, flanked by four younger, larger men in similar garb, whose gowns were golden yellow.

"Prime Minister Ashton, I was not informed of your visit."

Ashton smiled with warm affection. Here was the man he'd traveled through time and space in a flash to meet.

"Your Holiness, I apologize for our unexpected and unadvised arrival. It is a matter of great importance to the Buddhist faith that I am here."

The Dalai Lama listened and nodded. His face turned into a gently quizzical expression.

"May I inquire as to how you came in, Prime Minister? We did not see you at the entrance."

Ellie walked forward with Sam. She placed her hands together, touching her forehead, and bowed to the Dalai Lama. Sam did the same.

"Your Holiness, it was my husband Sam and I who brought Prime Minister Ashton directly to you."

The Dalai Lama gazed into Ellie's eyes, and then into Sam's, and he seemed to be somehow assessing their true nature.

Ellie smiled at the Dalai Lama, and he returned it with a knowing nod. He turned to the four men at his sides and stated that he wanted to be left alone. The four men placed their hands on their foreheads, bowed and departed, closing the door.

"I felt your vibrations during my meditation this morning. I expected your visit. You are from the world between, aren't you?"

Ashton watched the interaction, dumbfounded by the Dalai Lama's prescient knowledge and grasp of the identity of the Kudamaz couple.

"Prime Minister Ashton, you say to the world that you are on a path of peace. Outside is our pillar. It greets all our guests to the temple. It has the words 'May Peace Prevail on Earth' engraved on it. It is what we live by. I know that you have faced many threats. I know that your journey is still unclear. You think that you are on the path to enlightenment, however, your purpose is undefined. It is fuzzy in design. You have come here to show me your guests." The Dalai Lama gestured to Sam and Ellie. "These guests are ones who are from the spaces in between. You have done this in the hope that I will join your journey of enlightenment and peace."

Ashton opened his mouth and then closed it; he didn't know what to say. The Dalai Lama was all-seeing and appeared to know everything before a word was even uttered from him.

Sam stepped forward to fill the awkward pause made by Ashton.

"Your Holiness, your words are most accurate. Ellie and I are from a place between what is often referred to as heaven and hell. But I must say, your definition of us from the spaces in between is quite interesting. We exist outside of the universal plane and are not part of spacetime. We exist everywhere across the Universe at once, at every point across time up until this current point in the Continuum. Of course, access beyond this point in the Continuum is forbidden."

Ashton heard what Sam had said. Although he'd come to accept Sam and Ellie, he never really appreciated what they were. Until that moment. He replayed in his mind, '*We exist everywhere across the Universe at once, at every point across time*'. And what the hell was the Continuum? Sam's words truly staggered Ashton, and he gaped at the couple as if he was seeing them for the first time.

"And my wife, Ellie, is the Protector of Earth."

Realizing that Sam was divulging a deeper level of intelligence than he'd ever done to any other religious leader, Ashton touched Sam's arm and endeavored to pull him back on any further revelations.

"I think that's sufficient for His Holiness to appreciate the gravity of our visit."

Ellie listened but chose not to comply.

"Your Holiness, Sam is correct. I am the Protector of Earth, and my entire being is connected to everything on Earth, animals, minerals, plants, and, of course, people. I can communicate directly with atomic structures to build them up or break them apart. Like this, see..."

Ellie picked up a book from a nearby table. In her hands, the book's existence started to break down. Within seconds, it was nothing more than sand grains falling through her slender fingers.

The Dalai Lama watched, his eyes growing wider, but there wasn't the unbelievable surprise that Ashton would have expected.

"And you can restore it?" asked the Dalai Lama. Ashton could see from his sage expression, that he had absolute comprehension about Ellie's abilities in atomic connectivity.

"Of course, Your Holiness. See here..."

Ashton watched as the piles of sand on floor flattened, and then grew up, quickly forming the structure of the book again, until it was completely whole as if it had never been touched.

"This is understandable," said the Dalai Lama. "Your connectedness gives you immediate communication with the base elements."

Ellie smiled, pleased with such an erudite exchange.

"You know, Your Holiness, that everything is balanced between light and dark energies."

"I have felt that this is the way of the Universe."

"We constantly measure what is known as the Balance Shift. It is the light and dark balance of energies. We observe it to ensure that there isn't a dramatic shift to the dark, or even the light. Both are damaging to a world."

The Dalai Lama nodded, adding, "Even in the light, there will be a shadow, and when we are in the light, we are defined by the dark. Otherwise, we cannot be seen."

"Yes, Your Holiness. Your words are very wise. I see you have traveled to the far reaches of the universal plane, and almost touched my world."

The Dalai Lama smiled peacefully, and then shook his head, with a touch of sadness in his aged eyes.

"I have felt the vibrations of your world. But, alas, I've never traveled there."

"I am sorry, Your Holiness, but this is the way. For anyone on the universal plane, our world cannot be reached."

Ashton regarded the interplay, and suddenly, irritation tingled within him. He'd come here to get the Dalai Lama's buy-in, not give the Kudamaz couple the chance to have a friendly chin-wag about existentialism.

"And that is why my guests here are so very, very important," interjected Ashton. "They don't just pop out of their world on a whim. Our meeting today is crucial to Earth's future."

Ellie frowned, irked by Ashton's interruption, then continued to speak.

"You Holiness, Prime Minister Ashton has created a movement called

Freedom Earth. He has eradicated terrorism and organized criminal activity. He has pushed forward mankind's evolution. A shift to the light and a continuance of Earth in a stable position has been the result. We want to ensure that the goal of peace is achieved. We have seen religion become divisive, and we wish to change this. To make all religions about goodness, not piety, suffering, and the forcing of one religion over another, thus creating wars and death. Our intention is to support Prime Minister Ashton, to unify all religions under the theme of one religion: humanity and love for our fellow man. And to embrace all countries' religions under the philosophy of Freedom Earth."

The Dalai Lama looked thoughtful. "And you, Ellie, believe this to be the way for us all?"

"Absolutely, Your Holiness. That is why we have given our full commitment to Prime Minister Ashton's endeavors in unifying religions."

"How did the other religions react?"

"Very positively, Your Holiness. We have the majority of the faiths in agreement that this is the way forward. Lifting human minds toward enlightenment and crushing the need to enforce one nation over another will end war, terror, and death. This is a true path to ensuring peace really does prevail on Earth."

The Dalai Lama walked over to a chair in the corner of the room. He sat down and stared at Ashton, Sam and Ellie. He did not say a word. He closed his eyes, and his lips moved to pronounce silent words. He then opened his eyes and looked straight at Ellie.

"Ellie, being of the in between, I know you speak the truth. You are of light. You are of goodness. I cannot refuse."

The Dalai Lama turned to Ashton.

"You have my support, Prime Minister."

A knock at the door brought Ashton out of his reverie, back to the present moment in his Downing Street office.

"Come in."

Cumberford entered with a gentleman.

"Prime Minister, may I introduce Dr. Adnan Al Shirawi, Head of the Muslim Council of Britain."

Ashton looked up. He realized that all the other leaders had been a walk in the park. Now the fun really started.

Chapter 71

Ashton knew there are moments when all past presumptions seem to root themselves in reality. All those times when he'd said 'perhaps' or 'maybe', giving equal consideration to a situation, are in the blink of an eye totally eradicated. And in their wake, they leave behind just prejudice and discord. Feelings formed over a lifetime of formalized indoctrination are finally and unassailably cast in stone.

Ashton stood in front of Dr. Adnan Al Shirawi and attempted to banish the inner hatred he'd harbored against the people of his kind and faith. Of course, it didn't help that Saudi Prince Khalifa, another Muslim, had arranged his abduction and attempted murder at Buzz Academy just a few days before.

Throughout his time in politics, Islam and terrorism had been synonymous. They were virtually interchangeable. You're a Muslim so you must be a terrorist. Or, you're a terrorist so you must be a Muslim. It was a simple and effective logic, auspiciously avoiding those moments of 'innocent until proven guilty'.

Ironically, the biggest terrorists of all, Al Nadir, had been run by Salim Al Douri, a sadistic evil megalomaniac, who had no affiliation to Islam or any other faith. But he'd come from a Middle East country, where Muslims were in abundance, and he had a funny sounding name. Following the aforementioned logic, he had to be a Muslim and a terrorist. Even if he'd never exploded a single bomb, and lived his life as a monk, he'd still have been labeled a terrorist.

Ashton loathed Al Douri. But oddly, on a deeper level and one he didn't want to admit even to himself, he had held a form of admiration for the Al Nadir super-terrorist. Particularly due to his creation of a new pop culture category, the celebrity terrorist. It had made him as much known for his sultry, good looks worthy of a GQ model, as he was for his global atrocities.

Remembering those Al Nadir days, Ashton shuddered inwardly. He stepped forward. Dr. Al Shirawi placed a hand out to Ashton, and a magnanimous smile crossed his face. After a brief pause, Ashton took Al Shirawi's hand and shook it. He tried to smile, but again, it turned into his customary smirk. Ashton pulled away and gestured for Al Shirawi to take a seat.

Ashton examined Al Shirawi. A tall man, middle fifties, salt and pepper short cut hair, angular face with a long nose, and full, expressive brown eyes. His clothes spoke of money. He wore a charcoal grey suit, tailored to perfection in a cashmere weave, with a crisp white shirt and understated navy silk tie. Ashton didn't like him. The man was undoubtedly a player.

Al Shirawi smiled with a little too much geniality for Ashton and positioned himself with a bounce onto the sofa.

Ashton took the easy chair opposite and watched Al Shirawi, without a word, for a few seconds more. Ashton was irked. Al Shirawi's manipulation of the seating arrangements caused him concern. Most attending a meeting with the PM would have seated themselves at his desk. Opting for the sofa suggested a more informal engagement, befitting of a family member or close friend.

Al Shirawi, still smiling, looked at Ashton.

"Prime Minister, I am wondering why I was summoned here tonight. I was given no other indication as to the purpose other than a veiled threat that 'I would be removed as leader of the Muslim Council'. Have I done something to offend you?"

Al Shirawi's stare interrogated the PM but Ashton detected no direct animosity. In fact, his stare held a calmness and a sense of inner peace that Ashton couldn't fathom. He reasoned that the Muslim leader should be annoyed, or at least a bit truculent at being commanded to attend something he knew nothing about. Ashton thought, had the shoe been on the other foot, he'd have told Al Shirawi to take a hike.

Al Shirawi didn't speak further and seemed content to sit and wait out Ashton's response.

Ashton's phone pinged. Instead of ignoring it, as he would normally at the beginning of such a meeting, he brought it out, turned his face away, and focused on the contents of the new message that had arrived. Al Shirawi smiled softly and copied the PM. Ashton glanced up to see Al Shirawi engrossed in his phone. Ashton sneered a little annoyed

"The reason you're here is so that we can talk about religious unification under Freedom Earth." Ashton just said it. No frilly doily to dress it up with. No sugar coated 'slip into it' gently. Just stark and plain. *I'm unifying religion buddy, and you had better accept it.*

"Unifying religion? How can you unify something that is intrinsically divisive?" Al Shirawi frowned, confused, but in his eyes, he searched to learn more.

"By taking away the contentious elements," said Ashton. "By bringing you irrefutable proof of God's existence."

"I need no proof that Allah exists. He is within all of us. He guides our way."

"That is true, Dr. Al Shirawi. But what if I could present to you absolute proof of God's reign? That there are more things than a human can understand. That, as you say, we are all on a path and he does guide our way, and he has given us a means of gaining a clear direction."

Ashton stood up and walked over to his window.

Al Shirawi remained in thoughtful silence. Then he tilted his head to one side and glanced in Ashton's direction. "Absolute proof? A means of gaining a clear direction? Only Allah's messengers, the angels could deliver such confirmation and assurance."

"Oh Dr. Al Shirawi, I'm so pleased you said that." Behind the sofa, the air started to vibrate. "Why don't you turn around? There's some people I'd like you to meet."

Al Shirawi shifted himself to look over the sofa and gasped.

Slowly, the air started to sparkle, glowing brighter and brighter. Amongst the sparkle, an outline of something appeared and began to solidify in the light. Maybe a few seconds passed before the entire form could be clearly discernible, and a few seconds more until that form became Sam and Ellie.

Al Shirawi stood up, frightened and perplexed. He held onto the back of the sofa for support, fearing he may collapse.

"What trickery is this? How did you make this happen?" shouted Al Shirawi, stepping back, away from the strange humans.

Ashton smiled, beckoning Sam and Ellie forward.

"No trickery. And they made it happen, not me. Dr. Adnan Al Shirawi, meet Sam and Ellie, my emissaries of God."

Chapter 72

I walk forward to the well-dressed, attractive Arab man, who still cowers from Sam and me. I put out my hand and beam at him.

"Good to meet you, Dr. Al Shirawi."

Sam, at my side, also goes to shake his hand and greets him in fluent Arabic. Al Shirawi appears at ease by hearing his mother tongue and returns back to the sofa.

I sit down on the sofa next to Al Shirawi, Sam takes a seat next to me, and Ashton settles into his easy chair opposite.

"That's better, isn't it? I'm sorry if we startled you."

Al Shirawi stares at me and then Sam. His hand touches mine tentatively as if he's asserting I'm real.

"How did you do that?"

I'd scanned Al Shirawi in the Observation Room back in Kudamun, prior to our meeting. He'd had an outstanding career as an oncologist, but he'd been unable to cure his own wife of bowel cancer. After her passing, he'd invested more time in religious pursuits, and had eventually become an Islamic scholar, undertaking a further doctorate at Oxford that examined Islam in the modern world. His scholarly work had been recognized globally, requiring him to travel extensively. Many governments around the world had him as an advisor, and his unyielding stance against fundamentalism had earned him a stream of death threats. They had come from those parties whose ideology, borne out of a lack of education, had misinterpreted the Surahs. Reducing those important words of the Qur'an to little more than village folklore and failing to truly understand those peaceful Islamic tenets.

From Al Shirawi's questioning face, I can see that Al Shirawi, both a man of science and religion, is trying to reconcile what he's just seen with his own knowledge and experience in both fields.

I realize Al Shirawi needs a clear explanation of Sam and I.

"Dr. Al Shirawi, it is how we are. We are made from light, and through light is how we travel. We come from a realm beyond the universal plane. And it is a place where no one within the physical world can go. We live outside your level of perception."

"Beings of light," says Al Shirawi. The look of revelation on his features gives away his thoughts. He closes his eyes for a moment as if collecting his composure and his opinions in unison.

"As Muslims, we know that Allah created angels from light. In The Hadith, our prophet Mohammed, peace be upon him, declared that, 'The angels were created from light'. You are mala'ikah, a messenger of Allah. An angel. You said that you reside at a level of existence beyond the perceptible world. In the Qur'an, this place is *alam al-ghayb*, the hidden world. A place that we as humans are unaware of."

I watch the Muslim leader pause on his words, as he processes what's actually happening to him. I smile with reassurance, and touch his hand, gradually holding his in mine. His eyes widen. He pulls away, half scared but half in awe. He shakes his head as if he has no right to touch me.

"The prophet Mohammed, peace be upon him, saw Jibreel. He told of this being of light, the one guiding him. And now I meet you. What does it mean? I cannot begin to understand why this…"

Unable to finish, Al Shirawi falls to his knees and genuflects with reverence and humility in front of Sam and me.

"Please, Dr. Al Shirawi, there is no need for that," I say, feeling awkward.

"But you are the messengers of Allah. I must bow down to you." Al Shirawi speaks without raising his head.

"Dr. Al Shirawi, please stop that. Sit back up here. There's something we have to talk to you about, and it's central to the next steps in Earth's evolution."

With reluctance, Al Shirawi returns to his position on the sofa and stares hard at me as if I'm a strange and rare artifact. I pat his knee, and he looks horrified by my tactile response. I grin and enter into my ecumenical sales pitch.

I cast a sideways glance at Ashton, who has remained un-customarily quiet throughout the discourse. He is fixed with unnerving intent upon Al Shirawi and hardly acknowledges our presence at all. I check out his Balance Shift. Almost no change. I bury my concern and review Al Shirawi's Balance Shift.

It shows a man who holds a strong amount of white light energy, but darker energies are trying to encroach in different places. It may have been his initial bewilderment and annoyance at being summoned by Ashton. Or perhaps, he knows many people hate him because of his faith, and this brought him pain, enabling darkness to enter. Anyone of these occurrences has caused a seepage of dark energy.

Then, as I watch Al Shirawi, his white light energy floods in, almost obliterating the dark completely. I can literally feel his soul infusing with love and hope. Such a pull of energies make me realize this is why unification is so important. It is the creation of peace and true enlightenment for all.

Al Shirawi's face suddenly becomes glowing and joyful, reflecting the state of his inner soul.

"Am I the chosen one? Am I the next prophet?" Al Shirawi mumbles his words, half to himself, as he smiles with almost euphoric abandon.

"Well, Dr. Al Shirawi, put it like this, we haven't just popped onto the universal plane for a quick chat. There is a significant reason behind our visitation. You are the one we need to help us achieve our mission."

"Me? You need me? How? How can I help? I am but a humble scholar. I am no one!"

I notice, out of the corner of my eye, Ashton's eyebrow raises sardonically. He smirks into a glass of whiskey he's poured just for himself without enquiring on the drinking needs of his guests. Riled by his behavior, I move around to give the PM a superb view of my back. I can hear his low harrumph, as I continue.

"Oh, Dr. Al Shirawi, you are very much someone. We want to see religion unified on Earth. You said earlier that religion was intrinsically divisive and you're right, it is. But provide an overarching ideology that all religions can subscribe to, such as peace on Earth and an end to war and suffering, and religion is unified under that cause. Freedom Earth is that overarching ideology. In my world, we observe the Universe and every act of dark and light is counted."

"Counted?" says Al Shirawi. He is so eager to speak he doesn't realize he's broken into my speech. "In the Qu'ran, it says that, 'angels record the deeds of humans as long as they are on earth'. It says that, 'over you, there are watchers, noble writers, who know whatever you do. Over every soul, there is a watcher'. Are you a watcher?"

I look at Sam. I can feel his words burst into my head. 'Ellie there's a lot of misrepresentation going on here as to who we are. You know we're not angels. They're in a different place from Kudamun.'

'Well, you might not be. But as Protector, I certainly meet the description,' I quip, holding back a giggle.

Ashton turns. He seems to sense something. His eyes flash with irritation, and he narrows them at me. I smile, a small sedate reaction, although I feel like poking my tongue out. Or giving him the bird.

Ashton pushes into the conversation before I can respond.

"Dr. Al Shirawi, there are more things beyond heaven and Earth than we understand. You'll have to accept that and refrain from further inquiry. Ellie, you were saying?"

I glance at Al Shirawi. He looks a little lost and cheated, like a child standing outside a sweetshop, informed of the sweets inside, but told not to enter.

"As Prime Minister Ashton has said, we are here today to give full commitment to the movement of Freedom Earth. We have recognized the need for religious unification. Such an action is seen by us as a way to stop the religious persecution of others, and prevent the pain and suffering of wars fought over religion. It will be an end to mankind's future being determined by a set of doctrines and beliefs that have been imposed upon them. An end to the darkness that has resulted from giving up on one's true path, the path that lies within a person's soul, rather than a path that a person was told to follow. We know that through what we have seen on Earth, mankind is near a leap in its journey to enlightenment. Peace on Earth can only happen if religions unify and see their unified mission as one of love, connectedness, and humanity. Dr. Al Shirawi, will you stand by Prime Minister Ashton, and support his cause of Freedom Earth and religious unification?"

The lost little boy is gone. Al Shirawi now glows with happiness. He rocks back and forth with excitement as he listens. Enraptured by my words, he answers in a shaking voice.

"Allah, be praised! Oh, shining being of light, I will help in any way my mortal body can. Prime Minister Ashton, you have my word. I will ensure my Muslim brothers and sisters agree to religious unification under Freedom Earth. After tonight, this moment that I can barely believe, I will do anything for you. Will I see you both again?"

Sam and I nod.

"Yes, you will. As time moves forward, there will be more meetings. But for now, we have to say goodbye."

I have already invoked my shimmer, and Sam aligns in parallel to mine.

Through the twinkling lights, I see Al Shirawi drop again to his knees, giving way to his need to demonstrate his devotion and respect at the incredible spectacle he's been selected to witness that night.

As Ashton's private office becomes fainter, I can just make out Al Shirawi standing up and hugging Ashton in a warm embrace. The prime minister, so affected by this, appears to be crying with joy.

Or are those tears of happiness just a signal that he's getting that bit closer to his endgame?

Chapter 73

Ashton stared out the window of his office. A sheet of rain, as if Downing Street had been transplanted underneath a pixie waterfall in Ireland, greeted his view. Suddenly irritable, he muttered, "Oh, why can't that idiot Bishop meet me here? God, having to traipse all the way over to bloody Chiswick in this."

Cumberford looked up from his work. His mind was elsewhere, not in the moment, and he caught the last words of the PM's comment.

"Well, you'll be going by car. It's not like you're on foot, Prime Minister."

Ashton bit back resentfully. "If you'd been a better PPS, I wouldn't have to leave at all. Oh, ring him up. Tell him something's happened. He'll have to see me here, like it or not."

Cumberford shuffled awkwardly. He knew that the bishop had only just arrived, and he wouldn't be able to travel over. He knew Ashton knew it too. He was goading him on. It was a test on his tenacity as much as anything. Cumberford swallowed deeply.

"Well? Go on!" said the PM.

"Prime Minister?" Ashton turned around, as his Cabinet secretary, Redfern, marched into the room.

"Martyn, thank goodness. Call the commies and say I can't meet them unless they come here. Stoli, Beluga, whatever, just can't be arsed, not in all this damn rain. Get the bish here."

Redfern shook his head, and Ashton's eyes narrowed with menace.

"Not a good move, Prime Minister, if I may be so bold as to state. With your new energy source, we wouldn't want to be in bad favor with Russia. It will, after all, be their natural gas lines and solid fuel exports that'll take a beating when Quantum Force's power stations go online. It would be better to get them on our side. They could be a useful investment partner for Quantum, if so needed, of course. Everyone can win if we pull the diplomatic string."

Ashton listened, bristling with anger at the impudence of his Cabinet secretary. But as he allowed the words of Redfern to sink in, he realized his Cabinet secretary was quite a player. His diplomatic stance held a strength of purpose. Future-proofing his financial position and preparing Russia's opportunity to invest was a good move. It was better to have them in his camp than shooting the whole thing down.

"You may be right, Redfern. Very perspicacious of you. We need to keep the commies on our side. They've certainly got deep pockets, and they'll soon realize judicious investments in our new energy will give them good returns, maybe even better than their existing energy industry. It's going to come in for quite a hammering. And as we expand, their lucre will be most welcome."

"Quite so, Prime Minister. And you do have a rather large umbrella over there."

Redfern pointed to the coat stand and smiled. Ashton nodded and flicked a scowl at Cumberford.

"Come on, Cumberford. You can join me in Chiswick and hold the bloody umbrella."

"Yes, sir," muttered Cumberford, his eyes down.

"Prime Minister," said Redfern, "on the way, could you review these papers? Need to finalize the matter ASAP."

"What are they?"

"Oh, background legislation, HSE stuff. They're needing approvals from you prior to the coal-fired power station conversions to Quantum Force. If you wouldn't mind?"

"Sure. Right. Okay. I'll scan over them in the car."

Ashton folded the papers and tucked them inside his jacket. He pulled the curtain back. The torrential rain had abated. Only large droplets now fell intermittently.

"Cumberford, get the car around. I'll make a run for it. And don't forget that bloody umbrella!"

Redfern sniggered and Cumberford looked indignant. He straightened as he spoke. "Well, Stoli Elit vodka and Beluga was initially attractive to you. It's not my fault the weather's below par."

"Your diary arrangements are below par!" retorted Redfern. Ashton smirked in unison.

"That's not quite fair."

"Oh, shut up, Cumberford. Just take it like a man."

Cumberford caught the playful twinkle in Ashton's eye and blushed. He turned quickly away from the PM and Redfern, meaning to grab the umbrella.

Ashton, forever the consummate observer and people reader, noticed his flushed cheek. Still got the hots for teacher, eh? Ashton thought. He gave Cumberford's bottom a sharp tap to chivvy him along. The gesture was unexpected and caused Cumberford to clench in and jump slightly.

"My, my, Cumberford, we are a little jittery today. Need to sort out a good session of R and R soon."

Redfern laughed, but Cumberford didn't return with a witty retort. Too aware was he of his unhealthy and growing infatuation with Ashton, he could only walk fast out of the office, away from Redfern's mocking eyes and Ashton's tactile inclinations.

The PM's close protection security officers joined Cumberford and Ashton as they descended the stairs. Ashton didn't acknowledge them. He strode arrogantly to the front door. Cumberford followed a few paces behind. A police officer opened the door to the Jaguar that waited by the entrance. Ashton's bodyguard took the front seat as usual. Cumberford ran alongside with the large umbrella. Ashton dove in and looked up at Cumberford standing awkwardly with the umbrella.

"Well, get in. Don't you want to come too?"

Cumberford smiled widely and ran with eagerness around to the other side. He slipped into the leather seat and shoved the large umbrella between his legs. His joy at being invited to this secret meeting supplanted the uncomfortable feeling of the umbrella stuck tight between his big shins.

Ashton's driver sped off the second Cumberford shut the door. Two close protection Range Rovers with flashing blue lights maneuvered to sandwich the Jag between them, ensuring an absolute shield for the PM's vehicle.

"How far is Chiswick?"

"Twenty minutes at the most, Prime Minister," answered Cumberford, looking out of the window. He was still deeply embarrassed by the slippage of his emotional shield earlier.

"Right, let's have a look at this."

Ashton pulled out the briefing paper Redfern had given him. He pulled off the clip, popped it in his trouser pocket and started to scan read the papers.

Cumberford flicked through his phone and refrained from discussion.

Ashton noticed his silence but didn't comment until he'd finished reading Redfern's documents.

"Cat got your tongue?"

Ashton looked with smug amusement at Cumberford.

"Sorry, Prime Minister, I have a bit of a headache," replied Cumberford sullenly.

"Oh, sorry about that. Do you want a tablet?" Ashton dove into his briefcase for a painkiller and handed it over to his PPS. Cumberford picked up the water in the central armrest and took the tablet from the PM.

"Can't say I don't look after you."

"Thanks," said Cumberford, taking a further swig of water.

"Come on, Cumberford, cheer up, old boy. It's only a headache. You're not dying, are you? No good being down in the dumps." Ashton rubbed Cumberford's arm, and his cheek flushed up again. Ashton's brow arched with more than a little discernment. "This guy, Litinov, what do you know about him?"

Cumberford straightened up from his slouched position, opened his HoloTab, located a suitable file and invoked it. Within seconds, the car's interior lit up with a barrage of live photos depicting Bishop Litinov and his work with the Russian Orthodox community in London and beyond. Each live photo gave a few seconds into the life of Bishop Litinov and his auspicious charitable activities.

"Okay, background," started Cumberford, perking up as the powerful painkiller Ashton had given him took effect. "He's fifty-eight and comes from a very well-heeled family that moved to the UK in 1917 ahead of the revolution. They had to start all over, and his father became a self-made man, jewelry, minerals, energy, forex. You name it, he's dabbled. Mikael is the youngest of four brothers. Two are deceased. One lives in the States. No sisters. He claims the family's survival took him down the theological path. He realized the power of God and wanted to thank Him for saving his family. Studied at Oxford and did his doctorate in Moscow State. Went into a seminary in St Petersburg for four years and was ordained as a priest and finally a bishop."

"A good guy then?"

"Apparently, Prime Minister."

"Any dirt?"

Cumberford shook his head. "Squeaky clean, sir. More so than the others we've dealt with so far."

"Okay, that's enough, Cumberford. Put it away. I'll handle things. Play it by ear when we meet. Oh, and by the way, it's just the two of us, old chap. This is private. You stay in the car. It won't take long."

Cumberford frowned. Annoyance rippled through his face. Ashton realized that Cumberford had thought he'd be taken into the PM's confidence regarding his theological engagements. However, that was not going to happen. Ashton wasn't ready to reveal his unification plan, despite Redfern touching upon his understanding of it.

In a huff, Cumberford descended back into silence and the PM didn't press him, preferring to ignore his PPS.

A good few minutes passed. Ashton took the time to mentally prepare for the meeting. What would be his initial volley? The same old, 'we are not alone?' Or perhaps something deeper, something about his family's survival, a truth to touch him in a more personal way.

Suddenly, Cumberford erupted. "Why did you bring me along tonight if you weren't going to take me to the meeting?"

Ashton looked up at the very unexpected interruption. Cumberford's eyes were round and glassy, his face bulging and pink. He looked as if he was about to burst into tears.

"Cumberford, my dear! What's wrong with you?"

"I thought... Well, I... When you asked me to accompany you... Well, it's a secret meeting, but I thought you..."

Ashton placed a soft finger against Cumberford's chubby lips. His PPS swallowed, and his lips trembled beneath Ashton's touch.

"I do appreciate you, Cumberford. I can't do this without you. You know that, don't you?"

Cumberford's eyes grew wide with admiration.

Like a puppy in front of its master, thought Ashton. You silly boy.

Ashton moved his hand across Cumberford's face. The tips of his fingers lightly grazed his cheek. Cumberford brought his eyes up to the PM. Ashton could see that they shone with expectation, reflecting hidden desires now unveiled.

"Sir...Prime Minister... Erm, thank you." Cumberford's diction was sluggish. He looked away, again embarrassed.

"Now, no more outbursts. A wonderful future awaits us all." In sync with his words, Ashton squeezed Cumberford's thigh, smiled, and flashed a subtle yet potent signal of allure within his hazel eyes. Since Katzy's demise, his emotions pinballed any which way Ashton fancied, and he delighted in using his over sensual sensibilities to have a bit of fun and control those beneath him.

Cumberford held his look as if magnetized. Ashton detected a small quiver vibrate through his body. Then Cumberford opened his mouth, as if to say something, but Ashton noticed the car had stopped. He slapped a hand down on the leather seat.

"We're here! Okay, Cumberford, you come with me. You can hang around just outside the room. I'm not leaving you here to mope on your own."

Cumberford grinned, got out of the car and did his duty with the umbrella.

Six of the PM's close protection stepped simultaneously out of the two Range Rovers and positioned themselves around the PM. His personal bodyguard walked in front.

At the entrance, a large man with thick arms and tree trunk legs waited, unsmiling, alongside another man, who the PM recognized as Bishop Mikael Litinov. The bishop was also large in stature, but it was height, not muscle, that gave the bishop his imposing stance. He stood nearly six foot five inches, and although Ashton was hardly short, at six foot two, he felt dwarfed by him. Ashton pulled himself up straighter as the Bishop extended his hand out graciously and smiled.

"Prime Minister, welcome to the Russian Orthodox Cathedral. My apologies that this meeting couldn't have been sooner."

The prime minister walked in with Bishop Litinov, flanked on either side by his close protection team, with his personal bodyguard still leading in front. Cumberford followed in silence with the bishop's musclebound assistant.

The bishop gushed forth information about the cathedral, and how many new members of the congregation he had. He spoke incessantly about the charity work and how the Church was making a difference in bringing back faith and belief in God.

Ashton listened and made various pleasant remarks in keeping with an official visit. But he didn't enter into further discussion.

The bishop lead them through a room with a few chairs against the wall and two sofas positioned at right angles around an oak coffee table. It appeared to Ashton to be a waiting room.

"Here we are."

The bishop opened a door at the end of the waiting room to reveal a spacious lounge. A buffet of sumptuous foods, including the Beluga, was laid out on a long sideboard.

The PM spun around to Cumberford.

"Wait for me here. Okay?"

"Oh, I'm sure your assistant could join us," offered the bishop.

"I'm sure he couldn't," snapped Ashton.

"No, really, it's no problem. I have a lot of work to catch up on," said Cumberford, and he moved across to settle himself on one of the sofas.

"Prime Minister," said Ashton's personal bodyguard, "I'd like to join you." It was obvious that his bodyguard still remembered the incident at Buzz Academy. But he didn't know that Ashton could very well take care of himself.

"No. This is private. Actually, it's top secret. You don't have clearance."

"Prime Minister, in the light of recent occurrences, it would be prudent for me to check the room before you enter."

Ashton agreed. He looked at the Bishop, who threw up his hands. "As you wish. We have nothing to hide."

The bodyguard marched into the lounge, checked the windows and cupboards, and then signaled an all clear for the PM to proceed.

"Right, that's sorted."

Ashton clapped his hands together in his ritualistic gesture of 'let's get on with it.' Cumberford recognized the response. But the bishop, who wasn't trained in the PM's non-verbal instruction, stood looking quizzically at the PM.

Ashton moved the situation along. "Shall we?"

Bishop Litinov caught on. "Of course, Prime Minister." Before crossing over the threshold to the lounge, Litinov turned to his musclebound assistant. "Ensure that the prime minister's guests are looked after."

The assistant nodded and picked up the tray of glasses filled with juice on the sideboard in the waiting room. He placed the tray on the coffee table and handed the drinks around to the PM's men, who still looked concerned. With some hesitation, they took the drinks, sat down and, not wanting to appear impolite in front of the PM and the Bishop, sipped at them.

Ashton smiled at his men, nodded, and stepped into the lounge. Then, he remembered he hadn't sent his usual text to Ellie and Sam about when to show up. He'd told them to expect a text, and they knew he was going to be with the Russian Bishop that evening. He made a note to send it once he was inside and seated with the bishop. All the bloody business with Cumberford, and then Redfern stopping him about those papers, had put him somewhat out of step that evening. Still, mused Ashton, they could pop in any time during dinner. Anyway, less time with Ellie and her glaring eyes and facetious tone might not be a bad thing.

"Most gracious of you, Bishop Litinov, and thank you for your delightful hospitality!"

Ashton snatched a plate and ladened it with caviar and crackers. The bishop clocked his crude, selfish behavior.

"Leading the country certainly brings out one's appetite."

Ashton smirked. "It's all those meetings. No time to eat, you see. Got to grab a morsel when one can."

"I'm sure it must be difficult for you," said the bishop.

Ashton noted his apathy and bristled inwardly. Probably just Church pressures, considered Ashton. But the outstretched arm of the bishop proffering a large glass of Stoli Elit made the PM forget the moment of indifference.

They chinked glasses.

"Nazdarovya!"

Ashton arched his eyebrow as the ice-cold liquid slipped down his throat.

"Quality stuff, Bishop Litinov."

"Of course. Now, what did you wish to talk to me about?"

Ashton detected a harder edge to the Bishop's voice. Or was it his imagination? Ashton shook his head. No, his training had drilled out of him the notion of creative engineering by his mind. Always on alert, always primed, he'd definitely heard a change of tone in Litinov's voice.

Ashton turned his head to look at the bishop, and his vision wavered in front of him. Two bishops instead of one and both were talking. What were they saying? Something about a question? Who's asking a question? Did I ask a question? Or did the bishops? Where did the other bishop come from?

"Prime Minister, you wanted to talk to me."

Litinov stared hard at the PM. Ashton pitched forward as he attempted to place his glass down on the sideboard. He glared at the drink for a second, understanding what was happening, and lost his balance.

He scrambled to grab at Litinov, but the Bishop side-stepped out of his grasp.

"You stupid fuck! You have no..." Ashton slurred to a stop as his senses cut out.

Heavily, he thudded onto the wooden floor.

Chapter 74

The evenings are drawing out. The sky is still a vibrant cerulean blue, with just the faintest hint of drifting orange. Cottonball clouds puff up along the skyline near Westminster Palace, and pleasure boats with evening partygoers cut slowly through the waters.

Sam's hand is in mine. We walk through Victoria Tower Garden by Millbank alongside the river. I feel the air touch my skin, and the sun embraces the light particles within me. It's a beautiful evening and reminds me of our walks a few months ago when Sam and I were still human.

I recall that feeling, when I'd been incarcerated by Al Nadir, of knowing all those everyday things like arguing over the remote control and walks along the riverside would soon be gone from me.

I hold Sam's hand tighter, reaffirming our power. Together we're stronger.

I feel a sense of gratefulness. I'd been given a chance again to enjoy these small wonders.

'You okay, darling?' asks Sam in my mind. He knows me so well.

'Yes sweetness, just tripping down memory lane.'

'Good memories?'

'Some.'

We walk past Westminster Palace and across Parliament Square, still keeping hand in hand, navigating between the sweatshirts, suits and pencil slim skirts. We head toward our old stamping ground, St James Park.

The sunlight dapples across the oak trees, which have stood tall and resplendent for centuries, and eventually touches our hands, making our fingers glow a little. Together we feel the energy of life.

My bracelet, which Aby-od gave me to control my connectivity to everything, seems to glisten brightly and unexpectedly. The strange silver material of the bracelet's wide cuff is made from light particles arranged in a different configuration to anything humans could achieve. The creation of matter from light is a step too far for mankind.

But one day, if they're still around, perhaps.

I stare at the bracelet and the two crystals with mauve and violet hues sparkle and glow. If I look closely, I can see sparks of energy, as if inside the crystals are a Universe of twinkling stars.

I haven't taken off the bracelet since Aby-od gave it to me.

He warned me not to get too attached, but somehow, I feel it is a part of me, even though I don't need it. I have long stopped being overwhelmed by the vibrational resonances of the world around me. I can control my powers now and everything around me. But it reminds me of a time when material things meant so much.

'We used to come here for lunch, remember?'

Sam slips into my mind.

'Yes, I do. We used to meet in the St James Café over there. That was when I believed you were just a boring foreign office diplomat instead of some badass mother saving the world for a living!'

Sam laughs.

'Not still angry, are you?'

'Goodness, no. That's all water under the liar's bridge,' I respond in Sam's mind.

'Come on, I'll buy you dinner in the café, for old time's sake.'

'What about Ashton?' I glance at my phone. 'He still hasn't texted us yet.'

'Oh, when he needs us, he'll text. He's probably got his hands full anyway. You know what a political animal he is!'

Chapter 75

Litinov looked over to the door. His eyes widened, and he chewed on his bottom lip. A man built like a tank entered carrying a chair. He lifted Ashton off the floor with ease and hauled him into the chair. He fixed handcuffs to each arm of the chair, and then, to each wrist. He stood back to look at the PM.

"Excellent work, Bishop Litinov. Your country appreciates your cooperation in this matter."

Bishop Litinov flicked his head back and forth between Ashton and Tankman. He found it difficult to process that the figure in the chair was Richard Ashton, prime minister of the United Kingdom. He'd seen Ashton on television. He was a strong, single-minded leader who appeared to second guess any situation. Didn't see this, did you, Mr Ashton? The bishop gave way to a mean streak he'd festered ever since Ashton's name had been mentioned to him.

"Are you ready?" asked Tankman.

His voice was more of a deep rumble than a spoken word. He narrowed his eyes at the bishop, and Litinov could see his impatience flaring. He had no wish to test the patience of such a creature. He glanced back at Ashton. He dearly hoped his actions wouldn't carry consequences. Of course, he knew that such a notion was naïve. Repercussions from abducting the prime minister would be far-reaching and powerful. If his collusion was ever discovered, diplomatic immunity wouldn't cut it. He'd certainly be executed like all those Al Nadir terrorists he'd seen on television.

Litinov swallowed heavily, trying to lubricate the dryness in his throat, as he looked for the last time at the PM's unconscious body. He turned back to Tankman and asked, "Have his men been dealt with?"

"Yes, the gas has put them into lullaby land. So we must do this now."

Litinov nodded.

"Forgive me, Father," whispered Tankman, drawing his massive fist back.

"For Mother Russia," said the bishop. He closed his eyes and waited.

Tankman's curled fist met with the bishop's temple and Litinov collapsed. He then ring-tied Litinov's wrists and ankles, swept him up off the floor, and dumped him in a cupboard, leaving the door slightly ajar.

With the bishop out of the way, Tankman's attention focused on the PM, still unconscious in the chair. He slapped him hard a few times across the face with the back of his hand. Pain, he knew, was a good signal to the brain to come back into a conscious state. On the sixth slap, Ashton jerked and opened his eyes.

He took a moment to absorb every detail of the scene in front of him. An enormous man with a badly fitting jacket, with stains beneath his armpits and around the neck of his shirt, loomed over him. God, thought Ashton, hasn't the guy heard of deodorant? He held back a smirk, as it wasn't such a good reaction. The man was truly gigantic. He recalled seeing someone with a similar body frame but not the same face. Eyes, brown and deep set, thin mouth, blobby nose with flared nostrils, none of these features resembled the man he remembered, General Gregor Ivanov, Russian Ambassador to the UK and station chief for the GRU, Russia's external military intelligence service.

Ashton's gaze searched past Tankman. He could see the room was the same lounge he'd been in with the bishop. All the furniture was upright and there were no signs of a struggle. The bishop was nowhere to be seen. Ashton reasoned he'd either been complicit and had left or else, he was languishing somewhere in the house, either unconscious or dead.

Tankman stared at Ashton, unspeaking. Ashton returned the gesture. The two men glared at each other, taunting the other to make the first move. Ashton's piercing hazel eyes locked onto Tankman's dark brown orbs and did not waver. It was a game of chicken. Tankman drilled his stare, but Ashton was a consummate professional, unblinking and totally focused, Ashton remained strong, his stare a laser burning into Tankman.

Eventually, Tankman nodded his head, looked away, acknowledging a defeat of sorts. He stood up and turned his massive body at an angle, so Ashton couldn't see what he was doing.

Shielded to his actions, the first Ashton knew of them was the balled fist that struck his cheekbone at what felt like a hundred miles per hour. The chair tipped back and crashed onto the floor. Extreme pain like someone had caved in his lower back flashed through Ashton. His cheek throbbed, and dizziness kicked in. Ashton attempted to center himself. All his training of decades back suddenly took over, and adrenalin rose within him.

Tankman pulled the chair back upright. His fist connected with Ashton's right jaw, and then his left. Ashton tasted blood in his mouth. The chair dropped again. On the floor, the handcuff rode down the metal handle of the chair. Ashton remembered the paper clip he'd put in his pocket earlier. He maneuvered his hand downward and snatched it between his fingers, just as Tankman yanked the chair to its standing position again.

Another hit to the nose. It cracked. Blood streamed down Ashton's face. Tankman swung another left punch to his cheek, splitting it open. Ashton just took it. He needed to get on the floor again, so he could pick the cuff's lock. He couldn't do it upright; Tankman would see.

Ashton knew how to provoke Tankman. He didn't say a word. His silence infuriated him. He thundered at Ashton, his fist flying out again, this time to Ashton's right eye. Ashton's head pounded, and blood was all he could see. The force, however, threw the chair backward. Ashton prepared himself for the impact. His spine shuddered with pain, but his focus was on the lock. With his vision bloody, he had to rely on touch. He stuck the paperclip in and picked the lock the way his training had taught him. Ashton angled the paper clip at a ninety degrees, and pushed it into the lock. He turned it anti-clockwise, shoving the double lock bar out of the way, and allowing the first lock bar room to move. He flipped the clip rapidly in a clockwise direction, putting pressure against the first lock bar, pressing it down and out of the way of the ratchet teeth inside the locking mechanism of the cuff, enabling the mechanism to open. Ashton felt the cuff loosen. Tankman pulled the chair back up. Neither Tankman nor Ashton had so far said a word.

Tankman stood back, reached behind him and stuck a Gsh-18 semi-automatic 9mm in Ashton's face. Ashton recognized it as the sidearm of choice for the GRU Spetsnaz. So, the man was a Russian.

"You've gone too far. You've annoyed too many people!"

Ashton knew the voice. It *was* General Gregor Ivanov. But his face appeared completely different. Maybe nanotech, or a gene-therapy augmentation, thought the PM.

"Time for payback!"

Ashton felt the coldness of the gun against his cheek and stinging pain. Ivanov pistol-whipped him with anger. The chair toppled, and Ashton forced it to drop to the left-hand side. As the chair descended, Ashton released his hand and picked the second cuff's lock in seconds. Ivanov reached in toward Ashton, grabbing his shirt. But Ashton was faster.

His palm shot out and he delivered a strong, brutal uppercut to Ivanov's throat. In the same second, Ashton kicked Ivanov's fibula. He heard a crack, and Ivanov fell on his back, his breathing ragged. Ashton leaped on top of him. Giving him no time to bring his semi-automatic around, he straddled Ivanov, each knee on the top part of his arms, pinning him to the floor. Ashton twisted Ivanov's wrist rapidly around until it clicked, breaking, and he grabbed the pistol out of his hand.

Ashton pointed it at his knee and shot. Ivanov howled. Ashton turned the Gsh-18 and shot his other kneecap off. He wasted no time, blasting Ivanov's left and then right hand. Ivanov watched as his fingers flew off, showering him and Ashton in a waterfall of blood. Ashton jumped off Ivanov and pulled him back to prop him against the sideboard. Ashton then sat down on the chair and pointed the Gsh-18 at him.

"Okay, General Ivanov, this is how it's going to work."

Ivanov, although in phenomenal pain, looked amazed at Ashton's quick discovery through his disguise. He'd used the nano-cream perfected by the late Hans Stein-Muller of the nano-bomb fame to hide his features. He'd programmed the nanotech molecules inside the cream to create a larger nose, deeper eyes, and a thinner mouth, with a larger, rounder face. The nano-cream formed a base on which the material remolded over the top of a person's real face. Ivanov knew he didn't look at all like himself. So how did the prime minister see through his disguise? And where the hell did he learn those moves?

"I need to know who arranged this."

Ivanov gurgled a laugh. "You can ask, Prime Minister. It's a free world."

"No, Ivanov, it is not a free world. It is a Freedom Earth world. My Freedom Earth world. And no one fucks with my world. Who arranged this?"

Ashton didn't shout or scream. He was measured in his delivery. Ivanov said nothing, just smiled. Ashton looked at him. His knees were shattered and bleeding heavily, and his hands were a gruesome mess. He couldn't stand, couldn't move, couldn't fight. He couldn't do anything. Neutralized.

"Ivanov, I don't want to put you through any more pain."

Ivanov growled and tried to move, which caused him more agony. He groaned deeply.

"I didn't know you politicians could do irony," said Ivanov.

"I haven't always been a politician."

"I've realized that. Five? Six?"

"Does it matter?" stated Ashton, standing up. "We're all the same at the end of the day, aren't we?"

"I suppose so."

"And we reach our conclusions the same way, don't we?" Ashton moved over to the sideboard, took a silver corkscrew from where it lay alongside a bottle of Sauvignon Blanc, left the pistol on top of the sideboard and returned to face Ivanov.

Ivanov fixed on the corkscrew and nodded. He smirked.

"You and I, we are the same. Ready to do the necessary for our country."

Ashton squatted. He smiled at Ivanov. "Okay, so tell me who's behind this. Is this GRU actioned? Or are you guys playing mercenary?"

Ivanov just smiled.

With his eyes on Ivanov's, Ashton stuck the corkscrew into his thigh, just missing his femoral artery. Ashton watched for the moment of pain when the corkscrew pushed through his flesh. Ivanov grimaced but didn't scream. His eyes didn't register pain. Ashton withdrew the corkscrew and considered where next to plunge it in.

"You know you'll be executed? But it won't just be you, Ivanov. I will take your wife and your children, your twenty year old son, and your nineteen year old daughter. They will be executed with you. I know your daughter is married and has a new baby, an eighteen-month-old boy. He will be executed as well, along with his father. Everyone you love will be taken. They will be branded as terrorists. They will be made the property of Freedom Earth. My Freedom Earth army will take time to *really* enjoy your son, your daughter, your wife, and then finally, after they're done with them, your family will be executed."

Ashton smirked as he observed the reaction his words had on the general.

Ivanov paled and he shook his head.

"They have done nothing. They're not to blame."

"Collateral damage, General Ivanov."

Ivanov looked at Ashton. Was he bluffing? Ashton's emotionless hazel eyes stated a cold clarity. The PM did not lie.

Ivanov swallowed, opened his mouth, and then hesitated.

Ashton noticed the hesitation. He drove the corkscrew into another part of his thigh. Ivanov breathed sharply and scrunched up his eyes. Ashton ripped out the corkscrew and parts of Ivanov's flesh fixed on the metal spiral as it came out. Blood pumped out from the open wound.

"You have thirty seconds. After that, your entire family will be wiped out."

"It was an instruction from the Russian president. He is concerned about your new energy, and the impact it will have on our economy, our coal and gas exports. He wanted to warn you. 'Put the frighteners on you', as you say."

Ashton considered the intelligence. The Russian president implicated in a grubby abduction of the British prime minister. It was a hell of a bargaining chip for complete Russian financial buy-in to his Quantum Force. Ashton stared again at Ivanov. Something else was there. Something he wasn't telling.

"Is that all?" asked Ashton. Ivanov looked stunned. His expression told Ashton what he needed to know. "I won't hold back on your family's execution if you hold back on me."

Ivanov stared at Ashton. "But you said-"

"Tell me the rest," snapped Ashton, turning the bloodied corkscrew in his hand.

"Khalifa."

"The prince? The Saudi Prince!"

Ivanov nodded. Ashton was shocked, although not that surprised. Jensen did state there would be reprisals from Ashton hustling Khalifa out of the five billion. It seemed the foiled abduction in Buzz Academy wasn't the end of it. Now he knew Khalifa had a hand in this, Ashton realized the abduction wasn't all that had been planned.

"This wasn't just a warning, was it?" Ashton moved forward to Ivanov, who shook his head. Ashton brought the corkscrew up to Ivanov's face. "This was to be an assassination. Al Nadir die-hards or some other fanatics not bought into my ideology."

"Orders were to remove the energy threat completely."

"With me gone, Freedom Earth would fall apart. The country would be in disarray. The new energy roll-out would be stalled. It would give both Saudi and Russia sufficient time to bolster their defenses. Very neat plan."

"Yes, it would have been."

"But you didn't bet on me, did you?"

Ivanov smiled. "We didn't know you. We couldn't find out a background on you. Only as a lawyer and a journalist. Nothing else. And we looked *everywhere*."

Ashton thrust the corkscrew into Ivanov's cheek. The nanotech connection holding the molecules together within the nano-cream was broken. Sparks flew across Ivanov's false face. The nano-cream solidified as if Ivanov wore a silver metal mask, and then the structure broke down and turned to silver dust. Before Ashton's eyes, the mask disintegrated, revealing General Gregor Ivanov's real features. Dark blue eyes, elegant nose, and strong pronounced jawline. Ashton dragged the corkscrew out of Ivanov's cheek. Ivanov didn't react.

Ashton stood up and reached over to take the Gsh-18.

"Bit stupid to use this gun. You might as well have left your calling card."

"There's a Glock in the bag with typical ammo used by Al Nadir."

Ivanov indicated with his eyes to a bag on the sofa Ashton hadn't seen. Ashton turned around.

"Okay. So this was to be seen as a last-ditch attempt at retribution. Al Nadir's swan song."

Ivanov sighed. "And now it is mine."

Ashton smirked his habitual smirk, full of derision and condescension.

He aimed the Gsh-18 at Ivanov.

The general opened his eyes wide. Without the mask, Ivanov's eyes bulged, bloodshot. Ashton could now see agonizing pain had broken through the big man's tough resolve. Perhaps the nano-cream had been hiding the truth. The general looked at Ashton and rumbled a gruff pleading.

"Please, don't harm my family. I kept my word. I've told you everything."

"You know us politicians, our word is as reliable as a chocolate teapot!"

Ashton smirked. And blasted Ivanov straight through the heart.

Chapter 76

Chen looked down at Xiao. Two days gone and no further sign of contact. Chen now wondered whether his initial diagnosis had been correct.

His wife really was insane.

Their telephone call had precipitated a change. He'd attended the new investors meeting. His mind had been elsewhere but somehow, he'd still had enough of the Chen Chang charm to win over them and their deep pockets. After they'd signed the investment papers, he'd left his lawyers to handle the finer details.

His driver pelted down the A4 to get to Cromwell Hospital. The ride had been torturous. The car was jumping lanes, zipping between motorcycles and speeding up to a point where breaking suddenly would have had lethal consequences. But it was Chen's own fault. He'd given his driver carte blanch to drive however he liked to get him to the hospital as quick as possible.

Arriving, Chen leapt out of the car, hardly noticing anyone around him, and ran into the hospital lobby.

"Please slow down, sir," someone from the reception had called out, quoting something about health and safety. But Chen was past caring. He tore down the corridor, into the elevator and the punched the fourth-floor button.

He could feel his heart pelting against his rib cage. His throat was still dry despite the champagne lubrication after the deal was signed. The elevator doors opened, and Chen sped down the corridor, past the ward reception, where another health and safety conscious receptionist yelled, "Don't run, sir!"

Oblivious, Chen continued, only stopping when he'd reached his son's private room.

He burst in and saw his wife in a chair. Her eyes were glassy and red.

"Darling, tell me everything," said Chen, opening his massive arms to enfold his wife.

Lei wrapped her petite arms around her husband's huge frame. And then she pulled away and pointed to the monitor.

"It was there. I saw the word 'survival.'"

Chen watched his wife. Her chest rose and fell as she tried to contain the fear and hope that raged inside her.

"Have you seen it again? Or anything else?"

Lei shook her head.

"So you only saw this word once?"

Chen's tone signaled suspicion.

"Don't you believe me?"

Chen could see the hurt erupting in Lei's eyes. He didn't want to say that, especially not after his dreams.

"No, darling, of course, I believe you. I'm just asking, has there been any more contact? Any more words on the monitor?"

"Nothing."

Lei's despondency was tangible.

"Have you tried to repeat the things you did to invoke another reaction?"

"I've tried, God, have I tried. I've done nothing but try since I spoke to you."

Chen considered his wife and the trauma of everything she'd gone through. Maybe, despite his dream, his wife had imagined the entire episode.

"Lei, maybe you need to rest. Have a break from all of this."

"All of this!" shouted Lei, instantly aware that Chen was pushing her down a road she had no interest travelling down.

"This is our son!"

Chen looked down, exasperated. He tried to speak but Lei's guided missile of a mouth found its target and exploded onto Chen with powerful, blinding impact.

"You think I'm mad, don't you?"

Chen shook his head. "I never said that."

"You don't have to. Your eyes speak volumes. If you don't believe me then why did you come here?"

Lei's eyes burned holes in Chen's feeble defense.

"I wanted to tell you about my dream."

"Your dream?" repeated Lei, looking confused. "What are you talking about? What's your dream got to do with our son?"

"I dreamt about my past. I was shown again all the terrible things I'd done."

Lei's face paled.

"Through that hideous, visual journey of torture, one word resounded in my mind. Survival. I did anything and everything to just survive."

Lei's ebony eyes widened, and panic flashed through them.

"When did you dream all this?"

"Last night. That's why I came here immediately. The two events must be connected. We just need to figure it out together."

Chen put his hand out to Lei, but she drew away, acting like Chen's hand was diseased.

"Get out," Lei hissed.

"What?"

Chen couldn't understand Lei's flip in attitude.

"I said get out. Don't come here again."

"Lei, what the hell is wrong with you? You told me about the word on the monitor and I told you about my dream. It's obvious the two are connected. I believe you, Lei. I believe there really is a force inside Xiao. I don't know why you're being like this. I love you and I want to be with you and Xiao."

"Well…I …I don't want you! So get out now!"

"But why?" pleaded Chen, unable to comprehend the reason behind his wife's fractious behavior.

"Why? You're the reason why. You and your darkness. You've plummeted our poor child into a place of no return."

"What about the force? That's played a part too."

"It unveiled your darkness to Xiao and he couldn't take it. If you'd been an angel all your life, do you think we'd be sitting here now looking at our boy on the edge of death? No. He'd have been infused with light, love and happiness."

Lei's response was vitriolic and soaked in bitter sarcasm.

"What happened to your forgiveness? You said that I should never think I've caused his coma. 'It's all beyond our comprehension,' you said, 'but he will return back to us.'"

Lei listened, and Chen knew she was remembering her words a few days prior.

"Your dream," said Lei slowly, "you were shown what you've taken from others to survive?"

"Yes," said Chen. His great voice was now small and unsteady.

"Well, now we're being shown what is going to be taken from us, for this *thing...*" Lei's eyes darkened, and her mouth ran to a straight line. She no longer carried any warmth as she referenced the force.

"For this thing to survive."

Chen stared hard at Lei, who shook with hate-filled rage. She turned back to Xiao with tears flowing. Her voice dropped at least two octaves and came out more like a rumble of thunder than the soft, dulcet tones he knew.

"Our son."

Chapter 77

Ashton opened the door leading to the waiting room. The scene before him resembled a weird kind of clothed bacchanalian orgy. Ashton's close protection team draped lazily across each other on sofas and on the floor. With heads in laps and resting sensually on necks, it looked like they were languidly enjoying the afterglow of lustful activity. Across his primary bodyguard's chest was Cumberford, with an arm lying on top of his back as if his bodyguard had cuddled him close.

Had Ashton not been in serious pain, he would have roared with laughter at such a sight. As it was, Ashton urgently needed their assistance.

"Get the fuck up, you idiots!"

Ashton's sharp tone failed to awaken his sleeping beauties. He grabbed each and shook them hard.

His primary bodyguard was the first to wake. He jolted, not knowing where he was. Noticing Cumberford on top of him, he threw him back against the cushion with utter disdain. He stood up, still shaky, and looked around the room, stunned at all his colleagues knocked out by God knows what. He glanced to the right of him and saw the prime minister covered in blood with his face cut, bruised and swollen, and holding a gun. He gasped and jumped to aid his leader.

"Oh my God, Prime Minister, you're hurt. What happened?"

"GRU happened. General Gregor Ivanov. He's in there, dead," snarled Ashton. His primary bodyguard tried to help him, but Ashton pushed him away.

"Just make sure the room's secure and find that fucking bishop!"

His bodyguard nodded at the instruction and ran into the lounge as his fellow colleagues started to come around.

Ashton placed his hand on the door frame and looked from the lounge to the waiting room. His bodyguard checked Ivanov, but he could see he was dead, now just a bloody lump soaking into the carpet. His bodyguard flicked back a glance at Ashton as if to say, 'how did you do this?'

Ashton turned away, giving up nothing, and watched his security team wake up. Like his bodyguard, they disengaged from each other with certain disdain, and moved away, embarrassment burning on their faces.

"Good to see you all," said Ashton.

They turned in unison, took in the dreadful state Ashton was in, and literally sprang up to assist. Suddenly, everyone in the room was shouting orders, going for their sidearms, and calling on their mobiles. Activity for activity's sake.

Ashton watched, amused by their ineffectual performance. Would they have lasted in Ivanov's grip? That, he sincerely doubted. And these men were on his close protection detail. God, he'd have to have a talk with the head of security about a number of reassignments.

"It's all over, boys. Just clean up the mess in there."

Ashton pulled out his mobile from his briefcase, selected a contact, and hit dial.

"Cartwright, I have a special order under Freedom Earth to remove all of General Gregor Ivanov's family from the Russian Embassy and place them in a holding cell. Their crime is treason against Freedom Earth."

Ashton listened to Cartwright's protests, about it causing a diplomatic incident, that the embassy was foreign territory and Six had no jurisdiction. Ashton cut through his whiny objections.

"I've just been abducted and seriously attacked by General Ivanov at the Russian Orthodox Cathedral's house in Chiswick."

Ashton listened to Cartwright gasp and swallow. "Are you safe, Prime Minister?"

"Yes, I am now. Ivanov is dead. I killed him."

"Oh, good God. What happened to your close protection team?"

"Knocked out. Probably a derivative of fentanyl, undetectable, odorless and virtually instantaneous. I expect when I was inside with the bishop, they seeped it in. My boys wouldn't have known what hit them. Look, the Russians and Saudi Arabia-"

"Saudi Arabia? What the hell have they to do with it?" asked Cartwright, trying to get a fix on what the hell was happening with his leader.

"They were both in it together. Ivanov had direct instructions from

President Dimitri Gregarov himself, and Prince Khalifa worked with them, probably funding this GRUs off the books op. They wanted me dead to stop Quantum Force and protect their energy markets."

Ashton wiped away the blood dripping from his face with his sleeve. One of his security team appeared with a first aid box, but Ashton waved the fussing guard away before he could break Ashton's concentration. An ambulance siren sounded outside, and more sirens shattered the previous silence of the cathedral.

"Prime Minister, is Khalifa there?" asked Cartwright, automatically bringing up the private flight schedules to and from KSA.

Ashton hadn't considered the possibility that Khalifa was there, hiding and watching his torture. "Check the place for Prince Khalifa," screamed Ashton to everyone in the room. "He may be here. Get him alive!"

At the prime minister's word, they darted in all directions. Ashton hoped Khalifa was there, but he doubted he'd be so overtly complicit to be at the abduction.

"What do you need, Prime Minister?" said Cartwright.

"I need them to learn better manners. So we need to make some examples."

"I understand, Prime Minister. Both countries?"

"Both countries. 'Take no prisoners, make no excuses', that's our motto. Remember it! Russia and Saudi Arabia have attacked me personally, but they've also breached the Freedom Earth constitution. They committed terrorism on another Freedom Earth country's soil. By placing me at risk, they put the country at risk. And I can't have that. I had enough of it with Al Nadir. I'm not going back to those days again. Freedom Earth's laws within its structure have been violated. Both countries have committed treason of the highest order. You have my full authority to use the Freedom Earth army. Storm their embassies and incarcerate all within."

Cartwright sighed.

"You're worried about geopolitics? Reprisals? Well, I wouldn't be," Ashton continued. He slipped the phone into secure video mode and continued to transmit his current view.

Ashton heard Cartwright's sharp intake of breath as he witnessed what Ivanov had done to the UK's leader.

Cartwright joined the PM on the secure vid-line, and spoke rapidly. "Prime Minister, you must seek medical attention immediately, and leave this to us. Embassies will be hit at twenty hundred hours tonight." Cartwright stopped speaking. His voice dried. Transfixed by Ashton's injuries, he shook his head. "Sir, I can't believe they did this to you. How did you overcome Ivanov?"

A supercilious smile drifted across Ashton's face, despite the cut lip.

"Fortune favors the brave, Cartwright."

He refrained from further explanation. Cartwright didn't pursue the issue.

"Prime Minister, sir, we will deliver a retribution the like of which they have never seen. I promise you."

"Inform me when it is over."

"Yes, sir. Goodbye, Prime Minister, and I hope your recovery is a swift one."

"Getting swifter by the minute. Bye."

Sliding off the transmission, he heard activity inside the lounge. The voice was Litinov's, shallow and discordant.

"You cannot arrest me. I've done nothing. I'm a victim here!"

Two of Ashton's protection team pulled Bishop Litinov through the door from the lounge. He had a huge black-purple bruise down the left side of his face, and plastic ties still on his wrists. Indignant and mortified by the insinuation that he was involved with the attack on the PM, he shouted his protests.

The security guy ignored him and faced the prime minister.

"Found him stuffed in a cupboard. He was tied ankles and wrists. I released the ankle ties, so he could walk. It's obvious he's been hit, but he could be involved. He knew you'd be here. His hospitality sent us all to the land of nod."

Ashton nodded. "Premeditated, all of it. That bishop is up to his neck in it."

Bishop Litinov heard Ashton's pronouncement and scowled. "I'm the victim here."

"You certainly *took care* of my men!"

Ashton's bloody eye throbbed. The adrenalin that had got him through the last hour was dissipating. His body ached everywhere. A mother of all headaches was beginning to set in. The reason for his agony was the man in front of him, claiming innocence.

Ashton's hand struck out, slapping the bishop before he could maintain his composure. The force threw him into the bodyguard behind, who drew an arched eyebrow at Ashton.

"Take him away until I'm ready to *talk* to him."

The bodyguard steadied the shaken and remonstrating bishop to his feet. Litinov swung around, glaring at Ashton.

"What do you mean *talk* to me? You're not going to hurt me. I'm a bishop, a man of God."

Ashton pulled Litinov roughly around to face him straight on. He pointed to his own face.

"Look! Look at what your comrade, Ivanov, did. I came here to talk to you about religion, and I got this. My security team was knocked out. Ivanov told me he intended to execute me. And you say, don't hurt me. I'll do whatever it takes to get the truth from you. If it means ripping you apart bit by bit, I will find out your role in all of this."

Litinov listened and his face paled as if alabaster. He stared at Ashton and realized his words were no political bluff or posturing brinkmanship. In the prime minister's eye glinted pure sadistic menace.

This acknowledgment was all Litinov needed.

"Prime Minister, I'm sorry. I was forced into it. They threatened me. They said they'd burn down my church. My mother and father are still alive, and Ivanov was ready to kill them if I didn't cooperate. I couldn't refuse."

"That statement may just have saved your life."

Bishop Litinov, with eyes fixed to the ground, sighed and breathed deeply. Ashton tilted Litinov's chin upward. Shame and terror surfaced on his face.

"I have no wish to harm a man of God," Ashton continued. "You appear to be an unwilling party. Your statement is now in the process of being verified and, once confirmed, you'll be free to undertake your religious ministrations." Ashton pointed at the handcuffs. "Remove them."

His primary bodyguard looked amazed at the PM's benevolence but unlocked the cuffs without further inquiry.

Litinov understood how close he'd been to forfeiting his life. Emotions overwhelmed him. Ashton could see the Bishop's gratitude flowing through his body. His shoulders hunched forward, and he dropped to the floor.

Ashton watched, holding fast to a snigger that was building. It had been a while since anyone had genuflected in front of him in recognition of his humanity and generosity. In fact, come to think of it, thought Ashton, no one ever has. Oh well, first time for everything.

Litinov kept his eyes to the ground, averting the prime minister's.

Ashton placed a hand on the bishop's head, echoing the gesture of the Papal Father. He was of a different denomination, but the effect was almost the same.

Bishop Litinov shivered at Ashton's touch.

"Please, forgive me!"

Ashton heard the bishop's tremble. His compliance had been gained under duress. It was obvious. There had perhaps been a moment when Ashton uncovered the bishop's dislike of him, but it appeared to be more against the political establishment, than Ashton in particular.

"Please rise, Bishop Litinov. This is all quite unnecessary." Ashton indicated with his open palm for Litinov to get to his feet.

Litinov rose, at the PM's instruction, but his stature still appeared severely blighted. With shoulders sloping and mournful eyes, he resembled a peasant farmer before the rich landowner, grateful for whatever was thrown to him for his survival.

In Litinov's case, it was his life.

The PM caught movement in the lounge. A few seconds later, Ivanov emerged, still to be completely zipped up in a body bag. Ashton stopped to stare down at the Russian officer's face. He shook his head and sighed.

"All this animosity, this need to create war, when love, peace, and harmony should be our focus."

Litinov nodded. "True, Prime Minister. Those are our constants. It is what we as humans should be about."

Ashton walked into the lounge and sat on the sofa. He beckoned Litinov to join him.

"Life is about being what we're not. The pretend state. A masquerade to manipulate. And do you know why we're compelled to act so fake? To behave incessantly as if someone else? Because our lives are a lie, a falsehood established to keep us waiting and wanting. But we never ask the biggest question of all."

Litinov snatched furtive glances at the PM as if scared to look at him. But Ashton's words were inexplicably mesmerizing. He turned full on toward the PM as he spoke.

"What question, Prime Minister?"

"Why?"

"Why? I don't understand."

"I know you don't," said Ashton. "Very few do. And tonight, I was going to bring you into my confidence, and give you the enlightenment I have shared with your counterparts in many religions. The unfortunate, and quite frankly painful, altercation with comrade Ivanov robbed us both of that opportunity. If, however, our investigation proves your innocence, we may yet discuss this further."

Bishop Litinov stared at the PM's face, still bruised and bloody, and he dropped his head toward the floor, ashamed at the terrible assault he'd been complicit in staging on the prime minister.

"Your contrition is plain," said Ashton. "Let us await the outcome of our investigations. Then, I hope, we will talk more."

The PM signaled his security to re-cuff the bishop and take him away. Ashton caught a glimpse of panic in the bishop's dark blue orbs. He could see that hope was a mutual desire for both of them.

Chapter 78

Embassies had always been seen as 'hands-off' places. The inhabitants of these protected havens were regarded as 'above the law,' untouchable and impossible for the authorities to get at. On sovereign turf, they basked in the impotency of the UK's legal system.

Of course, that was before Freedom Earth. Ashton didn't just change those territory lines; he erased them completely.

When all those countries across the world hurriedly signed up to Ashton's brave new world, they signed away their sovereign sanctuary. Under new state laws, the Freedom Earth Army with the country's security services had the absolute authority to gain access to anywhere that was deemed a threat to a Freedom Earth country. With protected status and diplomatic immunity revoked, embassies were now just another building. And diplomats were fair game.

This realization was dropped upon those within the Russian and Saudi Arabian embassies when both were stormed simultaneously at twenty hundred hours, just like Cartwright had confirmed to the PM.

Within minutes of breaching the embassies, Cartwright's men located and took into custody Prince Khalifa and General Gregor Ivanov's wife, Tatianna. From the monitored video feed in the room, GRU operatives could see the abduction and attempted murder had gone south and quickly shipped out the general's family, but Tatianna remained, tucked into the panic room twenty-five meters beneath the embassy. She'd stayed behind initially to arrange the family's financials but didn't bank on the speed of operations. She didn't consider the embassy could be penetrated. A GRU officer had thrust her into the panic room and locked it when the gates at the front exploded.

The first recce of the embassy didn't produce Tatianna, but Cartwright had floor prints. An MI6 operative running SmartLens received the plans from Cartwright and noticed immediately the panic room accessible from the wine cellar. He indicated to another colleague and the two descended the stairs. Inside the wine cellar, they searched for the entrance to the panic room. Cartwright advised through their earpiece to 'look for an elevator'. A scratch on the floor indicated that one of the racks had been moved. Behind it was an elevator.

Inside, the operatives pressed on the button marked one. The elevator dropped the operatives down to where Tatianna waited. When it opened, they were faced with a massive titanium door with rivets the size of golf balls. It looked tough and impenetrable.

Cartwright, back in central at Vauxhall Cross, stared at the views his operatives in both embassies showed, flicking between screens to catch all the action as it played out.

At the Russian Embassy, he knew his men could blast through, but the amount of explosive needed to move the door could easily risk bringing the building down as well. He preferred the second option: talk the bitch out of the room.

A camera positioned above the door obviously transmitted back into the panic room. The operative smiled into the camera.

"Mrs. Tatianna Ivanov, this is the security services. You have to come out right now. We will not harm you. If you do not, we will explode this door to gain entry. You will most certainly die in this explosion. We are only making this offer once. You have thirty seconds to comply."

A slow hissing sound emanated from the door as the hydraulic locks pulled back, and the massive door started to open. On a sofa, sat calmly, was a tall blonde woman in a navy blue Juicy Couture two-piece lounge suit and Jimmy Choo house slippers. A Glock rested on the leather seat beside her. She carried a knowing smile, as she laid her hands on her lap.

The operatives entered, removed the gun, placed Mrs. Ivanov in cuffs, and led her back to the elevator.

Cartwright flicked his attention to the Saudi Embassy. His men had mowed down GID personnel and were questioning one of them to discover Khalifa's whereabouts. Amongst the howls of pain, the KSA security thug confirmed that Khalifa was upstairs in the master suite.

MI6 operatives burst in at a most unfortunate moment for Khalifa. But for the young girl enduring his advances, it was probably the best timing she'd ever experienced. Raising Khalifa off the bed with nothing but his indignity to cover him, the operative cuffed him and hauled him through the door.

Khalifa's protests in Arabic and English fell on deaf ears. Embassy staff quickly turned their faces away, hiding both their mortifying stares and their embarrassed giggles. Khalifa screamed of 'having someone's head for this'.

But the operative poked his ribcage, and replied, "Not in this country, sonny!"

Cartwright laughed as he watched the whole scene. That'll teach you to come here and shit on our soil, you dirty little towel-head. He picked up the phone to advise the PM on his successful extractions.

Chapter 79

His phone rang in a single persistent tone. Ashton looked down. Cartwright. The raids must be over.

"Yes?"

"Sir, Operation Inkspot is completed."

Inkspot, an interesting codename, thought Ashton. It was chosen because those embassies represented a dark spot upon the otherwise white paper gleam of Freedom Earth.

"Excellent. Anything to report?"

"Mrs. I almost gave us the slip in a sub level panic room. Mr. K was in a most unfortunate situation."

Ashton sniggered. "In flagrante?"

"Yes, sir. With an underage girl too. Dirty bastard."

"Tut-tut. Not very respectful behavior for a royal."

"We removed him as he was."

Ashton's snigger turned into a louder chortle. "Did you capture it?" he asked, hopeful of a viewing.

"Absolutely, sir. I'll send it over now."

The secure email arrived. Ashton clicked on the media file and his screen exploded with Khalifa's indignant voice protesting about his treatment. And he had a lot to protest about. Ashton's battered face still throbbed, but laughing was therapeutic.

Khalifa starkers!

It wasn't an everyday occurrence, and he wallowed in the prince's abject ridicule.

That aloof, pious and hypocritical peacock had been reduced to a figure of fun. It was a joy to watch, and the start of a journey of retribution that would see Khalifa rendered an enemy of Freedom Earth, and a common terrorist who had just tried to murder its founder. By the time Ashton was finished, no country in the world would give him sanctuary.

He'd already uncovered so much about Khalifa. The drugs, the heavy drinking and the pubescent prostitutes whom he forced into his vile perversions. Ashton had even discovered the names of the victims of all those little sex games gone wrong.

Of course, once he'd made sure the world had witnessed what a depraved little shit he really was, the prince would be publicly executed as a traitor of Freedom Earth.

"Thanks, Cartwright. Keep me updated once he's secure."

"Very good, sir. And, sir, make sure you're seen to."

"Yes, of course."

Ashton hadn't had time to go to hospital. He'd had one of his medical team treat him swiftly at the church. But he knew that, with a busted jaw, black eyes and a broken nose, he still looked a mess.

Swiping his phone, he invoked the video camera linked to his social media channel. Ashton spoke with determination into the camera.

"People of the United Kingdom and the nations under Freedom Earth, tonight I was subjected to a horrific attack. Those behind it had one goal in mind. To kill me. The perpetrators that left me in this state were General Gregor Ivanov, Russian Ambassador in the UK and GRU Station Chief, and Prince Khalifa Butti Al Faisal, Crown Prince of Saudi Arabia. Both are from countries who have signed up to Freedom Earth and understand that any form of terrorism, such as the attack tonight, will result in the full wrath of the law under Freedom Earth. And this has already started. The days of terrorism taking the upper hand ended when Al Nadir fell. Never again will terrorism draw a long shadow over the country and the people that I love.

"If anyone out there believes they can win with terrorism, I promise you, I will descend upon you with such brutality the likes of which you will never have seen. You will pray to die. Every act of terror delivered upon the UK or any other nation under Freedom Earth will face retaliation of a hundred-fold. There will be no trial, only raw justice, and death. You have been warned."

Ashton smirked into the camera.

"But for all of you good people who love this country as I do, there will be great prosperity, unprecedented unity, and happiness. We're entering a time of peace and harmony. Nothing will be allowed to stop this glorious era. As your leader, I swear I will do everything in my power to bring you the future you all deserve."

Ashton cut the broadcast with an endearing and lasting smile to the camera. He laid down the phone on the desk, bent forward and knitted his fingers together with ponderous thought. He knew what he'd done. He was the first ever leader to go live with a speech without the accouterments of political office. It would surely set a precedent in the days to come.

A knock interrupted his thoughts, and his comms director, Paul Dawes, dove through the door with a spectacular thrust as if his buttocks were on fire.

"Prime Minister, sir, that broadcast...What were you thinking?"

Ashton shrugged.

"Prime Minister, it wasn't stage managed, properly directed or shot by a media expert. And, sir, with due respect, you looked horrendous. Like you just walked out of a war zone. Why did you do it?"

Ashton ignored Dawes completely. Swiping his phone again, he asked pointedly, "How many hits did it get?"

Dawes checked his tablet for the updated figures.

"Globally, over a billion. In the UK, at least 30 million. Comments and likes have gone through the roof in hundreds of millions. I've never seen such an impact."

"Exactly," snarled Ashton.

Dawes detected his supercilious superiority. He stared at the data stream.

"Prime Minister, this is incredible. The hashtags #AttackonPM and #AshtonsFace are trending across all media channels. Twitter has gone crazy. Instagram is receiving millions of videos in response to your broadcast. Some are from other leaders pledging their support. Others are just everyday people standing by your words against terrorism. I do believe, sir, that the world has fallen in love with you!"

Ashton sneered, rolling back his lips, then he snapped up sharply.

"Any dissenters?"

"Hardly any to speak of. Maybe two percent, if that. You're loved, sir. No question. What you did...I can see now. Genius. Absolute genius."

"Of course. Now, follow up. Big it up. The world knows I've suffered for Freedom Earth. My own blood has been spilled. There will be no stopping the tide now."

Dawes departed to initiate Ashton's instructions, leaving the PM once again alone.

The prime minister's crackling synapses were rapidly working on configuring a new world that would be answerable to just one man: Richard Ashton.

Chapter 80

A ripple of heavy emotions hits me like a tsunami. My footing slips, and I need to cling to one of the crystal walls in my quarters.

After we'd had dinner in St James Café, Sam headed off to the US to meet up with Hutchinson. The US president had doubts about the new energy source and Sam had offered to iron out his concerns. He didn't have my global empathic abilities, so I know he hasn't experienced the same emotive wave. He may, of course, through our connectedness, have felt my reaction to it. I wait for the air to shimmer and I'm a little disappointed that it doesn't. However, it does reassert the notion that this isn't something out to harm me. If it was, Sam would've been by my side in a blink.

After steadying myself. I focus my intention to narrow down the source of what has caused such a sensation throughout the world. I follow the emotive energy path and find myself SearchSighting Ashton.

I draw in a sharp breath as his physical pain slaps me hard. At his desk, a phone in his hand, he stares outward to a rapidly closing door. One look and I can see he's been through a terrible ordeal. I take in his face. A cut beneath his eye, several inches in length, bleeds down his face. His jaw, once chiseled, now balloons on both sides with raging black-purple bruises across the lower half of his face. His nose, off-center and swollen, shows a fractured cartilage. And his right eye is bloody, bloated and black, with a lid that flickers lower, as if all it wants to do is sleep.

What has happened? As much as I hate Ashton's contemptuous, conceited attitude, as if he thinks he's some kind of supreme being, I can't bear to witness his hideous injuries. Looking at him brings back the memories of Sam and mine's incarceration and torture at the sadistic hands of Al Nadir.

I hardly realize I'm shimmering into Ashton's office; I just do it automatically. He needs my help and protection, and that's what I'm there for.

"Ellie! What a surprise."

Ashton tries to give me a wide smile, but his torn lip falls lopsided, and I receive the oh-so-typical sneer the PM delivers daily.

"Ashton, what the hell happened?"

Just as I speak, the air to the right of me vibrates and becomes denser. I know Sam's shimmering in.

"Prime Minister, I saw your broadcast. I'm so sorry."

Sam spurts out the words. He is oblivious to my presence for a second, his attention solely on the PM, just like his focus of old when he was an MI6 agent, when nothing but a target held relevance.

"What broadcast?" I ask.

Sam looks around at me, acknowledging my being there. Finally.

"Oh, hi, darling! The broadcast the prime minister just made to the world about his attack."

"What attack?"

I try to keep my voice low, but that I know nothing about this thing that's happened deeply annoys me. Why don't I feel Ashton's danger? Why was I just reviewing past observations to check on Balance Shift patterns, instead of focusing on the threat befalling a man who had striven for peace?

What is wrong with me?

"Darling, the prime minister was on live, just a few minutes ago. Didn't you see it?"

I shake my head, stunned and still annoyed by my total inability to recognize Ashton's predicament.

"Don't worry, Ellie. Only a billion people across the world did." Ashton smirks, but with his cut lip and busted jaw, the action looks demented.

"Yeah, okay, well I was busy in Kudamun. I can't be everywhere," I snap back, then realize how petulant I sound.

"Ellie, I know that," says Ashton. "How could you know what I've been through? That would be impossible. I mean, you'd have to be tracking me all the time. And I'm sure you've more important things to do than just surveilling me?"

The question is rhetorical, but underneath, Ashton was casting doubt on my ability. He is almost suggesting that, as he was so important, I should be his personal bodyguard.

Sam has his HoloTab invoked and starts to replay Ashton's video. Aimed at a darker area of the room, the video springs to life. I watch Ashton explain to the world why he's a martyr to Freedom Earth.

Then I hear the words, 'You will pray to die', and I'm there, in Al Nadir's hell hole. But instead of being incarcerated by Sabena, I'm standing next to Al Douri as he speaks to human Sam, bound and bleeding in a chair.

"Make no mistake, Sam. We'll fuck her body and then fuck her mind. She'll pray to die."

I watch as my husband closes his eyes on Al Douri's words, the torment too much to stand. I can see he doesn't want Al Douri to witness him cry.

As quickly as I'm transported to that dark place, I throw myself out of it, purposely not wanting to recall the rest of those moments.

Why did Ashton use those words? He's had access to the files of our abduction. He would have listened to and seen everything. But how could he know those specific words? They'd been said in a whisper to Sam. Was it just coincidence? I stare at Ashton, trying to piece together his motivation, whilst he and Sam watch the end of the transmission.

He flicks his head toward me. His eyes, although bulging and bloodshot, seem to be goading me.

"So now, Ellie, you understand."

I prickle at Ashton's patronizing tone.

"Saudi and Russia attacked you. What did you do to piss them off?"

My question, delivered with cold efficiency, is to the point. By Sam's glare, it seems he isn't too happy with my approach.

"I'm not sure I did Ellie," replies Ashton.

"You must have done something. They don't beat up a prime minister and try to kill him for being a good boy."

Agent Provocateur again. I'd learned that trick from old Sam. Ashton tries to straighten himself as if stature makes him look more honest. But he shudders as pain catches him.

"It was Quantum Force. They didn't like the fact it would jeopardize their energy revenues from oil and gas."

Sam leaps in before I can speak. "Understandable. But dreadful that they thought they could take you down, Prime Minister. We expected your text, but when we didn't receive it by nineteen thirty hours, we made other arrangements. We didn't want to burst in at the wrong moment."

"I never got chance to text. I'd been knocked out cold by then."

Sam nods. I watch him gesture to me.

I know what is next.

'No, Sam. Don't make me,' I say to him in my mind.

'Come on, sweetness. He's had it rough. You can see that. He'd be grateful.'

I look at Ashton and see what a provocative prick he was. But I realize I can't let him suffer.

'Yeah, okay, go ahead,' I agree.

"Prime Minister, would you like Ellie to treat your wounds? Put you back together again, so to speak."

"You make me sound like Humpty-Dumpty. But yes, if you could, Ellie. That would be wonderful."

Ashton's eyes are on me. If Sam hadn't suggested, and pleaded with me, I wouldn't have entertained helping, not after those words he'd said. I know they were said to get at me. They were his pointed yet veiled humiliation of me. Yes, they were said in a live transmission to the world, but they were really targeted at me. Ironic, that I never caught the broadcast.

"Of course I will," I find myself saying. I can't back out. I'd agreed. Sam had offered and it would anger him if I suddenly shimmer off. Which is exactly what I wanted to do. "Come here," I command to Ashton.

He catches my terse response. "If it's not too much trouble for you. I'd hate to keep you from more important things."

I cup Ashton's face in my fingers. I visualize his bones, muscles and nerves in my mind. I tunnel into the cells and begin to fix the damaged areas of his face. The swelling diminishes along with the bruising, and the bleeding vanishes as I instructed the blood to coagulate and the skin cells to knit together. Cells in his nose cartilage realign themselves and his nose jolts softly back into place without a shred of pain. I then concentrate on his body. He'd been pummeled hard by his attackers, and bruising was popping up everywhere. His back was in poor shape with some lower vertebrae misaligned due to heavy force. He's either been hit or fallen. I enter his bone and muscle cells through my mind and give them instructions on how to heal.

I watch Ashton straighten and finish the posture he was trying to achieve earlier.

"Wow, Ellie, you really are something else! Wouldn't get that on the National Health."

Ashton's joking indicates that he's already absorbing the benefit of my interventions.

"Yes, well, as you said earlier, you are very important, and we couldn't see you suffer any longer." I deliver my words covered in candy-floss. I don't want to give him an inkling of insight on my next inquiry. "Ashton, why did you say, 'You will pray to die?' That's a barbaric thing to say in a live broadcast. You are a peacemaker, a leader of Freedom Earth who champions peace and harmony. Why speak the words of a vicious terrorist?"

Sam stares back at me, eyes wide, amazed I'd known about that confrontation. Al Douri had, after all, hissed the words into my husband's ear, beyond the range of any microphone. I smile, as he asks in my mind, 'How did you know?'

Ashton's now perfect face displays puzzlement.

"I'm not sure I understand, my dear Ellie. Words of a terrorist? I spoke words that came into my head that I considered to be appropriate to detract anyone from even contemplating terrorism. Yes, I make no apologies. They were brutal, but they were necessary. If we are to stamp out terrorism, we must make a stand. I just used my injuries to show that no one, not even a prime minister, is immune from an attack. But if all agree to unite in peace and harmony, terrorism will never plague us again. You see, Ellie, to welcome the light, you have to step out of the dark. I've been to my dark place today. I took the world to that place. I gave them a warning. But now, we are all in the light. And that light will fill us all. Forever. Glowing brighter."

I observe Ashton, and then Sam's reaction. He nods.

The light, yes, I thought. We all want the light. But if you have too much light, you are blinded by it. And then what is left? Where are you left?

In the dark.

Chapter 81

Half an hour had passed. Ashton glanced at his watch. She must have seen it, he thought with bitterness. Not a call, even for the look of it. He knew she despised him, but to ignore him at a time when the world was rallying around him was insane. It was a precarious position to take.

After the last attack on him at Buzz Academy, his security had taken Natasha and the girls to a safe house in Berkshire. Abigail had apparently become restless and Natasha couldn't control her. In a fit of desperation, she'd bundled them all into her Porsche Cayenne and headed for her family home just outside Exeter in Devon.

Ashton learned of her movements through a few brief calls and texts. And that was pretty much it. Then hardly a word for nine days, except to inform him that Abigail was back in London, staying with friends in Knightsbridge.

With reluctance, Ashton picked up the phone. It rang twice. She answered with an acidic, "Yes?"

"Natasha, darling, how are you?" Ashton kept it civil.

"Okay, and you?" His wife's voice was bored and labored. She didn't want to talk.

"So you haven't heard about anything that happened?"

"No. What happened?" Disinterest dripped from her. Ashton could almost imagine her flicking through the pages of those brain-dead magazines she read, more taken with the latest fashion gimmick than the fact her husband was almost murdered.

Hatred built inside him.

In his mind was Ellie and Sam. So in love. Entwined. Supportive of each other. Ashton suddenly wanted a love like that. Unconditional. Always connected. He remembered Katzy. His lover had always cared, and although he thought it to be just a hot affair, Katzy, he realized, much too late, had really loved him.

And he had really loved her.

"I was attacked," said Ashton calmly, waiting for a reaction. Any reaction. A gasp. An 'oh, my darling'. Anything other than what he received.

"Really. Who by?"

Natasha was apathetic, without compassion or a shred of emotion.

Ashton had to quell his anger. He knew it was a marriage of convenience. He didn't kid himself that they had any love at all. It worked for both of them. He married into society, giving him the pedigree he needed for his legal and eventually political career. For her, he was eye candy and intelligence in one, a stimulating conversation to spice up those dreary dinner parties and tedious soirees.

"Russian intelligence backed by Saudi money. They almost killed me. Didn't you see my broadcast?"

"No. I've been watching The Voice. Was it on TV?"

"I broadcast live on my channel. Got quite a viewing. Have a look."

"Yeah, I will later. But you're okay now, right?"

Ashton struggled to hold back from shouting, 'I nearly died, you uptight, cold, narcissistic bitch'. Instead, he just said, "Yeah, I'm alright now."

"Good, darling. Well, keep in touch. Love you." Her romantic delivery sounded as if she was asking for a portion of foie gras in Harrods Food Hall. In fact, Ashton considered, that request would be delivered with much more passion.

"Love you too."

Titanium hard and Sabatier sharp in response, Ashton closed the line.

He sighed with innate sadness. He thought of his life. Of Katzy and how unfair a blow her death had been. On the edge of him finding true love, her passing meant that one moment of kindred, soul-connecting love had been irrevocably lost forever. Maybe, he'd searched for love too late in his life. Perhaps, he should have tried to have found real love earlier. Instead, he'd settled for a cold acceptance of what was needed to get on, and a continuous lust for anyone who attracted him for a moment's thrill. He lived a base almost feral existence when he could have had so much more.

At Chequers, earlier in April, Ashton remembered how Sam and Ellie had been with each other, arms draped, fingertips touching. A delicate gesture, but one with inherent defiance and a warning aimed at the observer: don't try to break our love, or we'll break you. He'd felt that strength. It wasn't just that they were Kudamaz, and beholding of powers he couldn't comprehend, it was more than that. When Sam had been human, he'd had that sparkle in his eyes that only true love can create. At official Foreign Office functions, where Ashton had seen them both together, the bond of love had been irrepressible.

Ashton thought of Katzy again, her laughing playfulness, and sexy nature, and knew he'd never experience those things again, and unexpectedly, started to cry.

He grabbed a tissue from his solid silver Ottoman tissue box and quickly wiped the tears away. Fearing that he'd be seen as weak, he balled the tissue and threw it into the litter bin at the side of his desk.

A brief rap on the door indicated he'd only just covered up his emotion in time. He delved within himself to find that place of resilience and emotive resistance, and encased himself within its citadel.

"Come!"

As seconds passed before the door opened, Ashton's strength surged up through him, hardening his bones, freezing his blood and darkening his eyes.

"Evening, Prime Minister, I saw the broadcast. You are now recovered? That is good to see. So quick? You must have good genes."

Redfern's clipped, authoritative attitude snapped Ashton's attention fully back into his usual mode of malevolence and manipulation.

Ashton glanced at Redfern. He had to stop this line of questioning immediately. Give him another bone to chew on, thought the PM. It was always the best route to bifurcate his Cabinet secretary's thought process.

"Yes, thank you. Fully recovered. Good genes, quite! Well, that and the experimental treatment those bio-engineers in Cambridge have been working on certainly came through tonight."

"Good to hear," said Redfern, taking the bait. "Prime Minister, for what they did to you, they must be punished to the fullest extent of the law."

"Oh, they will be. Those responsible have been incarcerated under treason against Freedom Earth. I'll take steps to interrogate, as per our usual modus operandi. State executions have been issued. We must show examples. This must never happen again."

"May I say, Prime Minister, had surveillance been better, this wouldn't have happened at all. Perhaps, you could consider some form of automated surveillance, a drone of some kind, linked to a central Freedom Earth artificial intelligence system."

Ashton raised an eyebrow, as he considered Redfern's proposition. It was very forward thinking of his Cabinet secretary, and certainly a job for his Kudamaz compatriots.

"Redfern, that is an excellent idea. If you excuse me, I have some calls to make."

Ashton could see the slight scowl on his colleague's face, but then a faint smile flitted across instead, before it vanished like stardust from a dying firework.

Chapter 82

Sam's phone rings out. We've barely been back in the apartment in Silent Waters a few minutes when the same Downing Street pest shows up again.

"I'm not going to be at his beck and call," I snap at Sam, as he answers yet another request from Ashton. "It's not on, Sam. We're Kudamaz now. You're not working for MI6, the government or Ashton. Why do you always feel compelled to go to him? It's like he's got a hold on you." I stare at my husband, and he fixes on me intently.

"He needs us. He's just been through a tough time. You saw him today. He was a shadow of his former self. He needs us more than ever, Ellie."

I sense Sam's energies pulling through the Reality Gap, and his soul force connects to its destination. I know where he's going. I align my energies with my husband's and we shimmer in unison.

"Ashton, what is it now? It's lucky we weren't off-worlding."

I don't give Sam the chance to be convivial. Ashton pouts forlornly like a petulant child wanting sweets and toys. What toy does he want today? I soon find out.

"I need your help to design a new surveillance drone system, something unobtrusive, almost friendly, but that sees everything. The attacks on me were caused by poor surveillance. I never want to make that mistake again. Can you help?"

Ashton looks at Sam and virtually ignores me. I bristle with annoyance.

"Of course we can help."

I roll my eyes and shout at Sam in my mind.

'Why the hell do we want to interfere? If he wants a fucking all-seeing drone system to spy on everyone, that's his business, not ours. We shouldn't be helping him make this. It's wrong. We're Kudamaz, Sam, and we shouldn't intervene in matters like this. It could unnaturally change the Balance. That goes against the Antediluvian laws of Kudamun.'

I can see Sam is purposely avoiding my telepathic rant. He loved engineering stuff when he was human, but as Kudamaz, he has all the capability he needs to make what Ashton desires. It's like he still has a human ego, and it's driving him.

"Prime Minister, we need to leave you to work on options, but we'll return soon."

I watch as Sam starts to shimmer.

I don't bother to look back at Ashton, but instead focus my energies and pull my soul force into Kudamun and our luxurious quarters.

Alone in our crystal-encased living room, I fume.

"Sam, I'm not doing it, and neither are you. You've done enough with the Harmon execution devices, and that execution stage we designed. We must draw back now."

Sam spins around at me, suddenly angry. I can't remember when he'd last been so enraged with me.

"I don't know why you're being like this! Do you think he's going to unleash a surveillance system to spy on the world?"

Sam spits his words at me. I purse my lips and scratch my forehead the way I used to when I was human. It's a phantom reaction, a recalling of memories of when Sam and I had been head to head in a heated quarrel.

"Yes, probably. Well, he could. He thinks he's the king of Freedom Earth. Goodness knows what he's going to do next." My argument wasn't holding strong, and I knew it.

"Ellie you're being paranoid. Ashton is a good man. He's been through hell tonight. You know his injuries. You repaired him. He didn't make that up. He's the victim, darling. He's been targeted because he wants to bring peace. And now you're against him. That surveillance he speaks of is to make the world a better, safer place. What's wrong with that?"

Aby-od appears in the doorway to our quarters. He looks at me and then Sam.

"Everything alright?" he asks tentatively.

I jump in using my powerful authority as the Protector of Earth.

"Aby-od, it's Ashton. He wants us to create some new surveillance system that he can use just because he's been attacked twice this month."

"Use for what purpose?"

Sam butts in, "For the betterment of mankind, Lord Aby-od."

"I see no problem if this surveillance device is used for good."

"But this breaks our Antediluvian laws. You know, non-interference, and all that."

"Ellie, those laws were broken by Aswa-da, and previously, Dimkur. But I appreciate your warning. As Protector, you have the final say in this surveillance device. If you have evidence it will be used for evil purposes, you cannot be involved. Do you have such evidence?"

My lips open slightly but close again. I have zilch on Ashton. Once again, it all comes down to what the Balance Shift is doing and may do. Right now, it's stable, in the white light zone, supporting the hypothesis that everything Ashton is doing is correct for the world.

I shake my head, and look away, resentful of any help that Sam was planning to give to the PM.

"Well, then, it is clear. Go ahead and assist Prime Minister Ashton in his campaign to bring peace to the world in whatever form that assistance requires."

Aby-od's eyes dart back to me. But, like a moody teenager, I return no eye contact. Without a word, I shimmer out of our quarters and head for the Observation Room.

Inside, I bring up the scenes from seven that evening inside the lounge of the Russian Orthodox Church. I watch as a mountainous man beats six types of shit out of Ashton. Then the PM quickly turns the tables. I catch the calculating look on his face, the sheer brutality of his actions, and the barbaric torture he uses to make the Russian talk. I freeze the scene as he shoots the Russian. I flick a few controls, and I'm in the room with Ivanov and Ashton. Time's on pause. I stare at Ashton. I look into his eyes, those windows on the soul so often spoken about in Earth folklore.

Deep into his eyes, I stare, hoping for a conclusion, a final statement of his intent.

His eyes reflect an abyss of nothing. An empty vessel. A man who has forsaken what he needs in life for what he *thought* he wanted in life.

For the first time, I feel sorrow for Ashton.

But also, I feel incredible fear; a vessel that's empty can be filled with anything.

Chapter 83

A bone-thin woman with a long, angular face and vacant eyes curled like a half-starved cat on the sofa in an ornate, high-ceilinged Georgian living room. Her attention had drifted momentarily to answer the phone to her husband. She zoned out of his wittering on about some attack on him. Always the bloody martyr, that man, she thought, concluding that it was just another episode of his political showmanship. She didn't think anything more about it. Her attention quickly affirmed itself back on the young, handsome guy on the talent show on TV.

"Oh, you're so mean! He sang like an angel," Natasha Ashton yelled at one of the judges who'd made a defamatory remark about the young singer's abilities. "And with a body like that, he could surely take me to heaven." She giggled and knocked back her drink, and smiled with sensual pleasure as she imagined what she'd do with that lithe, muscled eighteen year old.

A small child sat on the floor in front of the sofa and played with her dolls. She had a mop of curly, sunshine-gold hair and bright blue inquisitive eyes that requested attention, although the woman on the sofa couldn't be bothered to give her any.

From the left of the room, a carved door opened, and a portly, middle-aged lady stepped inside.

"Mrs. Ashton, I think it's time I put Mariella to bed. She really shouldn't still be up this late."

"Oh, Florry, sweetie, give her a minute more. She likes watching all those hunks with Mummy. Don't you, sweetheart?"

Mariella turned around, nodded and smiled, pleased to have received her mother's interest at last. Florry, the nanny, gave Natasha a reproachful stare, and settled herself down into a chair. "I'll sit here until they've finished squawking."

Natasha watched the nanny and shrugged. "Please yourself!" She yanked the cocktail shaker from the table behind the sofa and poured the remainder of the gin-vodka mix into her glass, and then down her throat. "Oh that's good," she gasped. She tried to pour more, only to realize the cocktail mix had run out.

Natasha swallowed and steadied herself, as she reached out to the nanny.

"Florry, sweetie, get me another. We've gone dry here!"

"I don't know the mix. Where's Chrispin?" she asked, indicating the absence of the resident butler.

"Night off maybe. Fuck knows. Come on, old girl, get me that drink," slurred Natasha, waving her empty shaker at the nanny. Disgusted with her employer's behavior, Florry leaped up to grab Mariella out of earshot of her mother's swearing. Natasha saw the movement as an opportunity and she thrust the shaker into Florry's hand.

"Good show. Fill her up!"

Florry took the shaker over to the bar in the corner of the room and poured a mix of vodka and gin, with elderberry fizz and lemon juice. She had no real idea what she was doing. But if it shut up the harpy on the sofa, then she'd done her job well.

She poured out the contents of her newly created drink into the glass and handed it to Natasha, who sipped at it. Her eyes widened as the mix hit her palette.

"Lovely, Florry, top it up," said Natasha, licking her lips without taking her eyes off the screen.

Florry made the mistake of sighing, and commented under her breath, "You've had enough already."

Natasha heard the sigh and the barely audible comment and spun around to face the nanny, viciously annoyed. "What's wrong with you?"

"Nothing, Mrs. Ashton," answered Florry hurriedly, as she recognized Natasha's state of mind and her proximity to Mariella. She bent down and swooped up the young child into her arms. Then she turned back toward the door, refusing to engage in further discourse.

Natasha sprang up from the sofa and stood between Florry and the door. Her brown eyes were wild and threatening.

"Don't fucking judge me."

With a glass tipping in one hand and a sharply manicured finger prodding in Florry's chest in the other, Natasha continued to scream.

"I don't need you to fucking judge me. You don't know what I have to put up with. You don't know me. You don't know my life. So don't judge what you don't fucking know!"

Florry turned Mariella's face into her generous breast to shield her from her mother's banshee rantings. The child didn't cry. She stayed silent, and buried herself into Florry's chest.

"Mrs. Ashton, I'm taking Mariella upstairs now. By the other thing, I meant no offense and I would never presume to judge you. Good night, Mrs. Ashton."

Florry made a hasty exit before Natasha had time to retaliate.

Sulking that the nanny had the last word, Natasha sank back into the sofa, poured the rest of the cocktail from the shaker and swigged it back, then stared at the TV. She wet her lips salaciously, taking in the gorgeous teenage group on stage.

"What I wouldn't do with you."

Grabbing the shaker, she pouted, seeing it was empty. She raised herself from the sofa and picked up the gin and vodka bottles. She stared at each, bemused about what to do next. Annoyed that the butler wasn't around, she lifted the gin bottle and took a series of hefty gulps. She repeated the process with the vodka, and then the gin again. Dragging both bottles, she lurched her frame back onto the sofa.

Through drooping eyes, as the alcohol took effect, Natasha garbled, "She thinks I can't be a mother. I'll show her tomorrow. I'll show her I can be a proper mother!"

Natasha slept in, as she did every morning. As semi-consciousness beckoned into her brain, she moved in a languid circular motion until she was in the middle of the bed. Her baby-doll nightie slipped down, revealing a cosmetically enlarged breast that looked unnatural and Barbie-like against her rake-thin physique. She opened one eye as sunlight streamed in. Slowly, she became aware of someone in her room, a figure she could make out against the window.

Squinting, she called out, "Who's there?"

"Mrs. Ashton, good morning. It's me, Tina. I thought you would you like some coffee?"

Tina, her maid, laid the tray on her bedside cabinet. On the tray was a cafetiere of Arabica coffee and a porcelain cup.

"Yeah, great. Pour it. Black, right? Couldn't face milk in the morning."

"Of course, madam."

Tina poured the coffee and handed it to Natasha. Embarrassed, the maid deflected her glance from her mistress' semi-naked body. Natasha hadn't bothered to rearrange herself to cover her upper torso, and unashamedly displayed the work that had cost her husband over twenty grand.

"What day is it?" asked Natasha, yawning.

"Saturday, Mrs. Ashton. It is a beautiful day."

"Yeah, yeah, looks it. Can you get out now?" snapped Natasha, standing up.

She clocked the mess her baby-doll was in and straightened the clothing back to cover herself up. Wandering to the window, she looked out across the garden and the countryside beyond to the sea.

"I'm going to take Mariella to the seaside today," she announced. But Tina had already left the room. Natasha padded, still sleepy, out onto the expansive landing. A door opened and Florry emerged with Mariella fully dressed and looking pristine.

Natasha remembered she had something to prove to Florry, something about being a mother.

"Hey, Florry, I'm taking Mariella today."

The nanny looked up and smiled. "Of course, Mrs. Ashton. She's all ready for you, whenever you like."

Mariella jumped up and down as she realized her real mummy was going to take her out. She so rarely spent time with her mummy, it was quite a treat when she did.

Natasha sauntered over to Mariella and Florry. She squatted down to get at her daughter's height.

"Sweetie, Mummy's going to take you to the seaside. Would you like that?"

Mariella beamed. "Oh, yes. And get me ice cream and candy floss?"

I don't fancy getting sticky and messy, thought Natasha. Well, not with ice cream and candy floss anyway, and a naughty grin slipped across her face. She suppressed her dirty mind in favor of being a mother.

"You can have as much ice cream and candy floss as you like, darling. It's Mummy's special treat. Just wait downstairs with Florry and I'll be with you soon."

Florry nodded. She took Mariella by the hand and descended the stairs.

A short while later, Natasha entered the playroom, garbed in black Diesel jeans, a pale pink Dior silk sweater and rose blush kitten heeled Manolos.

Florry stared at her. Well, that's not a mother taking her daughter to the seaside, decided the nanny. But she gave no inkling to Natasha of the thoughts rolling around in her head.

Natasha slipped into the car. Florry settled Mariella into the child's seat at the back. She held onto the driver's side door, stopping it from shutting.

"Are you sure you don't want me with you?" asked Florry. "Mariella can be a bit of a handful."

Natasha glared at the nanny, and then let her vitriol seep out of her perfectly pouting lips. "Florry, you're not the only one who can look after her. I am her mother, and I can handle anything. Go on, put your feet up. Watch some daytime crap on TV. I'll be fine, you'll see."

Natasha pulled the door out of Florry's hand and slammed it shut. She placed her foot on the accelerator and her Porsche Cayenne shot off up the paved driveway, out of the wrought iron gates and up the lane to the A30. As Natasha's car passed a black Volvo estate parked in a layby, the car pulled away and slipped into the lane a little way behind the Cayenne.

Florry watched them go and tried to subdue the apprehension rising within her.

Chapter 84

The man received the secure, encoded message. He invoked the crypto-cipher, and the message displayed, showing a photo and registration number. He clicked on the phone-tracking software, and a blip appeared on a road about twenty minutes away. He clicked on the blip and it showed a live image of a car. He indicated to his driver to get on, and they headed in the direction of the blip.

Natasha noticed the black car in her rear-view mirror, despite its attempt to shield itself behind several vehicles. She knew the lanes since childhood, and she knew all the shortcuts too. Slamming a hard left, she whooshed down a very tight lane. No one followed.

Slipping left and right, Natasha tracked the flow of the hedgerows at speed. She flicked on the voice recognition system, requested a text to Richard Ashton, and dictated it. Or rather, she screamed it.

"Next time you want to track me, teach your fucking sex pests how to drive first!"

Natasha headed into a bridleway alongside a field and traveled down, driving near to the main road but keeping to the fields for speed. After flinging her Cayenne through the puddles and mud, she arrived near Woodbury on the other side of Exmouth. Pulling onto the A376, she raced down the road, only slowing when she approached the speed camera near to the town.

She parked on the esplanade and trotted along with Mariella, taking in the seafront. Even to her bloodshot eyes, the views across the Exe River to Starcross and Dawlish made her stop and breathe in. Picturesque rolling hills, dotted white houses, golden beaches and glistening blue waters showed why this part of South West England was regarded as the English Riviera.

Mariella pulled at Natasha's arm. She pointed to the round ice cream kiosk on the corner by the esplanade.

"Mummy, can I have an ice cream?"

"Yes sweetie," muttered Natasha, distracted by the sailing boats out on the sea. Their calmness seemed to quieten her anguished soul. She thought about Richard and realized she still hadn't seen that broadcast, despite his plea for her to watch it. She took her phone out and loaded Ashton's social media channel. The video popped up.

"Mummy, *please* can I have an ice cream?"

"Yes, darling, okay…Oh my God!"

On the screen, her husband was showing the world what he'd gone through. At the time of her quick chat with him, she'd genuinely thought he was exaggerating, spinning her a yarn, the way he spun his political games. Always the victim. She never believed he'd actually been hurt. As the video played, she barely recognized him.

Unexpectedly, her heart cried out, and with it, her eyes filled with tears. She had to sit down on a bench to regain her composure. Mariella sat patiently next to her mother. Natasha looked down at her daughter, smoothed her curled hair and cupped her face with one bony hand.

"Oh, darling, your poor father. He's really been through hell."

"What's hell, Mummy?" asked Mariella, confused by her mother crying when seconds before she'd been so happy.

"It's a very bad place, darling, and your daddy went there yesterday."

Mariella's eyes were wide and questioning. "Did daddy come back from the bad place?"

"Yes, darling, he did."

"Oh good. Mummy, can we get some ice cream?"

Natasha stared down at her daughter, wiped the tears away, and tried to smile.

"Yes, we will. And after, we'll call daddy and tell him how much we love him."

"Yes, Mummy, we love daddy lots and lots."

Natasha nodded. Suddenly, a new dawning of recognition arose within her. She *did* still love Richard. She clasped Mariella's hand and walked with her to the ice cream kiosk.

"What flavor do you want, darling?"

"The white one, Mummy."

Natasha handed the Mr. Whippy ice cream to her daughter, who grabbed it greedily. Natasha decided on butterscotch. But she wasn't really interested in eating. She couldn't get Richard's attack out of her mind.

Natasha walked idly back along the pavement by the seafront. She flicked a look at posters advertising the various tribute bands playing at the pavilion theatre across the road. But Richard floated back into her mind. Mariella skipped a little way in front of her, singing and eating her ice cream.

Then, her much-loved ice cream plunged to the floor. In unison, Mariella fell. Or rather, she dropped, as if a great force had whacked into her.

Natasha threw her unwanted ice cream away onto some stones, ran over, and bent down to Mariella. She pulled her up, her hand beneath her head to support her, and she felt that it was wet. Drawing back her hand, Natasha saw blood. Bile rose, and her heart thundered. Her baby girl. What had happened to her? Frantic, Natasha looked around for assistance.

"Help me, someone, please!" Natasha screamed as she knelt and cradled her daughter in her arms.

A young guy with a kind face walked fast toward her, and an elderly couple on a bench behind struggled to raise their arthritic bodies to give support. A woman delivering sandwiches from a van flung open her door and called out, "Are you okay?"

Natasha stood up with Mariella, now motionless, blood dripping through her golden hair and down her small, cherubic face.

"My daughter fell and hurt her head!"

The young guy arrived, his phone already in his hand, speaking to the emergency services. Natasha looked around, dizzy and confused, unable to process what to do. She listened to the man talking.

"Yes, she may have had some kind of seizure. She lost consciousness and fell."

Natasha picked up snippets of people talking.

"She doesn't look too good, poor little mite."

"That's a lot of blood."

"I hope's she makes it."

Words circled, entrapping Natasha in bewilderment. Her mind spun like in a centrifuge.

"Where's that ambulance?" shouted the guy, as he searched up and down the street.

"It's coming," said someone else.

Up the road, the man in a black G class Merc with darkened windows doubled back and observed the crowd. The Glock with the Osprey silencer rested in his lap.

"Put her down here, love. You look like you're going to faint."

People pulled Mariella out of Natasha's weak arms. Not knowing what to do, she released her hold and the kind guy laid Mariella on a canopied bench at the side.

Shaking, Natasha dove into her bag. Richard, she thought, I must tell him. She hit on favorites and pressed RA.

"Richard, something's happened to Mariella. Some seizure, or a brain thing, I don't know. She just collapsed."

She listened to Richard's cool, authoritative tone, and she wanted to melt into his voice. "Is the ambulance there?"

"It's coming. Oh, Richard, I'm so sorry. I've been such a bitch. I saw the broadcast. I can't believe it. What they did…Once this mess is sorted out with Mariella, I'm coming back. We need to try again. I know you don't believe me, but when I saw the broadcast I realized what it would be to lose you. I do love you, Richard. I love you so-"

The man in the black G class Merc took the shot. Between the kind guy, the middle-aged sandwich seller and the elderly couple, Natasha was clean and clear in his mental cross-hairs. The high-velocity bullet tunneled into her chest, and into her heart. Natasha had neither the time to know what was happening nor the life to see the effect her collapse had on the crowd around her.

The kind-faced guy leaped back. The sandwich lady screamed. The elderly couple went catatonic.

The ambulance pulled up to the curb. The team inside turned their heads toward the commotion by the bench. They saw a skinny but attractive lady talking on her phone. Then suddenly, she crumpled. And then they saw the blood on her chest.

The ambulance team ran over, checking both the woman and the child on the bench. The team leader found the gunshot on the left side of the little girl's head.

"They've both been shot," said the leader sotto voce. "Get these people away fast. This is an active crime scene now."

He moved away from the crowd, who were being dispersed swiftly by his team. He touched his radio, and called in the shooting, requesting a SOCO Police Team.

One of the female members of the team stared at Natasha and was flooded with an image of her and the prime minister at the Academy Awards. She beckoned the team leader over.

"Dave, you know who that is?"

The leader looked again and recognized the woman.

"Oh shit! It's Ashton's wife." He turned back to Mariella. "And that's their little girl."

The female member noticed the mobile on the floor. A call was still in connection. She could hear a frenzied, angry voice on the other end.

Carefully, using a tissue, she picked up the mobile.

"Hello?"

"Who's this? Where's Natasha? What the hell is happening?"

The female member knew the voice immediately. She trembled.

"Prime Minister, I'm sorry. Your wife, she's been shot, and your daughter, your…" She couldn't finish, too upset by the scene. The team leader took over.

"Prime Minister, sir."

"What the *fuck* is happening? Some mad woman just told me my wife's been shot!"

Ashton's infuriated voice sounded loud above the chaos.

The team leader swallowed, and continued. "Prime Minister, I'm sorry to confirm that the woman you spoke to was my colleague. I'm from East Devon Ambulance Team, and what she said was true. I'm sorry, sir. Your wife appears to have been shot. I'm so sorry, sir, it looks like your daughter was also shot. Both died on impact, sir. They would have felt nothing."

The leader waited on the line for the prime minister's response. He seemed to be waiting a long time.

Finally, the prime minister returned. A voice of ice replied, "I'm coming down."

The line went dead, and the team leader stared at the phone, unable to comprehend the events that unfolded around him.

As he stood at the edge of the tragedy, a black Volvo estate drew up. Two men, suited and, by the outline of the holsters, well tooled up, came over to question him.

He couldn't tell them anything other than what he'd seen.

It was simply a day at the seaside that had turned into carnage.

The two men looked at each other with worried frowns. They knew they needed a better answer than that for the prime minister of the United Kingdom.

Chapter 85

Ashton remained immobile. His phone silent. His hands palm down on the desk. Back straight, shoulders square. Face immutable. Eyes ahead focused on years passed in duty instead of joy.

Ashton felt the tilt down, toward the abyss inside him. He drowned in the feeling. Suffocating. He welcomed it. He wanted his lungs to sear raw, sucking in air that wasn't there. He knew the agonizing vacuum he was in was just like before when he'd lost his beloved Katzy in March that year when Al Nadir's sadistic viciousness had raised its head and targeted him personally.

Natasha had said she loved him. Her words of undeniable truth touched him. She'd wanted to start over. She'd wanted to give their marriage another chance. They'd been on the precipice of reconciliation. But that chance, that chance to find love, like Katzy before had been snatched from him.

She'd gone. Ripped from him.

He had nothing.

He had no one.

Just that steady, solid thump. That resonance of vengeance.

He breathed in and out. Slowly. And let his soul drop and darkness wash over him.

A knock at his door sent a jolt through him, pulling him back to the present.

His chief security advisor walked in, his tone grave and respectful.

"Prime Minister, I have just heard. I am sorry for your loss. Please accept my condolences."

Standard empty words, thought Ashton wryly.

"Thank you." He paused. "Abigail. Has anyone checked on my daughter?"

The chief security advisor shook his head, worry popping out across his features. "No, Prime Minister. Our last understanding was she was with your wife in Devon."

Ashton paled. "She's here in London, staying with friends in Knightsbridge. I've no address. Track and find her."

His chief security advisor touched his ear. "The daughter is in London, Knightsbridge area. Track her phone, any activity on cards, get her location and collect her. Stat!"

His chief security advisor turned back to Ashton.

"Prime Minister, we'll find her. You can be assured of that."

Ashton glared at his chief security advisor but said nothing. His eyes delivered the cold, hard message that failure would bring.

With a swift nod, understanding the terms, the chief security advisor left to find Ashton's wayward daughter.

Ashton leaned back, staring at the closed door. Looking at his chief security advisor disappear through the doorway, Ashton issued a faint whisper of a smirk and then it vanished. His phone jumped off the desk. Ashton answered. His MI5 chief, Dudley Gibbs, had called to deliver an update report on ballistics.

"It's a GID tit-for-tat. Same ammo as they used in the Buzz Academy attempt. This is because we have Khalifa. What would you like to do, sir?"

"Where is he held?"

"Usual location for FA hostiles. Are you coming, sir?"

"Yes. I'm heading for Exeter, where my wife and daughter are. But I'll see you on the way to Northolt. Do nothing to him."

Gibbs harrumphed a little, not quite understanding the PM's instruction. "I'm sorry, sir, do nothing to him, you say? So, you don't require anyone to *talk* to him a bit? Make him more flexible for your requirements?"

"No, I don't," snapped Ashton. "Keep him in the cell, and don't go near him. Understand?"

"Yes, Prime Minister," confirmed Gibbs, and he rang off in something of a quandary.

Within seconds of one call, another came through. Ashton clocked it was coming in from President Hutchinson's private line.

"Richard, London Station just told me about Natasha and Mariella. Oh God, man, I can't believe those bastards got to them." The president gushed words of comfort to his close buddy, Ashton, and the PM took them graciously. "How's Abigail? They didn't get to her, did they?"

"Five is just searching for her now. You know she's quite a hothead."

"Rich, she's a free spirit, rather like my own Becca. They do as they like. You try to control them, and you'll only push them further away."

"That's true, Al. I sent them all into a safe house, and they damn near exploded. Abigail and Natasha, they don't see..."

Ashton stopped. He realized his tense was wrong. Natasha wasn't in the present. Natasha wasn't anywhere anymore.

He suddenly broke down. Tears rolling fast, heavy sobs reverberated across the Atlantic to his pal, the president.

"Oh, jeez, Rich. You need to take a break. Stop everything. Come over. Spend some time with me and Doloros. Stay at the ranch. Bring Abigail. Just chill, unwind and forget."

Ashton wiped the tears away.

"Nice thought, my friend. But I have to be here. There are the funerals to arrange. And Abigail...Oh, dear God. How am I going to tell...?" Ashton lost the words as he choked up again. His hazel eyes filled with tears.

"Rich, be strong. You're the most incredible guy I've ever met. Think about what you've done with Freedom Earth, the virtual eradication of terrorism, and Quantum Force."

Ashton interrupted. "You're behind me on that one, aren't you?"

"Absolutely Rich. We intend to align with your timescales. I had looked into phased intro, but hell, when the figures came in, they didn't stack. Nate and I discussed it. He was pretty against my phased roll-out, claiming I should be a pioneer, like you. And when I thought about it, he was right. This quantum energy thing, well, yeah, it is the most significant discovery in mankind's history. It's our duty to bring it as soon as possible to the people who count on us."

Ashton, despite the enormous sorrow inside of him, found the strength to smirk. Little BDSM-obsessed Nate had delivered, and now he was still on track with Quantum Force.

"But, Rich, you shouldn't be thinking about Freedom Earth, Quantum Force or any other initiative right now. You need to take time out to grieve properly. Throwing yourself into work is the worst thing you can do. God forbid, if it was Becca or Doloros, I'd shut everything down and mourn for a month."

Ashton listened. Yes, you probably would, you wet lettuce, he thought.

"I hear what you say, buddy, and believe me, I'm going to pull back. But there are still some things I have to do. I can't let them think they've won. There's going to be retribution, and it will come hard, fast, and brutal."

Gone was the soft sentiment Hutchinson heard earlier.

"I understand, Rich. A man's gotta do what a man's gotta do. But take care of yourself. Don't lose yourself in vengeance. That path leads to darkness."

Ashton saw a call coming in on his security line. It was from Five.

"Al, I have to go. I think they've just found Abigail."

"Are you sure it's her?"

"Absolutely, sir. Will you come down?"

Ashton's hand shook as he stared at his watch. "Yes."

In the car, Ashton played back what he'd been told. Five found Abigail amongst other young boys and girls in their late teens in a basement in a house in Pont Street. There was evidence of cocaine and substance abuse. All signs had showed excessive vomiting, defecation, paralysis, and eventual respiratory failure. Had Abigail heard about her mother and little sister? Had she taken her own life? Was it some kind of weird suicide pact, and it was just a coincidence that she chose now to enact it?

Ashton knew that coincidences rarely happened. As Ellie was always so fond of pointing out to him, everything is connected.

As thoughts circled and he analyzed the situation, he slowly realized he hadn't processed the fact that Abigail was dead. It was as if he'd pushed that fact to the back of the filing cabinet of his mind and kept his attention on other aspects pertinent to the case. Objectivity afforded no time for emotion. His time in British Intelligence had drilled that painfully into him.

He considered again the facts. Abigail knew her limits. Yes, she was wild, but she was never bloody stupid. She'd never overdose on her own. She'd been coerced, and the rest were there as a distraction. She'd been the target. Only they used a different weapon. He thought about the symptoms again and realized something was off. A cocaine overdose leads to seizures and a stroke. Cocaine is specific in what it attacks: the brain. The effects of overstimulation kick off tachycardia, the heart going into overdrive, and the brain tries to compensate for this effect of super-stimulation. It drops into psychosis, seizures and eventually death. Cocaine does not result in respiratory failure, considered Ashton, running down the typical poisons that did. Neurotoxins were well known for delivering that fatal impact.

Ashton opened the line to Five. Gibbs answered.

"Check for evidence of neurotoxins in the cocaine."

"Neurotoxins?"

"I believe this was a hit on Abigail made to look like a drugs overdose."

"Right, sir. We'll talk when you arrive. I see you are close."

Inside the shabby basement flat, Ashton stood. Forensics were already on the scene, but they parted the waves when Ashton walked in. Bodies were everywhere. Most were half-naked, covered in shit and sick. Partially eaten junk food lay scattered between bottles of vodka, JD, and Red Bull. What the hell did Abigail think she was doing messing with this kind of scum?

Ashton surveyed the room. None of the faces were Abigail. The Five officer that greeted the prime minister called over to him. "She's over here, sir."

Ashton maneuvered through the melee of bodies. He picked his way across the room, averted his eyes from the sheer human squalor and concentrated on the place where his daughter rested.

A soft sigh escaped his lips. She was fully clothed, albeit in a skimpy sparkly top and a tight Lycra black mini.

Her face displayed a journey of agony.

Beautiful eyes now protruded out of her skull as if someone had tried to suck them out with a vacuum cleaner. Heart shaped lips that had spoken such abuse and caused family disruption now jerked downward, a sign that paralysis had hit her suddenly. Vomit had pooled and crusted around the corners of her mouth and down her chin. Her slender body was twisted at unnatural angles, suggesting her body had convulsed violently.

He shuddered and looked away, knowing that Abigail's death had been neither peaceful nor immediate.

In his days with Six, he'd seen puffer fish toxin used on a fellow agent who'd been caught. He'd watched, unable to save his colleague for fear of revealing his position. Despite all that had passed, he remembered it vividly.

A horrible, excruciating death.

And now his own daughter had met the same fate.

He dropped to his knees and cradled her face in his hands.

"Oh, my darling Abigail. My poor little mixed up girl. I hope you have found your peace now."

He bent forward, closed her eyelids and lightly kissed her forehead.

"Goodbye, sweet Abigail."

Even before the toxicology report came in, Ashton was certain that the cocaine had been cut with a neurotoxin like tetrodotoxin or fuggy.

Ashton rose from the floor, aware that eyes were flicking toward him, reflecting pity. He sensed bile rising, and he swallowed down the feeling. He controlled his hurt and sorrow, keeping it contained until he could unleash it with an unrelenting force on the perpetrator who'd destroyed his family.

Chapter 86

One more stop before his plane trip to Exeter. Ashton had told Gibbs it was on his way, but he'd have made it even if it had been right out of his way. He wasn't going to miss this appointment.

He passed through the dark grey security gates of an installation, which, by its ambiguous appearance, could be anything from a warehouse packing factory to an electricity sub-station. No signage denoted the owner of the facility. Cameras doted in every conceivable position, and heavily armed guards and sophisticated biometric scanners at the entrance suggested that a little more than just baked beans were being packed there.

Ashton walked through quickly, flanked by guards in a diamond formation. He passed concrete cell after cell. No sounds came out. But Ashton realized that the cells were all soundproofed.

He smirked, pleased with this feature.

Gibbs met him by a cell marked, K. Ashton felt Gibbs' inspection. In the car, he'd descended deep into himself, and bricked up any glimmer of emotion. His feeling as to the loss he'd just suffered had been over-ridden by a singular drive to avenge his loved ones.

"Prime Minister, sir, thank you for coming. Again, my condolences on your loss."

Ashton held his hand up to halt Gibbs' personal sentiments.

He was not the prime minister.

He was not an MI6 agent, or a lawyer or a journalist.

He was a man who had one simple task to perform.

"Open it," commanded Ashton, and Gibbs opened the thick concrete cell door.

Inside, Khalifa sat, garbed in an orange jumpsuit and shackled to the arms and the legs of a metal chair.

He looked up as Ashton entered.

Apart from a small bruise on his face, he was, as Ashton had instructed, untouched.

Ashton shut the door. He stared into the cameras above and gave a cut across the throat action. The red light blinked off.

Khalifa turned around to see the cameras shut down. He flicked his eyes back to Ashton.

"Oh, I see the gloves are off," he sneered. "I suppose I should be afraid. But the truth is, despite your talk of Freedom Earth, I am still a Saudi Arabian national, and a member of the Royal Family of the Kingdom of Saudi Arabia. I have complete diplomatic immunity, and you cannot do anything to me."

Ashton listened and remained silent.

"You have not charged me."

Ashton let Khalifa talk. Let the little man ramble.

"You have no authority."

Still, silence from the PM. Khalifa squirmed. He was unsure of Ashton's next move. He straightened with indignance and bred-in pomposity.

"I am Prince Khalifa Butti Al Faisal, heir to the Saudi Arabian Kingdom. You have no jurisdiction over me."

Ashton looked across to a table holding his usual kit to get people talking. Khalifa followed his eyes.

"You cannot torture me. I have diplomatic immunity."

Ashton stood, nodded, and finally spoke. "You think because you have killed my wife and my daughters that I want to torture you?"

Khalifa drained of color.

"What…what do you mean?" He stuttered. "Killed your family? How can I have done this? I have been incarcerated in here since last night."

"But they are dead. Killed by your GID."

"No…no. This cannot be. I haven't done…" Khalifa shook his head, his mind racing to understand what was going on. Ashton could see the confusion, the worry, the fear.

He absorbed Khalifa's terror. Taking in his dread made Ashton stronger.

"My security services confirmed the ammunition was one used by your GID."

Khalifa made to stand, to protest that the prime minister had got it wrong. That there must be a mistake. The shackles kept him down in his seat.

"Prime Minister, I swear to you, I swear I did not order the GID to kill your family."

"But they did."

Khalifa dropped his head down and shook it softly. "I didn't…"

Ashton swung a glance at the table and sneered. A venomous look flickered across his face.

Then, he shrugged.

"But…I'm not going to torture you. You've nothing I need to know, so what's the point? You're of no use to me."

Khalifa wriggled around, still maintaining his innocence. But Ashton ignored his pleas. He reached inside his jacket and pulled out his Sig.

"No! You can't. This is murder. Assassination. I've done nothing. What do you want? Money? I'll give you anything."

"You have only one thing I want."

Khalifa looked hopeful. Everyone had a price. "Name it," he said smugly.

"Your life."

Ashton fired bullet after bullet into Khalifa, walking closer to him. He reloaded and continued to pelt another round into the dead body until the prince was ripped into pieces. By the time Ashton finished, he was standing over the body, covered in Khalifa's blood and detritus.

He stuck the empty Sig back in his jacket and vacated the cell.

Gibbs stared at the PM, unable to speak.

"Clean that shit up and send it back in a diplomatic bag."

Chapter 87

Ashton is calling Sam, as he always does when he needs something. We're in Silent Waters, working with the MD Modeler on the best design for the surveillance devices Ashton has requested. Sam nails a fantastic design. It's a little larger than a tennis ball, but still all-seeing. He's pleased with himself, and I'm in the process of giving him a loving kiss when Ashton's ID flicks up on his phone.

I groan inwardly and give the wind-it up motion to Sam. But he holds his hand up to stop my distraction. Sam's face pulls in, giving him a gaunt appearance, and his eyes darken as he listens. I stand up and move toward my husband, wondering what has transpired.

"Sir, what can I say? On behalf of Ellie and me, we are most dreadfully sorry to hear this. Of course, we'll be with you. Where are you? We'll be there."

Sam rings off and looks up at me, his face desolate.

"What's happened?" I ask.

"Ashton's family have just been wiped out by the KSA's GID. Natasha, Abigail, and little Mariella. All of them are dead."

I know I don't get affected by emotions the way humans do, but when I hear what's happened to Ashton, I feel genuine sorrow for him. I've had my doubts about him, and I still do, but he doesn't deserve what's happened to him.

First the attacks, his abduction at Buzz Academy and that horrendous assault at the Russian Orthodox Church, and now this. Someone hates Ashton, big time. Was it really the GID? Or a shadow from his past?

This makes Ashton more than a martyr to the cause of Freedom Earth. Now he's a victim. Ashton can show to the world the strength of his conviction in Freedom Earth in the face of his own personal tragedy. He's literally suffering for his cause.

I realize this new position, as devastating as the loss of his family is, delivers Ashton a new standing. No one can refuse him. He'll be given a clear path to whatever he wants.

A man who has lost everything has nothing else to lose. By that loss, he is given supreme strength. His opponents will no longer see him in the same way as before. His suffering will bring out their humanity. Through the virtue of the human condition, he will be the winner. His policies that were once discussed and pontificated upon will now be accepted without question.

The man who has lost everything will have won the world.

I look at Sam and remember that when he'd been an agent, he'd engaged in ME9 or false flag activities, a masquerade as the enemy, so that no one really knew who was behind a bombing, a shooting or an attack. It was a simple intelligence agency ploy known by all the security services across the world, and used countless times to push one country's political game against another's. Even I, as human Ellie, had been caught up in one of those dreadful false flags.

Is there a chance that this is some sick, gigantic play by Ashton, or parties unknown? The terrible fate that's befallen Ashton is just a means of getting a specific result?

"I'm just going to Kudamun. I need to check on something."

Sam looks dismayed and very annoyed.

"Didn't you just hear what's happened to Ashton? What's so important you need to vanish now? He needs us, and we've got to go and see him. Whatever it is you need to do, it can wait."

Sam grabs my hand and abruptly shimmers. I automatically connect my soul force, and I'm pulled to Ashton's location.

As it's a new location, we check the surroundings, especially for cameras, as well as people, before shimmering out and locking into the Reality Plane. A back corridor next to a fire exit is our best option.

Sam and I walk up the corridor, through double doors, and into the morgue. In my memory banks, the smell of formaldehyde comes back to me, triggering the memory of when MI6 had thought I'd died. They'd stuffed me in a morgue at their 'in the sticks' interrogation center. Only after I was reconstituted as the Protector did I remember that. Although, I didn't immediately recall the event. Sam's trigger when he told me the truth about his employers torturing me that Sunday back in March unlocked the memory in my databanks. But whilst I was human, the drugs Six gave me prevented recall of their cruel abuse.

I stare at Ashton. He doesn't acknowledge our entrance. He stands between two trolleys, one carrying a small child and the other carrying a thin, tall woman. He seems to be deep in prayer. I look at Sam, and he gives a solemn nod to continue. I don't feel very happy to be there. In fact, I feel totally awkward. This is a private place. Ashton should be on his own to grieve.

Ashton notes our presence and raises his head. I'm shocked by his face. His eyes are rimmed in red from excessive crying, and his cheeks are sunken and sallow in color. Seeing him like that, I know I'm crazy to consider anything other than Ashton being a victim of the horrendous assassination of his family.

"Sam, Ellie, thank you for coming down." His voice is small and humble. He reaches out his arms to both of us like we're now his family.

I move into his arms with Sam and we hug him. I tell myself not to read his Balance Shift; his Equilibrium will be out completely after this happening. But I can't stop myself. He fades to white, then dark etches out his being, and then stops. For a man who has suffered like Ashton has, his Balance should be far darker. But it isn't. Once again, it's in almost perfect Equilibrium.

I swallow, unable to know how to handle this constant Equilibrium position. Does it mean Ashton really is in tune and in Balance with himself and the rest of the Universe? I observe the energy lines around him and they're very dark. Almost menacingly so. I could expect that, as the morgue is a place of distress. It's a place of pain for the surviving ones who suffer after their loved ones have departed.

In the hug still, Ashton grips us. "Thank God I still have you."

We pull out of the hug, and Sam responds, "We're here for you always, sir. Anything you need, just ask."

I add, "Do you need us to hunt anyone for you?"

I stare at Ashton's reaction to my words. He shakes his head. "No. It's been taken care of." A vengeful glint in his tired, red eyes catches my attention. I want to question what exactly has been taken care of, but I don't pry further. "Just that you're both here with me now is enough." Ashton's voice drops into a sob.

Sam lays a hand on the PM's shoulder in a comforting gesture.

"Sir, how did they get to her? I mean, wasn't she under your security?"

Ashton turns away, unable to face either of us. I watch. It seem my husband has asked a vital question, and one I'm just about to ask.

Ashton is in turmoil with himself, which again, doesn't scan with his Equilibrium.

"Ashton, why wasn't she protected?"

I drill into Ashton, determined to know why he'd left his family so exposed.

"Look, it's complicated. She hated bodyguards. She always felt they were nosing into her life. She couldn't appreciate that they came as part of the package. We had massive rows about it. She always saw them as a nuisance, and an opportunity for her private life to be leaked. She followed my advice after the Buzz Academy incident. They went to the safe house, laid low for a while. But then Abigail..."

Ashton's eyes mist over, and he starts to cry again. I touch his arm softly.

"It's okay if it's all too early to talk. We understand."

Ashton looks torn, unsure of whether to continue. He sighs, smooths his eyes of tears, and stares at me.

"Abigail was always a problem. God knows what happened. How it happened. But Natasha found Abigail and one of the security chaps in bed together. Lines of coke by the bedside and empty bottles of whiskey on the floor. They'd obviously been on one hell of a bender. Natasha went bananas. She chased the security guy out of the house in his boxers. She screamed at me to get them all out of the house at that moment. Obviously, I couldn't comply. She stormed at Abigail, but she just laughed in her mother's face. She was still out of it and couldn't give a damn. Natasha ran around the house, grabbing her daughters, and hurled both into the Cayenne. She yelled that she wasn't spending another day in a house where my security guards were given carte blanche to fuck anyone they pleased. She blamed me. She really believed that the security chap had taken advantage of Abigail. But in truth, it had probably been the other way around."

From Ashton's flushed cheeks, I can see it wasn't easy to explain.

"Couldn't you have just talked to her? Convinced her of the importance of security?" asks Sam, shocked and saddened by what he hears. The security officer had abused his position of trust by what he'd done, irrespective of Abigail 'putting it on a plate.' That security officer's indiscretion had led to their deaths.

"Natasha was never a woman you could talk to easily." Ashton touches his wife's face. A softness breaks out across Ashton's face in an expression I'd rarely witnessed before. Stroking her face, he continues. "But you know, I'd give everything I have to talk to her again."

He strokes her a little longer, bends down and kisses her on the forehead.

This display of love is so out of character for Ashton, I don't know where to look. It makes me worried my former judgment has been completely wrong. I've read into things, seen things in Ashton that weren't there, just because I was searching for justification of my own existence.

What he's doing, in eradicating terrorism, bringing the faiths together and enabling a cost-efficient new fuel to stop oil and gas giants from wreaking continued injustices, is incredible. And uniting the world under a single goal of peace is inspiring. Maybe he is as balanced as his Equilibrium shows. Maybe he's part of a bigger plan that not even Kudamun was privy to. Maybe he's beginning an evolutionary path for Earth, as decreed by the Ancient Ones, with Ashton as the catalyst. I have to admit that many ideas run through me, but no answers.

"Did she have any security in Devon? Surely you didn't leave her with nothing?" asks Sam. I continue to ponder what it all means.

"Of course not. I put in several security personnel that I personally hand-picked from Five, with orders to keep her close and intervene only when needed. I couldn't use the typical wagons, the Range Rovers and Audi SUVs. She knew them all. Natasha acted the dippy blonde, but you could never fool her. If she'd got a whiff of surveillance, she'd have vanished completely, gone to ground abroad and I'd never have found her until she wanted to be found. I rotated the security personnel in a range of different cars for unobtrusive tracking. She was always under my eye."

"So what went wrong?" I ask, staring at Ashton, reading every nuance he projects. Ashton's eyes drift and, for a second, I think he's going to faint. This isn't the 'take no prisoners' arrogant bastard I know.

This is a man shattered to the core.

He shakes his head, puzzled and ashamed.

"I don't know. I've gone over it a million times. Security was just outside in the layby. They followed, but somehow, they managed to lose her. She was driving the Cayenne, and I can tell you, Natasha drives..." Ashton catches himself and sighs heavily, eyes glassy. "Natasha drove like a maniac. Forget Formula 1, those drivers had nothing on Natasha, when she drove she had no fear. I think she knew she was under surveillance. She sent me this."

Ashton pulls out his phone and shows us the last text from Natasha.

"I'm guessing the sex pest reference was about your security guys," I add.

"Yes, it was. But believe me, if she'd only let them do their job instead of trying to evade their surveillance, she'd be alive now. And so would Mariella."

Ashton looks down at the little body of his daughter.

"You know, she could be sleeping, couldn't she? I mean, if we all just forgot. If we imagined. That's all. She's just taking a nap. Dreaming. In another world. Oh God...Why?"

Suddenly, Ashton breaks down with heaving sobs. He slips to the floor and sits, his back against the cold concrete wall. His body shudders silently as tears take him over. Instinctively, I drop down and hold his hand.

"Richard, she's at peace. She didn't suffer."

Ashton, his head in his hands, shakes through pain.

"But my Abigail did. They made her suffer. Why? Why did they do that? Despite how she acted, she was only really a child. How could anyone be that evil?"

"Have you seen Abigail?" I enquire slowly, aware that Ashton's all-consuming pain is strangely affecting me. For one thing, I've started to call him Richard, and I see him as a human being rather than an egotistical, selfish prick.

"Yes. I saw her in that shithole she was in. They're doing an autopsy to confirm the cause of death. But I know the cocaine was cut with a neurotoxin. I don't need a path lab report to tell me, but I had to follow procedure."

"Can we do anything to help you?"

"Yes. There's something I need to know. What happened to them when they died?"

I listen, and I'm not surprised. I shake my head, and Sam states clearly in my mind, 'We can't tell him. No one must know that.'

"I'm sorry, Richard. That is on a 'need to know' basis, and you don't have a clearance level high enough. No one does. I'd breach the Order of Kudamun if I told you."

Ashton nods.

"It was just a thought. I had to ask. But you do know?"

I glance at Sam, as I measure how to respond. "Richard, I know what is needed to be known. They're all at peace now. Just remember that."

Sam interjects the conversation, diverting it rapidly in a different direction.

"Prime Minister, Ellie and I have devised an interesting model for your surveillance device. Would you like to see it?"

Ashton declines, waving his hand down.

"Just make it. I trust you. I trust you both more than I trust anyone in this world."

Hunched on the floor, with shoulders drooping, his body of such stature has now crumpled. Ashton's exhausted, in a condition I've again never seen before, not even when he fought with Ivanov. It is like I'm looking at a different person entirely.

His face no longer holds that smirk I loathe. Another expression has taken over. It is one soaked in sorrow and a begrudging acceptance he's no longer an impenetrable force. That he isn't unbreakable. And that whatever he does from now on, he knows his actions have consequences. He's paid the price of his smug, arrogant ways.

"Richard, when do you want the surveillance devices?"

Ashton seems to have floated off again. His mind is somewhere else.

"Sir, when do you want the devices?" repeated Sam, giving Ashton a gentle nudge.

"Oh, sorry. Yes, right, the surveillance devices. I need them as soon as you can get them to me. We need to be able to use the data here on earth. So whatever you can create, keep it within our technological frame of capability."

As Ashton speaks, I notice he's regained some of his strength. Work stuff charges him up. He makes to stand, pushes against the wall and stands straight, looking at me. I notice a hardness flicker back into his features, and that glint of vengeance I'd seen earlier comes back into his eyes.

"Feeling a bit better, Richard?"

"Yes, Ellie. Yes, I am. You know, it's strange, I always thought myself immune to terrible things. I guess I thought I was unbreakable. I wrapped myself up in goodness, focused on doing so much good. Freedom Earth, the religious unification, even my new energy will change mankind forever. A set of good actions, that cannot be denied. Don't you agree, Ellie?"

Ashton almost seems for a second to glare viciously at me, but I think I must be imagining it. Not this man, who dissolved in front of my eyes in a sea of pain.

"Of course, I agree, Richard. Who cannot?"

"Quite," says Ashton. I notice a little smirk appear, and vanish. Again, it has to be my crazy perception. "I really did believe I could encase myself in utter goodness, and only visualize goodness, and thus, keep myself free of experiencing any badness."

I tilt my head toward Ashton. "But no one can. You know that. There's always the Balance."

"Ah, yes, the Balance. That's what it's all about. Someone decided it was time I really suffered, and redressed the Balance in my life. Too much good.

Need a bit of hell on earth. Maybe one of your lot perhaps?"

The unexpected flint sharp tone in Ashton's voice throws me off guard. His personality seems to almost flip.

"No, Richard, that's madness. No one would do that." I try to hide the deep frown on my face.

Ashton nods. His expression is calm again, his eyes still full with tears.

"Forgive me, Ellie, Sam. I'm just looking for someone to blame. I'm just full of pain right now. The grief, it makes one think demented thoughts. After the funeral, I shall be more at peace with myself."

"Of course, sir, we understand," says Sam. Then he says in his mind to me, 'Sweetheart, I think we should leave him now.'

I agree.

"Richard, we're going to head off now and finish the surveillance drones for you. You need to be with yourself and the memories of your lovely family. Please don't feel you've been targeted by Kudamun. Everything you're doing is right. And you have all of us behind you."

I feel I need to say that. Ashton's mind is in flux. I want to give him a reassurance, a mental fuel to keep him driven but stable.

Sam and I start our shimmer, and Ashton waves us goodbye. His features are a masterpiece of melancholy. There isn't a sardonic smirk or a hard glint in sight.

As I shimmer into our London apartment, I can't help but think about what this new dynamic means for the future, and for the man who has lost everything but may have won the world.

Chapter 88

Lei shuffled her body across the sheet, swung her legs over the mattress and pushed back on her hands to launch herself off the bed. Standing up, she brushed the tears away from her face. Her pillow was sodden from all the crying. It seemed she'd never be able to stop. Did she cry whilst asleep? Lei wondered, flipping the pillow onto its dry side.

Every morning was the same.

That emptiness.

A longing for something that couldn't be found. But, oh, how she searched. She held positive to the thought of his return.

He's taking a rest; having a nap, she always said.

Day by day, trudging to his bedside, she ignored the tubes and equipment. Talking about films, football, newly released games, incessant drivel of the inconsequential dropped from her lips. Anything she could think of to inspire and ignite a glimmer of life back into Xiao.

It had been different at the beginning of May. They'd both held onto the belief that the force that had taken over Xiao would return him quickly. But that belief started to erode as days passed and Xiao remained locked in his coma.

That one glimmer of connection when Lei had seen the word 'survival,' had turned into the bane of their lives. Her husband's weird, inexplicable dream the night before the incident had only exacerbated an intolerable, intractable situation even further.

Eight days and still no contact. No sign there had even been contact. Lei eventually believed it had all been in her mind.

But what about her husband's dream? The contents of it had been a description of his evil. It sought to underline the fact that he was responsible. Chen was the cause of her boy's coma.

In the very inner reaches of her soul, Lei knew she was incorrectly attributing blame. Without true cause or evidence, Chen had become the fall guy. He was the one who could take the blame as, by his sins, the man had already been found guilty.

Lei had gone so far, and now her hatred of a man she used to love ate into her heart. She felt she had nothing left but a void filled with unanswered promises.

Chen entered.

He slept in one of their other bedrooms. He'd tried to sleep with Lei, holding her close when she sobbed herself to sleep, feeling her small but firm frame raise and lower as sorrow took its grip. Time progressed, and her sobbing had turned to low moaning, which she emitted with a gentle but persistent rocking motion.

And then her hatred took her over and she wouldn't let him touch her.

She didn't sleep, or if she did, Chen wasn't aware. He watched her all night, night after night, descend into a chasm of despair. She was a husk of a woman, not the towering strength he'd married. She'd fragmented in front of his eyes and what was left lived only to weep.

Where had that wonderful belief gone? That feeling of positivity and hope they'd both shared some three weeks ago?

Intransigence on the part of the force inside Xiao had unleashed such sorrow. If he could still believe a force was there at all. The force's inactivity had caused their failing faith. Xiao's condition hadn't changed. And now that the revelation that perhaps, he'd been the one to trigger Xiao's coma was firmed up in Lei's mind, she could barely hold his eye.

The love she'd had for him had turned cold, and hate started to seep in.

Chen knew she now blamed him totally for Xiao's current state.

"Are you going to him today?" Chen asked, trying to remain civil.

"Of course. Why do you ask?" Lei bit back sharply.

He watched as she rubbed the sleep out of her eyes. A last deposit of water fixed to her fingers. Chen noticed, and touched her shoulder.

Lei stiffened. Her back was a drawstring pulled tight against any emotion beyond the sorrow she harbored.

Reluctantly, Chen let his hand fall. "It's time you faced facts, Lei."

"Oh! And what facts are they?" she snapped back. "That our son, our normal, loving, and often annoying son, is in a coma caused by some unknown, supernatural ailment that no doctor can understand nor do anything about? And that maybe your dark, cruel past somehow triggered the onset of the coma? Tell me, are those the facts? Facts are things that are known, comprehended, and there is nothing that is known about our son. There are no facts to speak of, other than what is before our eyes."

"Lei, I know. I didn't mean-"

"What didn't you mean, Chen? You didn't mean to say that I should give up, lose hope, let things be, and accept that Xiao is gone. If those are your facts, there's the door. I've no place in my home or heart for a defeatist."

Chen rose up as he listened. His face sallowed and his eyes enlarged with hurt.

"Whatever you think of me, I will never leave you, Lei."

"If you believe our son is gone, you won't have to. I'll go."

Lei's lips trembled, but that was the only part of her that showed movement. Granite still, she stared at her husband.

"I don't believe that, darling," replied Chen. "You know I don't. But I can't stand you torturing yourself. This is tearing us apart. Whatever happens, I'll always be there. But this grief-infested misery must stop. I know when you're by his bedside, you're different. You're a shining light of positivity. But here, at home, you descend into a pit of sorrow and despair. All I ask is that you retain that positive vibe you have in the hospital back here. I know you are light, Lei. You are the lightest, sweetest soul I know, and I love you so very, very much."

Chen made a move toward Lei, grabbing her and holding her tight in his arms. Again, she stiffened. But his words broke through and she melted softly into his encasing massive limbs. Chen dropped his head deep and kissed Lei. Recalcitrance rippled through her at first, but eventually, she opened her lips slightly, allowing Chen access to her mouth.

Pulling her closer, Chen could feel her broken love undeniably healing against his body. He grasped her face. His fingertips touched the sides of her temples and cheeks. Lei's eyelids dropped. A sigh slipped from her lips from a place deep inside her, a place she considered banished forever from the flame of love.

"We will get through this together. We will survive this, Lei, but only love can be our savior."

Lei nodded in acceptance and understanding.

Chen smiled. His wife had returned. Now for his son.

"Come on, darling. Let's go to the hospital together today. It could be the day."

Lei held his hand, squeezed it and smiled. "It may just be."

Chen could see, from within her, a surge of unexpected positivity. Holding his hand, she brought his fingers to her lips and kissed them.

And dared to allow fragile hope back into her life.

The walk seemed endless. Lei had believed so hard in the words of Chen that morning, but in the stark fluorescent lighting of the hospital corridor, such confidence appeared misplaced.

Approaching Xiao's bed, she grasped hold of her husband's hand for strength. He took her hand to his lips and kissed it. Lei nodded, a glimmer of a smile on her face.

Her son's bedside was a place riddled with tubes and equipment and a slow beeping sound signifying that life was in there.

Somewhere.

Chen pulled the chair up for his wife. Lei flopped into the seat. The walk had sucked out her energy completely.

"My darling, Xiao, you are a boy who has brought light into my life. I need you back."

Chen sat in the chair next to Lei and touched the bedcovers, unable still to take the death-like limbs of his son in his hands.

"Xiao, my son, enough playing around. You need to come back. We love you, for all your faults." Chen's words brought a scolding glance from Lei, but, unperturbed, Chen continued. "We love you because of your faults. Without them, you wouldn't be you. You wouldn't be the Xiao we love."

Lei snatched up her son's hand, as flimsy as a piece of steak in a butchers. She ignored the disconcerting lifelessness and imagined him holding her tight, needing her protection and safety. She had a deep assurance borne of a mother to son bonding.

His fingers had once tightened and intertwined around hers. His blood had pumped faster with growing excitement, anticipating a new experience, a museum, zoo or amusement park visit, a shopping mall perhaps, or even an airport. So many options. With anticipation brought greater movement in his limbs, heightening his nerves, as he had waited with his mother to discover the world.

Lei created and captured those memories. She captured that moment. His hand tightening; she visualized the sensation in her mind. She brought through the energy of that feeling, that wonderful feeling of being needed by her son, into existence. She allowed the energy to flood through her. Closing her eyes, she concentrated.

Chen looked at his wife but asked nothing of her. He knew not to interfere when Lei was in the zone of peace.

The pressure on her hand was almost undiscernible.

She could have been mistaken. Lei opened her eyes and stared at her son's hand. Against her skin, she felt the faintest of presses.

"Xiao? Oh, my darling!"

Chen jumped at his wife's sudden exclamation. He watched his wife place her left hand over the top of Xiao's.

The pressing increased by a fraction until a slight movement flickered in his fingers.

"Chen, he's coming around! Oh my God, Chen, he's waking up. My boy, my Xiao, is coming back to us. Baby, darling, come back to me."

Chen observed the minuscule movement and called the medical staff for assistance. The senior nurse arrived within seconds and worked swiftly to extubate Xiao from all the tubing that had kept his body stable before he slipped into full consciousness.

Xiao's eyelids fluttered fast as if someone had just plugged him into the mains, and energy pumped through him. His arms flew up in search of an invisible embrace. The suddenness of his movements disoriented Lei. He had transformed from a still slab of inanimate human meat to a gangly jangle of limbs, moving uncoordinated and of their own accord.

It reminded Lei of those movies she'd watched as a teenager, like Frankenstein, where the corpse was reanimated. She looked at Xiao. His movements had become subdued, and he was turning his head slowly, purposefully, examining all around him.

Lei detected a subtle aloofness in his inspection. She ventured to address him directly.

"Xiao, darling. Mummy's here."

Xiao turned with labored deliberation toward his mother's direction and smiled with a degree of condescension.

"Mother, I'm so pleased you have finally got here. I have waited so long. I thought that time would not allow it to be so."

Lei didn't understand.

"Darling, what do you mean?"

"But time has allowed it. And those responsible know it to be so." Xiao stopped speaking as Chen came into his eyeline. With ire invested in every word, Xiao continued, "Those of your kind."

Xiao stared at his father, and Chen shifted uncomfortably.

"But there shall be change," Xiao continued. "It is written. Everything is connected. There will be consequences."

Lei grew concerned by her son's strong, mature voice. There appeared to be a poignant message in those ramblings. But she was either too emotional or too under-developed mentally to comprehend the meaning.

"Darling, what are you talking about? We don't understand you."

"Mother, it makes no difference whether you understand me or not. I am but a vessel given a voice. But what will pass, remains so. Survival is my goal. It has to be for the future to be. Can we go home now? I want to play on my games."

Xiao finished his seemingly prolific announcement with an extremely child-like request. His voice switched from deep and measured to bouncy and effusive. Lei was thrown back by his change of tone. His temperament, no longer aloof, grew suddenly agitated and impatient.

"I want to go home, Mummy."

Xiao's nagging, whiny edge had returned. Lei sighed, not really knowing how to handle the person before her.

"Darling, you've been through a lot. The doctors need to run some more tests to ensure you're safe to go home."

Lei touched Xiao's cheek, now flushed with a faint pinky glow.

"Son," said Chen, "what did you mean when you said, 'you're a vessel given a voice?' And 'Survival is my goal?'"

His inquiry brought forth a puzzled look on Xiao's face. "I don't remember. Did I say that?"

Confusion created wrinkles on Xiao's young brow.

"Yes, Son, you did. Just now."

"No, Dad, I think you're getting a bit senile. I was talking about my Play Station. I do miss it. Have there been any more games launched since I've been resting? Can we go to Hamley's and see what's new? Can we, Dad?" Xiao looked at his father's shocked face. Realizing he wasn't getting anywhere, he turned to his mother. "Can we Mum? Go to Hamley's?"

Xiao appeared to have dismissed any previous announcement as a figment of his parents' imagination, as well as, perhaps, their premature senility setting in. Lei, like her husband, displayed concern. But for Xiao's sake, she attempted to hide it behind a shallow smile.

"Of course, darling. When you're discharged, we'll go anywhere you want to. And we'll buy you any game you like."

Chen held his wife's arm, which had started to shake, but Xiao rapidly observed his father's gesture.

"Mum, what's wrong? You look worried. Why are you shivering?"

Lei glanced sideways at Chen, who shook his head. His dark eyes instructed her to refrain from revealing anything to their son.

Lei moved forward in the hospital chair and spoke swiftly.

"There's nothing wrong at all, darling. Mummy just felt a slight chill, that's all. Now let's have a look at all the new games on your HoloTab. I've brought it here for you."

Lei withdrew from her bag the new style, slim tablet, barely two millimeters thick and A5 in size. Made from high-tech nano-composites, it weighed little more than a piece of stiff card. But the tech inside those two millimeters was formidable. The tablet's auto-recognition system read Lei's face vectors and opened all the preloaded applications on the Tab's desktop. She clicked on HoloTab application, and the HoloTab apps floated above the tablet in suspended form. Lei pointed on the App for internet and then spoke the search command.

"Show Hamley's London, new PlayStation games."

The air above the HoloTab filled with front covers of all kinds of games.

"Action and adventure," said Lei, and the selection updated and reduced to illustrate games in Lei's requested category.

Xiao exclaimed little coos of delight as he observed the new titles floating in front of him. He noticed a new game based on the mythological world of Atlantis. He pressed the air, opening up the game. The sales video show-reel ran.

It was loud, and Lei stated hurriedly, "Mute".

Abruptly, the weapon sounds, explosions, and heavy bass music ceased.

"Definitely that one, Mum. It looks amazing."

Lei snatched a 'lost for words' look at Chen as she tried to piece together the fractured personality her son had acquired. Chen shrugged, equally baffled.

For now, at least, their son was back, almost a normal boy, and that was a blessing neither could avoid being grateful for.

Chapter 89

The wooden archway intermeshes together. One hue of the wood is fractionally darker than the other in an analogous representation of life and the tenets of religion.

"Although we dance in the light, we can't avoid making shadows."

That has always been Sam's phrase, and I never realized its importance until now. How that morning of March 22 changed everything, when the world seemed to rearrange itself around my invisible destiny.

I haven't materialized out of shimmer.

I want to spend time to look. I wasn't inclined to attend Ashton's family's funeral, feeling it is too private and intimate an event to warrant our attendance. But Ashton, being Ashton, had insisted we attend. I know Sam's a point of a degree forward from me, his quantum-self pulling his soul force faster than mine. I'm okay with a slight delay. It affords me the time to surveil without intrusive inspection from Ashton.

The overcast day matches the mood along the narrow, winding, and cheerless grey asphalt path. Dotted on either side, carved headstones from centuries ago, weathered by the climate, now lie crumbled. Forlorn piles used to be proud crosses. Inscriptions of loved ones by loved ones are forgotten, lost within the straggling chaotic threads of time.

I find this place I am shimmering into sad and desolate. It's something created to project and harvest emotions for the Balance. It enables humans to let go, to gain closure and finish their last chapter. Well, the last known to them, of course. But not the last chapter in one's journey.

I stare out at the church ahead of me. Its solid red brickwork gives a sense of steadfast security. A place, real, strong and true. Belief is transmitted through its structure. Even if a person isn't a believer, the force of the collective energies embedded in the walls empowers one to feel, almost by osmosis, the power that they have to believe in. It is an emotionally charged hand-me-down of religious acceptance.

I watch, still a few points out of reality, as black-clothed, grieving people walk up to Ashton to pay their respects. Behind him, armed, ready and rock-hard stand his close protection bodyguards. In front and at the sides is another selection of meaty marine types, arms crossed and they scanned the mourners, their Sigs already in their hands.

Ashton nods solemnly and receives their condolences with dignity and fortitude. Some shake his hand and hold his arm. Others kiss his cheek. A few break down in tears, requiring Ashton to hug them. With the pretty friends of Natasha's, I can see Ashton's lips going out for a kiss a fraction too quickly.

A rotund older lady, with a stern face and mean mouth, steps up in front of Ashton and I think I see him slink back a little as she approaches. She's probably a maiden aunt or mother-in-law.

"Ashton, I hold you responsible for this!"

Immediately, his primary bodyguard flexes, showing concern, but Ashton moves his hand out horizontally and shakes it, his sign to his security that she's close family.

Ashton attempts to shift his way out of the direction of her rant, but her tight, leather-gloved hand shoots out and slams him hard across the face. Ashton's primary bodyguard leaps out and makes to grab the woman. But a sharp, "Leave her," from the PM catches him dead in his stride. He returns to his default position by Ashton's side.

I can see she's used some force as Ashton's cheek brandishes the rosy imprint of her hand. The woman turns on her heel and marches away without saying a further word.

"Marigold, please!" shouts Ashton, running after her.

Ashton reaches his mother-in-law. He grabs her back to face him.

"What do you mean, I'm responsible? I didn't kill them. The Saudis did."

Marigold's face screws up in anger. Her fury explodes in a tirade of accusations.

"You did kill her. You and that stupid new energy. You must have known those people wouldn't just lie down and take it. You raided their embassy. You humiliated their royalty. What did you think? That you were untouchable? You, the great Richard bloody Ashton, had carte blanche to do anything? Did you think you were God? Is that what you thought? Well, you're not. And they've died because of your stupidity and arrogance. You might as well have pulled the trigger yourself because their blood is on your hands."

The woman who Ashton called Marigold wipes away the tears that stream down her face, and strides up the path leading to the church.

I watch as Ashton turns back to other mourners and tries to shield the mental pain Marigold has inflicted. A tall, kind-faced older man in his mid-sixties shuffles in front of the PM. I can see the immediate closeness and know, without consulting my databanks, that he has to be Natasha's father.

"Richard, I'm sorry about Marigold. She doesn't know what she's saying. I know it's not your fault. Come on, son. Let's go in."

The man who'd spoken so softly to Ashton nudges him in the direction of the church. Ashton nods.

"Thanks, Father. I'm pleased you're on my side. I don't know why your wife is always so belligerent. I've tried to be a good husband and father. It hasn't been easy. God knows I've been tested."

I watch as Ashton, wracked with inner sadness and regret, cries openly in front of his close family. The father-in-law rubs Ashton's back in a gentle expression of endearment and hugs him. Ashton wells up again.

I'm surprised by Ashton's sudden openness and wonder whether he will remain changed.

I notice Sam has shimmered into reality in an isolated area, just behind the church, and I target that area myself with materialization.

The vicar appears in the doorway of the church. I check him over as he reaches the PM and gives his 'deepest condolences.' His plump body, flushed pink cheeks on his circular face and bright, laughing eyes look like they belonged to a comedian, not a man of the cloth. I can imagine this strange little fellow in front of me having been waylaid by the Verger and thrust into the dog collar and gown, as the actual vicar has gone AWOL. Even the timbre of his voice suggests he's about to deliver a punch-line rather than commence a sermon.

Sam emerges from behind the church at the top of the path. I join him by his side and we walk over to Ashton and the vicar.

Ashton proffers a feeble smile, but then his face shrouds over, and his eyes hood with remorse.

He pushes out and hugs Sam and me.

"Thank you for coming. This is difficult. I need you both to give me strength."

I hold his arm. He is shaking. His eyes can't remain dry. The tangible pain he emits touches me.

I know there and then that I really have to rethink my view of him.

Chapter 90

The dark sentient crystal walls within the Hall of Etima-Si-Sig, the Hall of Dark Silence, awoke as Temenos strode through them. He reached a part of the wall where multicolored jewels were embedded, and they sparkled as he approached. Temenos swiped his hand through the air and immersive 3D images floated in front of him.

The images suggested that all was going extremely well on Earth. He took in the scene. Three figures hugged and then they pulled away and walked slowly toward a church.

A vibration grabbed his attention and the air beside him started to get denser. He felt a pulling, like a vortex of great power materializing. The air rippled and undulated like it was vehemently fighting with whatever was trying to break through.

Temenos waited, intrigued by the power of his Revered One. Within the air, something dark grew.

The battle had been won. The air had lost. A chasm of dark erupted into existence, suspended by its own energy in the air beside Temenos.

Two eyes ringed in red peered out of the darkness.

"Revered One, my lord, thank you for coming."

"Update," requested the booming voice in Temenos' head. It was so powerful; he could sense his own internal resonance vibrating in pain.

"All is as planned. The Chosen One has been fully accepted. All the players are now in place. The flip will make all that is theirs, ours. The rise will be unstoppable. Giznu will crumble. Etima will reign. We will change Kudamun for good."

The eyes creased slightly, and Temenos heard a thunderous laugh in his mind as the Revered One responded.

"True words, my friend. Your words have never been so true."

Temenos watched the red-rimmed eyes slink back into the darkness. The chasm shuddered, folded in on itself and disappeared out of Kudamun's plane.

Temenos breathed, long and deep, and tried to cancel out the sudden pain caused by the connection. His internal resonance quelled the flickering vibration of pain until it vanished.

Turning back to the images, still suspended, Temenos kissed his index finger and planted it on one of the people still walking with solemnity up to the stone archway of a church.

"Soon, my sweetness. Soon."

TO BE CONTINUED…

DON'T MISS THE MIND BLOWING FINALE TO THIS SERIES IN

THE SUM.

END OF BOOK THINGS

The Sum

Part Five * Book Five

Chapter 1

18 June 2017

The blonde, permanently tanned man known as Richard Ashton, British Prime Minister lounged back on the ivory leather sofa. The type only found in first class lounges and VIP club suites and he sighed contentedly. He pulled the casually slung seat belt a little tighter across his toned stomach as he noticed a slight dip in movement. He took in his surroundings. Much had happened in the past couple of months. And all for the good. *His good.*

Quantum Force, the incredible, abundant clean energy source had dramatically changed his fortunes, enabling little luxuries like the sleek, private jet he was on, and all the trimmings private ownership brought.

"Prime Minister, we'll be arriving shortly. Would you like anything before we begin our descent?"

Ashton smirked as he eyed up the raven-haired beauty at the drinks trolley. He licked his full lips salaciously. Well, a quick blow-job wouldn't go amiss.

The man seated opposite him looked up as the flight attendant spoke.

"G and T thanks, darling."

The man was Jensen Stalbridge, promoter of Freedom Earth and the PM's business partner and confidante. Unlike the PM, whose features were softer, bordering on effeminate, Stalbridge's features were sharper, angular, with a hooked nose that led up to searching, always interrogating eyes. He looked like an eagle on a constant hunt for prey.

"How about you, Richard? What're you having?"

"Just another glass of bubbly."

"You're getting a taste for the finer things."

"And why not? We're all entitled."

"And some are more entitled than others." Stalbridge laughed, knocking back his drink.

"I have no idea what you mean," said Ashton in a coy voice, and then the two men laughed raucously.

Startled by the sudden loudness, the attendant flicked her head back. She caught Ashton's eye. Finer things, why not? He motioned her over.

She leaned in towards the prime minster. "Yes, sir?"

"Listen, sweetheart, there is something you could do for me."

Stalbridge's eyebrows rose. "Rich, I'll go and...well, just check on those papers," he muttered hurriedly and got up. Heading for the back where the office paraphernalia was, he didn't turn around. The attendant noticed him leave.

"Sir, we'll be descending shortly. Could you take your seat?"

"Sweetheart, the only one descending around here is you." Ashton grabbed the attendant's head and pushed it forcefully down toward his crotch. "Now off you go," he said, unzipping his hand tailored trousers.

The flight attendant, too terrified to refuse, acquiesced without a further word.

Ashton's long arms stretched out across both cushions of the leather sofa and his head tilted back. He let out a deep groan. He could feel it. Beyond the climax, something else.

At that moment, it was blatant. Revealed to him. The surge that every human craves, but tries to hide. They shun even the mention. But deep down, Ashton knew humans wanted to control others. Dominate them. Hold the balance of life and death in their hands.

That was ultimate power. An unquestionable primal need unfettered by twenty-first century morality.

And he had it.

Chapter 2

11 Days Earlier

Reggie Wellwood looked out from the northern end of the Terrace in Westminster Palace. The expanse of Thames spread out before him, glistening in the morning sunlight. He'd stared out from this place before, when he had just been made a Member of Parliament. His life in politics had then been an unturned page. An expectation still waiting to be fulfilled.

He remembered watching the gentle waves and imagined streams of horses galloping just underneath the surface. Their eyes, the sparkles of light that caught his attention. He would be like them. Running ahead, sweeping up the top positions, being the star politician. His ascendency would shine bright over the palace.

But all that had been a lifetime ago.

His close-set eyes scanned wearily the horizon for movement. No airborne Surv-Motes out today. At least not around Westminster. Other parts of London would be under observation by the strange surveillance drones the prime minster had instigated almost immediately following the systematic decimation of his family.

Life in Westminster had become very different following that moment. He hadn't seen that much of the prime minister since then. Understandable, considered Reggie, trembling inwardly as he imagined how he'd deal with such a devastating act of terror. How does a man deal with his family's annihilation? Even in a hypothetical context, such a consideration delivered an unthinkable level of pain. Reggie knew, in truth, if he'd been in Ashton's shoes, he'd have been crushed to the ground.

Reggie recalled the days following the prime minister's return. The hushed whispers. The incredible respect, not pity, that Ashton received from not only his party faithful, but all the opposition as well. He was virtually venerated. A man who could do no wrong. A man who had suffered for peace and for his country. Everyone somehow felt that they had to honor whatever the PM wanted, for rejection of his wishes could be tantamount to treason.

Initiation of the Surv-Mote devices hadn't been something Reggie had wanted. As defense secretary, he thought, despite the PM's circumstances and the dreadful massacre, that it was a form of provocation and would only create more problems. But Ashton was not prepared to engage in any such discussion. Reggie shivered, remembering their conversation after the PM had returned from a short leave.

"Prime Minister, I'm not sure that this is necessary. We already have one camera too many as it is. Intrusion into the public lives of people has gone too far. These drone things...well, their lives won't be their own."

"Wellwood, do I have to remind you that terrorists are everywhere, and they can still get to anyone?"

Reggie looked down, embarrassed by having to face the PM about his family's demise.

"Yes, Prime Minister, sir, I know they can. But not all the people in the UK are criminals. Most are good people."

"Unfortunately, Wellwood you are naïve. Most people are not good, and they take no responsibility in their lives at all. When they eventually decide to live their lives with responsibility away from evil temptation and become law-abiding citizens, then their lives can return to be their own. Until such time, their lives are mine."

Ashton smiled at Reggie. It wasn't a joyous smile. Reggie could feel bile rising in his stomach. He nodded, accepting the inevitable.

Ashton slammed him hard on the back in a faux-comradery gesture. Reggie gasped, as his spine vibrated under the PM's impact.

"Good man. Will help with our civil defense agenda. Work with the home secretary and the energy secretary to make this a reality, old chap. I want it expedited without delay. First, the delivery of the Surv-Motes."

"Surv-Motes?" enquired Reggie, confused and still a little dizzy from the 'don't cross me again' endearment.

"Surv-Motes. Yes, it's the new people-friendly term for the surveillance automated drone. It's much more affable to the impressionable masses. I've even commissioned a public information advert on TV and across the web. A cute, cartoonish Surv-Mote zooming around, talking to kids and keeping people safe. We may even run production on the cuddly Surv-Mote toys and games. Make a killing at Christmas time!"

Ashton laughed at the joke. Reggie tried to laugh too. But the laugh mutated into a cough as his lungs tightened in his body, agitated by the PM's earlier hit, and he puffed and wheezed.

"You're in a bit of a state, aren't you, old chap? You do need to take better care of yourself."

Ashton proffered a chair to his coughing defense secretary and continued.

"So, as I was saying, Reggie, delivery of the Surv-Motes will be arriving Friday."

"That's very soon, Prime Minister," muttered Reggie through his heaving.

"Can't wait around. Need to get things moving." Ashton rubbed his hands together. The action completed his interaction with his defense secretary. It also signaled his closure to any argument, if anyone would dare to bring one forth.

Reggie stood up from his seat and left the PM's office in a numb silence. He likened the feeling to a visit to the dentist, when he'd just been injected with cocaine and had things done to him he had no control over. His mind floated on a peripheral consciousness, aware of things happening but not actually partaking in their activity.

Reggie slid out the PM's office and into Private Secretary Milburn Cumberford's domain. A thoroughly nasty little fellow, thought Reggie. All Oxford Blues, the classics and stiff upper lip. Reggie doubted he'd ever felt a true emotion in his life. He had a round, pudgy face, boyish in a way, which could display quite an affable even vulnerable appearance had it not been for those dead eyes of ice blue and the permanent condescending sneer he carried and delivered to everyone except for Cabinet Secretary Sir Martyn Redfern and, of course, Prime Minister Ashton. Two peas in a pod were Redfern and Cumberford, realized Reggie, as the cabinet secretary pushed past him in a hurry to jump at Ashton's next request, as always.

Redfern was the type of person who could probably remain immaculate in a 60-mph gale, thought Reggie begrudgingly. Tall, as one sees a basketball player, with an almost concave body despite gorging on the best fare in the Common's dining hall. His startling, green eyes reflected disregard and condescension to all except the prime minister, a man for whom he fawned and brownnosed unashamedly.

Redfern was a stickler for detail on everything. Nothing happened without him knowing and no one got to the PM without going through him first.

"Morning, Sir Martyn," ventured Reggie, wanting to appear the better man.

"Oh yes, good morning, Minister. Hope all is well in the world of defense?"

A slit of red venom curled across his face. The Redfern smile. It showed utter contempt for having to deal at all with Reggie. He could see, although he held his ministerial position, who really held the power. He was nothing but a minnow against the barracuda might of the cabinet secretary.

"Never better," mumbled Reggie.

"Getting those Surv-Motes sorted for us then? Good chap." Redfern flicked a conspiratorial look at Cumberford, who sneered, as expected, in return.

Reggie turned away from his colleagues. His face flushed with embarrassment. He was nothing more than an errand boy to them. He didn't have their public school sensibilities. He hadn't been brought up to bully, victimize, and belittle those around him. Respect for himself and others had been the code he'd lived by.

He heard the malicious sniggers behind him. Like being back at school, he thought, and closed the door.

Reggie returned from his reverie and sighed. The intelligence elite had their eyes and ears everywhere. No one could keep a secret anymore. Oh, how the world had changed in a few months.

His gaze bounded over the flowing river, and he had a sensation he'd come to recognize and, with reluctance, accept: being under observation. He moved his head toward the feeling, and a Surv-Mote popped up almost of out of nowhere in front of him and hovered just above the railings on the balcony. It had no sound, but human instinct always informed on its presence.

The Surv-Mote was a strange machine. It was like a tennis ball only a fraction larger and adorned with small apertures like the compound eye of a fly. The small eyes were nanocamera or nancams, and they picked up movement across a three-hundred-and-sixty-degree field of vision. If the Surv-Mote detected movement, its nano-eyes would suddenly flicker and flash independently. The Surv-Mote in front of Reggie was flickering and flashing but was not issuing any command. Had the Surv-Mote's surveillance of the scene indicated signals of movement above the threshold criteria of acceptable behavior, its real time data-feeds flowing back to Freedom Earth HQ would have analyzed by an artificial intelligence system, and according to the AI's established rules and current learning, a prediction on the likelihood of criminal activity would have been made. The Surv-Mote would then emit an eerie, high-pitched whine and announce, "Your actions are identified as unacceptable. Police have been called. Remain where you are."

It was now understood that since all data was streamed and stored at Freedom Earth HQ, insufficient evidence was a defense plea that had no standing in Ashton's brave new world.

The Surv-Mote's presence had disturbed his thoughts and Reggie no longer wanted to be outside. He wandered over and opened the door to return inside the Terrace. In his mid-fifties, of slight frame and average build, even the exertion of pushing down on the handle made him puff a little. Moving to the city after Ashton had given him the UK defence secretary position had brought back his asthma.

The pollution of the city hung uncomfortably inside him, constantly at the back of his throat. Before any talk, he'd cough, trying to clear the mucus, but that sour taste would still stick. If he got too irate or too passionate about a subject, the coughing would kick in rendering his delivery inadequate and embarrassing.

His doctor had given him various medicines but none of the remedies had been lasting enough. Only getting out of London would help, and that wasn't going to happen now.

All the ambition, the drive for stardom, had been burnt out of him decades ago by the ruthlessness of the political game. He wanted a quiet life. He was quite satisfied with being culture minister, attending nice, dignified events and getting paid for the pleasure. He really didn't want such a high-profile position. But with Godley's untimely demise, he was suddenly in the spotlight.

His appointment still bemused him. He had no experience in defense. No experience in anything really. As a minister, having too much knowledge was sometimes a disadvantage. You couldn't uphold the impartial position the role demanded. Far better to know a little but rely on your advisors for the drilled down details. That's how Reggie had operated, and although that ascendency to political stardom had evaded him, he'd been a survivor. Many of his other feistier colleagues couldn't claim the same.

It was, however, all very strange, his appointment. Reggie knew there were at least three other ministers who could do the job ten times better than he could. But it seemed Ashton wanted him. And lately, what Ashton wanted, he invariably got.

Chapter 3

Fluffy ice blue sofas.

They're everywhere, throughout Kudamun. Our quarters are no exception. We have our share of those requisite sofas, and I especially enjoy their fluffiness. It feels like I'm sitting on a cloud, although I've never done that. Not sure if I could, but anyway, that's the feeling the material projects. The Kudamaz love them. They push a sense of calm in your body, and when you sink into them everything feels so right.

So perfect.

I'm on the sofa, stretched out with Sam Noor, my husband. Kudamun is our home. Well, partly home. Our other home is Earth. You see I'm Ellie Noor, Protector of Earth, and until recently was just a hard-working businesswoman, with a husband whom I thought was a boring diplomat, who actually turned out to be a badass, 'saving the world' type spy.

Over the last few months things have changed.

Life has changed.

I've changed.

I'm not human anymore. I've taken the form of a Kudamaz-human hybrid attuned to every resonance vibration on Earth. Plant, animal or mineral including man-made things, I can connect to at the molecular level, and communicate with those base elements. I'm also quite a fighter, and I've cornered the market in rainbow light annihilation.

Sam is also Kudamaz but he's different to me. Instead of having light energy networks inside him, Sam's human makeup, his blood, bones, organs, and brain, through the reconstitution process, have been separately turned into Kudamaz energy rather than obliterated and recreated. Imagine a body is digitized and all that information is used to produce a super-pixelated image. Well that's my hubby. Sam's being is like a rasterized image, with every part of his human internal make-up recreated as billions of light cells instead of human cells. He still has the human scaffolding, but he's held together through Kudamaz energy.

We both use our shimmer ability to transport between Earth and Kudamun – an inner dimensional world out of time, space, and the known universe. The positioning of Kudamun was perhaps best summed up by the Dalai Lama, who Sam and I met back in May this year. He said, "you are from the world in between." That's exactly where Sam and I are from. The places in between. We are always there, just one degree out of the reality but hidden by the Reality Gap. That constantly fluctuating quantum field where the degree of tilt of shooting quantum particles keeps Kudamun from being seen by anyone in the physical world or the reality plane, as the Kudamaz call it.

I close my eyes and stretch my body down languidly toward Sam who is sitting into space. He tickles my feet as they nestle into his lap and I pull away suddenly, my eyes open and alert.

"Still makes you jump!" says Sam smiling with naughty delight.

"Yeah, a little. More a retreading of old memories. Difficult to shake."

Sam grips hold of me staring hard.

"Shake? Why would you want to?"

At that moment I didn't know why I'd made such a crass comment. The words came out of my mouth and it was as if I wasn't in command at the split second. I scowled, annoyed with myself.

"Of course I don't want to."

"Then why say it?" snaps Sam, the relaxation vibe has vanished.

"I don't know. I… I…haven't been quite myself. Everything that's happened. Al Nadir's obliteration, Ashton, the massacre, Freedom Earth. All that religious and new energy stuff. It's been a whirlwind even for us. I guess my head isn't quite clear yet. My databanks aren't blasting on all eight cylinders!"

Sam nods. "I know what you mean darling. It's been a wild ride."

"I know I got a lot when I become Kudamaz, but I had to give up so much."

Sam puts his arm out and drags me closer to him. I rest my head on his chest and try to hide the emotions building. The Kudamaz are not meant to submit to feeling emotion. The way in which we function is through our knowledge banks, reliving memories that are used to create energy to materialize into reality the emotion, and with it, our tears of joy or sadness.

I could feel the tears pricking at my eyes. I blink, and they sparkle away.

"I know you did darling. But there wasn't any choice."

I listen to Sam's voice. Pragmatic. Commanding. Infuriatingly sensual.

I curl my legs underneath me, and sit up, resting my chin on Sam's shoulder.

"I know. It's just sometimes I think - why me? Why did it happen at all. I know it had to, destinies are written. I'm aware of what I'm saying, and of course I'm grateful to Aby-od for saving me, but..." I stop and look into Sam's deep pools of dark brown.

"But..." repeats Sam, edging me on and he pats my thigh.

"I wonder what would have happened if I hadn't insisted on you coming back that Friday from Oslo. If I'd just accepted you were away on business. I'd probably still have had the nightmare, woken, had that awful experience with Aby-od and Aswa-da's wicked intervention, screamed and burnt my hand, but you wouldn't have heard anything. There would have been no revelation. Even if MI6 had seen, they probably wouldn't have put so much emphasis on it had I not known about your MI6 status. That moment changed it all. And it was down to my petulant, school girl tantrum that I wanted you back sooner. I really do think I caused it all."

Suddenly, I couldn't hold back. Tears drop and sparkle as fast as I produce them.

"I almost lost everything, Sam. My life, you. All because I wanted the last say on everything. I had to win. I just didn't want you away from me anymore."

Sam rubs my arm. "You didn't lose me sweetness. We got through it. We survived. Being Kudamaz is the most incredible experience I could ever have dreamed of. I love every moment."

"Don't you think about the things you've had to let go?"

"What, all those human things, like being hungry, tired, having aches and pains, using airports, getting stuck in traffic, handling politics."

"We still do that now..." I counter and grin, but Sam isn't smiling.

"Being afraid of dying."

Sam says it. It's a truth I know he values. Probably more than me.

"Fear makes you human." I say.

"But we're not human anymore Ellie. We have gained more than we have lost. You must be able to see that."

"I do, but even though you're not admitting it, I have lost too. My business for one."

"Ellie, sweetheart, you can't put losing your business on the same level as not being human."

"I'm not," I sound peevish, and I tone down the testiness in my address, "but it was still something I cared a lot about. Remember darling, it became my obsession, so much so, I didn't even realize you were spy!"

Sam strokes my leg. "Alright, point taken,"

I glance at Sam, turning my head sideways. I see he's considering what I've said. Ever the analytical mind, he retaliates.

"Come on sweetness, you're being myopic in your recall. You know you didn't lose it. You sold it. Ashton found you a great buyer."

I thought about Richard Ashton, British Prime Minister, and current pain in my backside. It was true, he found a very deep-pocketed tech company who happened to be branching into virtual warehousing. The blockchain capability I'd developed with my tech team was an attractive, differentiating feature. The acquisition made sense for them – cheaper to buy than to develop the new business organically – and for me. Being the Protector of Earth, I couldn't kid myself I could continue as CEO of Cloud Nine. I'd made sure all my staff were kept on and all were given pay rises. Securing Palmer Pharm, and their deal in several orders of magnitude larger than the twenty million I'd secured from their rival a month before made Cloud Nine a sought after asset in the tech world.

Sam and I never had money worries. And with the funds from the sell-off only boosting our very healthy bank balances, I decided to keep a small amount in trust, with the majority of the funds going to key charities I cared about. I left enough in our main bank account to pay for utilities. Even though we were Kudamaz and all intents and purposes were superbeings, we still had to pay the bills for electricity, gas and water on Earth.

Some realities stay constant!

"Yeah, I know he did. But besides you, Cloud Nine was my only love. I gave part of myself away when I sold it."

"I know you did darling, but we're beyond all that now."

I look at Sam. Beyond it, I think. Right. So that's why you always slip back into you MI6 agent mode whenever you possibly can.

But I say nothing. Just smile and grab his hand.

"I know."

"So you're ok."

"Yes and no."

"That ambiguity again, darling. You're fond of that."

I know what Sam's referring to. When I first explained about me becoming Kudamaz, and I spoke of Mark I and Mark II versions of Ellie. He asked, 'are you Ellie – yes or no'. I replied. 'Yes and no.'

"It's not intentional. It never was. But life isn't always black and white Sam."

"For someone whose life is about balancing dark and light, that's a hell of an ironic thing to say."

This time I do laugh. It was ironic, but it's also true. Lately I've been unable to discern dark and light. Nuances of grey were all I could pick up on. Actions that I thought were honed with evil intentions, have turned out to be delivering good. Ashton is a prime case in point.

"What do you think about Ashton?"

"What, as in do I think he's good or bad?

"Yes." I keep my response short, like I'm scared my mouth will run away again and say something weird, or out of keeping with who I am

"He's a good guy. No question. And one unlucky son of a bitch too. That stuff with his family. It would send a man crazy."

I stare at Sam, and turn my mouth up, unsure of his conclusion.

"You don't think he's good?"

"I don't know darling. He seems good. But there's a ruthless streak in him. I feel it."

"Ellie, he's a politician, of course he's going to be ruthless." I hear Sam's voice playing down my fear, dismissing it as my paranoia. My need to be wanted as the Protector. Couched within his voice is a mocking.

I stiffen as I listen.

"Don't think I'm a fool. I'm not paranoid, nor delusional. But Ashton is still an unknown quantity."

"Unknown! Ellie, we know him completely. The High Council cleared him to work with us on religious unification, Freedom Earth and Quantum Force. He's open and honest. Ellie, he shows his hand to us all the time."

I stare at Sam and cannot believe, with his constantly questioning background defined by his time in MI6, why he could just accept Ashton.

"Shows his hand!" I say, with scorn, raising an eyebrow at Sam "Well let's hope he doesn't have any cards tucked up his sleeve."

ARE YOU READY TO FINISH THIS RIDE?

Dear reader,

Al Nadir have been savagely obliterated. Ellie and Sam – the Kudamaz super couple – have overseen their demise personally. With stragglers mopped up by local forces, Al Nadir's reign of death, destruction, and darkness is over.

The world is on the brink of embracing global peace. Religious leaders are laying down their staffs of conflict and coming together under one unified, enlightening ideology: Freedom Earth.

A new energy source brings with it the promise of a completely fossil-fuel-free future, and, for the UK, economic security and reinstatement on the international stage as a major player with reignited power.

All of this wonder welcoming the world is down to one man: Richard Ashton, British prime minister, a man who carries, despite the impossible odds, a Balance Shift in a permanently perfect Equilibrium.

Are you ready to finish this ride?

The picture looks rosy, but something is lurking.

What evil web is Temenos spinning?

Ashton has suffered greatly but how far will he go for his peace drive?

Is he changing the world? For good? Ellie feels something dangerous is bubbling up. An indescribable sensation. A portent of doom.

Is she right?

Join Ellie as she seeks to uncover the truth in the final blistering, mind-bending instalment of this extraordinary series.

Take that final leap into *The Sum*, and you'll be pulled into a reality where nothing is really what it seems.

You won't believe what your eyes will read.

Hold on tight to the light…for you're heading for the dark.

GET OPERATION SNOWDROP FOR FREE

One constant throughout *The Trusted Thriller Series* has been **Operation Snowdrop**. If you haven't already accessed this 'Eyes Only' mission, now is your chance. Get the inside track on what really happened and get the real facts behind the mission that crossed the line.

If you want to get insider intelligence on Sam and Ellie next adventures, early bird discounts on all future releases in *The Trusted Thriller* series, access to competitions, or instant access to me, Michelle Medhat, then subscribe by hitting the link below and we can continue this journey together.

Operation Snowdrop Feedback

"OMG! Talk about edge of your seat, grab you by the ba... The author kept the book moving at a good pace with plenty of twists and an ending that will make you question the world around you!"

"Snowdrop is a fiercely paced book. Characters are dynamic, & powerful. A great spy thriller good versus evil gets blurred. Looking forward to next book."

"Kept me guessing and enthralled right up to the end. Looking forward to reading the next book"

"A very well written, suspenseful book. The description of the agents emotions and conflicts was very well done."

"I loved the constant adrenaline rush in this book. Looking forward to the next book."

"So similar to the situation in the world today that it's hard to read. Well developed"

"This book is exactly why I read new authors as often as possible. The intrigue and characters are heart-stopping. 5 stars +"

GET ACCESS TO OPERATION SNOWDROP
https://dl.bookfunnel.com/nz69zq8lp2

ENJOY THIS BOOK?
YOU CAN MAKE A DIFFERENCE

You have probably heard this before, but for an author, reviews really do make a difference. It takes no time at all to type in a few words, a sentence at the most, but it means the world to an author.

Honest reviews help others to find out about books they wouldn't have heard of before.

If you have enjoyed this book, I would be very grateful if you could leave a review on the book's Amazon page.

You can jump straight to the review page by hitting the link below.

LEAVE A REVIEW HERE
https://geni.us/IBdEELG

Learn more about Michelle Medhat

www.forever-connected.com
michelle@forever-connected.com

THE TRUSTED THRILLER SERIES

This Thriller Series is an edge-of-your-seat, ruthless, non-stop ride packed with gripping spy action, provocative sci-fi suspense, sex, political intrigue and amazing sci-tech to push Bond into the background! If you're searching for something that's nail-biting to the very end - you've found it in this extraordinary Thriller Series.

If you've read this book first, and haven't discovered the rest of the series yet, you need to read these books. Don't miss out, get them now and get the full story!

The Trusted (Book One – Part One)

He's a husband, a killer, and the only man who can save the world...

Sam Noor keeps his double lives separate with expert precision. But when the MI6 agent's wife discovers the lie, he fears that both his worlds may shatter. Distraught and conflicted, Noor concentrates on his latest mission and discovers a weapon that could cause a global catastrophe...

Drawn into the fight against a sinister terrorist group with powerful connections, Noor must uncover the faction's secrets by any means necessary. Even if it puts the woman he loves in the line of fire.

But Noor has no way of knowing that a supernatural war rages within his nation. And the winner could take charge of humanity's very soul.

Against forces that defy his reality, can Noor protect millions of innocents from a bloody end?

The Dominant (Book Two – Part Two)

One spy's war on terror could decide the fate of humanity…

MI6 agent Sam Noor isn't afraid to get his hands dirty to protect his homeland. While overseas interrogating an enemy terrorist, he's horrified to learn his beloved wife suffered the same brutal tactics from his own men. Determined to expose the betrayal and extract bloody justice, Noor uncovers an unbelievable fact: his wife died and somehow came back to life…

Swept up in an international power struggle, Noor goes rogue to uncover the eye-opening truth. The fallout from Sam's revenge ripples from the Oval Office through the CIA and MI6. As he fights tooth and nail to turn back the doomsday clock, cosmic forces wage their own battle for Earth's future. And Noor fears that preventing nuclear destruction may sacrifice the love of his life.

Can the maverick agent protect his wife and save his world from annihilation?

The Resonance (Book Three – Part Three)

World War III rages. What can she do to protect the innocent?

Ellie Noor's hope hangs by a thread. Tortured to within an inch of her life by sadistic terrorists, she's horrified to learn her husband's efforts to free her cost a half-a-million lives. But grief must wait as Ellie is swept up in an interdimensional attempt to stop all-out nuclear destruction.

Shocked to discover the key to saving the universe lies inside her, she becomes a potent instrument to respawn Earth's lost protector. But with the world's atomic arsenals locked and loaded, and sinister beings on the attack, she fears only an unfathomable miracle can halt humanity's extinction.

Can Ellie unleash her hidden power and prevent her planet's annihilation?

The Refracted (Book Four – Part Four)

She's now a fully-fledged Protector. But her formidable extraterrestrial powers may not be enough to save humanity from itself.

Ellie Noor longs for an end to the constant fighting on Earth. Now fully alien and nearly invincible, she and her superhuman husband are busy stamping out terrorist armies worldwide. But her heart breaks when a new global alliance for peace makes its first initiative a mass execution of its enemies.

Suspicious of the motives of the movement's creator, UK Prime Minister Ashton, Ellie's search for answers only leads to startling revelations. And her former-MI6-spy husband isn't helping matters by kowtowing to the British leader. With political havoc and cosmic dangers threatening, one wrong move could spell disaster for millions...

Can Ellie balance the forces at play before humankind is wiped off the interstellar map?

The Sum (Book Five – Part Five)

Earth is in harmony, its people free. But behind the mask of tranquility lurks a dark and deadly danger.

Ellie Noor fears her alien powers may not be enough to keep the peace. Brushing off her husband's insistence that she's just paranoid, the powerful Protector's suspicions prove correct when two high-ranking politicians are kidnapped. And when the lionized British Prime Minister announces the death penalty for anyone betraying his leadership, Ellie knows evil is closing in...

Battling the lure of the darkness that tries to claim her, she races once more to prevent the world from falling into chaos. But despite her extraordinary abilities, the human-alien woman is about to face her deadliest threat yet... herself.

Can Ellie stop benevolent calm from turning into bloodthirsty totalitarian terror?

A WORD FROM THE AUTHOR

This is quite an emotional time for me. This series is coming to a close, and the characters I've crafted over the years will finish their adventures. It is a strange feeling, after writing a series of such intensity, I've literally been living it in my mind for quite a while; then suddenly everything stops.

No doubt I'll have to find a way to get over that affecting void!

It's been said my series is like a trip into the weird, wonderful, and deeply twisted. I can understand this take. Writing it has been like a drug to me. Even after a hard day's work, I'd sneak over to my laptop or take out my notebook (if my eyes couldn't face a screen) and bash out the scenes converging in my brain.

And I'd get my fix.

Perhaps, that's why my books are seen as addictive. Maybe, through the words I've written that deliver such an instant rush, somehow that same adrenalin-pumping feeling has been transferred to the reader.

Who knows the wonders of that thing we call the mind?

My next book, *The Sum,* is the last in this series, although I'm writing a few more '*Operation*' style novellas focusing on key missions with MI6 agents Sam Noor and Matt Kinley, giving insights into their lives, prior to the 2017 events that kicked off in *The Trusted.*

But after these novellas are finished – four at the most – I will put Sam and Ellie to bed (a place they love to be!) forever.

Then I intend to start something completely new.

I've said before about music being important to me. Right the way through this series, there has been a companion playlist reflecting key chapters and scenes from the books. This has been built up, not through specific searches, but instead, through serendipitous moments and crazy coincidences. I'm a great believer in the connectedness of everything. I'm in good company. Leonardo Da Vinci said, "*Everything connects to everything else.*" It does at the quantum level, and through resonance frequencies within our cells and our brain, we're all connected.

Our world, the universe, and everything we understand about reality is much greater than the existing physics that attempts to give it interpretation and a form of definition.

Reality is something that is readily accepted, but its nature - why it is there - forms, for the majority of us, something incomprehensible. But strangely, talk to a child, and they 'get reality'. It's what they want to make of it. Take imaginary friends. Are they really imaginary? Or are children tapping into a frequency resonance through their minds to access a connection to someone or something else living outside our degree of reality, our degree of perception?

Here's a mind-boggling notion: do thoughts really create our reality?

Much in popular culture has been written on this point, and to debate this question, a much bigger platform than being an afterword at the end of a book is needed.

I don't know the answer. What I do know is we're all capable of creating amazing things. Of doing the incredible.

The power of being human is about stretching the limits of our own perceived abilities. Challenging what we understand. Changing for the better.

Bringing hope to a soul darkened by pain or misfortune.

Compassion is the bedrock of society.

At a time where, often unintentionally, our behaviors and thus, our values are defined by likes, sound bites, and memes, it is important to never forget the need to care for one another. To once in a while, pop out of that insular bubble smart phones have placed us in and open our eyes, empathize with our fellow neighbor, and truly comprehend the power of love.

Michelle Medhat

Find out more
www.forever-connected.com
michelle@forever-connected.com

Twitter @theconnected1 Facebook @michellemedhat

The Playlists of The Trusted Thriller Series

The Trusted
Everlasting – Take That
Secrets – One Republic
Have I Told You Lately that I Love You – Rod Stewart
Rock You Like a Hurricane – Scorpions
Khalina Lewahdina (Let's stay alone together) – Amr Diab
E.T. – Katy Perry
Solsbury Hill – Peter Gabriel
Angel with a Shotgun – The Cab
Only Love can Hurt Like This – Paloma Faith
Who Wants to Live Forever – Queen
Rule the World – Take That
Fighting Suspicions – Rebecca Ferguson
The Architect – Paloma Faith
Rewrite the Stars – Zac Efron & Zendaya
The Last of the Secret Agents – Nancy Sinatra
New Divide – Linkin Park
Army of Two – Olly Murs
Demons – Imagine Dragons
Shine a Light – Bryan Adams
Don't Stop Believin' – Journey
What Part of my Body Hurts the Most – Rob Fowler & Sharon Sexton
Please Don't Leave Me – P!nk
Set Fire to the Rain – Adele
Guilty – Paloma Faith
Almeno Stavolta (At Least this Time...) – Nek
Candlelight – Jack Savoretti
I Belong to you – Caro Emerald
Try – P!nk
Redemption – The Strange Familiar
Nothing Breaks Like a Heart – Mark Ronson (Feat. Miley Cyrus)
Many Shades of Black – Adele & The Raconteurs
See Who I am – Within Temptation

The Dominant

Secrets – P!nk
La Tortura (The Torture)– Shakira
L'Altra Dimensione (The Other Dimension) – Måneskin
Amor Eterno (Eternal Love) – Fonseca
My Immortal – Evanescence
Revenge – P!nk with Eminem
Killer Queen - Queen
So Am I – Ava Max
Any Way You Want It – Journey
Me – Taylor Swift & Brendon Urie
Lucy in the Sky with Diamonds – The Beatles
Some Guys Have All the Luck – Rod Stewart
Perfetto (Perfect)– Gianna Nannini
Half the World Away – Aurora
Raise Hell – Brandi Carlisle
The Pretender – Foo Fighters
Too Good to Lose - Rebecca Ferguson
Maybe – Lewis Capaldi
Something's Gotta Give – One Republic
Torna a Casa (Come Back Home) – Måneskin
I Want to Break Free – Queen
Amo Soltanto Te (I Only Love You)– Andrea Bocelli & Ed Sheeran
Love at First Sight – Kylie
Whisky Tango – Jack Savoretti
Wonder – Naughty Boy with Emeli Sandé
Retribution – Jeff Scott Soto
Ayami Beek (My Days With You) - Elissa
Wasted – Jack Savoretti
Light My Fire – The Doors
We Share the Same Sun – Stereophonics
Surrender – Paloma Faith
What Have You Done – Within Temptation
Out of the Frying Pan and Into the Fire – Meatloaf
Rockstar (Salim's Theme) – Nickelback
Radioactive – Imagine Dragons
Back for Good – Take That
Danger Zone – Kenny Loggins

What Doesn't Kill You (Stronger) – Kelly Clarkson
Sweet But Psycho – Ava Max
Welcome to The Jungle – Guns and Roses

The Resonance
Strong - Mark Kingswood
Hiding – Florence + The Machine
The Sound of Sunshine – Michael Franti & Spearhead
All of My Heart - ABC
Toxic – Britney Spears
Burn it to the Ground - Nickelback
On Top of the World – Imagine Dragons
The Scientist - Coldplay
Blood on My Hands – Jack Savoretti
Music's Too Sad Without You – Kylie Minogue & Jack Savoretti
Suspicious Minds – Elvis Presley
Girls Just Wanna Have Fun – Cyndi Lauper
Traitor - Daughtry
Torn – Natalie Imbruglia
Dear Mr. President – P!nk
The Prayer – Celine Dion & Andrea Bocelli
The Winner Takes It All - ABBA
Guilty – Paloma Faith
Strip Me – Natasha Bedingfield
Won't Get Fooled Again – The Who
Changing – Paloma Faith
Drops of Jupiter – Train
Liar – Camila Cabello
Bring Me To Life – Evanescence
Venus – Bananarama
WW3 – Paloma Faith
Find U Again – Mark Ronson (feat. Camila Cabello)
Get Lucky – Daft Punk (feat. Pharrell Williams & Nile Rodgers)
Dancing in the Dark – Bruce Springsteen
Rescue Me – One Republic
Superheroes – The Script
Get Outta My Way – Kylie Minogue
Set Fire to the Rain – Adele

Who's Crying Now – Journey
Pain is So Close to Pleasure – Queen
Dark Night of the Soul – Van Morrison
Maybe Tomorrow – The Stereophonics
One Last Kiss – Kylie Minogue
Any Other Way – Jack Savoretti
Truth Hurts – Bullet for My Valentine
Stuck in the Middle with You – Stealers Wheel
Firework – Katy Perry
Red Light Spells Danger – Billy Ocean
Breaking Your Own Heart – Kelly Clarkson
Everything is Broken – Bob Dylan
Simples Corazones (Simple Hearts) – Fonseca
Greatest Mistake – Jack Savoretti
When Love Takes Over – David Guetta (feat. Kelly Rowland)
Shine – Emeli Sandè
I Saved the World Today – Eurythmics
Cold – James Blunt
Hold Me Close – David Essex
We Are Bound – Jack Savoretti
The Power of Love – Huey Lewis & The News

ACKNOWLEDGEMENTS

The name that has made this book a reality is Sam Medhat, my husband. He is my inspiration and without him this series would never have been created. He is the one who listens to every word written. He is the one who endures my frustrations when I have writer's block. He is the one who is constantly woken up by my unsuccessful attempts at creeping into bed in the wee small hours after I've become lost in my writing world.

Without Sam, no writing would have happened.

Whilst writing this series, I lost my brother, father, and mother. None of them lived to see this in print, however their love is embodied within the words, and I hope, somewhere, they can see the result of the faith they had in me to achieve.

I would like to thank my fabulous editor, Ceri Savage, who has been with me on this journey and who has been incredible in her support and advice.

Michelle Medhat

Printed in Great Britain
by Amazon

83095394R00233